LEFT AND LEAVING

For
Fin and Sam
Sylvie and Enzo

Acknowledgements

My sincere thanks to: Caroline Oakley for her encouragment, editorial expertise and friendship; everyone at Honno for continuing to support my writing; Cardiff Writers' Circle for constructive criticism; Stephen May and Eddy Walsh for taking time away from their own writing to read this; Ramesh Pydiah, Medical Photographic Manager at UCLH; Dr. Michael Shapter – sorry Mike; and The Weakerthans for the music.

Finally, thanks to Jim for helping fathom the desires and motives of people who exist only between the covers of this book.

LEFT AND LEAVING

Jo Verity

HONNO MODERN FICTION

First published by Honno
'Ailsa Craig', Heol y Cawl, Dinas Powys, Wales, CF64 4AH

1 2 3 4 5 6 7 8 9 10

ISBN 978 1906784 98 0

Published with the financial support of the Welsh Books Council.

Cover image: © Getty Images/Andrew MacDonald, 2007
Cover design: Graham Preston
Text design: Elaine Sharples
Printed by

1

Vivian hadn't seen Nick for over a week.

'Miss me?' he said, planting a kiss on her cheek.

'Not at all,' she said.

It was a shame, but she hadn't. And her week had been simpler for not having to factor him into it.

She took his coat and hung it on the peg. 'How was Oslo?'

'Stockholm,' he said.

She had no idea why he'd gone to Sweden. Or why he'd been to Newcastle the previous week. They'd agreed, a while back, that banging on about work got them nowhere. They were both permanently under pressure and 'a trouble shared' was merely an additional burden.

'Did you get off with lots of sexy Swedes?' she said.

'Just the one.'

A double bluff? Surely the very possibility should arouse a twinge of…*something*. No? At least she didn't spend hours moping or roiling with jealous suspicions. (And yet. Once in a while, a film or poem or piece of music tweaked – for the want of a better explanation – *her heart*, leaving her feeling short-changed, regretful that she didn't crave more from her lover.)

'I've never been to Stockholm,' she said.

'Stylish city. But bloody cold.' He pulled a hat from his coat pocket and jammed it on his head. 'I was forced to buy this.'

The khaki hat, lined with fake fur, had earflaps and a peak that could be fastened back. He turned to face her, jutting out his chin, gripping the bowl of an imaginary pipe, fixing his gaze on an imaginary fjord. 'What d'you reckon?'

Nick Mellor was handsome. Dark hair, grey eyes, straight nose, white teeth. He was tall, too, a plus point for Vivian who was five-eight.

1

She'd been introduced to him several years ago, at a dinner party thrown by mutual friends. It was a set-up, of course. She'd grown accustomed to being a project for couples who wanted the whole world to be as happily paired as they insisted they were. She and Nick had hit it off and things had progressed from there.

In the beginning, they'd made time for each other in their busy lives but, as they both scrambled up career ladders, the need to be deemed indispensable became a full-time job. They got on well enough but, as time went by, they spent less and less of it together. Her phone logged a string of texts confirming this. 'Still at work.' 'Shattered. Can we leave it tonight?' She often wondered why they bothered. On the other hand it was easier to be part of a couple than to explain why she wasn't. But, unless something changed, whatever they had wasn't going anywhere. Two more young professionals without the energy or desire to make their relationship flourish.

'Mmmm. Something smells good,' he said.

'Duck *confit* with a red wine *jus*.'

'Blimey, that's impressive'

'Waitrose,' she said. 'Just in case you think I've morphed into a domestic goddess whilst you've been away.'

'It still smells good.'

After they'd been together for a year or so, the question of their living together had come up. It was what couples in their mid-thirties did, and there were half-a-dozen reasons why they should. But, with the property market threatening to nosedive, they'd agreed that it was the wrong time to sell, and that it would be wiser to hang on, to see how things panned out.

To be truthful, Vivian had been relieved that they'd found a credible reason for leaving things as they were. She'd never been good at living with other people. She'd disliked those obligatory years of student flat-shares – the chaos, the lack of privacy, those alien cooking smells. As soon as she'd qualified and found a job, she'd rented a studio flat in Finsbury Park, preferring the hassle of a flap-down bed to housemates who left damp towels on the bathroom floor and bags of rubbish mouldering in the kitchen. She'd recently heard of a couple who, despite marrying, had continued to live separately. It wasn't as crazy as it sounded.

Five years ago, when her mother died, Vivian had discovered she was the beneficiary of her life insurance policy. (In making plans, her parents had assumed her father would be the first to go – not unreasonable as he was so much older than his wife.) The six-figure sum had enabled her to buy this flat. It was a bittersweet route to property-ownership, but there was no doubt her mother would have approved of her spending the money in this way.

'How's your dad?' Nick said as they sat down to their meal.

'Okay. I think. I haven't seen him for a few weeks.' She glanced up from her plate. 'I'm going down on Saturday. D'you fancy coming?'

She watched him struggle to frame his excuse. 'Saturday. Mmmm. Damn. I've got…this, this *thing…*'

She held his gaze until he looked away. 'It's time I told him about Cologne.'

'It's definitely on then?' he said.

'Yes. I'll go in January.'

'How d'you think he'll take it?'

'I have no idea.'

When the possibility of her working in Germany came up, Nick hadn't seemed concerned but she wondered whether he was still as sanguine.

'*You're* okay with it?' she said.

'Sure.' He smiled. 'It's no more of a problem than if you worked in…in Glasgow. In fact, Cologne is probably nearer than Glasgow.'

What sort of an answer was that?

'So what are your plans for Christmas?' he said.

They were barely into November. Forward-planning wasn't his thing and she was surprised by his question. For a moment she wondered whether he was planning to whisk her away. Somewhere hot. White sand beaches. Azure seas.

'Why?' she said.

'The guys in work want me to go skiing.'

'Oh.'

'Actually they asked me months ago and I said no. But someone's dropped out. I sort of assumed you'd be spending Christmas with your dad.'

'Yes, I suppose I shall,' she said.

'Look, Vivian, I won't go if…'

'Of course you must go,' she said. 'Christmas is no big deal. It's just another day, after all.'

Christmas loomed ahead, an iceberg in the winter fog. If she didn't spend it with her father, he would be on his own. She suspected that he wouldn't care but, fanciful though it was, she felt that, in abandoning him, she would let her mother down.

Annaliese Carey – her mother – hailed from Munich and, as a child, Vivian had adored the family's German Christmases. They'd made her feel special. Interesting. Different. No one else she knew woke on the sixth of December to find their shoes filled with sweets. No one else opened their presents on Christmas Eve. No one else ate goose and dumplings for Christmas dinner, or hung picturesque wooden decorations on their tree. (Always a real tree that touched the ceiling and filled the house with the dark scent of Bavarian forests.)

Even after leaving home, when Christmases had stopped feeling 'special', she'd returned to celebrate with her parents, arriving as late as was possible on Christmas Eve and finding an excuse – parties, friends, even work – to escape on Boxing Day. Her mother must have seen through her excuses but she'd never pressed her to stay longer.

Nick kissed her cheek. 'Let's make sure we do something special for New Year.'

'Yes, let's,' she said.

Belsize Park Tube was a ten-minute walk from Vivian's flat. If there were no hitches on the Northern Line, her journey to work took thirty-five minutes.

Friel Dravid Associates' offices were located off the Caledonian Road. The building had begun life as premises for a firm of carriers whose horse-drawn carts conveyed goods from Kings Cross railway station all over the city. When horses were superseded by motor vehicles, the owner had sold the building to a circus impresario who – or so the story went – had used it to house an elephant until planning regulations had overtaken him. Percy Friel had acquired the property in the early sixties when he and Bharat Dravid were setting up Friel Dravid. They'd restored and refurbished it (the scheme had been written up in the *Architects' Journal*) and the quirky building became known as 'The Elephant House'. By the time Vivian joined the firm, Dravid was dead, Percy Friel had retired and his son, Howard, had taken over.

When Vivian arrived at work, Ottilie – the office manager – was in the kitchen, arranging showy chrysanthemums in a gigantic glass vase.

'They're stunning,' Vivian said.

'They were pricey, but they'll last,' Ottilie said standing back and squinting at the bronze blooms. 'White's classier. But you know me. I can't resist a splash of colour. Howard's looking for you, by the way.'

Vivian bit her lip in mock trepidation. 'Oh dear. What have I done now?'

She knew she'd done nothing wrong. She also knew that Howard Friel, who could be a hard taskmaster, trusted her to do a good job. He liked her, too, and they'd become friends. He sometimes moaned to her about his children – both in their thirties, both something in the baffling world of City banking. 'Where did we go wrong? They don't have an iota of creativity between them. Or a jot of social conscience.'

'He's in his office. Could you take him a coffee?' Ottilie nodded towards the industrial-scale coffee machine that kept the office buzzing throughout the day.

Vivian poured two mugs of coffee and carried them up the spiral staircase to the first floor. As usual, the door to Howard's office was open and he was seated at his desk.

Howard Friel was sixty-two but with his wiry frame and abundant iron-grey hair, he could have passed for fifty. He had a quiet, authoritative manner which set him slightly apart, as if he were an anthropologist observing humankind. Yet he was approachable and open-minded, ready to listen and, when asked, to give an opinion. Vivian sometimes pretended to herself that Howard was her father. It would have made more sense if he had been.

He looked up from his screen and beckoned her in. 'Coffee. Wonderful.'

'You wanted to see me?' she said.

He signalled for her to sit down. 'We should try and fit in a Cologne visit before Christmas. You, me and Ralph. We need to meet the contractor. Firm up the schedule. Maybe we could take a look at offices. Get a few viewings lined up.'

'Sounds good.'

'Cara's keen to tag along. Would that be okay with you?'

Vivian meant it when she said, 'Of course. It'll be fun.'

Cara, Howard's wife of thirty-odd years, was a jewellery designer. She was a handsome, buxom woman. Always laughing. Everyone cheered up when Cara was around, jingling with jewellery and oozing vitality. The couple exuded an aura of well-being which infected everyone around them. At the office summer party, asked by a young man (who had downed too many glasses of Pimms and who was a week away from his own wedding day) for her recipe for a successful marriage, Cara had replied 'Shared baths. Dancing in the kitchen. And a firm hold of the leash.'

Vivian, also a little drunk, had tried to imagine what her parents would have come up with if anyone had asked them the same question. She had not the faintest idea – but then she had no idea whether her parents had considered theirs to be a successful marriage.

2

Gil tapped his pockets. A few weeks ago he'd locked himself out and since then he'd taken to frisking himself before pulling the door shut. Keys. Wallet. Phone. I.D. His mother would be proud of him. He was fifty-one years old, and she lived on the other side of the world, yet she still nagged him to eat a 'proper' breakfast and to get his hair trimmed when it reached his collar. (Skype was a mixed blessing.)

He jabbed a thumb on the light switch then hurried down the two flights of stairs, taking up the daily challenge to make the front door before the switch popped out and stranded him in darkness. *Yes.* Five days in a row. He was heading for a record.

Bending, he scooped up the leaflets strewn across the scuffed vinyl. At the tenants' most recent 'hall and stairs' meeting they'd agreed to keep on top of this menace. He glanced through the batch of flyers. Cabs, takeaways, 'scrap' gold for cash, dry cleaners, men with vans, and men with drain-rods. A reflection of the aspiration – and desperation – of North Londoners in twenty-ten. Having made sure that there were no genuine items of mail amidst the junk, he dropped the lot into the bin that they'd all pitched in to buy.

Leaving the house, he descended the half-dozen steps to the pavement then slipped through the gate in the iron railings and down the stairs to the basement flat. He rapped on the door. Beyond it, Feray was shouting at the kids. He couldn't make out what she was saying, or whether she was speaking English or Turkish, but he knew she would be threatening them with reprisals if they didn't shift. It was the same every weekday morning.

When she came to the door she looked frazzled, a frown darkening her eyes, her lips set tight.

'What is their problem?' she said, shaking her head.

'God, you look sexy when you're angry.'

She arched an eyebrow and held his gaze. He'd persuaded her to do just that when he'd last photographed her. 'Come on,' he'd said. 'It makes you look hot. Like Gardner or Bacall.' 'Bullshit,' she'd said, but she'd complied and the portrait – he'd gone for black and white – took pride of place on her living room wall.

'You coming in?' she asked.

'Got to get to work. I wondered whether you'd like me to cook supper tonight. For all of us.'

Her expression softened. 'That'd be nice.'

James and Melissa were bickering in the background. Their complaining voices evoked the sniping that had gone on between him and his sisters when they were this age.

'Six-thirty-ish?' he said.

She nodded.

He leant forward and kissed her hastily on the lips. 'Gotta go.'

Pulling his collar up around his ears, he shoved his hands in his jacket pockets and headed for the bus stop.

On days like this, when the pewter sky squatted no more than a few metres above the rooftops, he had to remind himself that, of his own free will, he had *chosen* north London over New South Wales. But his misgivings were constantly short-lived because, between leaving his top-floor bedsit and getting dragged along in the rip tide of commuters, he regained the certainty that this was where he wanted to be.

Gil had drawn his first breath at the Royal Free Hospital in Islington. (When he'd checked, he'd discovered the site had long since been redeveloped as luxury flats.) His mother kept the unfeasibly small identity bracelet that proved this in the bottom of her jewellery box, the essential information presented in block capitals. 26 – 4 – 1959. MALE. 6LBS 11OZS. GILLON PAUL THOMAS.

When he was a toddler, his parents had hijacked him,

9

transported him to the other side of the world then set about brainwashing him into believing that he belonged in that technicolored land of opportunity. He knew now that the time he'd spent in Australia – first in Brisbane, then in Coffs Harbour – had, in effect, been a stretch in an open prison from which it had taken him forty-odd years to escape.

He'd arrived in London by way of several European cities, each a potential new home. Rome – too full of itself. Paris – too stylish. Berlin – too prescriptive in its permissiveness. Amsterdam – too damn easy. He'd saved London until last, like the favourite chocolate in the box, knowing that he wouldn't be disappointed.

He waited at the bus stop with the restless crowd, each of them fine-tuning their position, making sure to be well-placed when the bus turned up. Racehorses jostling at the starting tape. He peered up Fortress Road. From here he was only able to see a couple of hundred yards before the bend in the road cut off his view, keeping alive the hope that a 134 was a matter of minutes away.

Sometimes, to prove that he could, he walked the three-quarters of a mile to Camden Town and picked up a bus there, where he had the choice of several. On one occasion there'd been a snarl up – road works or a 'shunt' – and he'd covered the distance faster than the crawling traffic. He'd used a Transit van as a pacemaker and, having set himself the challenge, he'd jogged part of the way. (That was a while ago now, and on a sparkling spring morning.)

After ten minutes the bus – a matching pair, in fact – arrived and he hauled himself up the stairs. Even after living in London for five years he still got a kick out of riding on the top deck. An extra kick if, as today, he managed to get the seat at the front, above the driver. As the bus lurched on, he planned what he would cook for Feray and the kids. They'd be hungry so it should be something quick and filling. Maybe, to save time, follow it with a ready-made dessert. Melissa was picky – Feray was getting quite worried about how little she ate – but she had a sweet tooth. Chocolate was always a winner. Okay. Pasta with a tuna and tomato sauce. Profiteroles. And, for Feray, a carton of fresh pineapple – her favourite – if there were any to be had by the time he got out of work.

The bus dropped him, along with a dozen others, at the corner of Hampstead Road and Euston Road, outside the glass and steel edifice that was the administrative hub of the hospital. He fell in with the stream of people making their way through the revolving doors and on through the atrium café to the bank of lifts. The coffee smelled good and he was tempted to join the queue but it was an expensive indulgence. The money he saved could go towards tonight's meal. Besides, he was trying to cut back on his caffeine intake – shaky hands and cameras didn't sit happily together – a vow which he made every Monday but which he invariably broke by Tuesday morning.

The lift *bing-bong*-ed its arrival and a subdued cohort shuffled in, reluctant to return to the grind after the weekend. The capsule ascended, the air inside prickly with perfume. Gil, who was averse to any aroma apart from coffee and cigarettes this early in the day, was glad to get out at the third floor. Checking the time on the clock above the door, he entered the open-plan office that served as base for several of the hospital's non-clinical functions. It was a dreary room. The ceiling was oppressively low and, despite the expanse of windows running down either side, daylight failed to penetrate to its centre. Today, as on all but the brightest of summer days, the lights were on.

The Medical Photography Department amounted to a couple of desks, three PCs, a colour printer and a photocopier in the corner nearest the door. People were surprised to learn that the hospital employed only two photographers but, as Gil explained, doctors were type-A individuals. They could afford expensive digital cameras – nowhere near the spec of the big Nikon beasts at Gil's disposal but good enough – and increasingly undertook

11

their own photography. He foresaw that, before long, his function would be redundant. But there was no point in getting steamed up about that until it happened.

'Good weekend, Gil?' Terry called across from 'Health and Safety'.

'Not bad. Saw a great exhibition at the Tate.'

A maxillofacial consultant for whom Gil did a lot of work had given him two tickets for the Muybridge exhibition. 'Another dropped bollock,' he'd explained. 'My wife informs me we're off to a wedding. No use to me. Thought you might be interested.'

Gil had invited Feray to go with him. 'What about the kids,' she'd said. 'They're on their own every day until you get in from work.' 'I know but it's…different at the weekends.' He'd persisted, the kids joining in, rather too enthusiastically, he'd thought, promising to phone if there was the slightest problem.

They'd gone but Feray had been twitchy. They'd spent barely an hour looking at the photographs before she'd said, 'I think I'll head back. But you don't have to come.' He'd sulked all the way home and, instead of spending the night with her as he often did at weekends, he'd gone out for a few beers then returned to his own flat, slamming the front door and stomping across the hall to make damn certain she heard him. Tonight's meal was by way of a peace offering.

Gil's boss, Kevin Lisle, wasn't in yet. Kevin had recently become a father and fractured nights were taking their toll. One of the few things that Gil remembered clearly from the days when his own kids had been newborn was the constant leaden-headed exhaustion. Another was the *what the hell have we done?* cloud that hung over him and Janey, darkening every day.

He switched on his machine and typed in his password. F.A.L.C.O.N.5.3.9. The model and registration number of the fourth-hand Ford he'd raided their savings to buy in nineteen eighty-nine. Janey, sleep-deprived and permanently on the verge of tears, was still breastfeeding Polly. It hadn't taken much to push her over the edge and that car (God, he'd loved that car) became a cipher for everything that was wrong between them; every way he'd failed her.

The usual assortment of email awaited him. Requests from clinicians to photograph patients or write images to CD. A reminder that his 'flu jab was due. An invitation to contribute to a colleague's leaving gift. Information on a cross-infection course he was booked to attend. Nothing out of the ordinary.

His first task each morning was to check the images he'd downloaded at close of play the previous day. Depending on what they were required for – patient records, lectures or displays – they needed cropping or resizing. It was a routine chore and an undemanding way of easing into the day.

That done, his time was spent photographing patients. This took place in the hospital a couple of hundred yards away, on the opposite side of Euston Road. His 'home' there was a studio on the lower ground floor where patients attending the various clinics came to be photographed. If they were incapacitated or unable to come to him, he took his equipment to the ward or the operating theatre.

The commute between hospital and admin building took place several times a day. It was a crazy arrangement but Gil looked forward to it. He enjoyed rejoining the outside world for five minutes, dicing with death as he negotiated four lanes of traffic. It also gave him the opportunity to snatch a sneaky fag. Theoretically, he'd given up smoking. Both his mother and Feray (although they'd never met or even spoken) were on his case and, seven months ago, they'd extracted his promise to quit. But by some distorted logic he'd persuaded himself that a few drags taken in this limbo-land didn't count; that the damage the occasional Euston Road puff did to his lungs was nothing compared with the traffic fumes he inhaled.

As he was preparing to make the first trek of the day, his phone chirruped an incoming text from Kevin. They'd had another bad night and he'd be late in. Gil would have to cover but he didn't mind. Taking a few extra photographs was a piece of cake compared with what Kevin – poor sod – was going through.

Gil had decided to become a photographer when, at the age of twelve, he was given a battered Pentax K1000 by a neighbour who had tired of the hobby. His father had helped him rig up a darkroom under the stairs and, with the aid of a couple of library books, he'd learned how to develop and print his work. Cartier-Bresson and Robert Doisneau were his idols and he'd daydreamed of tooling around Europe, capturing the spirit of the age – always in black and white. He imagined reproductions of his work adorning the walls of student bedrooms, smoky bars and cafés. And his stuff wasn't bad. (His photograph of his mother pegging his father's work shirts on the clothesline took second prize in the *Gazette*'s annual photographic competition.) But somewhere along the way he'd been distracted by girls and music and beer and, by the time he'd dealt with all that, he'd been forced to modify his dreams.

Taking photographs of leg ulcers or radical surgery couldn't be described as pleasant but, given his aptitude with a camera and lack of squeamishness, Gil didn't mind. On the occasions when he was called in to photograph a rare condition or groundbreaking surgery it could be quite fascinating. He was good with patients who found the hospital environment intimidating and were reassured by this middle-aged guy with his down-to-earth manner. Once they'd identified his accent, they were keen to chat about visits to family and friends in Australia, and naturally there was incessant cricket and rugby banter. He wasn't heavily into sport but it was a useful means of easing patients through the unavoidable indignities of the process. The pay wasn't great but it was sufficient for his needs. No. He wasn't a latter-day Doisneau but he was doing a useful job, and there were worse ways to earn a living.

At five o'clock Kevin, evidently delighted to have an excuse not to dash home, offered to finish up. 'You get off. I owe you one.'

'That'd be great,' Gil said, picking up his jacket. 'I'm cooking supper tonight.'

'Special occasion?'

'No.'

'Aaah. Blotted your copybook, eh?' Kevin winked and tapped the side of his nose, conveying his customary 'women are the enemy' message.

Gil felt a bit of a shit when he went along with Kevin's 'us and them' rubbish. His boss wasn't a bad bloke but Gil didn't care enough about him to embark on a crusade to put him right.

'You and Feray must come over soon. Meet Jack.'

Kevin held up a glossy A4 print of a baby's face. Baby Jack's eyes were barely open and he sported a roll of fat running across the bridge of his nose and above his eyes, making it look as though he'd gone the distance with Mike Tyson. He wore a beanie which was way too big, its stark whiteness accentuating the purplish-pink of his skin. The hat had two ears sewn to its crown and 'Jack' embroidered in blue on the front in case, Gil supposed, Kevin and Debbie forgot their son's name.

'He's got a cheeky little face, don't you think? He's going to be a proper Jack-the-Lad.' There was a hint of desperate hope in Kevin's prediction, as if all his problems would fade away once his four-week-old son was into sex and drugs.

'He's a real beaut,' Gil said, giving Kevin the reassurance he craved and himself a chance to make his getaway.

3

When Vivian emerged from the Tube station, it was raining. Less than an hour earlier the skies over Belsize Park had been streaked with winter sunshine but, whilst she'd been making the subterranean journey south, the weather had changed.

She set off briskly, dipping her head against the rain. Her father's house was a twenty-minute walk from the station, via a dreary stretch of main road and a series of humdrum streets. She'd covered the route dozens of times and could navigate with her eyes shut.

Almost immediately beads of water were dripping from her hair, snaking down her neck and inside her collar. Checking that she had enough cash in her purse, she retraced her footsteps and slipped into the mini-cab office – little more than a cubby hole – located next to the Tube station. The bearded man seated behind the grille was studying a Sudoku puzzle. Behind him, in the gloom, two men in padded anoraks were hunched over a chessboard. The front man looked up but said nothing.

'Farleigh Road, please,' she said.

He turned, speaking sharply to one of the chess players who, eyes still on the board, lifted a set of keys from one of half-a-dozen hooks screwed into the tongue-and-grooved boarding behind his head.

Unbolting the door, the driver emerged from his secure enclosure. 'This way please, madam.'

She used the firm when the weather was foul or she was pushed for time, but anyone new to Abbas Mini Cabs might have lost their nerve as they were led along the pavement and round to the side street where the anonymous vehicles were parked.

'Farleigh Road,' she repeated as the driver opened the rear door of a tired-looking Toyota.

The car pulled away, wallowing on its spongy suspension, and she remembered that she'd meant to call in at the Sainsbury's Local opposite the station to pick up something for her father – a bar of milk chocolate or a puzzle magazine or a net of satsumas. These small offerings had become a ritual and she pictured him glancing at her empty hands, childishly disappointed.

The cab smelled of air freshener, the sickly scent exacerbated by the heater going full blast. Farleigh Road was only a couple of miles from where she'd grown up. The low-rise streetscape of south-of-the-river London, its hugger-mugger terraced houses, its down-at-heel shops, were familiar territory. She stared out of the window. It wasn't worth engaging with the driver on such a short journey. What was the point of talking about the rain or the traffic or the state of the nation? All he wanted from her was the fare and a tip. All she wanted from him was to be delivered safely to her father's door. He'd be relieved by her silence.

Although it was barely four o'clock when the cab pulled up, lights glowed in most of the houses along the terraced street. Number eighteen, however, was in darkness. A passer-by might think no one was at home. But her father was a stickler for switching off unnecessary lights and she knew he would be in the kitchen at the rear of the house – the place where he spent most of his time. She'd phoned before getting on the train to let him know that she was running late. On hearing this, he'd launched into his customary 'No need to toil all the way down here. You've got enough to do.' There *wasn't* any need. She *did* have plenty to do. But that wasn't the way it worked.

Her father had moved here a matter of months after her mother's death. Vivian had suggested he wait a while before taking such a radical step, to see how he felt in a year, which seemed to be standard advice following bereavement. He'd been pushing eighty-two when he was widowed. Most old men would have been content to sit tight, cocooned in memories. Not Philip Carey.

Once mooted, the notion of moving set in his mind like a dollop of concrete in a drainpipe and he'd forged relentlessly ahead with the sale of the house which she still hazily thought of as 'home'.

His neighbours had expressed surprise when the board appeared in the front garden, shocked to learn that not only was he moving but that he intended living *alone* in his new home. Octogenarian widowers were expected to throw in the towel and retreat to sheltered accommodation or a small bungalow. Certainly not a three-bedroomed house with awkward stairs and a sizeable garden. Once they'd got over their surprise, they'd praised his courage in 'battling on alone', obviously assuming that he couldn't bear to remain in a place steeped in his late wife's presence.

A broken heart wasn't what drove him – Vivian was sure of that. He was moving because it suited him to move. When the time came, he methodically whittled down the thirty-one years that he'd shared with Anneliese, systematically purging her from his life, or so it seemed to Vivian. He left her to take whatever of her mother's personal belongings she wanted and, as they bagged the remainder – clothes, books and knick-knacks – ready for the charity shop, she had been the one who was weeping.

She stood on the step, experiencing, as she always did when she came here, a blend of apprehension and reluctance. She sighed. Had she come first thing, she would be back in her flat now. But she'd allowed the morning to drift away in a fug of coffee and newspapers. Then, when she'd taken a jacket to the dry cleaners, she'd run into a girl from the Pilates class that she sporadically attended and been persuaded to go for lunch at the Italian Café.

Despite the set of front door keys entrusted to her 'just in case', she wasn't comfortable with letting herself in to her father's solitary world. She rang the bell and peered through the stained glass panel at the top of the door. After what seemed too long, light from the kitchen flooded the hall and she watched his silhouette growing as he made his way towards her.

He opened the door a few inches and studied her warily before slipping the chain off its rail. 'Vivian?'

'Of course it's me,' she said.

It seemed colder inside the house than out and the air smelled of fusty dishcloth. She took off her jacket and draped it over the newel post, hugging herself and shivering. 'You should put the heating on, Dad. I pay huge amounts of tax so you get your winter fuel allowance.'

Ignoring her remark, her father led her into the kitchen. It was warmer in here, the windows fogged with condensation. The source of the heat was one of the burners on the gas cooker. Her father had stationed his chair – a prosaic winged effort, upholstered in serviceable beige fabric – in front of the cooker, as if it were an open fire. On a stool next to him were his newspaper, spectacles case, several library books and a packet of cough sweets.

'Sit yourself down,' he said. 'I'll make the tea. I haven't had mine yet. I waited for you.'

The implied criticism of her lateness. The suggestion that tea was rationed and that he was only allowed one cup per afternoon. She'd been in the house a matter of minutes and already the skirmishing had begun. While he was filling the kettle, she took one of the two dining chairs that were tucked under the formica-topped table and placed it alongside his, watching him fussing with mugs and tea bags.

She would never forgive her father for being old. He had been fifty, her mother twenty-five when they married. That was their choice. But then they'd been selfish (or careless) and, the following year, produced her.

Even before she went to school, she noticed that her father neither looked nor behaved like other dads. He had grey hair and a little moustache. He wore a tie and shiny, lace-up shoes. He raised his hat to ladies in the street. Other dads laughed and played and made themselves available. They took their children swimming or to the park or taught them to play tennis. Hers drilled her in good table manners, insisted she change into slippers as soon as she came in and trained her to be silent when he was reading. By his demeanour, he made it clear that 'fun' fell outside his remit. He was a thief because, by being old, he had stolen something from her.

Anneliese Krüger had been Philip Carey's second wife. Vivian knew little about Elspeth, her predecessor, except that she came from Dumfries and, after fourteen years of marriage, she'd upped and offed back to Scotland to marry a cousin, taking their two sons, Richard and John, with her. As a child, when asked whether she had brothers or sisters, Vivian had answered 'no', simply not understanding that these men, twenty-odd years her senior, who occasionally came to visit her father, and to whom she'd barely spoken, could be her brothers. As far as she was concerned, she was an only child. Even now, at the age of thirty-six, she felt the same way.

Her father took four digestive biscuits from a tin on the worktop and placed them on a plate. 'How's that young man of yours? Mick, isn't it? The journalist?'

'It's Nick, Dad. And he's a literary agent, as you well know.'

His memory was perfect but he did this sort of thing all the time. It was as if he wanted to trivialise her life.

He waved a dismissive hand. 'I can't keep up with you.'

'I've been seeing Nick for *three years*. What's to keep up with?' She shouldn't rise to the bait but it was out before she could stop herself.

'*Seeing*.' He shook his head in mock despair.

They drank tea and nibbled the biscuit allocation. Whilst her father described a documentary on Wellington bombers that he'd watched the previous evening, her thoughts drifted to the difficulties that Friel Dravid was having in obtaining planning permission for a spa hotel near Dorchester.

After a while her father stopped talking and closed his eyes. She stared at the digital clock on the cooker, the burble of the gas and the *plink* of the tap as it dripped into the sink the only sounds to penetrate the congealing silence.

It seemed that each time she came they had less to talk about. The past – a natural source of conversation between fathers and daughters – would never be a comfortable country for them to revisit together. Yes, she had happy memories but, without exception, these involved her and her mother. What was the point in asking 'Remember the time...?' to someone who'd played no part in the story?

There *was* something she needed to talk to her father about and her opportunity came when, eyes still shut, suddenly he said, 'Are these latest cuts affecting you?'

'We're okay. We've got enough to keep us going for a while.' She cleared her throat. 'Actually we've had some good news.' (Not strictly true – the firm had learned of its success a couple of months ago.) 'The firm's won a competition. For a gallery in Cologne. Quite a prestigious job.'

He nodded. 'Well done. I expect your German will come in useful.'

'Yes. I've been over a couple of times. To look at the site and talk to the client.'

He turned to look at her. 'You didn't mention it.'

'No. Well. We were up against stiff opposition. There wasn't much point in getting our hopes up prematurely.'

'So you'll be traipsing back and forth I suppose. Or can everything be done on the internet these days?'

'We can do a lot from London. But Howard's talking about opening a small office over there. It would make sense to have someone on the spot.'

She waited while he processed the information.

'You'd be the obvious choice,' he said.

He was right. She spoke perfect German. She had no husband. No children. No commitments – except, of course, to him.

Vivian might as well be an only child. Richard – who was something to do with engineering – lived outside Edinburgh. John had just recently taken up a post at the University of Toronto. They both sent her Christmas cards. But so did her dentist. In fact she saw her dentist twice a year and the last time she'd seen her half-brothers was at her mother's funeral. She still didn't understand why they'd trekked down from Scotland for someone who was all but a stranger.

'Yes,' she said. 'And it would strengthen my position should the firm need to slim down.'

Job security had nothing to do with it. She'd been heavily involved with the project from its inception and was eager to see it through. But job security was a reason he would understand.

'You must do what you have to do,' he said.

She tried not to notice his hands, the delta of veins visible through the papery skin. The razor nicks on his scraggy neck. Encased in his brown chair, he resembled a shrivelled kernel inside a nutshell.

'I'll be back every couple of weeks,' she said. 'And it'd be a temporary arrangement.'

'A bit like me,' he said and gave a mirthless laugh.

At six o'clock they shared a scant supper of jam sandwiches and out-of-date almond slices and, shortly after that, she escaped, her spirits lifting as the door banged shut behind her.

The rain had stopped and the wind was chasing skeins of cloud across the moon. It was much colder. She headed for the station, walking as quickly as she could, taking oversized breaths, the air scouring her throat. She fished her iPod from her bag and pushed the buds into her ears. Scrolling through her 'favourites', she chose The Weakerthans to accompany her home.

4

Gil's flat consisted of a good-sized living-dining-bedroom and, opening directly off it, a miniscule kitchen and rudimentary bathroom. In summer it was stifling. In winter, when the temperature plummeted as it had last night, the bedding felt damp and his breath misted the air. The oil-filled heater made next to no difference except to send his electricity bill soaring. In theory, heat from the flats below should help to warm his, but any rising heat simply kept on rising, leaking out of the roof and into the skies above Kentish Town. Despite its shortcomings, there was something satisfying – romantic, even – in its simplicity. He suspected that the place contravened every safety regulation in the book but he wasn't going to make waves and risk eviction.

Gil had spent his first months in London working in pubs and cafés. With luck and persistence, he'd eventually secured the job at the hospital and been able to afford a room in a house-share. His housemates were medical students and, after a few months, when pounding hip-hop and pubic hair (never his) embedded in his soap were getting too much, one of the hospital porters had put him on to this bedsit.

He'd arrived with a rucksack and a holdall and, for a while, he'd held out against acquiring 'stuff'. This place came with a bed and a few bits of furniture but inevitably his belongings had multiplied. TV set, armchair, a dated (but superb) sound-system, an old Fender acoustic – all second-hand. A laptop and broadband connection – pricey but essential for keeping in touch with his children and his mother. Far too many books, CDs and DVDs. If anyone asked him to describe his home he'd put it somewhere between a teenager's bedroom and a junk shop.

If truth were told, he was too old for this stripped-down life. Men of his age owned property; joined golf clubs; pottered in garden sheds

23

and polished cars. If he'd toughed it out with Janey, if he'd stayed in Coffs Harbour, he could be doing just that. But they'd both accepted that the marriage was over. Janey was happily remarried to a bloke she'd been at school with, whilst Gil was doing what he might have done twenty years ago had he not impregnated Janey Burnet, the sexy young waitress who worked at the café down by the Marina.

After a week of dank, colourless days when the sluggish air had seemed to be depleted of oxygen, today was crisp and clear, the sky the mid-blue of the plumbagos that his mother grew outside her back door. In the street, vehicles parked nose to tail were frosted over and yesterday's litter was edged with ice crystals transforming each discarded cigarette packet and bus ticket into glittering treasure. He guessed that the temperature was way below zero and, by the time he reached the bus stop, his nasal passages felt scalded by the freezing air.

Freddy Kimura – an orthopaedic surgeon whom Gil liked for his dry wit and penchant for modern jazz – asked whether he'd be able to stay late to photograph a procedure.

'Sorry it's last minute, Gil, but I wasn't sure the patient would show.'

'Something unusual?'

'Only a laminectomy – but it's a tricky one. It'll make a great case study. He's signed the consent form so no problem there. I've spoken with Kevin. He said you could take time in lieu.'

Gil had half-wondered whether he'd wander down to the South Bank this evening – *Peeping Tom* was showing at the BFI. But he wasn't set on it.

'You're on,' he said. 'Kick-off time?'

'Four-ish. I'll ring you when we're ready to start.'

Gil's morning forays across the road whetted his appetite for the outdoors and when Kevin thanked him for agreeing to stay late, he took the opportunity to ask for an extra half hour for lunch.

'Sure. And thanks for doing Freddy's thing. I'd have done it myself but...' Kevin closed his eyes and yawned.

Baby Jack certainly had his father on the ropes.

24

Dropping his point-and-shoot in his pocket, Gil pulled on his old beanie and hurried out through the revolving door. It was still cold, frost lingering in the canyons between buildings where the winter sun failed to penetrate. He headed for Regents Park, a fifteen minute walk away.

This corner of the park, abutting Euston Road and opposite the Tube station, was always busy. On summer days, every bench was taken, the grass a sea of escapees from offices, and tourists taking a breather before pushing on to the Zoo or Madame Tussauds. Today certainly wasn't sitting weather. People were on the move, striding out, shoulders hunched, hands deep in pockets.

Earlier in the year, Gil had identified a spot near the fountain that was good for people-watching. The tumbling water seemed irresistible and there was always a crowd around it. He made his way there and wasn't disappointed. A group of teenagers – Russian or Polish – were fooling around, the boys threatening to toss a pink knitted cap into the fountain. Sneaking out his camera, he grabbed a shot of the hat sailing through the air above its owner's up-stretched arm, and another as it hit the water.

Gil had set himself a project. 'Headgear.' It was the type of assignment given to photography students in their first semester but he was enjoying having something to go at. He had no idea what he would do with the pictures. He'd need permission from each of his subjects if he wished to exhibit them. He understood why. Even so it was a bitch.

But he today he wasn't here to take photographs and, walking on a little further, he found a seat in the lee of a yew hedge which faced the sun. He took a sheet of paper from his inside pocket, noting how warm it was to his cold hand. He checked his watch. Ten minutes before he needed to start back.

His daughter's email had been there this morning when he'd logged in to his Hotmail account. He'd scanned it quickly then printed it out, folding it away in his pocket, trying to put it out of his mind whilst he photographed leg ulcers and malignant moles.

The sun, although welcome, was having little effect on the temperature. Pulling his collar up around his ears, he slouched down into the warmth of his coat and read what Polly had written.

Hey Dad,

I was going to phone but we don't seem to be very good at talking to each other these days, do we? It's weird to think of you shivering while we're on the beach. Thanks for the latest pics. Your flat looks pretty neat.

I have some BIG NEWS. I'm thrilled and I really, really, REALLY hope that you'll feel the same way. <u>I'm going to have a baby.</u> You're going to be a grandfather!!!! Mum was OTM when I told her and you've got to be too. Chris and Adam don't know yet. I guess boys don't get excited at being uncles, specially as she won't be playing for Oz. Yes. It's a… GIRL. Due in March. So I won't be getting over there to see you in June like we planned.

I hope this changes things enough for you to want to come back. I don't expect you to live in Coffs but I want my daughter's grandfather to at least live on the same continent.

Another thing you should know – Gran isn't so good. After your visit home she seemed to get smaller. And she forgets things. She's started letting people do things for her, which is totally not her. She misses you, Dad, and she's not going to live forever.

I haven't mentioned a bloke. That's because he was long gone before I even knew I was pregnant. I have no intention of telling you or anyone who he is. I'm doing this on my own so, if we're to stay in touch you'd better accept it. There. Good job I didn't phone.

Don't bother getting back to me unless you have something nice to say.
P x

He folded the letter and returned it to his pocket, closing his eyes. This was crazy. Polly didn't stick at anything for more than five minutes. Was she capable of being a mother? And what about money? How would she support herself? Where would she live? With Janey? Who, and where, was the bastard that left her in the lurch? Round and around it went, dredging up memories.

It was Janey's day off and they'd arranged to meet for lunch. She'd been waiting for him when he came out of the *Gazette* office. He could picture her now. Shiny brown hair. White blouse. Pink shorts. When she'd told him that she was pregnant, his first thought had been to deny that it was his, the way a kid denies breaking the classroom window with a leg drive. *It wasn't me, miss.* 'Perhaps you've made a mistake,' he'd blurted out and Janey had started sobbing. He'd wanted to run. And he might have done, had she not been clinging to him. Disbelief was followed by distaste and then suddenly – from out of the blue – *pride*. Wasn't this was what his gender had evolved to do? Procreate? Polly had been born and her miraculous presence compensated for all the crap. For a while anyway. And when the scales were beginning to tip again, along came twin sons.

A young woman pushing a pram stopped near Gil's seat, rocking the pram gently with one hand whilst talking on her mobile. By turning his head slightly, he was able to study her. She finished her call and perched on the end of the seat, keeping a safe distance between them. Rummaging in her bag, she took out a chocolate bar and a tangerine.

She might have been younger than Polly (it was hard to tell) and for all he knew she was the *au pair*. But something about the way she tucked the blanket around the sleeping baby, her absorbed expression and the exhaustion etched across her face, told him that she was the mother. She'd taken off her gloves to peel the fruit and he had a clear view of her left hand. No ring. This could be Polly in six months time.

The baby roused and gave a fretful whimper. The girl lifted it out, swaddling it in layers of blanket. She didn't seem to notice that he was there as, muttering the nonsense that came naturally to women when they held a baby, she kissed the tiny forehead.

'How old's the baby?' he asked.

He felt her give him a quick but incisive inspection before deciding that he wasn't a threat. 'She'll be five weeks tomorrow.'

'How are you doing?'

She smiled. 'We're doing fine, thanks.'

Gil stood up and for the first time he could see the tiny face, pink and cross and new. He'd felt indifference when Kevin had shown him the photo of Jack but now, looking at this scrappy little thing cradled in the girl's arms, his eyes welled.

Reaching in his pocket for a tissue, he blew his nose violently. The noise made the child jump and turn her head towards him.

'Sorry,' he grimaced. 'My wife used to get mad at anyone who woke the kids. Funny how you forget all that stuff.'

'You've got children?'

'Three. A daughter and twin sons. They're grown up now.'

'Grandchildren?'

'No.' He hesitated. 'Actually – just this morning in fact – I heard that my daughter's expecting in the spring.'

The girl smiled, temporarily banishing all signs of fatigue. 'That's wonderful. Congratulations. You must be thrilled.'

'I'm still getting used to the idea.'

He felt the cold lump of his camera in his pocket and, for a second, thought of asking the girl if he could take a photograph of her and her baby. He sensed that this moment, here in Regents Park, might one day prove to be significant. No. He didn't want to freak her out.

'I'd best get back to work,' he said. 'Take care of yourselves.'

He hurried off, turning to look back only when he reached the park gate. But she had already gone.

5

The lecture was due to start at six-thirty. Vivian had decided that she couldn't spare the time when Howard stuck his head round the door. 'Ready?'

She shook her head and indicated the files heaped on her desk. 'I really ought to—'

'It'll still be there in the morning. Get a move on.'

'You're the boss.'

'What's on the menu tonight?' he asked as they bundled into a cab.

'"Globalisation and the Architect". Ned Rasmussen.'

He sighed. 'Oh dear.'

'You always say that. I don't know why you bother going.'

'To see and be seen, like every other bugger there. And be under no illusion. Rasmussen's in it for the same reason. Plus a juicy fee, of course.'

'You're horribly cynical,' she said.

'Well I doubt whether anyone positively *wants* to hear about globalisation and the architect.'

'*I* do,' she said. 'Listen.'

She was clutching a pamphlet which she tilted towards the cab window, the street lights illuminating the paper. '"The rapidly expanding economies of the developing world are shaping new cities at unprecedented speed and scale. Western architectural practices have been popular choices for signature buildings and master-planning in both the Middle and Far East. Will the focus remain on imported approaches or will there be a shift to more local solutions?" That's got to be right on the money.'

He patted her knee. 'We may have won a minor competition, Vivian, but Friel Dravid isn't a global player.'

'We could be.'

'No. We couldn't. Nor would we want to. And I shan't fret too much if Foster, Gherry and the like lose out to the locals. Therefore I suggest we sit back and enjoy the pretty slides.'

Howard was right. They should leave skyscrapers in the desert to the big boys. A small firm like Friel Dravid would be well advised to stick to what they did well and not overreach themselves. The German job was modest but it would enhance their reputation and pull in more work in Europe – unless the Euro-zone went down the pan.

The lecture was well-attended. Rasmussen was a good speaker, his thesis clear and well formulated. The slides were excellent. When she sneaked a glance at the audience, she suspected that several of them, including Howard, were dozing, soothed by his mellow voice.

It was getting on for eight o'clock by the time they emerged into Gower Place.

'A few of us are going for a bite to eat,' Howard said. 'You're welcome to join us.'

She smiled. 'Thanks, but I think I'll head home.'

'Of course.' He nodded knowingly, clearly assuming that she was dashing back to Nick. 'See you in the morning.'

The sky was clear, the air sharp with frost and, by the time Vivian had crossed Gower Street and turned left into Euston Road, the warmth of the lecture room had seeped away. She shivered, suddenly wanting to be home. What was in the fridge? Eggs? Cheese? Maybe she'd call in at Budgens and see if they had a packet of salmon fish cakes. Comfort food for a chilly evening. Increasing her pace, she set her sights on the red, white and blue roundel above the entrance to Warren Street, looking forward to swapping traffic fumes for the fug of the Tube.

When she reached Tottenham Court Road she waited at the crossing opposite the station. It was a complex junction where four lanes of northbound traffic became six and flew off in all directions, whilst beneath it, out of sight, a road tunnel conveyed east- and westbound traffic. It was a nasty but necessary crossing for those wanting to get to the station.

A swelling huddle of pedestrians was waiting, ready to scurry to the traffic island, a temporary safe haven where they would regroup for the second half of their hazardous journey. Vivian checked her watch. Ten past eight. With luck she'd be home by nine. Her new boots felt a little too snug, the soles too thin. Perhaps she should have gone for a half-size bigger. She looked up at the sky, ambient light making it impossible to see all but a few stars. And planes, of course, winking their way to or from Heathrow. She stamped her feet attempting to restore the circulation to her aching toes. *Come on.*

At last the traffic slowed and the red man changed to green. The convoy of pedestrians stepped off the pavement but she paused, glancing to her left, not trusting the drivers to obey the lights. They did, all but one car which was positioned, somehow, between the diverging traffic flows, as if the driver had been unsure whether to go straight ahead or bear right. She watched as it kept coming until it was halted in its tracks by the raised kerb of the island. Then it exploded.

The procedure had gone smoothly and Gil was satisfied that he had all the shots that Freddy had requested. It was getting on for eight and rather than toil back over the road, he took the lift down to the studio where he locked the camera safely in the metal filing cabinet. He'd call in here for the camera card first thing tomorrow.

That done, he climbed the stairs to the ground floor. Now that outpatient clinics were closed, the bustle of the working day had been replaced by a slight melancholy as the hospital settled into its night shift.

Gil paused, making up his mind what to do. It was cool in the reception area, the revolving door drawing in fresh air and

31

expelling stale as a dwindling number of staff and visitors came in and out. He shivered and buttoned his coat to the neck. It was too late to head for the South Bank and, pooped after his long day, he was ready for home. He was relieved that Feray was out this evening. She was a sweet, caring woman and he enjoyed her company but he had some thinking to do and he needed to be sure of his own position before sharing the news of Polly's pregnancy.

His bus stop was on the far side of Tottenham Court Road and he was within fifty yards of the crossing when an all-enveloping *boom* came at him from all sides and up through the pavement beneath his feet. He heard glass shattering then nothing but a hissing in his ears, as if he'd dived through a plate glass window into the deep end of the swimming baths.

Instinctively, he moved across the pavement, away from the hospital building and its looming glass walls, trying to calculate where the immediate danger lay, anticipating a second blast. A man on the pavement ahead of him pointed towards Tottenham Court Road and shouted something which Gil couldn't make out through the hiss in his ears. Pedestrians began running. His instinct told him to run in the opposite direction, away from the obvious danger, nevertheless he followed them.

Traffic was still moving along Euston Road. Cocooned in their own worlds, drivers were taking a while to grasp that something had happened. Some were slower than others to react and Gil watched a car shunt into the one in front. A cacophony of horns started up.

When he reached Tottenham Court Road he saw a burning car, its roof ripped off. It was belching black smoke and the tarmac around the vehicle was strewn with shards of mangled metal. Tracers of burning fuel snaked across the road. He identified a car door, still intact, lying on the pavement. The stench of fuel filled the air. Glass crunched beneath his shoes. People were sitting on the pavement. A motorcycle lay on its side. Vehicles that had been travelling up Tottenham Court Road were abandoned as drivers bolted. Someone was screaming. The street was well lit yet, amidst the chaos of heat and smoke and panic, it was impossible to make sense of what was going on.

A young woman pointed at a bystander who was using his phone to film the car. 'How can he do that? Someone's been burned to death in there.'

'We should move back,' Gil said. 'There may be more explosions. Let's try and persuade them to move away.' He indicated a cluster of onlookers who were mesmerised by what they were witnessing, shocked into immobility.

'Best move back, folks,' he shouted. 'It's not safe here.'

To prove him right, flames started to engulf the vehicle on the far side of the burning car.

'What about him?' The young woman nodded towards a figure lying in the road next to the kerb. He was wearing a helmet and leathers and had, presumably, been riding the motorcycle.

Gil's ears were still hissing but he could hear better now. 'He shouldn't be moved,' he said.

Most of the crowd had moved well away from the burning vehicles, some of them sitting on the pavement. Sirens could be heard, growing louder and louder. The whole area was clogged with abandoned vehicles. He could see three buses – evacuated he hoped – parked amidst the chaos of cars and vans. The traffic must be snarled up for miles. It was difficult to see how emergency vehicles could get anywhere near.

'Well we can't leave him there,' the young woman said, pointing towards the inert form.

Together they eased the biker onto the pavement, away from the burning fuel.

'Should we take his helmet off?' she asked.

'Best not. We don't want to risk doing more damage.' He turned to look over his shoulder, in the direction of the screaming woman. 'I wish someone would shut that bloody woman up.'

He watched the girl walk purposefully towards the hysterical woman, impressed by her composure amidst the bedlam.

Swirling smoke made it difficult to make out what was happening on the far side of the road. Gil guessed that the kiosk selling newspapers and tourist tat outside the station had been damaged because sheets of paper were rolling and curling across the road, some catching fire and spiralling into the air before drifting into the darkness.

The noise of sirens had swelled to an ear-splitting pitch. Blue and red lights flashed as emergency vehicles appeared from side streets. Motorcycles wove between the lanes of abandoned cars. Police were arriving in numbers, pouring out of white vans. Their torsos looked bulky beneath their fluorescent tabards and Gil guessed they were wearing flak jackets. He felt horribly vulnerable. His coat and beanie scarcely protected him from the cold let alone exploding cars.

The girl was back. She'd succeeded in quietening the woman who was now sobbing at her side.

'Is she hurt?' he asked.

'Her knees and hands are grazed. And she's lost her bag.' Her deadpan delivery made it clear that she didn't think much of this useless woman.

'It's tan leather,' the woman said, 'and the clasp's shaped like a cat.' She pointed at the crossing. 'I was there when…' Her voice tailed off and she clamped both hands to her mouth.

'I'm sure it'll turn up.' Gil put an arm around her shoulder in the hope of preventing another spate of hysteria. He turned to the young woman. 'You okay?'

'I think so, apart from my ears. D'you think it was a bomb?'

They turned to look at the wreckage.

'Yep. It was a bomb,' he said.

'What should we do now?' she said.

'The area's bound to be sealed off. Nothing'll be moving. There could have been other…incidents. In fact the whole Underground network will probably be closed down. I guess we'll be stuck here for a while'

'Shouldn't we see if we can help them?' the young woman said, pointing towards two motionless forms lying on the traffic island.

It was too dark to pick out details but those poor people, who now resembled piles of sandbags, must have been no more than ten metres from the car when it went up. The steel railings, there to protect pedestrians from the traffic, were totally mangled and it seemed likely that the victims were dead.

'We should leave that to the professionals,' he said gently.

Sensing that the girl wouldn't be satisfied unless she was doing something, he said, 'Why don't you take…' He squeezed the woman's shoulder, prompting her to say her name.

'Irene,' she said.

'Why don't you take Irene along to A&E? She needs patching up. D'you feel okay to walk, Irene? It's down there,' he pointed, 'only a coupla hundred yards.'

'I think so.'

'Good on ya,' he said, slipping into the Aussie chumminess that worked so well with patients.

'What will *you* do?' the girl asked.

'I'll wait here with him,' he said, nodding towards the motorcyclist. 'Grab a medic. I'm Gil, by the way.'

She held out her hand. 'Vivian.'

6

Vivian took stock of the waiting area. Measuring no more than fifteen metres by ten, it seemed small for such a huge hospital. Grey metal seats, linked together in banks of four, stood against the walls, and in rows across the room. There was seating for about forty people and most of it was occupied. Fluorescent lights, set within the grid of ceiling tiles, cast a flat, yellowish light that made everything look lifeless. The place smelled of hotdogs and disinfectant and, like every hospital she'd ever been in, it was too hot.

Staff hurried purposefully through the waiting room, their shoes squeaking on the vinyl flooring as they disappeared through the double doors or down the corridor in the far corner. Nurses were checking people in, assessing injuries, taking names and details. When it came to their turn, Vivian learned that Irene Tovey was fifty-six years old and lived in Upton Park.

'Next of kin?' the nurse asked.

'My sister, Lillian. Lillian Dobson.' She gave an address in Maidenhead.

Vivian had expected her to say her husband or her children but, glancing at Irene's hand, she saw that her ring finger was bare.

'We'll sort you out,' the nurse said, studying Irene's grazes. 'Not too bad. But it's as well to clean them up.'

Irene Tovey had probably been a pretty child – rosebud mouth and blue eyes, that sort of thing – but now, in middle-age, her features seemed too small for her plump face. Short, highlighted hair in an easy-to-manage cut. Tiny pearl earrings, hardly worth wearing. Navy coat and shoes to match. Unadventurous. Neat. (Even now, amidst the horror and chaos, she was fidgeting with the sleeve of her coat, using a tissue to dab something off it.) Vivian occasionally came across 'Irenes'– working at the bank or behind the reception desk at the dental surgery. Women who didn't quite fit in the twenty-first century.

'Are your hands painful?' Vivian asked when they returned to their seats.

'Sore more than painful.'

Vivian hoped that Irene would offer to clean up her own wounds – they *were* very minor and the nurses were under pressure – but it was apparent that the woman wasn't ready to relinquish her place in this drama.

An elderly man wandered in. He was bleeding from a head wound, dribbles of blood congealed on his forehead and cheeks. Another, followed, clutching his arm tight against his chest. Vivian felt like a *voyeur* as she watched these distressed and confused people assembling around them and she turned her attention to Irene. 'D'you need to phone anyone?'

Irene raised a hand to her lips. 'My phone's in my bag. And my money. And my house keys.' Her voice grew agitated as she listed her missing possessions.

Vivian feared that mention of the wretched bag, and the consequences of its loss, would set her off again and she tried to calm her. 'I'm sure it'll turn up.' She pulled out her phone. 'Here. Use mine.'

Irene took the phone, staring at it as if it might do something unexpected. 'I've not used one like this.'

'Shall I get the number?' Vivian asked.

'Thanks.' Irene closed her eyes, her face contorting with the effort of remembering. 'Tsk. Silly me. You'd think I'd remember my own sister's number.'

'I expect it'll come back to you in a minute.'

Vivian retrieved her phone. The incident – or a version of it – would be all over the news by now. She ought to contact Nick. And her father. They had no reason to think she would be anywhere near Warren Street this evening, nevertheless she should tell them where she was. Howard, too. If he'd gone to Charlotte Street he must have heard the explosion and he knew she was heading for the Tube.

Suddenly she wanted to get away from Irene and the dismal waiting area. 'I'm just popping outside for some air,' she said.

Irene's face flooded with apprehension. 'You'll come back, won't you?'

'Of course.'

Two policemen were stationed near the exit. 'You okay, Miss?' one asked. His face showed no emotion, no reassurance, and, for a second, she experienced a childish dread of having done something wrong.

'Yes, thanks. I'm keeping a…friend company. I have to make a few calls.' She held up her phone to confirm her explanation.

'Don't go too far, will you? We'll need details of everyone who was in the vicinity.'

'Sure.' She hesitated. 'D'you have any idea who…?'

'No, Miss. Not yet. Our priority is to make the area safe.'

She stood at the top of the steps leading down to the pavement, enjoying the chill after the fug in the waiting room. The whole area must have been sealed off because Euston Road was devoid of traffic. Two helicopters circled overhead, lights winking, spotlights trained on the ground. Their blades stirred the air, creating an unpleasant sucking feeling in her ears. If she looked to her left, towards Tottenham Court Road, she could see flashing blue lights reflecting off the surrounding buildings. An occasional siren wailed. The night smelled of burning fuel.

She wondered what had happened to the biker. She hadn't been brave enough to study him closely but he'd been lying very still on the pavement. People must have died. Whoever was in the car, for a start, and those in the vehicles closest to it. Then there were the pedestrians on the traffic island. She'd seen chunks of burning metal flying through the air – huge lumps of shrapnel – but, until now, she'd avoided picturing the damage done as they hit human flesh. She felt shaky, queasy.

Both Nick and Howard had left messages asking her to get in touch. Despite their trying to sound off-hand she could tell they were anxious. Nothing from her father, though. She smiled. It would take more than a bomb for him to lash out on a call to a mobile.

She'd been in Cambridge on 7/7 and remembered how all the networks had gone into meltdown. But this evening she had no trouble getting through to Nick. She explained, quickly, what had happened, reassuring him that she was perfectly fine, playing down how close she'd been to the car.

'So where are you now?' he said.

'At University College Hospital. A&E.'

'But you said you weren't hurt.'

She told him about Irene and her promise to wait with her until she'd been patched up.

'I'll come and find you,' he said.

'There's no need. Getting here's bound to be a hassle. What are they saying on the news?'

He filled her in on what had been reported. The police were being cagey but this was the only explosion. 'Apparently there was no warning and so far no claims. They haven't ruled out an accident of some kind.'

'It was a bomb,' she said. 'Deaths?'

He hesitated. 'Four so far. And whoever was in the car. Several on the critical list.'

Once more he offered to come but she wouldn't have it, promising to call again when Irene had been sorted out.

Next she spoke to Howard, again making light of her escape. He'd been on his way to Pescatori in Charlotte Street and had heard the explosion. Details had filtered through to the restaurant and he and his friends had cut short their evening.

'There,' he said. 'Perhaps in future you'll have the sense to accept my dinner invitations.' Concern was evident in his teasing reprimand. 'And don't even *think* about coming in tomorrow. I shall only send you home.'

Finally she phoned her father. It was late but he usually had a nap in the afternoon and rarely went to bed before midnight. She had decided not to mention the explosion unless he did. Judging by his rant about the Co-op and the argy-bargy he was having with them regarding an insurance premium, he hadn't yet heard the news.

'It's gone eleven,' he said. 'Was there anything in particular?'

'Did you go for your 'flu jab?' she said, hoping that he would take that to be the reason for her call.

'I went on Monday. The nurse was an incompetent idiot. My arm's still bloody sore.'

She warned him that colder weather was forecast, reminding him that the central heating was there to be used. 'I'll be down to see you soon,' she said, surprising herself by adding, 'sweet dreams.'

She interrogated her Blackberry for the latest news. Accounts were sensationalist and scaremongering; they contained few facts. But the world demanded instant news and instant comment.

She shivered. What if she forgot about Irene Tovey and slipped away? She had no need of treatment and she doubted whether she could make a useful contribution to the enquiry. Irene was a grown woman. She would manage.

An intercom squawked and she turned to find that the policeman had come out to join her.

'Feeling better, Miss?' he said. He seemed more approachable now as if, with her as the only observer, he could lower his mask of inscrutability.

'Not really,' she said. 'I don't know how you can do this for a living.'

'You get used to it. Or rather you work out a way of dealing with it.'

40

'I feel a fraud,' she said. 'I'm absolutely fine. Like I said, I'm just here keeping someone company. I'd never met her until… this.'

'Very kind of you, Miss. I'm sure the lady appreciates it. In my experience, this sort of thing brings out the best in people.'

'I'll be getting back,' she said. 'I promised I wouldn't be long.'

'Well you make sure you have a cup of sweet tea when you get home.'

More people had arrived in the waiting area. Every seat was taken and newcomers were standing or sitting on the floor. Irene was nowhere to be seen.

Vivian went to the desk. 'I'm looking for Irene Tovey.'

The receptionist ran a finger down a list. 'She'll be outside one of the treatment rooms if you want to join her.' She pointed towards a corridor to her right.

Vivian, still feeling queasy, realised that venturing down that corridor would increase the likelihood of her seeing something grisly. 'I'll wait here,' she said.

The policeman had mentioned that she would have to make a statement. It would be sensible to note down what she'd seen whilst it was fresh in her mind. If nothing else it would pass the time. Finding a wall to lean against, she took her notepad from her bag and turned to a clean page.

'You're still here.'

She might not have recognised the man had he not been clutching a handbag, the clasp shaped like a cat. She hadn't had time to study him in the chaos but now she could see that he was a little older than she'd thought.

'Where's…?' He held out the bag.

'Irene. They're seeing to her now.'

'Is she okay?'

'More scared than anything.' Vivian nodded towards the handbag. 'You found it.'

'It was on the pavement, right where we were standing.' He looped it over his shoulder.

A doctor approached them, hand raised. 'Hey, Gil. They called you in?'

'I was heading for my bus when it kicked off. What's the story back there?'

The doctor glanced at Vivian and she guessed that he was censoring his reply. 'We're coping,' he said. 'Everyone stayed on and anyone who could get here came in. I'm on my way to grab a coffee then I'll get back to it. Nice handbag, by the way.' He grinned as he hurried off.

Vivian noticed the ID tag on a cord around Gil's neck, half-hidden by his jacket. 'You work here?'

'I do.' He held out the tag for her to read.

'"Gil Thomas. Medical Photographer."'

'That's me.' He inspected her front, as if expecting to see a similar tag, frowning officiously. 'And you are…'

'Vivian Carey. Architect.'

He raised his eyebrows and nodded as if her reply explained something he hadn't previously understood.

'I'm not very good with blood,' she said. 'But I suppose you're used to seeing nasty things.'

'I guess so. I usually get to look at the patient's file beforehand – know what to expect. Mind you an atrocity like this gets to everyone, no matter how used they are to seeing "nasty things".'

'Did the biker…?'

He paused a second, holding her gaze. 'It wasn't looking good. They're working on him now.'

'Here?'

'Yes. Most of the casualties are here.' He jerked his head towards the rear wall of the waiting room. 'The ambulance bay's out back. That's one good thing about it. It couldn't have happened closer to a hospital.'

A headache that had been building at the base of her skull, began to throb in earnest. She'd not eaten since lunchtime – a feta and bean-salad wrap which Ottilie had fetched from the sandwich bar around the corner. That was eleven hours ago and now she was feeling both sick and ravenous at the same time.

As if he could read her mind, Gil took a packet of crisps from his pocket and offered them to her. 'You look as if you're going to pass out. You need to eat.'

Thanking him, she tucked into the greasy crisps.

'You should drink something too.' He produced a bottle of mineral water from another pocket. 'Here.'

She took it, noting that the bottle had been opened, a little of its contents gone, but, after what had just taken place, it seemed absurd to fret about hygiene. 'Thanks.'

'Look,' he said, 'why don't I see if I can speed things up? After all, you're only here because I wished what's-her-name on you.'

'Thanks. You'll be her hero when she sees the bag.'

She watched him cross the room. He wasn't much taller than she was. Skinny. Grey hair – too long to be stylish, too short to be 'cool'. Baggy cords. Black Doc Martens. Australian? New Zealander? Nice smile. Nice voice.

7

Gil was surprised that the girl – Vivian – had stuck around. She didn't look the Good Samaritan type. He'd imagined that, having offloaded her charge in the hospital, she would grab the chance to escape.

Injuries sustained in explosions were brutal and his suggestion that she escort screaming Irene to A&E had been primarily to protect both women from sights that would haunt them forever. After they'd gone, he'd ventured across the road to the traffic island. One glance at the bodies, slumped and inert, had confirmed his fears. The only blessing was that the pedestrian route was some distance – perhaps ten yards or more – from where the car had stopped. When he'd returned to the biker, he'd spotted the lower part of a leg, its foot still encased in a trainer, lying close to the burning car and he'd been thankful that Vivian and Irene hadn't seen it.

The hospital had been one of many involved with treating the injured on 7/7. That was before Gil's time. Over a few pints not long after he'd started the job, Kevin had told him how bad it had been. 'Worst I've ever seen,' he'd said. The events of that day had highlighted failures in communication and coordination. As a result, procedures had been reviewed and revised. Dealing with the unexpected would never be easy but at least this time it was above ground and, as he'd mentioned to Vivian, it couldn't have been closer to a hospital.

He found Irene sitting in the corridor outside one of the treatment rooms. As predicted, she was delighted to be reunited with her handbag and clutched it tight as if expecting a passing doctor to snatch it from her. He reassured her that Vivian was still there, then that he'd had a few words with the nurse in charge and she was next to be called.

'Could you tell Vivian I shouldn't be long?' she said.

'Sure,' he said.

On his way back to the waiting area, he bumped into a nurse he knew quite well. She told him that the explosion had been heard, and felt, throughout the hospital. It was easy to imagine the panic that must have broken out amongst the patients, some of them a dozen storeys up, many, no doubt, recalling the Twin Towers as the wards were put on 'code red' should evacuation be necessary. He was glad he hadn't been the one who had to call it.

Vivian Carey was concentrating on a notebook, unaware that he was watching her. She was an unusual-looking young woman. Tall and rangy. Her shiny hair made him think of the lacquered box that his mother used for her stationery. It was so black that he might have suspected that she dyed it were it not for pure white hairs here and there at the temples. It was cut in a severe bob, the short fringe exposing her forehead and accentuating her eyes, which were a little too far apart. She wore a rust-red velvet coat, tight black jeans and boots. No jewellery. No makeup. Her look – her style – said *take me or leave me*.

As he approached she looked up. 'Will she live?'

'I think so. Will you? You look very pale.'

'I've got a headache. I'm beyond tired. And I have a terrible craving for a fry-up.'

'That's me, every Saturday night,' he said.

The statement – unfounded as it happened – would have gone down well with Kevin but not with this grave young woman who probably had, in that instant, labelled him a misogynistic roué.

Two police officers – a man and a woman – were working their way around the room, asking people exactly where they had been, and exactly what they had seen, when the car blew up. When it was their turn, Gil explained that he'd been fifty yards away and had only witnessed the aftermath.

'Anything you saw, no matter how insignificant you think it is, may be vital,' the woman said patiently.

Gil told them as much as he could and then gave his contact details.

She turned to Vivian. 'What about you, Miss?'

Vivian said that she'd been waiting to cross the road. 'I thought it best to jot down a few things.'

The policemen nodded approval. 'Well done, Miss.

'D'you need anything else?' Vivian asked when she'd finished going through her story.

'Not at the minute. Someone'll be in touch within the next twenty-four hours about making a full statement. If we could just have your details.'

She gave an address a couple of miles from Gil's own. But London was like all cities, changing from affluence to just-scraping-by within the space of a block or two. Belsize Park was for the well-to-do whilst Kentish Town – his part, anyway – wasn't.

'Notes, eh? I'm impressed,' Gil said when they were alone again. No one else had been so prudent, so focused, he would put money on that. 'You're very observant.'

'Yes, I am,' she said in a matter-of-fact tone. 'But don't forget I was alone. If I'd been with someone we'd have been talking and my mind would have been on other things. Not that there was much I could tell them. The fact that I noticed that it was a pale-coloured car – white or silver – makes no difference because they can see that for themselves.'

'Maybe. But it validates anything else you tell them.'

She frowned. 'The lights were red. I don't know what made me wait.'

Gil could see that Vivian Carey expected things to make sense.

The waiting area was less crowded now and they were able to find adjacent seats. Gil checked his watch. Midnight. The police had their own forensics team but, as anticipated, the medics had wanted him to take pictures too. He'd texted Feray to let her know where he was and that he was hanging on for a while in case he was needed again. He'd been in two minds about telling her. He'd mentioned that he might go to the movies after work but if she were listening out for him, sooner or later she would start to worry. The last thing he wanted was to add to her concerns. She already had enough on her mind what with the kids, her job and her ex-husband's unreliability.

'What will you do when Irene shows up?' he asked.

'How d'you mean?'

'I get the feeling that she's counting on you.'

'What for?'

'Well, I can't see her jumping on a night bus and heading back to…wherever.'

'Upton Park,' she said. 'Now she's got her phone back she can call her sister. Or she must have a friend.'

'I don't want to alarm you but I think *you* may be her new best friend.'

Irene emerged from the corridor, hands and knees bandaged. Her face lit up when she spotted them.

'So, are we finished here?' Gil asked.

'Yes,' Irene said. 'I told a nice policewoman everything I could remember. She said they'll need to talk to me again. And I can get these dressings changed at my surgery.' She patted Vivian's arm. 'Thank you so much, dear. I wouldn't have coped without you.'

'I'm sure you would,' Vivian said.

Gil noticed that, although she'd allowed Irene's arm to rest on hers, she'd pulled back a little, as though preparing, at any second, to break away.

Irene turned her attention to him. 'And I can't thank you enough, Gil, for finding my bag.'

'My pleasure.'

This was where he could bow out. Go home and maybe sneak into Feray's bed and snuggle against her. Forget all this until tomorrow. Vivian Carey and Irene Tovey were nothing to him. Okay. The orbits of their lives had briefly overlapped but that was all. Nevertheless, he felt responsible for lumbering Vivian with this pathetic yet oddly determined woman. And he had to confess that he was becoming fascinated by this solemn girl whose hair he had a yen to touch.

'Let's put our minds to getting home,' he said.

'They don't need you?' Vivian said.

'No. There's nothing more for me to do tonight.'

Keeping the media at bay after a major incident was hospital policy. The rear access lane to the ambulance bays had been cordoned off and police were preventing unauthorised individuals from getting anywhere near incoming casualties.

It was a different matter on the Euston Road side of the building. Despite police officers being strategically stationed outside entrances to both A&E and the main reception area, journalists had congregated on the pavement and were accosting anyone entering or leaving. During their interviews, the police had asked them not to talk to anyone. Dream on, Gil thought. Chequebooks would soon come out and make resistance impossible.

'C'mon, ladies,' Gil said, 'best head in that direction.' He pointed east, away from Warren Street.

Shepherding the two women down the steps, he forged a way through the clamouring journalists. A couple of them made as if to follow but they soon gave up, returning to join the rest of the pack. Taking Irene firmly by the arm, he began walking briskly away from the hospital, Vivian following a few paces behind.

He could walk home from here in forty minutes and he guessed that Vivian would have no qualms about sorting herself out. But Irene? Upton Park wasn't an easy place to get to at this time of night. Underground services stopped around midnight – not that he could see her braving the Tube after ten – and night buses weren't pleasant places for solo women.

'Okay,' Gil said. 'We've shaken off the paparazzi. What next?'

'Should we try and find cabs?' Vivian said. It was freezing and her vapourising breath was caught by the street lights.

'Oh, dear,' Irene murmured.

Gil guessed that splashing out thirty quid or more for a taxi would leave Irene short for the rest of the month. 'Do you know anyone living around here? Someone who might put you up? Given the circumstances, I'm sure they wouldn't mind being woken.'

'No,' she said.

'You don't work around here?' he persisted.

'Our office is at London Bridge. I was up this way visiting a girl from work.' She lowered her voice as if it were an embarrassing secret. 'She's had a big op.'

Gil looked at Vivian in the hope that she might come up with something but she shrugged and shook her head.

He shivered, suddenly desperate for a leak. 'We need to get out of the cold,' he said. 'We could try the station. Or there's an all-night caff just off Eversholt Street.'

He would have put money on the girl turning down his suggestion. A cab would get her to Belsize Park in twenty minutes if she were keen to get home to someone.

'Do they do fry-ups?' Vivian asked.

'Famous for 'em,' he said.

As they crossed Euston Road, Irene – who was in the middle – linked arms with them both as if they were friends out on the town and, thinking what a bizarre night this was turning out to be, he steered this three-linked human chain towards its destination.

He'd frequented this particular greasy spoon when he'd been working at The Cock Tavern, often stopping for something to eat after a late night, much as they were doing now. But that was several years ago and he was thankful to see that the place was still in business.

The three of them ordered the 'full English', Irene coyly opting out of the baked beans – 'they don't agree with me.' When the food came, he was surprised how well she coped considering that her hands were bandaged.

'Those journalists were despicable,' Vivian said.

'It's what readers want. Instant news and to hell with anyone's feelings. I worked on a newspaper for a while and I'm ashamed to say I was as bad.'

'Which paper was that?' Irene asked.

'Coffs Harbour Gazette.'

Irene frowned. 'Coffs Harbour?'

'Yep. Half way up Oz, on the right hand side.'

'I've been there,' Vivian said.

'You're kidding.'

'No. I worked in Sydney for a year. Before I came back I drove up as far as Mackay. I stopped off in Coffs Harbour and I've got photos of the Big Banana to prove it.'

Irene looked bewildered and Gil explained that forty-odd years ago some bright spark had dreamed up the notion of erecting a giant-sized banana to encourage motorists to stop at his roadside banana stall. 'It's a ridiculous great thing but it did the trick. Everyone who drives down the Pacific Highway knows the Big Banana.' Gil turned his attention to Vivian. 'You didn't make it to Cairns?'

She grimaced. 'I'm afraid I got bored.'

He was delighted by her honest answer. 'Same here. So when was this?'

'Two thousand and one. April.'

'Don't suppose you can remember where you stayed?'

'The Comfort Inn.'

He must have looked surprised because she added, 'I said I had a good memory.'

'My sister Louise worked there when her kids were young,' he said. 'She did split shifts to fit in with school hours.' He made a quick calculation. 'It must have been around that time. She might have booked you in. Tall woman? Red hair?'

'My memory's not *that* good,' she laughed and he noticed that she looked less strained now, had some colour in her cheeks. 'Were you living there then?'

'I was, actually. We probably passed each other in the street.'

'I knew it,' Irene chipped in. 'We were *meant* to meet. I was in a pickle and God answered my prayer. He sent me two guardian angels.' She pointed triumphantly first at Vivian and then him.

Vivian shot him an eloquent glance, the same thoughts obviously running through her head. Did this weird woman really think that their meeting justified the murder of innocent strangers?

Irene went off to find 'the little girls' room, and he and Vivian had a few minutes alone.

'How d'you see it going?' he asked.

'I can't see her making her way back to Upton Park, can you? And she's not going to sit here on her own all night.'

'You're right. I'd offer to take her to my place but I've only got a bedsit. I don't particularly want her bunking up with me. I don't think that's part of the divine plan.'

She smiled and he noticed that her teeth were uneven, her right incisor overlapping her front tooth. Her generation tended to have the slightest dental imperfections corrected – it would have been a simple orthodontic procedure – but he found the asymmetry attractive.

'Should *I* offer her a bed? It's the only way I can see of getting home tonight.' She yawned. 'And it's the sort of thing guardian angels do, after all.'

He was pretty sure that rescuing lame ducks wasn't Vivian Carey's normal practice. 'Don't let me push you any further into this. I'm already feeling bad.'

'A policeman told me that horrific events bring out the best in people,' she said. 'He didn't specify how long the effect lasts or when I can revert to being my normal mean-spirited self.'

'I'd say tomorrow morning. Around ten.'

When Irene returned and Vivian put the suggestion to her, she said that she 'couldn't impose', that she didn't want 'to put anyone out'. But she didn't take much persuading.

'Shall we make a move?' Gil said.

Vivian took out her phone. 'I should give my boyfriend an update.'

This started another outpouring from Irene. 'He won't want me getting in the way, dear.'

Vivian assured her she wouldn't be in the way of anything as her boyfriend lived elsewhere and, in any case, she had a spare room.

At Irene's insistence, before leaving the café they exchanged phone numbers. Gil had been through this ritual so many times after nights out, scrawling numbers and email addresses on old bus tickets or receipts. He'd hang on to them long after he'd forgotten who 'Charlie' or 'Emma' or 'Phil T' were, or until whatever he was wearing went in the wash and these scraps became wodges of papier maché in the corners of pockets.

They were close to three main line stations and, although it was late, they had no difficulty in finding a taxi. No sooner were they inside than the driver began grumbling, telling them how the explosion and subsequent traffic diversions had ruined his night, as if the whole thing had been staged to inconvenience cabbies. Once the topic was mentioned, there was no stopping Irene who, leaning towards the sliding window as if she were in the confessional, gave him a graphic account of their evening.

'Thank you for taking care of me, Gil,' Irene said when the driver stopped to let him out in Camden Town. 'And for finding my bag. I don't know what I'd have done without you. I shall say a prayer for you. Both of you.' She clasped him in an awkward hug, her bandaged hands on his shoulders and her head against his neck and he caught a whiff of floral scent and antiseptic.

He eased himself away from her determined embrace and stood on the pavement. 'Now you take care of yourself.'

Vivian was watching from the corner of the back seat, looking vaguely amused. He wondered how the rest of the night would go for her and Irene up there in Belsize Park. Good luck, he mouthed and winked. Then feeling that it wasn't quite enough of a farewell, he leaned into the cab, not entirely sure what he was going to do. She solved his dilemma by taking his hand and shaking it in a firm, cold grip. He slammed the door and as the taxi pulled away, she raised her fist to her ear, thumb and little finger extended in the universal *I'll ring you* gesture.

8

Vivian crawled under the duvet and phoned Nick.

'I'll come,' he said.

'Why?'

'I don't like to think of you on your own.'

She told him that she wasn't on her own and explained about her guest. 'We couldn't abandon her.'

'*We?*'

'*I. I* couldn't leave her there all night. And a cab to Upton Park would have cost a fortune.'

'Surely the police could have driven her home.'

'It was mayhem, Nick. People were dying. The police had better things to do.'

'Okay. But I don't see why *you* had to take her on.'

'She's a woman who needed help. It's no big deal.'

He seemed to get the message. 'Sorry. I'm worried about you, that's all.'

'Look,' she said, 'let's have lunch. I'm taking tomorrow – I mean today – off. I'll come in and meet you.'

'Damn. I've got to go to Manchester first thing.' He hesitated. 'I could probably reschedule if…'

'No. It was just a thought. I've got to get some sleep now.'

She closed her eyes, instantly becoming conscious of her body. Her feet were icy. Her head and her back ached. The fry-up, so delicious while she was eating it, now sat leaden in her stomach. Her lips felt numb and she could feel – *hear* – her blood pulsing somewhere behind her ears.

The events of the evening started playing through her head. *The crossing. The car, veering towards the island. The explosion. The bodies.* Once set in motion she couldn't stop the images going round and around, a continuous loop driven by adrenaline and fatigue.

She rarely slept well and some nights, after a sleepless hour in bed, she hauled her duvet into the living room, nodding off in front of mindless night-time television. Tonight, not wanting to risk being joined by Irene, she took her iPod from her bag, eventually falling asleep to Chopin nocturnes.

After breakfast, Irene seemed reluctant to leave. 'I'll phone work and tell them that I won't be in until Monday.' She held up her bandaged hand. 'I wouldn't be much use with these, would I?'

Despite being hampered by bandages, Irene had taken charge in the kitchen, humming to herself as she stacked the dishwasher.

After her restless night, Vivian was on edge and this grated. Determined to make the point that she was host here and Irene guest, she said, 'Was the bed okay? Were you warm enough?'

'I couldn't have been cosier. Better than the Ritz. Not that I've ever stayed at the Ritz.'

'No bad dreams?'

'I slept like a log.'

Vivian was surprised and the tiniest bit intrigued by this woman who had been reduced to hysterics by the loss of a handbag yet seemed to have erased last night's shocking events from her memory.

'You mentioned you work near London Bridge,' Vivian said.

'Yes. For Brooking and Laverty. Commercial accountants. D'you know them? I'm their "Jill of all trades".' She hooked quotation marks in the air.

'You enjoy the job?'

'I love it. Such a friendly crowd. It's hard work, mind you, but we have great fun.'

'What d'you do in your spare time?'

'God's work,' Irene said, as if it were on a par with flower arranging.

Vivian struggled to keep a straight face and to summon up an appropriate response. But Irene seemed not to expect one. 'When I was at school,' she said, 'I dreamed of becoming a nurse. And I did become a nurse. In a way. You see my mother suffered terribly with her nerves, and when my father passed on she couldn't manage. So I stayed at home and nursed her until she joined him. Eighteen years.'

'You have a sister, don't you?' Vivian said.

'Yes. Lillian's older than me.'

'Didn't she take a turn?'

'She's married to a soldier – well he's ex-army now – and they were living in Germany. She popped back whenever she could but she had her own family to take care of.'

'It must have been hard,' Vivian said.

'Mum needed me. We needed each other.'

Vivian stood up, thinking to bring an end to the conversation, but Irene hadn't finished.

'By then I was too old to start nursing training. I took a little part-time job in Boots and signed up for a secretarial course. At night school. I met someone and we "started a relationship".' Again she hooked the air. 'We got engaged. We'd even set the date. Booked the reception and everything. But…well, he changed his mind a few days before the wedding.'

'That must have been…traumatic,' Vivian said, disconcerted by Irene's readiness to reveal details of what amounted to failure.

'I admit I was shaky for a while.' Irene smiled. 'But it all turned out for the best. Everything happens for a reason, doesn't it? We just have to put our trust in Him.' She pointed towards the ceiling. 'He knows what's best for us.'

'How was it for the best?' Vivian said, irritated by the presumption that she shared Irene's beliefs.

'Colin abandoned me but Jesus gathered me to Him. He healed my sickness. Made me whole again. Since then, He's been my rock. Look how He sent you and Gil to help me last night.'

56

Vivian had had enough of this peculiar woman who never stopped talking. To be honest, she was rather creepy. Fearing that, were Irene to realise that she was staying home, she would never be rid of her, Vivian resorted to subterfuge. 'Sorry to rush you, Irene, but I need to leave. I've got a ten-thirty meeting with clients.'

Irene tutted. 'You poor thing. It's not right after what you've been through.'

Vivian looked at her watch. 'I'd better get a move on.'

They walked to the Tube, Vivian embroidering her story, pretending that her meeting was in Hampstead and that she was going to catch a bus.

When they reached the station, Irene became tearful, clutching Vivian and hugging her, thanking her for the umpteenth time for her support. 'I'll remember you in my prayers, dear.'

Having talked Irene through the simplest route back to Upton Park – 'Change at Bank then Mile End…' – Vivian waited at the barrier until she had disappeared down the escalator. Alone at last, she bought the *Guardian* and the *Independent* and returned home.

The newspapers devoted pages to the explosion, although few hard facts had emerged. She made a cup of coffee and switched on *News 24*. Six people had been killed outright; twenty-three injured, two of them critically. The utilities people were sure that it wasn't a gas leak, the MOD that it wasn't a World War II relic. It was very likely some kind of a terrorist action. *But why target a traffic island?*

A car horn, then another, sounded in the street below. Vivian went to the window. The refuse lorry was manoeuvring between rows of cars parked, bumper to bumper, on both sides of the road. Half-a-dozen vehicles had become corralled behind it and, without room to get past or turn around, the drivers had no option but to crawl along. No doubt this happened every Thursday morning but she could count on the fingers of one hand the number of times she'd been at home to see it.

Nick phoned from the train. He was clearly avoiding discussing the explosion presumably fearing it would lead them back into stormy waters. They arranged to get together on Saturday then, with little else to talk about, their conversation lapsed into a series of hesitant silences and Vivian was relieved when his train entered a tunnel and he lost signal.

Shortly after that, her phone rang again, the screen displaying a number that she didn't recognise. It was Irene, letting her know that she was safely home and thanking her again for her kindness.

'Anyone would have done the same,' Vivian said.

'No, dear. They wouldn't.' Her declaration was laced with conviction. 'How did your meeting go? I've been thinking about you all morning.'

'Very well, thanks. Actually I'm just on my way back to the office.'

Vivian was annoyed with herself for letting this woman intimidate her into first telling a lie then embellishing it with another. She'd assured Nick that Irene Tovey was a timid woman. She was. But she was also tenacious. A barnacle – inconspicuous yet immovable.

Irene rambled on. She'd made an appointment to have her dressings changed. Her sister was coming up from Maidenhead to help her shower and wash her hair. 'It'll be nice having company over the weekend. I suppose you'll be seeing your young man. Nick, isn't it?'

Vivian couldn't recall mentioning Nick by name but they'd discussed many things last night. 'Yes.'

'I expect you're busy,' Irene said.

The woman was lonely and yet Vivian couldn't wait to finish the call. 'Yes. I am rather.'

'Well, I won't take up any more of your time. I'm going to ring Gil now. He was so sweet last night.'

'Say hi from me, won't you?'

58

'Of course. 'Bye for now.'

After lunch the police phoned asking whether it would be convenient to come and take her statement. Within the hour, two plain clothed police officers were ringing the bell.

She went through it again. It didn't take long because there was little she could tell them. When she'd finished, one of them asked, 'You didn't see anyone getting out of the car when it slowed down.'

'No.'

'And you didn't see how many people were in the car?'

'No. All I saw was a car failing to stop.'

They thanked her for her time and handed her a card with a number to ring if she needed to 'talk to someone' – a box that she assumed had to be ticked.

After they'd gone, she couldn't help feeling that they had expected more of her and that she had failed them.

Gil was eating a sandwich and downloading yesterday's work when Irene Tovey rang to thank him for finding her handbag.

'All part of the service,' he said. 'So you finally made it home.'

'Yes. I'm just having a bite to eat.'

'How are the hands?'

Whilst she talked, he scrolled through Freddy's pictures, adjusting and cropping them.

'I've just come off the phone to Vivian,' she said. 'Such a sweet girl. So thoughtful. She sends her love by the way. D'you know, I feel as if I've made two new friends. I was thinking it might be nice if we could all meet sometime. A little reunion.'

'Why not? But in the meantime, you take care now.'

When Gil had a few moments to spare, he went to find out what had happened to the biker. Policemen were a common sight in and around the hospital but today there were more of them than usual, pacing unhurriedly through the reception area and stationed in twos at the entrances and the ambulance bay. Reassuring yet, at the same time, alarming.

Up on the third floor in ICU, phony jollity, a feature of the other wards, was replaced by an air of purpose. The staff spoke softly and moved silently about the corridors. The lighting was subdued. Everyone was focussed.

The sister stood at the desk, checking notes on a screen and monitoring visitors.

'Did the biker make it?' Gil said.

'Are you a relative?' Her face gave nothing away.

He lifted his ID. 'I came in with him last night.'

'He's stable,' she said. He knew he would get no more out of her.

Black coffee kept him going but by four o'clock he was starting to make mistakes. When Kevin asked if he'd like to leave early, he jumped at the chance.

A diversion remained in operation around the scene of the explosion, blue and white tape strung around the crossing. The bus stop that Gil normally used fell within the cordon. Warren Street station had reopened during the morning and he could have taken the Tube to Kentish Town, but since childhood he'd disliked confined spaces and, as he grew older, his aversion had become stronger. He couldn't put his finger on anything which might have caused this phobia – he'd never been locked under the stairs; he'd never fallen down a well or been trapped in a tunnel. It was inconvenient at times but he could generally work around it. Today he headed north, picking up the diverted 134 near Robert Street.

It was stuffy on the bus and, as it ground its way up through Camden Town, Gil had to make an effort to stay awake. He'd managed to get five hours sleep last night which, when he was a younger man, would have been plenty but now he was shattered. It had been near two o'clock when he got home. He'd been careful to make no noise as he crossed the hallway (directly above Feray's basement bedroom) and crept up the stairs to his bedsit. He'd pictured her curled on her side, hair spread across the pillow, irrationally disappointed that she'd taken him at his word and gone to bed.

Gil had encountered Feray Kennedy soon after he moved in. He'd been on his way to work and she'd been taking the kids to school. They'd regularly bumped into each other after that but it was some time before they'd had a proper conversation. In the beginning she was reticent. Wary. He'd done most of the talking, clowning around, trying to earn a smile which, when it came, wiped years of strain off her handsome face. He discovered that although she'd split up with her husband some time ago things were not good between them. Kennedy was unreliable, regularly missing maintenance payments and failing to turn up for scheduled visits with the children. As a result, she lived in a constant state of unease, mistrusting everyone, and it had taken him some time to convince her that he was an okay guy. Later they joked that he'd had to learn 'Feray-whispering' in order to win her trust. After a while, they'd become friends. James and Melissa liked him, and he them, which was Feray's priority for any new friendship. One night, after a family meal and when the children were safely asleep, they'd become lovers. There was no 'moon and June' about it, no promises or expectations. They were grown-ups, happy to be together for the time being and that was good enough.

Once home, he heated a bowl of mulligatawny soup in the microwave and checked his email. Janey had written demanding to know why he hadn't got back to Polly. 'She's in pieces waiting to hear what you think. What are you trying to do to her? Don't you care?'

He was on the point of firing off a reply – 'Where the hell were you when she was deciding to keep this baby? D'you think it's a good idea for her to be lumbered with a child?' But what would that do to Polly if she got a sight of it? And Janey just might make sure she did.

He took a beer from the fridge and re-read his daughter's email. She not only expected him to be delighted that she was pregnant but she was also suggesting that he return to Australia, blatantly using his mother's age and frailty as leverage. It was a big ask and it had come out of the blue. She might be fretting at his silence but it was barely thirty-six hours since he'd received her ultimatum. *'Don't bother getting back to me unless you have something nice to say.'* He needed time to think this through because he had to get it right.

Gil had always made his own decisions and own mistakes. He couldn't deny that he'd been a flaky dad, yet he'd managed, somehow, to do enough not to alienate his children. He'd been delighted and surprised when Polly had mentioned, six months ago, that she wanted to come to London next summer. He accepted that it probably had more to do with having somewhere to stay on her European travels than missing him, but it proved that she didn't think he was a complete waste of space. He'd hoped that, spending time with him in London, seeing him in his new habitat, would go some way to validate his decision to come here. But now this.

Agony Aunt crap wasn't his forté but he was being pressed for an instant decision on a vital issue. It would be good to talk it through with someone who would understand.

Feray knew more about him than anyone in the northern hemisphere. When they'd become lovers it had seemed only fair to let her know what she was taking on and, by the same token, she'd told him that her ex-husband had treated her badly and left her mistrustful of men. She'd refused to elaborate but she'd mentioned his foul temper.

She was his obvious choice as confidante. They'd been together for a couple of years now and it had been good for both of them.

They'd agreed, right from the beginning, it would be foolish to look too far ahead but any decisions he made concerning the future couldn't fail to affect her. Could he suddenly ask her whether he should pack up and head to the other side of the world? It wasn't fair to dump it on her and expect her to be objective. It would be cruel to get her agitated when nothing might change.

Who else was there? Kevin? Mmmm. Perhaps not. In fact, definitely not. Mention a baby and, in his post-natal condition, Kevin would start sobbing and book him on the next flight to Brisbane.

Gil wasn't short of acquaintances – mates, male and female, with whom he could share an evening at the pub or a curry or a gig. He thought of these as his 'here and now' friends. They knew him as the laid-back Aussie bloke who enjoyed a night out once in a while. And that was all they needed to know. All he wanted them to know.

He finished his beer, shucked off his shoes and stretched out on the bed. Having ruled out the 'phone a friend' option he had no choice but to mail Polly, tell her he loved her and explain that he needed more time to get his head around her news. She'd doubtless take his procrastination as a negative response but he'd have to take that chance.

Vivian Carey flashed into his mind. Now there was one cool woman. She'd been – or appeared to have been – unfazed by last night's mayhem. While all around her were going to pieces, she'd *made notes*. He had to hand it to her. It had been good of her to offer Irene a bed too, although he was sure the idea hadn't crossed her mind until he'd mentioned it. Maybe he'd give her a call. Check how she was making out. She'd done that 'phone me' thing when they parted company in Camden Town and she didn't strike him as the sort who did anything unless she meant it.

He heaved himself up and switched on the lamp. His jacket was on the floor where he'd dumped it. Scooping it up, he rooted through the pockets until he found the paper napkin inscribed with her number. He checked the time on his mobile. Six-thirty. He thumbed in the digits, not sure what he was going to say if she answered, not even sure why he was phoning.

'Yes?' Her voice was neutral

'Hi. It's Gil.' He paused, giving her time to process the information. 'From last night?'

'Oh, yes.'

'Did I wake you?'

'You did actually.'

'Sorry. I was just wondering how you're feeling today.'

'Tired. Jittery.'

She used words sparingly as though she thought they were a commodity not to be frittered away and it was impossible to gauge whether she was pleased or annoyed to get his call.

'Did you go to work in the end?' he said.

'No.'

'How did it go with Irene?'

'It went.'

'As a matter of fact she rang me at lunchtime. She suggested we three get together for a coffee sometime,' he said. 'What d'you think?'

'I've had enough of Irene but I'd like to have coffee with you.'

From most women this might have sounded like a come on but from Ms Carey it sounded no more or less than the truth.

9

Next day, when Vivian suggested they get on with sorting out the Cologne trip, Howard insisted on leaving it until the following week. Ottilie kept foisting cups of coffee on her and asking if she 'fancied anything to eat'. Ralph offered to give her a lift home although it was miles out of his way. Everyone at the Elephant House treated her as if she were recuperating from an acute illness. Their relentless consideration irritated her. She neither expected nor needed this pastoral care and she was thankful when it was the end of the day.

Vivian and Nick had spoken several times since his return from Manchester. In the course of these conversations she'd given him a fairly full account of Wednesday evening. She hoped that, having satisfied his curiosity, they could put the incident behind them but when he arrived at her flat on Saturday morning with a bouquet of lilies she feared that he, too, was going to treat her like an invalid.

'God. A few more seconds and…' He hugged her and she wanted to hit him.

She was searching for a tall vase for the lilies – had he forgotten how much she disliked their cloying scent and unnatural perfection? – when he came into the kitchen holding up a postcard card, the text in its centre surrounded with a wreath of roses and forget-me-nots.

'"I am the way, the truth and the life." He pulled a face. 'What are you doing with this sentimental tat?'

'Irene left it for me. It's scratch-and-sniff.'

He drew his thumbnail across the card and held it to his nose. 'Phew. That's rank. You assured me she wasn't a weirdo.'

Vivian pictured Irene, waving a bandaged hand as she disappeared down the escalator. She'd intended consigning the mawkish object to the bin but Nick's suggestion that anyone with religious conviction and poor taste was deranged seemed arrogant and callous.

'She's not a weirdo,' she said, pinning the tract to the notice board, making a big thing of getting it perfectly straight. 'She's lonely. Devout. Sad, I suppose. That doesn't make her weird.'

'Maybe not.' He folded his arms. 'So what was the guy like? The one who was with you?'

'Like? Oh, I don't know. Australian. Middle-aged. Thoughtful.'

'A good match for your Irene, perhaps.' His comment was unnecessary and tinged with spite.

Making out that Irene was weird was one thing but she couldn't have Nick sniping at the man who, spotting that she was going to faint, had given her his crisps. 'Actually, he's rather interesting. He's a medical photographer. I liked him.'

Maybe sensing that it was unwise to continue on this tack, he changed the subject. 'What does your father make of it? He must be relieved you weren't hurt.'

'What is this? The third degree?' She glared at him. 'If you must know, I haven't told him.'

He looked surprised. 'Don't you think you should?'

Her father would certainly have heard about the explosion by now but, as it had no bearing on his life (his criterion for assessing the relevance of anything) he wouldn't give it a second thought. What was the point in telling him she'd been there? He'd simply get steamed up which would do his blood pressure no good at all. Worse still, it would give him the perfect excuse to vent his racial prejudices.

'Why?' she said.

He held up his hands in submission. 'Only asking.'

Overnight, clear skies had given way to racing clouds and, although the thermometer had risen, a raw wind was blowing from the east. Despite the weather, they wrapped up warm, deciding to go ahead with their planned visit to the Heath, Vivian hoping that a brisk walk might dispel her restiveness.

For the past few days her appetite had deserted her and she'd been getting by on coffee and toast, but by the time they'd stomped up Haverstock Hill she was famished and they stopped at The Coffee Cup for brunch. A copy of the *Daily Mail* had been left on the window sill and, while they waited for their omelettes, she flicked through it. On page two there was an interview with a 'survivor of Wednesday's atrocity', a certain Irene Tovey, who praised (and named) her 'two guardian angels'.

'Are they allowed to do that? Without getting my permission?' she said.

'Aren't you being a bit naive? Look, Vivian, I honestly think you should talk to your father. He's going to find out that you were there and he won't be happy that you kept it from him.'

'Dad doesn't read the *Mail*.'

He squeezed her hand. 'Maybe not. But I bet his neighbours do.'

Vivian wasn't surprised that Irene had talked to the press. It was clear that the woman craved attention, something the journos would have latched onto straight away.

She sighed. 'I suppose you're right. I'll go down and see him tomorrow.'

She glanced at Nick, expecting him to look disappointed and to reveal that he'd planned something special for their weekend. At the very least to offer to go with her but all he said was, 'Good idea.'

Almost as soon as they got onto the Heath, it began raining, icy raindrops slanting down, numbing Vivian's cheek and dripping off her waterproof onto her jeans. The paths were fast becoming etched with miniature rivulets, the backs of her jeans splattered with mucky grey shale flicked up by her boots. Only dog walkers and joggers were committed enough to be out here in the numbing wind. They marched on, up towards Kenwood House, pretending for a while that they were finding the weather invigorating. 'The last time we were up here was for *Die Fledermaus*,' she said, only remembering when she saw his puzzled expression that she'd come with Howard and Cara.

Before long they fell into silence. There was no reason for this. Nothing had happened. Yet they had somehow, by tacit consent, become joined in a battle of wills, each determined not to speak first. It was a futile, hazardous contest. Vivian knew she could put an end to the nonsense in seconds. All she had to do was grab his hand and admit to being a moody cow. But she didn't do this because she couldn't bring herself to touch him.

Was she having some kind of breakdown? She did feel wretched. Ottilie had warned her that she would probably suffer delayed shock. 'You've had a horrid experience.' Vivian had shrugged it off. 'I'm fine. Honestly.' Perhaps Ottilie was right and this rawness, this certainty that, were she to speak she would start crying, was a result of Wednesday night.

In the end, Nick broke the silence. 'Jeez. I'm freezing to death. C'mon. Let's go home. I'll cook supper. Or we can get a takeaway if you'd prefer.'

'Indian?' she said, that one word demolishing the ridiculous barrier that had sprung up between them.

They walked off the Heath and on to Hampstead Lane, picking up a cab which had stopped at Kenwood House to drop off a couple of tourists. On the way back, they apologised to each other for being grumpy – even though it was clear that whatever had caused their silent falling-out was more than grumpiness.

Vivian inspected the selection of ready-prepared meals. A salad would suit her but it was Sunday and her father would expect something traditional for his midday meal. So. Bangers and mash or shepherd's pie? She chose the pie, adding a pack of frozen peas and a strawberry trifle to her basket.

'You made the second page, I see,' her father said before she was over the threshold.

'I didn't know you read the *Daily Mail*.'

'I don't, but every other bugger seems to. Three neighbours have already knocked the door and donated their copies. They seem to think I'm keeping a scrapbook.' He indicated the neat pile of newspapers on the kitchen table. 'I didn't let on that you hadn't told me. Wasn't going to give them the satisfaction.'

She waited for his reprimand and when it didn't come she said, 'I didn't want you fretting.'

He shrugged. 'Well, you weren't hurt so there was no need.'

Feeling a surge of gratitude for his unsentimental reaction, she gave him a rundown on her part in the affair. She could see from his face that he wasn't much interested. She wasn't hurt and Warren Street was a foreign country to an octogenarian living in Tooting.

However one aspect of the story did take his fancy. 'This woman,' he prodded the newspaper, 'she sounds like a lunatic.' Squinting through the lower part of his bifocals he read, "I was terrified. I thought I was going to die. I prayed to God and he sent me two guardian angels – Vivian Carey and Gil Thomas.'" He put the paper down. 'What did you do? Fly in wearing a halo?' He chuckled at his own joke.

Vivian suggested that, for a change, they eat lunch in the dining room, a cramped little room that smelled of dusty carpet and which her father rarely used. For once, it didn't feel damp in here and she touched the radiator. It was tepid, the thermostat set on 2, but it had been on recently which was something. Whilst he wasn't looking, she tweaked the valve to maximum, gurgling pipes confirming that the heating was on. The outlook from the window was restricted by the wall of her father's kitchen on the one side and his neighbour's on the other. Consequently next to no daylight penetrated the room and, in order to lend it some cheer, she switched on a table lamp.

'It's nice and warm in here today, Dad,' she said when they sat down to eat.

He gave her a shrewd smile. 'Ahhh, well. I knew you were coming.'

The pie had been a good choice. She took only a small portion whilst her father steadily ploughed his way through the rest.

When she was growing up, he'd been a stickler for good table manners, fastidious to the point of obsession, changing immediately if one speck of food found its way onto his clothing. She watched him now, scooping up the soft food with his fork, lowering his head towards the plate. She noted the splashes of gravy on the front of his shirt, the peas that fell from his fork and rolled across the table cloth, leaving a faint trail in their wake. She shouldn't find the sight and sound of an old man enjoying a hot meal distasteful. But she did.

'Now if *I* had a guardian angel she might like to change my bedding before she flies off again,' he said after they'd cleared the table.

Generally, if he had something to say he came straight out with it and she found this unexpected whimsy irritating.

'You only have to ask, Dad,' she said.

He'd laid out clean linen on his bed – the double bed that he'd shared with her mother. Thinking about it now, it seemed not quite...*nice* for a woman in her mid-fifties to sleep with an old man of eighty. On the other hand, how did a couple get round to agreeing that they no longer wanted to sleep in the same bed? Perhaps when one of them was ill? Sleeping with someone was the cipher for romantic love, so what did it signify when a couple exchanged one bed for two? That the physical side of the relationship was no longer important? Her parents had always slept in the same bed. Did that mean her mother had loved her aged husband – in every sense of the word? It was hard to believe.

She stripped the bed. The linen smelled musty and, when she

70

removed the bottom sheet, a shower of tiny white flakes drifted to the floor. Dried skin? *Ughhh.* She bundled the sheets into the laundry basket. When she came to put on the pillowslips she discovered that she was one short but had no idea where her father kept them.

How little she knew of his day-to-day routine. He employed a cleaner – a Polish woman called Teresa who worked for several people in the neighbourhood and whom she had never met. Teresa came every Wednesday morning but Vivian wasn't sure exactly what her duties were. Washing? Ironing? The place wasn't immaculate, there was only so much anyone could do in three hours, but the kitchen, bathroom and his bedroom – the rooms he used most – were always presentable. On the whole, he was managing remarkably well for a man of eighty-seven who, until five years ago, had depended on her mother to service his needs.

When she came downstairs, he was dozing in the kitchen. She wanted more than anything to go home but she couldn't sneak away whilst he was sleeping. She filled the kettle and took two mugs from the cupboard, clattering about, making sure to rouse him.

'Tea?' she said, watching whilst he surfaced.

'Yes, my darling,' he said, eyes still closed, voice slurred. He reached out his hand as if expecting someone to take it then, when no one did, let it drop back on the arm of the chair.

My darling? His words stopped her in her tracks. He'd never, not even when she was a child, called her anything but 'Vivian'.

'Would you like a cup of tea, Dad?' She spoke louder this time.

When he opened his eyes he seemed confused and she realised that, half asleep, he'd thought she was someone else. 'Yes, please,' he said.

She handed him a mug of tea. 'I was thinking I'd spend Christmas with you.'

He started his usual silly game. 'You don't have to.'

71

And she joined in. 'I know I don't. But I want to.'

They batted untruths back and forth until the matter was settled. She would come on Christmas Eve. 'I'll see you before then, Dad. We can make a list of what we need and I'll get it delivered.'

'Could you take a look in the shed before you go?' he said. 'Something's had a go at my hosepipe. Rats if I'm not mistaken.'

She didn't fancy fumbling about in a dingy shed, looking for rats. 'It'll be too dark to see anything. I'll do it next time I come.'

'You said earlier that I only had to ask,' he said. 'I've got a decent flashlight—'

'No Dad,' she said. 'Next time. I promise.'

Vivian liked Mondays. Whilst those around her grew morose as Sunday afternoon gave way to Sunday evening, her spirits lifted. Weekends were formless, unstructured and in some way... unsatisfactory, but come Monday she knew precisely what was expected of her. It had been the same when she was at school.

She'd had a few wobbly days at the tail end of last week but all that was behind her now. As she ran her bath and sorted her clothes for the next morning, she thought through what she had to do in the coming week. First thing in the morning, she must contact West Dorset District Council. Then she should get after Howard and Ralph about the Cologne trip. They ought really to go this week – or the beginning of next at the very latest. Leave it any longer and they'd find themselves tangled up with Christmas.

She was getting into the bath when her phone rang. It was Gil Thomas.

'Tell me to sod off if it's too late,' he said.

From the background noise she guessed he was in a pub.

'No. It's fine.'

'We should get that cup of coffee soon, don't you agree?'

She watched a raft of bubbles slowly rotating beneath the tap.

Were she to think too hard about this she knew she would find several reasons why it was a bad idea.

'Vivian? Are you still there? I haven't frightened you off, have I?'

'No, you haven't. And yes, we should.'

'Terrific. How are you fixed this week?'

'What did you have in mind?' she asked.

'I was thinking – large Americano. No milk, two sugars.'

It wasn't especially funny but she couldn't help smiling. 'There's nothing in my diary for tomorrow.

'Me neither,' he said.

'Where?'

'How about Camden Town? Six-thirty-ish?'

They arranged to meet at Caffè Nero in Parkway. It was a safe, neutral kind of place to meet a man she didn't know, and not far from home if the meeting proved to be a mistake.

10

Gil wasn't sure why he wanted to see her again but she'd sneaked into his thoughts a dozen times over the weekend. Not in a 'she's hot' way. If anything, she was cold, even mannish – although it was a tad unfair to judge her, bearing in mind the bizarre circumstances of their only meeting. Besides, she was, he guessed, young enough to be his daughter.

His daughter. Polly.

He'd started out emailing Polly but abandoned that and Skyped. He needed to talk to her and to gauge her reaction to what he had to say. She had to see that he was taking her news seriously. That, although he loved her and always would, it was a big thing to get his head around. That she must allow him more time to get it straight. It was a high risk strategy and it had failed. Within minutes of establishing contact, she was sobbing and ranting, accusing him of being heartless and selfish. And, within a few more minutes he had given up, detaching himself from the pixellated image on the screen, wondering when, or why, he'd stopped feeling like a father.

He'd been back to Coffs Harbour twice since moving to London. The kids had given him a hard time on his first visit, refusing to see him, then, when they did, keeping their distance, treating him like a criminal. By his second visit, they'd become too caught up in their own affairs to spare him more than an hour, here and there. They were older – Polly almost twenty and the twins, fourteen – and they'd cooled off a bit. Perhaps they'd seen that their mother was happier with her new man than she'd ever been with him.

His own mother, bless her, had never tried to persuade him to come back. His sisters, both born out there, were Australians through and through. Maybe she thought that having two of her three children

74

(along with seven grandchildren) living within fifty miles of her wasn't a bad score. He spoke to her regularly and, okay, maybe she *was* a bit forgetful at times but only stuff that didn't matter and he was cross with Polly for using her to shame him into returning.

He hadn't told Feray about the baby yet. Everything was so up in the air – more so after the Skype session – and it seemed vital that he resolve things with Polly, or at very least in his own mind, before he did. He'd not told her about Vivian Carey either. Well he *had*, but only in a sketchy, dismissive way. When he'd described his part in Wednesday night's incident, he'd included her in the catchall 'I helped a couple of women find a taxi'. Nor had he mentioned that he'd arranged to meet one of these women for coffee.

He was at Caffè Nero ten minutes early, in no doubt that Vivian's 'six-thirty-ish' would be six-thirty. He'd made up his mind to dress as he would on any other working Monday but somehow he'd ended up wearing his black jeans and the chambray shirt which Feray said made him look like – correction, 'a *little* like' – Paul Newman. He'd even found time for a haircut. Well, it was time for a trim.

Vivian was two minutes early, pushing the heavy glass door open and striding in, scanning the crowded coffee shop. He raised his hand and stood up, as straight as he could, making the most of his five-nine.

'Hello again,' he said, holding out his hand.

She took off her green leather glove. 'Hello.' Her hand was cold.

'What can I get you?'

'Tea, please. No milk. I've been drinking coffee all day.'

'Anything to eat?'

'Yes. Choose something for me.'

He was struck, not for the first time, by her way of saying things which, coming from any other young woman would sound flirtatious but from her sounded authoritative.

'You're not allergic to nuts? The edible kind, I mean.'

She looked puzzled for a second then smiled. 'Oh. No. I'm not.'

He inspected the selection behind the Perspex screen. Muffin? Flapjack? Croissant? They all looked rather 'end-of-the-day' but he wondered if her request was a test of his decisiveness and he chose a chocolate twist and a *pain au raisin*.

'How've you been?' he asked, lowering the black tray onto the table.

She shrugged. 'Tetchy. Any little thing sets my nerves jangling. I'm snapping at everyone.'

She leaned forward and cut both pastries in two, pushing half of each towards him in an unexpectedly intimate gesture. 'How have *you* been?'

'Tetchy.'

'You seemed so together,' she said.

'It's not the bomb.'

She raised her eyebrows.

'It's my daughter. She's pregnant. The bloke's scarpered. After five years of hating my guts she suddenly wants me to go back to Australia. Be the perfect grandpa. My ex-wife is giving me a hard time about it too, although it's nothing to do with her. Oh, and my mother may be losing her marbles.'

He hadn't intended it to come out like that – petulant and whingeing – but at least it gave her an instant snapshot of his family situation.

'It must be hard, you here, your family in Australia.'

'No. It's easy, actually. Up until now, that is. But Polly's given me this ultimatum. Come back now or don't bother.'

'How old is she?'

'Twenty-two. Same age her mother was when she was born. Same circumstances, too, except I stuck around.'

He couldn't believe he was telling her this stuff. The idea was to learn more about her but so far all he'd discovered was that she didn't suffer from a nut allergy.

76

'What d'you think of my tie?' he asked, struggling to find less treacherous territory.

She inspected it. 'Not very interesting. I wouldn't have had you down as a diagonal stripe man. Or polyester, come to that.'

'I'm not. It turned up at the hospital today, along with a pair of navy socks with those little diamonds down the sides. Gift-wrapped. Presents from our mutual friend.'

'Poor Irene.' Vivian took a bite of the chocolate twist. 'What am I talking about? She's creepy. Did you see the article in the *Mail*?'

'Yes. They've been ribbing me in work all day. Still, if thinking we're angels helps her, I can hack it.'

They chatted and by the time they'd eaten the pastries and drunk second cups of tea, he'd established that Vivian was thirty-six – older than he'd imagined – and an only child. Her mother was dead and her father lived in Tooting. She was bilingual in German. The information had emerged in a matter-of-fact fashion entirely in keeping with her style.

By seven twenty-five, there were only a few people left in the café. The staff were bustling around, making a big show of sweeping the floor.

'Chucking out time,' he said. The hour had passed too quickly. 'What are you doing now?'

'Going home, I suppose.'

'I'll walk you.'

'You don't have to. I'm used to getting myself around,' she said, winding a green scarf around her neck.

'I don't doubt it. But I'd like to.'

She held his gaze. 'Why?'

She was on her own patch, it was early evening and they were a mere well-lit mile from Belsize Park. No point in pretending it was an act of chivalry. Whatever reason he came up with had better be as near the truth as he could make it because she would see through any bullshit.

'Why? Because I enjoy your company. I like the way you give straight answers to straight questions. You're clever and you don't try to hide it. You scare me a bit, too.' He dragged the palms of his hands down his cheeks, feeling the roughness of his twelve-hour beard. 'I'm not doing very well here am I?'

She kept her eyes on his face, letting him flounder.

'And I think you have the most remarkable hair. I want to touch it. See if it's as cold as it looks.'

He saw himself through her eyes – a weird, middle-aged hair fetishist – and he half-expected her to walk away.

'It's just hair,' she said leaning towards him so that it swung away from her cheek. 'Go ahead.'

He shoved his hands deep in his pockets and laughed. 'I can't now, can I?'

'I'm freezing,' she said. 'Shall we start walking?'

They walked north, leaving the trendy shops and restaurants of Camden Lock and entering the scruffy no-man's-land around Chalk Farm.

He pointed to the squat bulk of the Roundhouse to their left, aglow with gaudy lights. 'I saw Alice Cooper there a couple of weeks ago.'

'Alice Cooper?'

'You're too young. *I'm* too young. But it had to be done. And it's a great venue. Pretty handy for you.'

'It is. But I rarely go.'

'You're not into music?'

'I am, but I never seem to find time.'

'What type of thing d'you listen to?'

He felt embarrassed by the banality of his conversation.

'Emo. Sad stuff. D'you know The Weakerthans?'

'No, I don't think I do.'

'Canadian. They've been around for a while.'

Her enthusiasm around the topic was surprising and endearing. She'd seemed too earnest to be suckered by pop music.

'You?' she said.

'You'll groan.'

'I won't. I promise.'

'Blues. Jazz.'

She groaned and they laughed and he felt the bond between them strengthen.

They started up Haverstock Hill. The wind bent the branches of the plane trees that lined the pavement, the force of it making the going harder.

'You said your father lives in Tooting,' he said. 'What does he do?'

'Not much. He's eighty-seven.'

'*Eighty-seven?*' It was out before he could stop it.

'Yes. Obscene, isn't it?'

'Well—'

'The plan was that he'd die first and that I'd have my mother to myself for twenty-five more years. That was *my* plan anyway.'

They plodded on up the hill. Vivian's long legs enabled her to steam along and, by the time they reached Belsize Park station, Gil was out of breath.

'Down here,' she said, indicating a turn on the left.

Street lights illuminated a terrace of three-storey houses with wide frontages. The houses had graceful windows and balconies above the front doors. As he'd imagined, it was a different world from his down-at-heel neighbourhood.

'This is me,' she said, stopping at the wrought iron gate of Number 15.

He noted the three meter boxes located beneath the front window, the only ugliness spoiling the elegant facade. 'Which flat?'

'First floor.'

'Nice neighbours?'

'An old lady below. Middle-aged man above. We keep ourselves to ourselves. It works fine but Mrs Sachs won't live forever and

79

Malcolm could decide to take up tap dancing. It's easy to get out if you're renting. Not so easy if you have to sell. Especially with things as they are.'

He was surprised to hear she owned this flat. The mortgage for a two-bedroomed place in this location must be exorbitant, especially as, from what he'd gleaned, she lived alone. Few of his acquaintances owned property and those that did had been forced to move way, way out to find something affordable.

'Will you come in?' she said.

He'd been wondering whether she would ask and how to respond if she did. He wanted to accept but something made him hesitate. 'I've promised to meet a friend at my local around nine-ish. Can we do it another time?'

'Sure.' It was impossible to tell whether she was relieved or disappointed by his refusal. 'How will you get back?'

'I'll walk. It can't be more than a couple of miles. I'll cut through Prince of Wales Road. Forty-five minutes, max.'

They swapped email addresses and shook hands. Now that he knew her mother had been German, he understood where some of her mannerisms – the hand-shaking thing and the candour – came from.

When he reached Kentish Town Road, he texted Feray to let her know he would be home in ten minutes. He gave no reason for his late return but she assumed that he'd been working late, and it was simpler that way.

'You let that Kevin take advantage of you,' she said when he let himself in.

She was standing with her back to him, dropping cutlery in the drawer, and he pulled her hair away from the nape of her neck and kissed it.

'I'll take advantage of *you*, if you like.'

She wriggled and laughed. 'Ouch. Your hands are cold.'

She turned to face him and he pulled her to him, kissing her again, this time on the lips, firm and long.

'What's that for?' she said.

'Does there have to be a reason?'

'No.'

They kissed again.

'D'you fancy cheese on toast?' she asked.

'Fantastic.'

The sound of canned laughter was coming from the living room where the kids were watching television. It was snug down here in the basement and the normality of family life, the warmth of Feray's body were, in that instant, the most desirable things in the world.

'Okay if I stay tonight?' he said.

His request seemed to surprise her. They'd fallen in to the habit of sleeping together at weekends and but rarely on weekdays.

She pulled back and, reaching up, took his face between the palms of her hands, thwarting any attempt he might make to avoid her gaze. 'Are you okay?' she said.

'Why d'you ask?'

She shook her head. 'I ask you a question – you ask me a question back again. You do this all the time, Gil. It makes me feel like I'm nagging. It's not good. Something's not right. Is that why you're late home?'

Feray wouldn't understand about Vivian. He didn't himself. Instead he told her about Polly's pregnancy and her demand that he return to Australia. She would have to know sooner or later and it might explain his distraction.

She listened and, when he'd finished, she took a piece of cheese from the fridge and began grating it violently.

'Aren't you going to say anything?' he asked.

'When did you find this out?'

He pretended to think. 'Ummm. Middle of the week, I guess.'

He reached out to take some grated cheese and she slapped his hand hard – too hard for the minor offence. 'Why didn't you tell me before?'

'I dunno. Maybe the explosion rattled me more than I realised.'

He watched her expression soften at his phony justification.

'Have you decided what you're going to do?' she asked.

'No. Not yet. It's…complicated.'

'Okay. What d'you *want* to do?'

'That's easy. I want to carry on as if nothing's changed. Is that a terrible thing to admit?'

'Terrible? No. But things *have* changed. You can't deny it.'

'You asked me what I wanted to do and I told you.' He was irritated by her smug observation. 'If you must know, I didn't tell you about Polly because I didn't want you getting in a state.'

'A state? About what?' She placed two pieces of bread on the rack and shoved the tray under the grill. 'I'm not pinning my hopes on you if that's what you think. I'm not that stupid.'

They both had their backs to the door and didn't notice Melissa come into the kitchen.

'Are you two fighting again?' she said.

'You should be in bed,' Feray said. 'Tell your brother to switch that rubbish off.'

'Don't forget it's cookery tomorrow, Mum.' She pointed to a list fixed to the fridge door by a magnet shaped like a cupcake.

'You've had all evening to do this. You're old enough to sort it out for yourself,' Feray said, grabbing the list, opening and banging cupboard doors as she gathered ingredients and slammed them down on the worktop.

'What's on the menu?' Gil asked. It wasn't fair to take it out on Melissa.

'Chocolate brownies.' The girl glanced over his shoulder. 'Something's burning.'

He rescued the toast but not before the smoke alarm had set up its piercing warning.

He imagined Vivian Carey's flat as it would be now. Calm. Neat. Peaceful.

And, an hour later, when he and Feray made love, he imagined how it might feel to rest his cheek against Vivian Carey's cold, black hair.

11

Vivian detected an increased nervousness around public places. Warnings not to leave luggage unattended, to be on the lookout for suspicious packages, were more in evidence. She was aware of commuters furtively inspecting station platforms and scrutinising each others' bags. Anyone from the Middle East was the focus of ill-disguised scrutiny.

The story circulating on Twitter was that it had been a botched job. That a suicide bomber, driving to his target destination – possibly one of the main-line stations – had prematurely detonated explosives strapped to his body. This theory raised as many questions as it answered but, once out there, it gained credibility and the police seemed happy to let the rumour run.

Gil mailed her most days – a few lines or a comment on something he'd seen. Nothing heavy or intimate, more like passing the time of day. Attached to one of his mails was a photograph of youngsters fooling around near a fountain. The picture was full of life and movement. It hadn't crossed her mind that his photographic skills might extend beyond the technical requirements of his job. He was a nice guy. Easy to be with. It would be good to see him again. He hadn't mentioned another meeting but she guessed that he was waiting for her to raise the matter.

Irene, too, kept in touch. Vivian regretted having given the woman her number and always diverted her calls to voicemail. But that didn't stop the texts coming. Or the gifts. A pair of tights and a pack of toothbrushes (to replace the ones Vivian had given her that night). A bottle of peach-scented hand cream – Boots' own brand. A calendar with a different picture of a stately home for every month of the coming year. Each gift was accompanied by a tract and a coy note on a sheet of pink notepaper.

Gil had received gifts, too. 'She wants us to get together,' he wrote in one of his mails. 'How did you respond?' 'I didn't.'

The trip to Cologne was firmed up. The four of them – Cara was coming too – would leave early next Wednesday morning and return late on Thursday. Ottilie made appointments for them with the client and the contractor, and also arranged viewings of a couple of offices both of which incorporated living accommodation.

Cara mailed, suggesting that, at some point, Vivian 'ditch' the men and they go shopping. Vivian explained that they were on a tight schedule but Cara wasn't one to accept work as reason not to have fun and, in the end, Vivian agreed that she would try.

Work was frantic. Everyone involved in the building process was struggling to get things done before the two-week Christmas break. To make things more difficult, the weather was causing problems with deliveries of materials, and pouring concrete was out of the question due to the freezing conditions. On top of that, there was the inescapable round of Christmas parties which Howard liked his staff to attend but which were no more than networking opportunities.

The trip to Cologne went smoothly. At home, she and her mother had always spoken German to each other but, since her death, Vivian had had few opportunities to use it. She was concerned that she might be rusty. She needn't have worried. After a hesitant start, she was soon into her stride and, although most of the people they dealt with spoke English, she knew that her fluency impressed them.

It appeared that Cara had primed Ottilie and their appointments had been shuffled to leave a couple of hours free.

'I expect you know Cologne well,' Cara said.

'Not really.'

'D'you have family in Germany?'

'My mother's older sister lives in Munich. And I've got two German cousins. But we don't really keep in touch.'

'No? That's a shame.'

When Vivian was growing up, once in a while letters had arrived from Germany. She'd been taken with the envelopes lined with tissue paper. (How could – why *should* – German envelopes be so different from their English equivalent?) Her mother and Tante Steffi's handwriting were identical, as if every German schoolchild was taught to write by the same teacher.

Then there was the stamp ritual – cutting (never tearing) the corner off the envelope, floating it in a saucer of water until the paper saturated. *Be patient Vivian, you'll damage it.* Next the most enjoyable part – sliding the stamps off the paper, the glue slimy on her fingers. Drying it between sheets of blotting paper. Sticking it in her stamp album.

The letters themselves, written on flimsy airmail paper, were of little interest. The snow was late this year. Her cousin had done well in his music exam. Tante Steffi had fallen off her bicycle and grazed her knee. It was dull stuff.

She and her mother, never her father, had visited every couple of years, spending a week in a characterless suburb of Munich. When her mother died, Steffi came to the funeral but since then they'd done no more than exchange birthday cards. Maybe it *was* a shame. She had little enough in the way of family. Perhaps she should make more of an effort.

One of Cara's friends had recommended they go to Apostelnstrasse. 'Apparently the shops are very elegant and there are several jewellers which might be worth a look. I've checked and it's not far.'

Apostelnstrasse turned out to be a narrow street, snarled with traffic. Cara was disappointed with the jewellers – 'Very passé…' – but they happened across a smart coffee shop where the Apfelstrudel and pungent coffee made up for the disappointment.

On the way to link up with Howard and Ralph, they passed a shop window displaying stylish winter hats. The day had been bright and clear but now, as the sun was setting, the air felt dangerously cold. Vivian had checked the weather forecast and packed a warm hat. Cara hadn't, and complained that her head was aching with the cold. Ten minutes later they emerged from the shop, Cara looking stunning in a grey Cossak-style hat, faux fur with a velvet crown, Vivian carrying a small bag containing a knitted beanie – navy blue with a jade green fleecy lining.

'That's nice. For Nick?' Cara said.

'Maybe. I'm sure I'll find someone who'd like it.'

On the flight back, they discussed which property the firm should rent, Cara insisting that they choose one which had room for guests.

Howard smiled and kissed his wife's cheek. 'Why don't we let Vivian decide?'

'I liked the first one,' Vivian said. 'It's cheaper and it's nearer the site.'

'The living accommodation's pretty tight,' Ralph said.

'Yes, but I shan't be spending a lot of time there. It's only somewhere to eat, sleep and shower.'

Been offered a couple of tickets for the Roundhouse tomorrow. Romeo and Juliet – *RSC. Not Alice Cooper but great reviews. Free? Fancy it? Gil.*

She checked her diary. Tomorrow. 6.30pm. Damn. A 'Christmas nibbles' do in Holborn. The Roundhouse sounded far more interesting.

She mailed him back. *What time?*

They arranged to meet in Belgo Noord, a bar on Chalk Farm Road opposite the Roundhouse. It was a single-storey building sandwiched between Italian and Thai restaurants. Vivian had passed it scores of times but its drab green façade and the limp

Belgian flag hanging above the entrance had never tempted her inside.

The place was packed. It was hot and noisy. There was a strong smell of garlic and fish – presumably the mussels, advertised as the speciality of the house.

Gil was standing just inside the door. 'Hi,' he said and they shook hands.

She looked around, taking in the exposed pipework and industrial-style detailing. In direct contrast, the bar staff and waiters were dressed as Trappist monks.

'I'm not getting it,' she said.

'It's Belgian,' he said, as if that explained everything.

His tired-looking anorak was unzipped and beneath it she could see a navy shirt and yellow bow tie.

'Nice tie,' she said.

'Thanks. I wasn't too sure.' He tugged at the bow, squaring it up and flattening it against his shirt collar. 'Tricky things. Only took me and Freddy ten minutes to tie. Surgeons aren't as good with their hands as you might hope. But I thought I should make an effort for the Bard.'

'How did you get the tickets?' she asked.

'Perks of the job. You'd be surprised how often doctors fail to check their diaries. They're constantly double-booking themselves.'

'So they give you their tickets?'

'Yep. They see me as a charity case. I'm badly paid. I'm from a cultural wasteland. In fact I'm doing them a favour.'

'How?'

'I turn them into philanthropists.'

They caught up with each other's news. She told him about her trip to Cologne and he told her that he'd made no progress in patching things up with his daughter. They drank beer and ate crisps and she found herself thinking that were she going with

88

Nick, they'd be eating in some *chi-chi* restaurant, each of them preoccupied with what was in tomorrow's diary.

They made their way across the road and found their seats in the packed auditorium. Vivian couldn't remember the last time she saw a live performance of *Romeo and Juliet*. (Probably when she was at school.) The Roundhouse was an iconic venue and this was a startling production. Live music, pyrotechnics and video imagery more than compensated for the minimal sets, and by the time the lovers lay dead, she had forgotten that she was sitting in a defunct railway shed.

'Thank you,' she said afterwards as they shuffled towards the exit. 'I loved it.'

'Well you should really thank Mike Newham and his lack of forward planning.'

They were only ten minutes walk from her flat and she'd been debating whether to invite him back for that promised drink. But tomorrow was a working day.

Gil solved her dilemma. 'Will you be okay from here?'

The route was well-lit and there were plenty of people about. 'Of course,' she said, experiencing a tug of regret. 'Goodnight. And thanks again.'

'Goodnight, Vivian.'

She cleared her throat. 'Last time, you said you enjoyed being with me. I enjoy being with you too.'

'Good,' he said. 'You can take me out next time.'

'It's a deal.'

He leaned forward and planted a kiss her on the cheek. 'That's settled then.'

Gil had watched enough middle-aged saddos go gaga over girls young enough to be their daughters. On the day his divorce came through, he'd vowed never to tangle with any woman more than ten years his junior. He'd also promised himself that he would be straight with Feray. It was as well to lay down a few ground rules and, until now, it had been easy to stick to them.

This Vivian Carey thing, coming as it had out of the blue, had wrong-footed him. He'd understand were she the kind of woman who drove a man's brains into his boxers. But she wasn't. In fact men (he used Kevin Lisle as his benchmark in these matters) might be turned off by her candour and near androgyny.

So what was going on? Was it the challenge? The thrill of the chase? If so, he'd better knock it on the head right now because challenges were for round-the-world yachtsmen and chases ended up with someone getting hurt.

And yet. He found himself planning interesting places to take her. Things to tell her. Gifts he might buy her – modest things like a postcard from Tate Modern or a packet of multicoloured paperclips.

It had taken willpower not to suggest walking her home after the play. He'd wrestled with the dilemma throughout the final act. She might have felt obliged to ask him in for the promised coffee. He should have accepted her invitation last time when it was eight o'clock and when 'a coffee' meant just that. At eleven the agenda wasn't so clear-cut.

Their email correspondence kept ticking over. Her replies, prompt and witty, made him think that she was happy to continue their association. And that made him happy. He wanted to see her again but he wasn't sure how to go about it. Mike's tickets had given him the perfect excuse, but the last thing he wanted was to come across as a creepy old perv.

He'd let it ride. Leave it up to her.

'Had any thoughts about Christmas?' Feray asked.

'Why?' Gil said.

She glared at him. He was doing it again – answering her question with one of his own.

'No. I haven't had any thoughts about Christmas.'

'Well here's what the kids and I are doing.'

She gave him a rundown of the commitments she had with work and the children over the holiday period. 'We'll be spending Christmas Day with Mum and Dad.'

'That'll be nice.'

'Mum said you're more than welcome. She can't cope with the idea of anyone being on their own on Christmas Day. I'd like you to come but I'm not going to get into a fight about it, okay?'

A similar invitation had been extended last year but he'd had a legitimate reason to dip out. A mate of his, a journalist he'd worked with back in his days on the *Gazette*, was in London researching a book on orphans who had been shipped to Australia under The Empire Settlement Act. Andy had been delighted to spend Christmas with him and together they'd reeled around the pubs of north London. Whatever they did (neither had much recollection of the detail) served the purpose of passing the day – and the next day, too.

He'd met Feray's parents a fair few times but he'd never been to their home. As far as they were concerned, he was a neighbour who gave their daughter a hand now and again when she needed something doing. He guessed that they knew there was more to it than that. The kids were a source of information if they wanted to probe but maybe it suited them to maintain the pretence that he was a just a friend. Turgut and Munire Ergen were hardworking, down-to-earth people (he worked in the dry cleaners, she in the bread shop). But Christmas Day? To be honest he'd rather spend it listening to Miles Davies and sorting his photographs.

His face must have revealed his reluctance because she added, 'You've got two weeks to come up with an excuse.'

The stand-off with Polly continued. Janey, too, was behaving like a petulant teenager, ignoring his emails and refusing to take his calls. Needing someone whom he could trust to tell it like it was, he phoned his younger sister.

Despite the five-year age gap, he and Louise got on well. Always had. He suspected, although they never discussed it, that what bound them together was their dislike – maybe that was too fierce a word – of their sister, Rachel. As a kid, Louise had been a tomboy, always off with the boys, playing cricket or fishing for crabs. This had irritated Rachel. What use was a sister who preferred kicking a football to dressing up like a fairy? The irony was that Louise, without making any effort, had turned into a real beauty. She'd had her pick of the boys and had ended up marrying Dan, one of Rachel's old flames.

'Hi, stranger,' she said. 'Good to hear you.' Her voice was as clear as if she'd been speaking from the next street.

After they'd exchanged niceties, he told her about the baby and Polly's ultimatum. 'I said I needed time to get my head round it. That pissed her off big time.'

'Actually I ran into her a few weeks ago,' Louise said, 'and I have to say she looked washed out. It did cross my mind that she was pregnant.'

In all his ponderings, he'd never wondered how his daughter was faring in her pregnancy. 'She was okay though?' he said.

'Seemed to be. I was on my way to work and we didn't have much of a chat.' She paused. 'I wouldn't expect her to tell me stuff like that anyway. She knows we're close, you and I. Since you left, she and the twins have been pretty wary of me.'

'Left? As in left Janey or left Oz?'

'As in left *them*, Gil. Kids are egocentric little bastards. We were no different. When Gramps died I thought he'd done it to spite *me*. All that changes when you have kids of your own, of course.'

Gil guessed she was adding the silent rider *for some of us, anyway*.

'How's Mum,' he said.

'Pretty chirpy. She's talking about taking a trip to Sydney after Christmas. Something to do with her quilting class.'

'D'you think she knows about the baby?' he said.

'I'm sure she doesn't. We speak most days. She would have told me. And she'd be knitting, too.'

'Does she see much of my kids?'

His need to grill his sister on his children's habits filled him with sadness. But he'd chosen to leave. What did he expect?

'They drop in occasionally. The boys more than Polly, I think. That probably has to do with food. You know how she loves feeding people.'

'And Rachel?'

'Oh, Rache is Rache. Busy organising us for Christmas. We're all going to hers. I've had my instructions. What presents to buy. Food to bring. Time to arrive. And we've all got to promise we'll have a good time.'

Poor Louise. He knew that her perfect Christmas Day would be spent with her nose in a book. She'd be happy with a cheese sandwich for lunch and a stroll along the shore with Dan and her children as the sun was going down. But she'd go along with Rachel's demands for the sake of their mother.

'Look, Gil, I've got absolutely no right tell you what you should do, but...'

'I'm a selfish prick and I should come back to Oz and face my responsibilities.'

'Something along those lines,' she said. 'I'm being selfish, too. I miss you.'

Louise never did that 'wasn't it great when?' or 'd'you remember the time?' thing. She was one of the few people he knew who anchored themselves in the present, content to make the most of now, rather than fretting about what had been or would be.

'Thanks, sis. Can I ask you a favour? Could you not mention the baby to Mum or Rachel?'

'No worries. That's up to Polly. Oh, I take it you're still bunked up with your neighbour. Feray, isn't it?'

'We're hardly "bunked up". It's pretty much an open relationship.'

She laughed. 'Whatever.'

12

Vivian was checking the fenestration schedule for the gallery when a call came through on the office landline.

'Someone from St. George's Hospital,' Ottilie said.

For a second she thought it must be to do with the explosion but, when the voice on the other end asked 'Is this Vivian Carey? Daughter of Philip Frederick Carey?' she knew that it wasn't.

'Yes.' Vivian said. 'What's happened?

'Hello, Miss Carey. I'm Doctor Ababne. I work in A&E at St George's. Your father's broken his hip, I'm afraid. We've just admitted him.'

'He's all right?'

'Yes. A little confused but he's in no danger.'

'What happened? Where was he?'

'He fell. That's all I can tell you I'm afraid. As I said, he's slightly disorientated and I'm sure he'd feel reassured if you were here with him. Or is there someone else…?'

No. There is no one else.

'I'll come now,' she said. 'It might take me a while to get there.'

'No hurry. We'll let him know you're on your way. That'll lift his spirits.'

Howard thought she should take a cab but it was getting towards rush hour. 'Tube's quicker,' she said.

'Off you go,' he said, shooing her away with his hand. 'We'll cope. Sort your father out. Hips can be nasty when you're old.'

By the time she reached the hospital it was five-thirty. The waiting room for A&E was bigger than the one at UCH although it smelled the same and was just as hot. The seats were occupied mainly by men in work clothes or mothers with children. Everyone looked either apprehensive, resigned or plain bored. Not surprising as the scrolling screen opposite the entrance informed her that 'The waiting time to see a doctor is currently three hours.'

The receptionist found her father's name on a list and directed her down a warren of corridors to 'Assessment'. This turned out to be a large area subdivided by curtains suspended from tracks into, perhaps, a dozen bays, each big enough to take a hospital trolley, a small desk and a chair. The curtains were made of floral-patterned fabric, presumably to cheer the place up, but they looked merely domestic and out of place.

Staff in white coats or blue uniforms bustled about, intent on whatever it was they were doing. There didn't appear to be anyone monitoring or directing members of the public. She wandered down the centre of the room, glancing to left and right. *Where is he?* No one stopped her. No one demanded to know what business she had there. Bearing in mind the rigorous checks everywhere else in the city, the lack of security here was alarming.

She found him in the fifth cubicle on the left. Head tipped back and eyes closed, he was half-sitting, half-lying on a trolley, propped on several pillows and hooked up to a drip. His lower half was covered by a cellular blanket and the sides of the trolley were fixed upright like the sides of a cot. Were it not for his wristwatch she might not have been sure it was him.

The watch was a Timex, which he'd had forever. As a child she had been captivated by its expanding strap, gazing transfixed when he'd pulled it on, mesmerised by the way it more than doubled its length, then shrank to grip his wrist. He'd forbidden her to touch it without his permission. But on one occasion she'd come across it on the bathroom window sill and had been unable to resist. The cold heft of it. How its scissoring innards were exposed when she stretched it. How, when she folded it first one way, then the other, it became a rippling serpent. She hadn't heard him come upstairs. He'd lectured her about respecting other people's possessions, his tirade bouncing and echoing off the tiled surfaces. Then he'd

96

confiscated her new torch, locking it in his desk drawer for a whole week.

She positioned the chair next to the trolley and studied him. His mouth gaped. Where were his dentures? He wore a grubby grey shirt, open to the second button. The blanket had slipped a little on the one side revealing a sliver of pale, hairless skin at his waist and it was apparent that he was naked from there on down. This shocked her. Maybe it shouldn't have. Nakedness was no big deal in a hospital. Her father had damaged his hip (left or right?) so they needed to get at it easily. But he was a fiercely private man and he'd hate to be seen like this, even by his daughter, and she adjusted the blanket to cover the bare flesh.

After her mother's death, she could hardly bear to be with her father. She hated him for living, for casting the shadow of his old age across her life. She'd contemplated running far, far away, but something – love for her mother? A sense of responsibility? Fear of criticism? Superstition? – prevented her from running further than Belsize Park.

Time had gone on and she'd been unable to sustain that level of loathing. It would have worn her out. The hatred had modified to chronic exasperation seasoned with blame. To be fair, he'd demanded little of her, and he'd proved to be remarkably robust for such an old man. Good health wasn't, however, a guarantee against accidents. This fall, or something like it, was bound to happen sooner or later. It was too much to hope that he would die, healthily and independently, in his own bed. No one did, did they?

She watched the clear liquid, drip, drip, dripping from the bag into the tube taped to the back of his hand. Was this all that was keeping him alive? She could try fooling herself that everything would be all right – but it wouldn't, no matter how this played out. Through no fault of her own, her life was about to change. Her mother should be the one sitting here, having to deal with this. Marry an old man, bear him a child then vanish when things were on the point of getting difficult. It wasn't on. So why not walk away now? Disappear. No one knew she was here. He was in safe hands and they couldn't force her to take responsibility for him. Could they?

'Drink,' he moaned. Eyes still closed, he turned his head towards her and murmured, 'Thirsty,' his voice frail, his toothless consonants imprecise.

'I'll fetch someone,' she said.

His hand reached out, flapping feebly yet impatiently. 'Drink.'

'Miss Carey?'

She turned to see a young man holding a large manila envelope. 'Yes,' she said.

'I'm Doctor McKenzie.' He had a Scottish accent. White coat a size too big, stethoscope slung self-consciously around his neck, he looked like a ten-year-old on his way to a fancy dress party.

They shook hands. 'What's he done exactly?' she said.

'Your father has a fracture of the left femoral head,' he said, easing two X-rays from the envelope. Jamming them into the clip above the light-box behind the trolley, he flicked a switch. 'There.' He traced a barely visible line running like a thread of cotton across the ethereal image. 'See?'

'The doctor I spoke to on the phone said it was his hip,' she said.

Perhaps she should ask him to fetch someone who knew what they were talking about because she couldn't believe this child did.

'Yes. Well. "Hip" is shorthand for the hip *joint* but, if we're going to be dead accurate, it's the head of the femur that's damaged.'

'I'd like us to be "*dead accurate*" if that's possible,' she said, glad to find a target for her anger. 'So what happens now? And what's the prognosis?'

Her questions seemed to throw him as if, in identifying the

98

injury, his job was done. He glanced around. 'I need to get one of my colleagues to talk to you about that.'

'My father's asking for a drink. Can he have one?'

'I'm afraid it's nil by mouth until we complete the assessment. The drip ensures that he doesn't get dehydrated.'

'He's *thirsty*. His mouth is dry. He wants liquid in his mouth not his hand.'

He shook his head. 'I'm sorry. I'll find someone to explain what'll be happening from here on.' And, having discharged his duty, off he went.

Her father was rousing and she guessed that whatever medication they'd given him was wearing off.

'Hello, Dad.'

'Vivian,' he said. 'I'm so thirsty. Can you get me a drink?'

His lips were scaled with dry skin and she felt wretched. 'In a minute, Dad.' She took his hand, hers sweaty, his cold and dry. 'What happened?'

'I tripped. Fell.' He shifted slightly on the trolley and his faced distorted with pain. 'Oh, God, oh, God.'

This was ghastly. She felt like a torturer, standing there, doing nothing to alleviate his pain or his thirst.

'Drink. Drink. Drink,' he intoned, over and over and over, and she wanted to cry.

She waylaid a passing nurse. 'My father's desperate for a drink.'

The nurse glanced into the cubicle. 'He's nil by mouth, love. I'll bring you sponge and you can moisten his lips.'

She wanted to scream *stop telling me he's nil by mouth* but instead, fearful that the nurse wouldn't come back, she went with her, returning with water in a stainless steel bowl and a synthetic sponge wrapped in cellophane.

Some people knew instinctively how to make ill people comfortable. The right things to say and do. They had no qualms about flesh, saliva, blood and worse. Vivian wasn't one of those people. *Moisten his lips.* Having steeled herself to touch his slack mouth, she was doing reasonably well until he grabbed the sponge from her and began sucking it. In her haste to take it from him, she spilled the water on the blanket.

'How are we doing?' Another doctor, a woman this time. Older. Wearing a headscarf and carrying a folder. Vivian glanced at the tag clipped to the pocket of the doctor's white coat. Doctor Ababne.

'*He's* in pain, semi-conscious and thirsty,' Vivian said, 'and *I* don't have a clue what's going on. Apart from that *we're* doing brilliantly.'

The doctor gestured for Vivian to sit down. She explained that her father had been given a pain-killing injection which had made him woozy but, until they'd decided when to operate, he couldn't have anything to eat or drink.

'Who makes the decision?' Vivian asked.

'I do.' Doctor Ababne consulted her notes. 'Mmmm. Considering his age, I'm inclined to leave it a day or two. Let him get over the shock of the fall. Give us time to run some tests.'

'You have to operate?'

'It's standard procedure for this type of fracture. As soon as we locate a bed, we'll take him up to the ward. And I'll get someone to bring him a drink.'

Vivian felt a surge of gratitude. 'Thank you. I'm sorry…'

The doctor shook her head and smiled calmly. 'Don't apologise. You've had a shock too.'

A nurse – a different one – brought a jug of water and a plastic tumbler. Also a 'bottle' made of compressed paper. 'In case he needs a wee. Don't worry though. We've popped a pad on. Just in case.'

Sponges. Bottles. Pads. Vivian wasn't sure she could do this.

After a few sips of water, her father became more alert. More restless, too, fidgeting on the trolley, moaning, complaining that

100

his back was aching and that his feet were cold. Vivian folded over the bottom of the blanket and tucked it beneath his heels, taking care not to lift his legs in case the movement caused more pain.

'Tell me what happened, Dad' she said, taking his hand again.

After his morning coffee, needing to tighten a screw on a door hinge, he'd gone in search of a screwdriver. (The small one in the kitchen drawer wasn't up to the job.) The path leading to the garden shed was damp and slick with moss. On the way, he'd slipped and gone down heavily on his left side.

'Lucky I wasn't on my way back. I might have stabbed myself.'

Vivian let herself in. This was the first time she'd used her keys – the first time she'd been alone in this house. It was near midnight but the kitchen table still held the remnants of her father's breakfast – toast crusts on the willow patterned plate, dregs of tea in a mug, a bottle of cod liver oil capsules. Relics from a bygone era. Before the Fall.

She'd established more or less what had happened. After he fell, his neighbour Mrs Francks, the 'prying woman' for whom he'd never had much time, had heard his cries and gone out to check. She'd phoned for an ambulance. The paramedics had gone through her house and climbed over the garden fence to get to him. If not for her, he might have lain there all day. He might have died of hypothermia.

It was bitterly cold in the house and she studied the boiler controls, scrolling through the functions until she found 'constant'. The boiler fired up and the pipes started clicking into life. Her father would be horrified at her profligacy but there was no chance of her sleeping unless she could get warm. She needed to eat something, too. Neither the fridge nor the bread bin offered anything inviting but there was an unopened bag of porridge oats in one of the cupboards. Golden syrup too, in a sticky tin. She measured oats and water into a pan and lit the gas ring. Whilst she stirred the thickening mixture she tried to remember what the nurse had told her to bring to the hospital next morning.

Sweet and bland, the porridge soon dispelled the hollow feeling in her stomach and warmed her. The house was starting to feel warm too.

Now she allowed herself to consider the implications of her father's accident. At best, he faced a rocky few months or more – at worst a loss of independence. Whatever the outcome, and whether she liked it or not, she would become his lifeline. Richard wasn't going to pop down from Scotland with clean pyjamas. John wasn't going to fly over from Toronto to check the mail and make sure the pipes weren't frozen. 'Vivian Johanna Carey' was the name in the next-of-kin box on the hospital admission form. There was no escaping it.

She couldn't be expected to put everything on hold, could she? She had a job to hold down. A life to live. It was important that she set down the ground rules, made it clear what she was, and wasn't, prepared to do. She'd visit the hospital at the weekend. Maybe sleep at the house on Saturday to keep it aired and to organise his washing. He'd have to endure weekdays alone. It was his own fault. If he'd not been such a resolutely antisocial man, he'd have a crowd of friends, other old people happy to visit him, delighted to while away a couple of winter hours in a cosy hospital ward.

She had yet to tell her half-brothers what had happened. Their contact numbers would be in her father's address book. But it was late and she was too tired to think. She would do it first thing tomorrow.

She ventured upstairs. Her father's bed was unmade and the room smelled stale. She couldn't sleep in there. The bed in the spare room had been stripped and she located bedlinen in the bottom drawer of the tallboy, draping it over the radiator to air whilst she found an old but clean bathrobe to wear in bed. It was her habit always to carry a toothbrush in her bag so, more or less ready for sleep, she went downstairs to lock up.

The back door had been bolted but not locked – a conscientious paramedic she assumed, or perhaps Mrs Francks. She must remember to go round in the morning and thank her for all she'd done.

13

Gil woke in Feray's bed. Dawn hadn't broken but the flat was illuminated by a pale radiance. When he sneaked into the kitchen, he saw that a couple of inches of snow had fallen during the night. It covered the small yard, transforming the dank area into something brand new. When he opened the front door, the steps up to street level were topped with plump, snow-pillows. He drew his robe around himself and grinned. The arctic cold made his teeth ache but he didn't care because snow was up there in his all-time top ten.

Last evening Kennedy had taken Melissa and James to a show – something in the West End – and they'd spent the night at his flat. It was his 'Christmas treat'. The children had been worked up for days. Probably, Feray was quick to point out, because he'd never done anything like it before. She'd been twitchy, fretting that something would go wrong or that he'd fail to get them to school on time this morning. Her reservations, Gil guessed, were exacerbated by the fact that her ex-husband had a new girlfriend and she didn't trust them to 'behave' in front of the children. Gil had tried to take her mind off it by picking up a 'two-dine-for-a-tenner' meal from M&S. The offer included a bottle of wine. He'd chosen the red and watched Feray relax a little more with each glass before (thanks to the kids' absence) they'd indulged in noisy and inventive sex.

He carried two mugs of coffee into the bedroom. 'It's snowed.'

Feray heaved herself up, pushing her hair back from her face. 'Damn. The kids' feet will get wet.'

She was naked, her skin dark against the white duvet cover, her nipples erect in the chill of the cold room. He felt himself stir beneath the robe, torn between making love and getting to work on time. Feray made the choice for him, taking her phone from the bedside table and ringing her son to make sure that he and his sister had survived the night, nagging them to leave in good time for school.

The snowfall, although forecast, had caught London on the hop and played its customary havoc with public transport. Staff and patients were late getting to the hospital and schedules had to be shuffled but, despite the inconvenience, everyone was upbeat and there was an air of *bonhomie*.

The cold snap had begun several weeks ago, launching an outlandish array of cold weather gear onto the city's streets. Evidently today's snowfall had upped the ante and sent everyone rooting around for yet wackier knitwear and headgear. Even senior staff (normally booted and suited) had got into the swing, looking sheepishly pleased with themselves for breaking the dress code.

Gil wasn't fussy about what he wore. He needed a couple of respectable outfits for work and he was addicted to his Doc Martens but, aside from that, he dressed out of charity shops. Why wouldn't you? Last weekend, noting that the temperature was set to drop, he'd invested in a bright orange sweater (hand knitted, he liked to think, by someone's granny) and a red, heavy-duty fleece, both from Shelter in Kentish Town Road.

Following the buzz of the snow came news of a lottery win. Gil paid two pounds each week into a syndicate organised by the X-ray Department and it had come up with five of the six numbers in last night's draw. The winnings would be shared between ten. It wasn't likely to change his life but his life was okay the way it was and £268 wasn't to be sniffed at.

During his lunch break, he called in to see the biker. For a week following the explosion it had been touch-and-go whether the lad – Tyler Freeman – would pull through, but now he had been transferred from ICU to a four-bedded ward. He was doing okay but he still faced tedious weeks in traction followed by months of physio – not an appealing prospect for a twenty-two-year-old kid, already out of his head with boredom. After the immediate drama of their son's accident, his parents seemed to have lost interest and his girlfriend and workmates (he was a gas fitter) were only able to visit at weekends.

For the past couple of weeks the boy had been drifting in a fuzz of painkillers. Now that his medication had been reduced, he was beginning to grasp the possible consequences of the accident. No one knew yet how long he would be in hospital or whether he would regain full movement in his leg. Whichever way it went, he would be off work for months. It was tempting to remind him that he was lucky to be alive but the boy was too young, too confident of his own immortality, to buy that. His primary concern was his beloved bike, its remains now rusting in a scrap yard somewhere in south London. Earlier in the week, Tyler had asked Gil to help with the insurance claim.

Gil's sons were both mad keen on speedway racing. Janey had gone ballistic when, for their last birthdays, he'd sent them each a hundred dollars to add to their bike funds. She'd accused him of trying to buy their affection, adding 'You won't be the one lying awake, wondering if they're splattered all over the highway.'

Her accusation wasn't far off the mark. He did want his sons to think well of their absent father. He could still remember his all-consuming desire to get his own bike, and the loathing he'd felt for his father when he'd tried to stop him. He'd rather the boys didn't ride motorcycles but when had parental wishes ever got in the way of a child's obsession? They'd get their bikes whether he helped or not and the extra cash might ensure that the ones they got were roadworthy.

Medical matters occupied enough of Tyler's days and Gil made an effort to avoid them. Today they discussed the snow and flicked through a gadget magazine, speculating on how Gil might spend his lottery win, agreeing that he wouldn't get much for his money, debating whether it might be more fun to blow the lot on scratch cards on the chance of a big payout.

He kept these visits short. He didn't want Tyler becoming dependent on him. He never specified when he would return, anxious not to make promises he might not be able to keep. He wasn't sure why he'd forged a bond with this lad. Okay, he'd happened to accompany him to the hospital that night but there had been no need to take it further. He supposed he must be going soft. It didn't take much to superimpose Chris or Adam's face on that of the broken boy in the bed.

At five-fifteen there were no outstanding 'request' forms in the wire basket on the reception desk. All he had to do now was return to the office, download the day's images, then that was him finished.

'Gil?'

Turning, he saw Irene Tovey advancing towards him from the corner of the waiting room.

'Irene? What are you doing here?' He held out his hand but she ignored it, grabbing him in a scented clinch.

'I took a half day for Christmas shopping. I was up this way so I decided to call in. On the off-chance.'

He might have been anywhere in the building and he was amazed that she'd located him. 'How did you track me down?'

'I explained to the woman on the desk that you and I are old friends. She said I might find you down here.'

H&S had a reputation for being overly officious. They were forever threatening 'swift action' against anyone who divulged staff details to members of the public. But they had a point. Often patients were scared or angered by what was happening to them. Occasionally they took it into their heads to lash out and anyone, from consultant to hospital porter, was a potential target. Whoever was on the reception desk had, without checking with him, blithely pointed this woman in his direction. Maybe they considered a photographer didn't merit the same protection as a doctor. But policy was policy. And, come to think of it, Irene was out of order too. 'Old friends'? That was naughty.

In the beginning, he hadn't been too bothered by her calls. She wittered on and all he had to do was toss in the odd 'wow' or 'really' or 'that's terrific'. But then the gifts started turning up. A pen. Socks. A key fob in the shape of that fish symbol. They made him uncomfortable. He didn't want the wretched things and he'd shoved them in a desk drawer until he could think what to do with them. Three weeks on and her calls were becoming more frequent. She was getting to be a pain in the butt with all that 'guardian angel' and 'divine providence' baloney.

'I'm going to treat you to coffee and cake,' she said. 'A little pre-Christmas celebration.'

It was five-thirty. He was tired. He had a stiff neck. All he wanted to do was get home.

He looked at his watch, frowning as though dismayed by what he saw. 'Is that the time? Sorry, Irene. Gotta go. I promised my girlfriend I'd be home early this evening.'

It was an unimaginative excuse, but one sentimental Irene might go for.

But it seemed not.

'Can't she spare you for half an hour?' she said. 'Just thirty little minutes?' She made an odd, pouty face, and he noticed blobs of lipstick – a crude shade of purplish crimson – glistening at the corners of her mouth.

He shrugged with what he hoped would be interpreted as regret. 'Wish I could stay, Irene, but Feray's a stickler.'

'Oh. Well. That's a shame. I was so looking forward to seeing you. Still…' She gave a bright, brave smile and fished her gloves out of her bag. 'I mustn't hold you up. I wouldn't want to land you in her bad books. I'll get on home.'

She turned to leave and, as she did, he imagined her in a pokey flat, phoning Vivian to tell her he was so under his girlfriend's thumb that he didn't dare keep her waiting, even to have tea with an old friend.

'You're right, Irene. Half an hour won't hurt. There's a coffee shop on the ground floor.'

The cafeteria was a no-frills affair available to both staff and visitors. The Formica-topped tables and plastic-seated chairs gave it an institutional ambience. Despite the efforts of the cleaner swishing a mop aimlessly across the tiles, the floor was slippery with snow melt and a yellow sign warned of the danger. By this time of day, the place had a world-weary feel to it.

'My treat, don't forget,' Irene said as they queued at the counter and, although he didn't want it, Gil took a chocolate-chip muffin.

When they were seated, Irene said, 'You'd better phone your girlfriend – Freya, isn't it? I don't want her after me.' Again, that bright little smile.

'Feray,' he said. 'It's Turkish.'

Keeping up the charade, he texted Feray, not to tell her that he'd be late – she'd want to spend the evening with her kids anyway so he'd planned to keep out of the way – but to thank her for last night, childishly satisfied to be putting one over on Irene.

Several staff members hailed him as they passed, which clearly impressed his companion. 'You're a very popular man,' she said.

To occupy the time, he told her about his job, explaining how it brought him into contact with most of the hospital staff. Then he turned the conversation to her. 'You mentioned that you work for a firm of accountants.'

'Yes. We're a small firm. By today's standards, anyway. Three partners, four accountants, a couple of part-timers and two of us in the office.'

'And you enjoy working there?'

'I do. We're a proper family. I've been there for fifteen years.'

She took a tiny diary from her handbag. There could barely be room to write more than a word or two on each page, yet she scrutinised it as if it were her days were so crammed with appointments that she might easily forget what she was doing. 'It's our Christmas meal next Tuesday. The fourteenth. We always have it at the Spaghetti House in St Martin's Lane. D'you know it?'

Gil shook his head.

'It's lovely. You should go some time. The partners treat us and we exchange our Secret Santa gifts. That's what I've been shopping for today.' She tapped the carrier bag that she'd placed on the table. 'It's a scented candle. Everyone loves candles, don't they?' She dropped the diary back into her handbag.

'What d'you do for Christmas?' he said.

'Me? I always spend it with my sister and her husband in Maidenhead. My nephew and niece are grown up now. It'll be just the three of us.' She glanced at him. 'I expect you'll be celebrating with Feray.'

Hearing her drop Feray's name so casually into the conversation, stirred a sensation of unease.

'I've really got to go,' he said, tapping his watch. 'Thanks for the coffee.'

'My pleasure. Oh. Before you disappear, can I twist your arm? Our choir's doing a sponsored carol sing. We're going to sing non-stop for six hours. It's for *Open Doors*. Have you heard of them?'

He shook his head.

'They send bibles and religious literature to Christian communities who are suffering persecution for their faith.'

She took a folded sheet from her bag and handed it to him.

'Fantastic,' he said.

He added his details below the half dozen names already on the list. 'Why don't I give you the money now?' He pulled a handful of coins from his trouser pocket.

She shook her head. 'That wouldn't be right.'

But he was adamant, insisting that he'd like to make a donation to such a worthy charity, more than happy to shell out three pounds to pre-empt another meeting with this silly, thick-skinned woman.

14

It took Vivian several seconds to remember where she was. She'd slept intermittently. The bed was comfortable enough but last night, with so much on her mind, she'd found it difficult to let go. It had snowed during the night, which on any other morning would have thrilled her but today it threatened to be an additional complication to what would be a difficult day.

The house was warm thanks to her decision to leave the heating on overnight and after a bath and a breakfast of porridge and coffee she felt ready to face the day.

She phoned Howard. Despite the weather, he was already at the office. She brought him up to date on what was happening and promised that she would come in as soon as she'd been to the hospital.

Next she tried Nick. Her call went straight to voicemail and, wondering where he might be this early in the morning, she left a message sketching out yesterday's events and promising to call later.

She made a list of things her father would need. Toiletries. Towels. Pyjamas and dressing gown. Slippers. No – he wouldn't be walking anywhere for a while. Reading and writing matter. Would he need money? She'd never had anything to do with hospitals and had no idea how it worked. When her mother had been admitted for an unspecified gynaecological problem, she'd forbidden Vivian (a student at the time) to visit her. Bodily functions were taboo in the Carey household, particularly anything to do with 'down there' and Vivian had been only too glad to avoid seeing her mother in what might, for both of them, be embarrassing circumstances. Anneliese Carey had only been in for a few days and they'd never talked about it afterwards.

She went in search of the things on her list, conscious of her ignorance of her father's habits and routines. Spectacles, for instance. The ones he'd been wearing when he'd gone to the shed had, by some miracle, survived the fall. But did he need a different pair for reading? And what about teeth? There were a number of denture-related products on the bathroom shelf – toothpaste and tablets in a metal tube and a brutal-looking toothbrush – but which were necessary? Collecting a survival kit for her father should have been straightforward but she was at a loss. In the end she dusted off the holdall that she found on top of the wardrobe and filled it with what she hoped would get him through the next couple of days.

Before setting off, she spent ten minutes checking and re-checking that everything was in order. She would be back here in forty-eight hours but she was unfamiliar with the ins and outs of the house. Her father would be livid were he to discover that she'd left the heating on but burst pipes posed a greater threat than his wrath.

Having called next door to thank Mrs Francks for her prompt action and to fill her in on the current situation, she phoned for a cab.

Last night, by the time a bed had been found for her father, Vivian, intent on escape, had simply followed the 'way out' signs. Now she spent a frustrating fifteen minutes navigating her way through the sprawl of ugly buildings, negotiating lifts and labyrinthine corridors. Before this whole business was over, she would probably be able to do this with her eyes shut – a depressing prospect.

It hadn't occurred to her that there might be set visiting times and when she reached the nursing station she was told to come back between three and eight o'clock. Holding up the bag, she explained why she was there and that she wouldn't be able to return until Saturday.

The nurse sighed. 'No more than five minutes.' She consulted a chart and pointed down the corridor. 'He's down there. Third on the left.'

There were four beds in the side ward. Two were empty, rumpled bedding suggesting their occupants weren't far away. The third was concealed behind closed curtains. Her father's bed was next to a window, which was obscured by a venetian blind.

He was propped up on several pillows, eyes closed, arms outside the covers and neatly at his side as if he were lying at attention. There was a livid bruise on his cheek, another spreading up his arm from his right hand. He was wearing some sort of washed-out garment, the pattern barely discernible. She'd imagined that his pelvic area would be protected in some way – a frame, perhaps, to keep the bedclothes away from his hip – but there was no sign of anything like that.

She stood at the foot of the bed. 'Dad?'

He opened his eyes and gave a little smile. 'Vivian?' She was thankful to see that he was wearing his dentures.

He went to raise himself up but winced and gave up. 'I think my specs are in the drawer.' His hand reached out to the locker at the side of the bed.

The drawer contained tissues, a small bar of soap, a worn towel and his glasses. Noting how grimy they were she said 'I'll give them a wipe, shall I?'

'Please.'

She did the best she could with a tissue and a few drops of water from the jug on the locker. 'There.' She handed them to him. 'How are you?'

'Moving is agony. But so is lying still. They've given me a shot of something, but it's not working. And that doesn't help.' He nodded towards the bag suspended from the bed frame. It was half full of brownish liquid and, for a split second, she couldn't think what it was.

'Have they mentioned an op?' she said.

114

He frowned and cupped a hand to his ear. 'What?'

'Oh, nothing.' Maybe Dr Ababne had had second thoughts about operating. Either way, it was their job to tell him, and their problem to deal with him when he objected.

'I've brought a few things.' She dumped the bag on the chair next to the bed and began decanting its contents. 'Towel. Wash bag. Pyjamas. Pen and paper. And these were on the kitchen table.'

He peered at the two library books she was holding up. 'I've read them,' he said, as if she should have known. 'Did you bring my mints? My mouth's dry.'

'I'll bring them next time.' She poured water into a beaker and offered it to him. 'Here.'

He told her what they'd given him for breakfast, grumbling that they didn't have his favourite cereal and that the toast was cold. He was propped at an awkward angle, neither sitting nor lying, and watching him struggle to raise the beaker to his lips and tilt it without spilling its contents, she wondered how he'd managed to feed himself.

The nurse bustled in reminding her that her time was up, lingering to make sure that she left.

'We'll take good care of him,' she said as if Philip Carey weren't there.

Irritated by the woman's disregard for her father, Vivian smiled at him and touched his hand. 'I have to go to work now, Dad. I shan't be able to come tomorrow but I'll be in on Saturday.'

When she bent to kiss his forehead, his skin was damp to her lips and he smelled sour.

He grasped her arm, pulling her towards him, whispering in her ear. 'You will come back?'

'Of course. On Saturday. They've got my number so they'll let me know if…if there's anything I need to know.'

She'd spent less than ten minutes in the ward yet she felt exhausted. Panicky, too. She was registered as next of kin and she would be fooling herself if she imagined that anyone was going to share this with her.

'You have to tell his sons,' Howard said. 'He's as much their father as yours. I know it's not easy for them but they should share some of the burden.'

He was right, and she would contact them soon, but there was no point in counting on them for anything.

'I feel dreadful,' she said. 'I'm letting you down. I've already missed two half days because of Dad. And there was that day after the bomb.'

Howard caught her hands in his. 'Vivian. Things happen. If I'm not concerned why should you be?'

'But Cologne? What if this drags on and—'

'It's not essential that you're on the spot from day one. We'll work around it.'

'But the office. We've signed the lease.'

'Why don't you let me worry about that?'

She poured a mug of coffee, resolved to tackle the backlog on her desk. But her thoughts repeatedly drifted to the hospital then gathered speed, racing full tilt towards Christmas and beyond.

She Googled 'hip fracture' – and wished she hadn't. Nothing told her what she wanted to hear. None of it promised that the patient would make a full recovery in no time at all and that life would chug along as before.

Nick phoned late in the afternoon saying how sorry he was to hear of her problems and apologising for not getting back to her sooner.

'I've promised to take a new client to a publishers' party after work. Introduce her to a few people. Same old, same old. It'll be finished by eight, eight-thirty. Why don't we have dinner afterwards?'

She knew what that would involve. They'd eat too late then end

116

up at her flat (or his) and feel obliged to have sex because it had been a while since the last time.

'I'm shattered, Nick. I need to go home. Let's leave it until tomorrow.'

He didn't argue.

She cleared up a handful of routine matters, knowing that, if she attempted to tackle anything complex she would make a mess of it and have to do it again tomorrow. Before leaving for home she checked through her emails and found one from Gil.

Up for making a snowman? Gx

He'd attached a picture of himself looking ridiculous in skiing goggles and a hat with reindeer horns protruding from its crown. His face was at a crazy angle and the cars in the background were heaped with snow, and she guessed he'd taken the photograph today.

She replied, explaining what had happened since she'd last been in touch.

Within minutes he rang her. 'Where are you now?'

'Still at work. Just finishing up.'

'Me too. Look, I expect you're bushed but…'

'But what?'

'I could come and pick you up. We could get a bite to eat.'

She was exhausted but if he came now and they ate right away, she could be home by eight-thirty.

'I'd like that,' she said.

'I'll get a cab.'

'You'll need to know where my office is.'

'I already know,' he said and reeled off the correct address.

She was waiting at the front door when his cab pulled up and didn't put up much of a fight when he instructed her to get in.

'You look done in. Let's get you home.'

They hardly spoke on the drive back to Belsize Park. But it was a comforting, comfortable silence. She relaxed for the first time in twenty-four hours, pleasantly drifting nearer and nearer sleep and, by the time they arrived at her flat, it was all she could do to get out of the cab.

Once they were in, she slumped on the sofa whilst, without prompting, Gil found a duvet and draped it over her. 'You need food. Something quick. D'you have bacon? And eggs?'

'I think so.'

He disappeared into the kitchen and from the gentle *clunks* she guessed he was investigating the cupboards. She heard the kettle boiling and the clatter of pans and, in no time, he returned with two plates of spaghetti carbonara. As she swallowed the first mouthful, she realised that, apart from a couple of bowls of porridge, she'd eaten nothing substantial for forty-eight hours.

After they'd finished she gave him a full account of her father's fall. He listened attentively and without interruption, and she couldn't stop it all spilling out.

'I don't see how I can do this on my own. My half-brothers are hundreds of miles away. I barely know them. I have no idea whether they'd be willing to help even if they could. I shall spend all my time on the Tube. We're opening the Cologne office next month. How's that going to work?'

She drew her knees up, burying her face in the duvet.

'Doing nothing probably doesn't come easy to you,' he said, 'but maybe you should let things settle for a few days. Wait until he's over the immediate shock. See which way things are going to go. Try not to get too far ahead of yourself.'

She looked up. 'You're saying he might die?'

'No, I'm saying give it a few days. Then talk to your dad. Be honest with him. He'll appreciate that you can't drop everything. Surely he wouldn't want you to.'

'You don't know my father. He's a selfish old man. It's not even as if he likes me. And, d'you know, I'm fine with that. Now, suddenly, he needs help. If that involves disrupting my life, he won't give it a second thought. Great timing. Thanks, Dad.'

'He doesn't like you?'

'No. He never has.'

'What about you?'

'I hate him.'

She expected him to pat her on the head and say she was talking that way because she was overwrought. That, deep down, they must both like and love each other. That the father-daughter relationship was complicated but special. Instead he took the dishes into the kitchen, returning with two mugs of tea.

'Black, no sugar, is that how you like it?'

'Yes, it is.'

She was surprised that he remembered and that, once again, he'd seen that she'd needed to eat quickly, not hang around waiting for a late supper in the West End.

'The pasta was delicious, by the way,' she said.

'Most people keep bacon and eggs in the fridge and pasta in the cupboard. It's one of my emergency meals.'

'What are the others?'

'*Other*. Bacon and eggs.'

He knelt next to her and studied her face. 'That's better. You've got a bit of colour in your cheeks.'

She snuggled under the quilt. 'Thanks for sorting me out. Sorry I'm being so useless.'

'I like useless women. They make me feel…useful.' He looked at his watch. 'I'm going to push off. Leave you to sleep. Hey, you'll never guess who turned up at the hospital this afternoon. Our mutual friend.'

'Irene? What did she want?'

She listened whilst he described his meeting with Irene.

'You'll have to watch out,' she said. 'She fancies you.'

'D'you reckon?'

He minced across the room, clutching a make-believe handbag and patting his hair.

Vivian laughed and clapped her hands. 'Brilliant.'

'Thanks,' he said, bowing, 'you've been a truly wonderful audience. Now, if there's nothing more, I'll be on my way.'

He paused in the doorway. 'I'd offer to hang around. Keep you company. But you might say yes and things could get confusing.'

15

Vivian had told him something of her history. He knew that she was an only child, that her mother had died fairly recently and that she and her father weren't close. She'd hinted at a solitary childhood without friends or fun. Reading between the lines, she attributed this to her father's age and attitude. 'He was more like a grandfather than a father. And not the indulgent kind either.'

He had been raised by young, energetic parents amidst the rough and tumble of their growing family. As immigrants, they'd had no one around to lend a hand when times were tough. Half the people in their street were in the same position and neighbours quickly became surrogate aunts and uncles, grannies and granddads. His parents had been easy-going and the house always teemed with people. As a kid, when he fell out with his mum and dad – as all children did – there were a dozen 'aunts' and 'uncles' on hand to give him a cuddle and a glass of pop and send him back into the fray. It had all gone pretty well until puberty kicked in.

Vivian's assertion that she *hated* her father had surprised him. From what he'd seen of her she seemed innately self-possessed. Look how she'd kept her cool on the night of the bomb. This made her outburst all the more startling. She must really detest the old man to let fly like that. Or was it merely a generational inevitability? Polly was doubtless telling someone how much she hated *her* father at this very moment. It was a little different, though. She'd had always blown hot and cold with him – understandable considering that first he'd walked out on them then, when they'd pretty much got over that, he'd buggered off to the far side of the world. (That wasn't the whole story but his daughter had been determined to see it that way.)

Vivian's antipathy appeared to have been constant and

unfaltering whilst he hoped Polly's was temporary. Pregnant, her body awash with hormones, his daughter was allowed – almost expected – to be melodramatic. Once she held her baby in her arms and those atavistic emotions came flooding in, as they surely would, her view of the world – currently so black-and-white – might soften. But he shouldn't count on it. In the short term, he must deal with her ultimatum. Long-distance communication wasn't getting him anywhere. If he could swing the time off, he'd look for a cheap flight after Christmas. Sit down and talk to her face to face. The lottery money would come in handy.

Christmas was two weeks away. Severe weather and the swine 'flu epidemic dominated the front pages, and the Ashes series was getting interesting. No organisation had yet claimed responsibility for the Warren Street bomb. 'Why would they?' Kevin said. 'Who'd want to claim a cock-up?' As the incident slipped out of the spotlight, Gil concluded that the British were happier being scared witless by snow, pestilence and Mitchell Johnson's bowling than by something they couldn't get a handle on.

Feray was in a foul mood. The kids had had a great night out with their father. They hadn't stopped talking about the show and the 'all-you-can-eat' meal in Chinatown beforehand. They were pestering to do it again. Tanya, the girlfriend, was obviously young and pretty and Melissa constantly banged on about 'Tanya's gorgeous hair' and 'Tanya's trendy shoes' and 'Tanya's amazing handbags'. She'd come home with one of Tanya's cast-offs – a skimpy top encrusted with sequins. Feray had banned her from wearing it outside the flat and this was causing a lot of friction, which had spilled over, affecting pretty much everything. Anyone stepping out of line got it in the neck and Gil was keeping out of her way until it had settled down.

Shivering in self-imposed exile at the top of the house, he put on all the clothes he could rustle up and tried not to think about Vivian Carey.

Divorcing Janey hadn't resolved his conviction that he was inhabiting the wrong life. So he'd cut and run. It had seemed the only thing to do. Once he'd settled on London as his new home, he'd been determined not to recreate his former existence. Starting the thing with Feray might have been foolish but neither of them was looking for an enduring relationship – just good sex and someone to share a meal and adult conversation. It was working fine.

So why was he allowing this girl to bug him? She was fifteen years younger than he. She had a boyfriend and seemed obsessed with her job. She was brusque, and frank to the point of rudeness. She rarely smiled and he had to work bloody hard to get a laugh out of her, as if she considered light-heartedness a failing. Perhaps he was making a big deal out of nothing. Maybe she was simply a gawky, gloomy, ambitious, humourless woman.

The supermarket shelves were loaded with Christmas goodies. Evidently, for the next few weeks, the population of Kentish Town was expected to exist on a diet of sausage rolls, whole smoked salmon and weird-flavoured dips. There was an obsession with mass catering. Suddenly everything came in 'bumper packs' and Gil was pushed to find a small-ish wedge of Brie and the malt loaf to which he'd become addicted.

At weekends, he generally cooked up a pot of stew or hearty soup. Whilst it was simmering, it warmed the flat and gave it a homely smell. He made plenty and by adding odds and ends he eked it out well into the week. It was typical Boy Scout cooking. To show that he hadn't lost the knack of preparing grown-up food, if he had a little cash to spare, he treated himself to something more sophisticated. Today he dropped a couple of sirloin steaks and a pack of flat mushrooms into his basket.

When he reached the checkout, everyone ahead of him had a heaped trolley and the queue had ground to a standstill. He was losing patience when he caught a glimpse of a tall, dark-haired girl on the far side of the shop. He was on the point of abandoning his place and going to join her when she turned and he saw that she looked nothing like Vivian. The incident caused his spirits to soar then plummet and, like it or not, he was thinking about her again.

No snow had fallen since Wednesday, but neither had the temperature risen above zero. Only major traffic routes had been gritted but compacted ice was making side roads lethal. For many, the weekend was their first opportunity to clear the snow and by mid-morning the rasp of spade on stone paving could be heard everywhere. When he got home with his shopping, a couple of his fellow tenants were clearing the pavement in front of the house. They rustled up another spade and he joined them, chipping and scraping and trickling salt on the steps up to the front door. Apart from 'hall and stairs' meetings, they all kept themselves to themselves but today camaraderie was in the air and Oskar, the guy from the flat below, brought out mugs of coffee.

Gil had decided to invite Feray to share his steak and mushrooms. After a meal and a few glasses of wine, she might be more ready to reveal what was troubling her. The steps to the basement were slippery and he made his way cautiously down to her front door. When he knocked, there was no reply and when he let himself in there was no sign of her or the children. Everything was neat and tidy. Feray's rubber gloves were draped over the empty dish rack on the draining board and the pedal bin had been emptied. The plug switches were off. He opened the door to Melissa's room, expecting to see the usual chaos of clothes and books and felt pens but everything had been put away. James's room – the same. He checked the kitchen table for a note to explain their absence knowing that he wouldn't find one. It was as if the little family had gone on holiday. Or simply gone.

Should he be concerned? No. When he saw the three of them

yesterday morning they were arguing but that was nothing new. He could text her but *where the hell are you* was one of the things they'd agreed never to get into. She'd had every opportunity to tell him if she had plans for the weekend, yet she'd chosen not to. Well, that was her choice. Suddenly, feeling that he shouldn't be there, he locked the door and hurried up to his flat.

He unpacked his shopping. He'd bought a couple of pounds of carrots from the greengrocer's next to the Tube station. He'd make spicy carrot and lentil soup. Plenty of chilli flakes. Maybe add some chorizo – he had a chunk left from last week. Flicking through his vinyl collection, he chose Dave Brubeck and started chopping carrots.

From the moment he'd caught sight of the girl in the Co-op, he'd known that he would contact Vivian again. He might have left it until tomorrow or Monday but Feray's absence seemed to be an omen, a signal that he should go ahead and do it right away.

He scrolled down to her number and thumbed the dial button.

She answered immediately. 'Gil?'

He liked knowing that his number was stored and tagged on her phone. 'Hi. How's it going? How's your dad?'

'I don't really know. When I phone all they say is he's "comfortable" – whatever that means. Actually, I'm on my way to the hospital now.'

He could hear something jangling. An earring perhaps or something around her neck. She was breathing heavily and he pictured her striding out, shiny hair bouncing.

'How are *you* feeling?' he said.

'Frustrated, mainly. I still have no idea what's going on.'

'It's the weekend so probably not a lot, I'm afraid. Hospitals go on hold, Friday to Monday. But don't let on that I told you.'

'Look, thanks again for Thursday,' she said. 'I slept for twelve hours after you left.'

'Good.'

He'd made his enquiry and they'd exchanged pleasantries. This would be the natural place to end the conversation.

'Is your boyfriend with you?' he said. It was a weird question coming as it did out of the blue but she didn't seem to notice.

'No.' She paused. 'He's not keen on hospitals.'

Gil hadn't realised until that moment quite how much he disliked this so called boyfriend. 'Really? I rather like them myself. All those sick people. All those egomaniac doctors and sadistic nurses. All those germs.' Now he was being silly but it was worth it to hear her laugh.

'Would you care to take him off my hands?' she said.

'Your boyfriend?'

She laughed again. 'No, idiot. My father.'

What had begun as a run-of-the-mill enquiry was mutating into something more intimate and affectionate, and he felt reckless with the possibilities this presented.

'Need a bit of moral support?' he said. 'I'm not doing anything much.'

'That's very thoughtful, but I'm staying at my father's house tonight.'

The flat was fragrant with coriander. He could see water dripping from the icicles hanging from the guttering on the house across the road.

'I could pop down if you like,' he said.

A vacuum cleaner hummed in the flat below.

'You must have better things—'

'If I bring my ID, I might be able to wheedle some information out of them.'

'Well…if you're sure.'

She explained that she needed to collect a few things from her father's house and would probably get to the hospital around three-thirty. She gave him details of the ward and he said he would come and find her.

St George's was about a far away as it could be. He felt ill at the prospect of the Tube journey but buses – it would involve three if not more – would take forever. An overground line ran through Kentish Town station and, when he checked, he discovered that it ran direct to Tooting. (Another omen perhaps?) He could walk to the hospital from there.

He showered and put on a clean shirt and jeans. He shaved, his stomach jittery like it used to be before Saturday night dances at the Greenhouse. He was a kid then, desperate to lose his virginity and not choosy. In the end it had been with a girl with buck teeth and a yellow dress – Sally? Suzy? – and it was all over in ninety seconds. Summer 1975. He was sixteen.

Chris and Adam, his sons, were seventeen. Last time he'd been with them they'd towered over him, lanky and good-looking, brown-haired and blue-eyed like their mother. They'd have no trouble finding girls and he imagined that their 'first time' had been a lot less disappointing than his.

Before heading for the station, he gave fate a final chance and knocked on Feray's door. No reply.

16

As soon as her father spotted her, he began complaining, his voice raised as though he were addressing the hard of hearing. The bed. The nurses. The lack of privacy. 'And they've done bugger all about my hip. I might as well be at home. In fact I'm going to discharge myself.'

The youngish man in the bed opposite had clearly had enough. 'I wish you would, mate. Give us a bit of peace.'

The other two occupants of the ward smirked and murmured assent.

Vivian found her father's petulance exasperating, nevertheless she was affronted by the hostility shown by these strangers.

'He's eighty-seven and he's in a lot of pain,' she said.

She felt her colour rising and when she turned her back on them, they sniggered, clearly delighted at her discomfort.

'You have to be realistic, Dad. It's a nasty break. The doctor told me that they might have to operate but they want to be sure you're over the shock before they do anything.'

She hadn't intended blurting it out but he needed to understand that going home wasn't an option.

'They may have told *you* that they're going to cut me open but it's the first *I've* heard of it. What about patient confidentiality? I may be old but I'm not gaga. I'm going to make a formal complaint.'

'Shhh, Dad. Please.'

People were coming and going, tidying lockers and chatting across the beds, bringing out Tupperware containers and Thermos flasks. The three men had evidently been here long enough for their visitors to be familiar with hospital routine. Her father watched the comings and goings over her shoulder, now and again craning his neck to get a better sight of what was going on. She feared he might, at any moment, comment on them and their medical conditions.

To divert him, she showed him what she had brought.

'Your mints. The *BBC History* magazine – I thought it might have some interesting articles. Clean towels. And I bought you a couple of pairs of pyjamas.'

'I already have pyjamas if you'd bothered looking for them.'

'They're tatty, Dad. One of the tops is torn under the arm. Half the buttons are missing.'

'They're perfectly functional.'

He was raising his voice again and, rather than provide the ward with further entertainment, she didn't challenge him.

'I picked up your post,' she said, offering him a few items of what was obviously junk mail.

He peered warily at each one as if it might contain momentous information. 'Is this all?'

'Were you expecting anything?'

'No.' He frowned. 'No. I don't think so.'

'I spoke to Richard and John yesterday. Put them in the picture.'

'You phoned Canada? How much did that cost?'

'I don't know. It doesn't matter.'

'And?'

'They both sent love, of course. I've promised to keep them up to date.'

When she'd contacted her half-brothers they'd shown polite concern for their father, asking what they could do to help. They spoke with pronounced Scottish accents, which surprised her although it shouldn't have as they had been children when their mother took them back to Scotland. 'Let me know if there's anything he needs,' John had said. 'I'll get it sent. You mustn't be out of pocket.' He'd meant it kindly but the implication that money was her principal problem showed a failure to grasp her predicament. He'd suggested they keep in touch by email. 'It'll be cheaper and it avoids the difficulty with the time difference.' He was right but it felt as if he preferred her not to phone in case direct contact brought him too close to something he'd rather keep at a distance.

Vivian kept an eye on the clock above the swing doors. Gil had said he'd be here around four-thirty.

Yesterday, she and Nick had spent a pleasant enough evening together. They'd ordered in from the new Thai place on Finchley Road and watched a movie. After breakfast, Nick had produced two tickets for *Cinderella* at Sadler's Wells. 'I know you wanted to see it. I managed to wangle a couple of house seats for tonight. It'll take your mind off things.'

Why hadn't he mentioned the ballet last night when she'd told him her plan to stay overnight at Farleigh Road? Even this morning he could easily have offered to exchange the tickets but instead he'd sulked, saying that he didn't see why she needed to spend the night in Tooting. 'Why so caring all of a sudden? You don't like the man.'

What he said was true but his readiness to bulldoze her into doing what he wanted irritated her. 'I'm sure you'll find someone else to take,' she said.

When Gil had called she was still smarting from their tiff. She was feeling sorry for herself and his offer to keep her company had been irresistible. Now she was doubting the wisdom of accepting. Introducing her father to Gil would give him an open goal for mischief making.

'I was telling a friend – an acquaintance – that you were here. He's going to be in the area and he may drop in and say hello.'

'Do I know him?'

'No. But you'll like him. He's Australian. A medical photographer. He works at UCH.'

He frowned. 'I don't understand what you're saying. Why is he coming here? Does he want to take my photograph?'

'No, Dad. He's a friend.'

'What's this one called? Mick? Rick? Or Dick?' He threw his head back and laughed.

What had she been thinking? This wasn't going to work. Saying that she needed the lavatory, she left the ward and was looking for a quiet corner from which to phone Gil and put him off when she saw him leaning on the desk at the nursing station, chatting with two nurses. He was wearing the red fleece from the snow photograph, shapeless jeans and black boots. A canvas satchel hung from his shoulder. She passed men like Gil Thomas in the street a dozen times every day – middle-aged, greying, bad clothes, nondescript. Anyone who didn't know might take him for a postman or the man who read the gas meter.

As she watched, he dipped his hand inside the neck of his jacket and fished out an ID badge on a wide cord. He showed it to the nurses, one of whom took a ring binder from the shelf behind her and flicked through it. He said something and the women giggled. Vivian guessed he was quizzing them about her father and, from what she could see, he was making headway. As if feeling her gaze, he turned, raised his hand and smiled his easy smile.

'Hello,' she said. 'I was on the point of telling you not to come. He's being thoroughly obnoxious. I'll apologise in advance.'

'Vivian,' he said, 'you mustn't worry about me. I can look after myself, and I'm not going to judge you by the way your father behaves. Does he know I'm coming?'

'Yes. I told him you're a friend.'

She led him down the corridor to the ward where Philip Carey was sucking a mint and flipping the pages of the magazine. Calm, controlled, alert. The perfect patient.

'Dad, this is Gil Thomas. Gil, this is my father, Philip Carey.'

The men shook hands and Gil brought a second chair from the stack in the corridor and placed it alongside hers. 'Sorry to hear about your accident, Mr Carey. Rotten luck.'

'It was,' he said. 'Tell me, how do you two know each other? I get to hear very little about my daughter's life, Mr Thomas.'

She shot Gil a *see what I'm up against* glance but he seemed unperturbed.

'We met after the explosion,' he said. 'Vivian came into A&E with a lady who'd been injured.'

'I see. So you haven't known each other long.'

'No. Not long.'

Her father nodded and Vivian felt herself tensing in anticipation of his next question.

'And have you met her young man? Nick?'

'Not yet. But I'm looking forward to it.'

'He's quite a go-getter.'

'Good for him.'

Gil had already removed his fleece but now he pulled his sweater over his head tousling his hair, which made him look younger, less ordinary somehow. She started to relax. Here was someone who knew how to play her father's game.

Gil unbuckled his satchel. 'I don't know what you like to read, sir, but I wondered if this might help while away a few hours.' He took out a fat, well-thumbed hardback and passed it to the old man. 'It's seen better days but it'll have all the right words in the right order.'

Her father put on his spectacles and studied the book, turning it over in his hands. '"The Complete Sherlock Holmes".' He opened it and inspected the contents pages. '"A Study in Scarlet.", "A Sign of Four." Years since I read Conan Doyle. I shall enjoy this. Thank you.'

They discussed the Ashes series, Gil updating her father on the latest score. She couldn't recall his ever attending a cricket match, or sports event of any kind, but he seemed interested and made a few pertinent remarks.

Gil showed him how to set up the radio service on the bedside device, guiding him through the process several times until he was able to do it unaided. Telephone and television were also available – at a price – and Vivian offered to pay but he insisted that the radio was all he needed, especially now that he had Holmes and Watson for company.

Gil was struck by how out of place Vivian looked surrounded by hospital paraphernalia – a creature out of its natural habitat. She spent the whole visit perched on the edge of her chair, as if ready to bolt at the first opportunity.

He was bemused by the picture she'd painted of her father and of her relationship with him. He'd assumed she was exaggerating but he had to admit there seemed to be little warmth between them. She made no move to plump the old man's pillows or stroke his hand. They shared no private jokes or reminiscences. He sensed no underlying bond. Whatever course the old guy's treatment took, whatever its outcome, daughter and father faced a tough few months and he felt for them.

They left when the evening meal was served, Vivian promising to visit the following afternoon, her father telling her not to bother.

'Thanks for being so tolerant,' she said as they waited for the lift. 'He loves winding people up.'

'Don't be too harsh on him. He's angry with himself for falling. Until the other day he was in charge of his life, now that's been snatched away. Hospital's not a great place when you're old. It should be but it isn't. Being stroppy's his only way of showing he's alive and kicking.'

With the onset of darkness, the wind had strengthened. It had been unhealthily hot inside the hospital but it wasn't long before the cold penetrated his jacket and sweater. Jeans were worse than useless in these conditions and he wished he'd worn his old cords.

They made their way across the car park, towards the exit. 'Let me have that,' he said, taking the bag containing the old man's

133

washing. Ridiculous though it was, carrying it made him feel more connected to her.

When they reached the main road, she turned left, away from his return route to the overground station. In the distance, he could make out a Tube sign. She'd naturally assumed that he'd come that way. When they reached the station, he would hang around until she'd gone and then back-track.

The shops were closing, shutters rattling down on the Christmas frenzy. Hunched figures scurried purposefully along or cowered in bus shelters, shifting from foot to foot. It started to snow – huge, feathery flakes blown horizontal by the wind.

'Here.' He reached out and brushed snowflakes from her hair and pulled up her hood. The coat was dark green, somewhere between a duffle coat and a parka, and the fur around the hood felt real.

'Is it far to your dad's house?' he said.

She clasped the hood under her chin, snowflakes catching on the fur. 'Not too far. Fifteen minutes if I walk quickly.'

The snow was settling on the pavement, outlining every paving stone with a crisp, white border. 'You can't walk in this. You'll freeze to death.'

He pointed to an illuminated sign on the far side of the main road, next to Sainsbury's. Road Riders Cab Services. 'Pander to an old man. Get a mini cab.'

'How old *are* you?' she said.

Forty-eight? Forty-six? What would he gain by lying?

'Fifty-one.'

'Yes. I guessed you were around fifty.'

'Fifty-two next April.'

'You're still younger than my half-brothers.'

Was that how she thought of him? A brother?

'So you'll get a cab?' he said.

She turned to face him. 'Look. Why not come with me? We'll order in.'

The smell of something spicy. Fairy lights, swaying in the wind. The gentle *spat* of snowflakes striking the plastic bag.

'Sounds good,' he said.

The cab driver was a cautious man. 'Rectory Lane too steep. I go long way round. Only charge standard rate.'

It was warm in the car. The wipers flipped back and forth at double speed, barely clearing the windscreen. Something meandering and Middle Eastern was playing on the radio. The snow, whirling and eddying in the headlights, was hypnotic and Gil felt pleasantly disorientated.

'Here. On the right.' Vivian's voice roused him and they stopped in front of a terraced house.

The driver asked for six pounds but Gil gave him ten, thanking him for delivering them safely. 'You take care, now.'

'Thank you, sir. I go home. My wife is worrying.'

Gil could tell from the piles of snow to either side of the path that it had been cleared since the last fall but several centimetres of fresh snow had already accumulated, and the gate needed a good shove to get it open.

A light glowed in the room above the front door. 'I left a lamp on a time switch,' she said. 'I don't suppose it fools anyone.'

She took keys from her bag and unlocked the door, and they stood in the hall, the snow from their boots melting and forming puddles on the mosaic tiles.

17

When Gil took off his boots Vivian saw that his red socks were thinning at the toes. His feet looked small – perhaps size eight, like hers – but broad and with a high instep.

'I'll hang this on the radiator, shall I?' he said, unzipping his fleece.

'Yes. Tea or coffee? There's only instant, I'm afraid.'

'Instant's fine.'

She filled the kettle, took two mugs from the cupboard and wondered why she was here, in her father's house, with Gil Thomas. He'd toiled all the way to St George's to keep her company. He'd been patient with her father and concerned for her when it started snowing. He was certainly a kind man. But that didn't explain why she'd invited him back to the house.

'Will they deliver in this?' she said.

'Someone's always prepared to take a risk if there's money to be made. But if it keeps snowing, it'll get less likely I suppose. Maybe we should start ringing round.'

She had no idea which was the best home delivery place and they ended up sifting through the recycling bag, searching for flyers. Third time lucky, they ordered Indian from Masaledar in Tooting High Street. Whoever took their order seemed unperturbed by the weather and promised to get the food to them within the hour.

'I expect it will be disgusting,' she said.

'Are you always pessimistic?'

'Better than being disappointed.'

She pushed her father's soiled washing into the machine and set the machine to hot wash. When it was done, she would have to drape it on the radiators. Not ideal, but with no tumble drier that must be what he did when the weather was bad.

Until the night of the accident, she'd not been in the house without his being there, keeping an eye on her, telling her what to do. As she opened drawers and cupboards, searching for this and that, she came across things that she'd not previously noticed. Instructions for the washing machine, copied in black marker onto a recycled cornflakes box. Strips of paper stuck inside the cupboard door, listing its contents. A cardboard box filled with sheets of newspaper that had been tightly rolled and tied in a knot.

She showed Gil the stash. 'What d'you think these are?'

'Paper sticks. For lighting the fire. They did that sort of thing in the war,' he said. 'How old would he have been then?'

'He's eighty-seven now so…' She did the maths. 'He must have been sixteen when it started.'

'Was he in the forces?'

It was an obvious question yet one she couldn't answer.

When she was growing up her father rarely mentioned the past. Occasionally he'd compared the rigours of his schooling with what he considered to be the failings of hers. His criticism had no relevance because his schooldays belonged in a history book. He'd never talked about the war and she hadn't asked. It was one more thing on the long list of things they hadn't discussed. When she was old enough to appreciate that not once but *twice* in the twentieth century, the two sides of her family – joint donors of her DNA – had been intent on killing each other, it had been too thorny a topic to confront.

And later, when she was an adult? Her father's life history – or anyone else's for that matter – was of little interest to her. She failed to understand the current obsession with genealogy. What difference did it make that your great-grandmother was a scullery maid or that your father was a soldier? *Who Do You Think You Are?* Silly question. You were you. Your life was what you made of it.

'I don't know. I suppose he must have done. Weren't all adult males called up?'

She could see that Gil was surprised by her ignorance.

'Yes. Unless they were unfit. Asthmatic or short-sighted or flat-footed.'

'He's none of those. Was your father in the war?'

'He was born in thirty-six,' he said, seeming almost embarrassed to let slip that his father was much younger that hers. 'Dad and his sisters were evacuated to Wales. They were those little kids you see in old news reels, with luggage labels tied to their coats.'

'It must have been grim.'

'Not at all. They landed up with a terrific family and had a wonderful time.'

Whilst they set the table, Gil told her what he'd found out from the nurses.

'They'll make a final assessment on Monday and operate on Tuesday if everything's looking okay.'

'That's almost a week since he fell.'

He paused. 'Sometimes old people don't last more than a few days after a fall like your dad's. The medics can't afford to waste time operating on someone who's very likely…'

'To die?'

He nodded. 'Like most things, it boils down to hard cash. And they've got their stats to consider. They can't have too many patients dying on the operating table. It doesn't look good for the hospital.'

'You're saying they don't operate on no-hopers.'

'That's about the size of it.'

Their meal was delivered by a figure – distinguishable as a man only after he'd spoken – in a bulky hooded jacket. He arrived in what looked like a Land Rover. Gil rummaged in his pocket but Vivian insisted on paying. 'No. This is on me. You got the cab.'

They prised the lids from the foil containers and as the aroma of garlic and spices escaped, she wondered what her father would make of this culinary invasion of his meat-and-two-veg territory.

The food wasn't exceptional but it was well cooked and there was plenty of it. On her way from the Tube, she'd picked up enough groceries to see her through the weekend – bread, milk, eggs, a carton of pea and ham soup – imagining she would be eating alone tonight and going to bed early. Looking for something to complete the meal, she raided the cupboard and found a tin of peaches and another of evaporated milk.

'What's a "cling peach"?' she said.

Gil explained that peaches could be classified into 'freestone', when the flesh separated easily from the stone, or 'cling' when it didn't. 'Cling peaches are firmer. Better for canning.'

'I've never met a peach buff before,' she said.

'My mate grows them. He lives in California. We spent a holiday there. You can learn a lot about peaches in two weeks.'

Her phone chirruped. The text was from Nick. He hoped that her father was okay and that she was safely back at his house. He'd speak to her tomorrow. He didn't mention where he was or what he was doing but she suspected he was at Sadler's Wells. It would be interval time about now and she pictured him in the foyer, drink in hand, 'new client' by his side.

They bundled the debris from the meal back into the carrier bag. 'This needs to go in the bin,' she said.

Snow had drifted against the back door and, when she opened it, a miniature avalanche cascaded onto the floor. It was still snowing, the flakes smaller now, less dreamy and more businesslike. She flicked on the outside light. What had, a few hours earlier, been a small garden dotted with nondescript shrubs was now an icy desert, punctuated with glittering snow-dunes. The only sign of life in the silent world was a trail of footprints – cat? fox? – running diagonally across the garden. *Where the snow lay dinted.* Dinted. Was that the word?

Gil came to stand behind her. 'Jeez. Too cold to build a snowman.'

'We can do it in the morning.'

He paused before replying 'Are you sure about that?'

'You can't set off home now. You'd die of hypothermia.' She tossed the bag of rubbish towards the dustbin then closed the door. 'Let's mop up this snow before our feet get wet again.'

Gil followed her into the living room. Were he at home, he would certainly insist a guest stay over on a night like this, even if it meant sleeping in a chair. Vivian had asked him to stay because it was the sensible thing to do. He must keep that firmly in his mind.

The room felt cold after the fug of the kitchen. 'Can we light the fire?' he said. 'I'm a sucker for fires. We could make paper sticks.'

The coal scuttle, a grey metal affair, was half-full of coal. Split kindling was wedged on top of it with a box of matches balanced on top of that. This was evidently a functioning hearth, nevertheless Vivian insisted on holding a twist of smouldering paper at the base of the flue to make sure the chimney was drawing. He watched her, thinking that whatever she did, she did meticulously. Any building she designed would stand for a thousand years.

They were setting the fire – paper sticks first then kindling and finally a few lumps of coal – when Gil's phone vibrated, signalling an incoming text. For once he was happy to see Irene's name on the screen, relieved that it wasn't Feray demanding to know where he was.

'Irene. Again,' he said. '"God keep you safe and warm in this dreadful weather."'

Vivian sighed. 'She really is getting to be a pain.'

'She's lonely,' he said. 'She doesn't have a lot going for her. Or a lot to look forward to. She must be anxious about what the future holds for her.'

'I'm sure my father's been lonely and anxious too but he's just got on with it.'

'There's no comparison. Your father's lived a full life. He's had a wife. A career. And of course he has you. You may not like the idea but he must find that reassuring.'

She shrugged, grudgingly conceding his point.

'The bomb was probably the most thrilling thing that's ever happened to Irene. That was almost a month ago now. I think she's trying to keep the excitement going by staying in touch with us.' He expected Vivian to mock his cod psychology.

Instead she said, 'You think I'm being mean?'

'No. But maybe it helps if we understand why she's the way she is.'

'She doesn't help herself by being so…needy,' Vivian said. 'If she backed off a bit, I'd be more sympathetic.'

'Really?' he said.

She laughed. 'No.'

It took several matches to get the fire going but soon it was convincingly alight, the room smelling of soot and sulphur.

'Let's watch the news,' she said, 'find out how bad the snow is.'

She switched on the television, apologising that the set was ancient and only received analogue services.

'Your dad's going to need a new one when they switch over,' he said. 'Maybe good to get that organised while he's in hospital. He'll be housebound for a while.'

'How long will they keep him in?'

'They'll have him up and walking as soon as they can. If everything's looking good, he won't need a lot of medical attention and they'll move him to rehab.'

'Rehab?'

'He'll need to regain his confidence.' He paused, recalling wards full of frightened people whose hope of active old age had been snatched from them by a fall or a stroke. 'He'll be using a walking frame for a while.'

She shook her head as if to disperse morbid thoughts and he

141

guessed that she wasn't ready to consider what lay beyond the next few days.

The news showed the country at a standstill. Trains cancelled, motorists stranded, airports closed. The Met Office talked of another day of heavy snow and advised people to stay at home. High street retailers were already calculating the loss in pre-Christmas sales.

They switched off the lights and pulled the sofa close to the fire, sitting one at either end, watching the flames and taking turns to add lumps of coal. Were it not for the television, it would be easy to believe that the world stopped beyond these four walls.

'Tell me about you,' she said.

'You know pretty much everything.'

'Were you *born* in Australia?'

'No. London. My parents emigrated when I was one. Ten pound Poms.'

She looked puzzled.

'You're too young,' he said. 'Next question.'

'Why "Gil"? Is it short for something?'

'Gillon. I know. Weird. He was the hero in a book Mum was reading the week I was born.'

'I like it,' she said. 'The name and the reason for it.'

'Good. Next.'

'Are you married?'

'Divorced. Quite a while now. One daughter – twenty-two. Twin sons – seventeen. Mother alive. All still in Coffs. Moved back here five years ago. Said daughter threatening to disown me if I don't return to Oz.'

It sounded like a walk in the park when he told it like that.

He was watching the coals, glowing orange, red and purple, but he was conscious that she was looking at his face.

'Why did you come back?' she asked.

He picked up the tongs and placed three more lumps of coal on the fire, watching as some kind of chemical reaction took place, releasing green-grey smoke to spiral up the chimney.

'I suppose I imagined I'd catch up with the Gil Thomas I might have been if my parents hadn't emigrated. Have you seen *Sliding Doors*?'

She frowned. 'But there already would be one Gil Thomas in London, living that alternative life. That was the point of the film. There couldn't be two. It wouldn't work.'

Again, her scrupulous attention to detail. 'You're right. It wouldn't. But my life in Australia wasn't working either.'

'Has running away solved anything?'

'Up to a point.'

He expected her to berate him for cowardice but instead she said, 'Maybe I should run away to Australia.'

'You'd hate it.'

'D'you think so?'

'I know so.'

She was tenacious. 'You must still have family in this country. Are you in touch with them?'

'Nope. Did you know that Thomas is the ninth most common surname in the UK? I have the perfect excuse not to find them. What about you? D'you have family in Germany?'

'Yes. But…'

'See,' he said. 'Loners, both of us.'

She laughed. 'You're no loner. You're a people person. D'you have a girlfriend?'

The question caught him off guard. 'How d'you mean?' he said.

'I'll take that as a yes.'

She disappeared to dig out bedding for him. He'd offered to sleep on the sofa, making out that he liked the idea of spending the night by the fire, thinking that by his sleeping downstairs any ambiguity would be removed from the situation.

He heard her footsteps as she moved about overhead and he wished he'd been straight with her about Feray.

He checked his phone. Feray had texted an hour ago, asking if he was okay. It was late but not too late to phone her, especially as she was concerned for him. He hesitated. The conversation would start with a casual inquiry but then she would ask where he was and he would end up lying, pretending he'd gone to visit Kevin and been stranded by the snow. Instead he texted. *Meal with mate. No buses home. G x* It wasn't so far from the truth.

18

Vivian drew back the curtains to reveal a cloudless sky and a startlingly white world. The sun had barely risen and the garden was in blue-white shadow. The lower half of the windowpane was etched with fractal forms of ice-crystals. She touched the glass with the tip of her tongue. It stuck for a fraction of a second, first burning then freezing as the ice melted to leave a peephole.

Farleigh Road lay beneath the flight path to Heathrow. The grumble of jet engines was the backing track to this area of south London, yet today there was no sound of planes, no vapour trails. She guessed the airport was still shut. Last night's news had shown footage of despondent travellers stacking up in the terminals. She felt some sympathy for them but their temporary inconvenience was more than compensated for by the beauty of unsullied skies.

The house, too, was silent. There was no hint of the snoring that had been coming from the living room when she stood on the landing at midnight, listening.

When her father moved here, the bathroom had contained a leaky shower, not much more than an articulated hose looping up from the taps to a bracket on the wall. He agreed it had to go but when she'd suggested he install a walk-in cubicle, he refused. What did he want with a shower? She didn't waste energy trying to persuade him. Now, as she ran her bath, she tried to work out how she was going to wash her hair, eventually kneeling in the bath, dipping her head forward, dousing it with water from a plastic beaker.

When she went downstairs, the living room door was open and Gil was in the kitchen making tea.

'Good morning,' she said. 'How was the sofa? Were you warm enough?'

'Terrific. I woke a couple of times and stoked the fire. I felt like

John Wayne, sleeping out on the prairie. Without the coyotes.'

She made them bowls of porridge then watched Gil write his name on the surface of his with a trickle of syrup.

'That looks fun,' she said.

'It's how I learned to write my name.' He nodded towards her bowl. 'Give it a go.'

'My name's too long.'

'You could write "Viv".'

'No, I couldn't.'

She liked her name now but, as a child, she'd hated it. Particularly the shortened version. Whilst Roses or Chloes or Isabellas were told they had 'pretty names', hers was, 'unusual'. When she'd quizzed her mother on her choice, she'd said that her favourite film was *Gone With the Wind*. 'Why not Scarlett?' she'd asked. 'Your father,' was her mother's reply.

'There's a towel on the stool if you'd like a bath,' she said.

He went upstairs and she heard the rush of water. The washing festooned around the radiators was still damp and she did the rounds, turning everything over. With luck it would be ready to put away by the time she left.

Gil's satchel was on the armchair, alongside the pile of folded bedding. She flipped back the top of the bag, pulling it gently open – not prying, simply looking to see what a man like Gil Thomas chose to carry with him. A shabby *A–Z*. An airmail envelope with an Australian stamp, his name and address in old lady handwriting. Black socks. A pair of boxer shorts. It seemed he'd come prepared for an overnight stay and she was cross at his presumption, remembering after a few seconds that she'd suggested he come back to the house.

She was washing the breakfast things when he reappeared.

'Is there anything needs doing? Fetching? Carrying?' he said.

'It's all under control, I think.' She paused. 'We could make that snowman.'

She rummaged in the cupboard under the stairs and found a pair of wellingtons and the old walking boots her father used in the garden. She wondered if Gil would object to wearing an old man's boots – she was squeamish about that sort of thing herself – but he laced them up without appearing to give the matter a second thought.

It was cold – well below zero, she guessed – but there was no breath of wind. The air felt pure, as if the snow had imbued it with medicinal qualities. The area of garden nearest the back door was in full sun and they chose a spot right outside the kitchen, deciding their snowman should peep through the window.

As they plodded about, scooping up snow, she regretted destroying the perfection of the garden but that was soon forgotten as their creation took shape. It was the right kind of snow for the job, each handful melding firmly to the evolving form. Within no time at all they had fashioned a stylish figure, tall and lean, with human proportions. They rejected coal eyes and carrot nose, instead modelling his features directly from the snow, burnishing his white face with the back of a tablespoon until it was as smooth as human skin.

When they were done they stood with mugs of coffee, admiring their achievement.

'He's a cut above your average snowman,' Gil said.

'He is. He's more…a man of snow.'

Gil suggested that, before he left, they clear the front path. They searched the shed for suitable tools, Vivian trying not to think about the rats. Eventually they unearthed a stiff broom, a spade and a short-handled coal shovel. They also came across two heavy-duty plastic sacks containing coal.

'They must weigh ten kilos,' she said. 'How on earth did he get them here? He can't have carried them.'

'Your dad's obviously a resourceful man,' Gil said. 'I'll put one by the back door. Could come in handy over the next few weeks.'

They started clearing the path. The untrodden snow was easy to sweep away but the trail of footprints leading from gate to front door was compacted ice and hard to shift, and it wasn't long before the noise of chipping and scraping brought Mrs Francks out from next door.

'I thought I heard voices last night,' she said. 'How's your dad going on, dear?'

Vivian gave her a bulletin and explained that she wouldn't be back until the following weekend. The woman's glance kept straying over Vivian's shoulder towards Gil and it was evident that she was more interested in him than in Philip Carey.

'I could pop in now and again if you like,' she said. 'Put your mind at rest.'

Vivian imagined her father's reaction were she to allow anyone, even the woman who had saved him from freezing to death, to poke around his house. 'That's kind of you, but there's no need.'

'Well, you know where I am if you change your mind.' She gave a tight-lipped smile. 'You're making a good job of that,' she called to Gil.

He looked up and raised a finger to his forehead. 'I'll do yours for a tenner, missus.'

Vivian contained her laughter until the woman had closed her front door. 'What was that accent? Polish? Russian?'

'Russians don't shovel snow any more. They buy art and football teams.'

'What if she'd called your bluff?'

'The odd tenner always comes in handy.'

It was midday. There was no reason for Gil to stay any longer. It wasn't as if she could offer him a decent lunch. He would go to the hospital with her if she asked, she was sure of that, but it was out of the question. *You remember Gil. He happens to be in the area* again *today, Dad.* Her father wouldn't wear it.

Gil rooted through his satchel. 'My camera's in here somewhere. Before I go I should take some photos.' He made no attempt to conceal the bag's contents, lifting out the socks and underpants to get to the camera beneath them, and she felt ashamed of her earlier snooping.

He took several shots of the snowman, bending and leaning until he was happy with angle.

'Very professional,' she said.

'Now you,' he said, turning the camera towards her. 'Hood down, please.'

Without arguing, she shrugged off her hood, her cheeks flushing as she looked directly at him, guessing from the gentle whirr that he had zoomed in on her face. She experienced a frisson of pleasure. Now he possessed an image of her.

'My turn,' she said, holding out her hand.

'You don't want a photo of me.'

'Don't make a fuss,' she said.

The camera was a Canon, similar to her own. 'I thought you'd have something high-powered,' she said.

'I do. It's a Nikon D300S – a bit cumbersome for everyday use. But I wouldn't want you thinking I'm a camera geek.' He ran his fingers through his hair and turned to face her. 'How d'you want me?'

She did what he had done, zooming in until his face filled the frame, but when she saw him on the tiny screen, he was the meterman again, as though the camera had filtered out the qualities that made him special.

'Group shot?' he said.

'Group?'

'You, me and Snowy.'

He went into the kitchen and did something to the camera before balancing it on the draining board. As a red light winked away the seconds, he hurried out and they stood on either side of their man of snow – three faces peering through the window.

*

149

Unblemished snow covered the steps to the basement. So Feray hadn't come back last night either. When Gil had texted, he'd been intent on not explaining where he was and it hadn't crossed his mind that she might not have returned home.

It was punishingly cold in his flat. Still wearing his fleece and hat, he turned the heater up to 'max.' and lit the gas under the carrot soup, stirring it to dredge the residue off the bottom of the pan. Whilst he waited for the soup to heat through, he went over it again. Feray's overnight absence was unusual but when he'd gone down yesterday the flat had been immaculate. She'd obviously gone somewhere with the kids. She might even have mentioned it.

When he'd finished his meal, he called her. Her phone was off so he left a message letting her know he was home. He wasn't going to feel bad about last night. He'd visited an old guy in hospital, been stranded by the snow and kipped down on a friend's sofa. What was there to feel bad about?

He made a cup of tea, put Mingus on the player and phoned Vivian. She answered straight away, as if she were holding her phone in her hand, waiting for his call.

'Hello,' she said.

She was breathing noisily and, in the background, he could hear the wail of a police siren.

'Did you get some lunch?' he asked.

'Yes. I did.'

He heard a man's voice asking 'Who is it?' and he pictured her holding the phone away from her mouth as she lied, 'It's Ottilie.'

Then she was talking to him again, her voice bright and businesslike. 'I've just this minute met Nick at Tooting Broadway Tube. I told him there was no need to toil down here but he insisted. We're on our way to the hospital. Then we'll go straight home. Okay?'

Message received and understood. She was making sure he

knew that it had been Nick's idea to join her, and that they weren't going anywhere near Farleigh Road. This meant she wouldn't have to explain the snowman or risk a second encounter with Mrs Francks who would enjoy letting him – Nick – know that Vivian had entertained a man last night.

Of course she would still have her father to contend with. He'd make jolly sure that this Nick guy knew she'd brought a man along with her yesterday. Still she was smart enough to pass it off as the ramblings of an old man on strong medication.

'Well, give your dad my regards,' he said, playing it straight, not risking tripping her up with a flip remark.

'I will.' She paused briefly. 'I'll see you soon?'

'Yes. Soon.'

He washed and dried the dishes and tidied everything away. What would she make of his place if she ever came here? Feray complained that the posters made it look student-y and cluttered. She wanted him to get a rug to cover the threadbare patch on the carpet. He'd resisted and anyone seeing it for the first time might be put off by the transitory quality that he'd made such an effort to maintain.

He loaded the photographs onto his laptop and scrolled through them. Several pictures of the snowman. Vivian. The one she'd taken of him. The shot through the kitchen window. Then back to Vivian. She stared out at him, as if she were weighing him up, her face solemn and timeless, only the colour saturation and the cut of her coat pinning her in the twenty-first century. He edited the image, converting it to black-and-white. *There.* It could be 1936 or 1947. Was it her hair? Or her features? Could features date?

He zoomed in on the image of his own face. If she were to have a picture of him, he'd prefer it not to be this one. He could Photoshop out the grey of his hair and the dewdrop hanging from his nostril. He could intensify the blue of his eyes, which seemed to be fading with age. But no amount of airbrushing could make him look more distinguished.

Needing milk for tomorrow's breakfast, he went to the corner shop, a scruffy little place that smelled of damp cardboard and where the proprietor sat behind a grille, looking mournful. Gil was a regular and they exchanged a few words.

'How's it going, Saeed?'

'Slow.'

For the umpteenth time, Gil wondered how this man made a living. He supported the shop whenever he could – milk, a sliced loaf, the odd jar of peanut butter – but like everyone else around here, he was on limited funds and there were a couple of supermarkets only a block away. He took a pint of milk from the fridge then mooched down the narrow aisle looking for something else to bring his total up to a few pounds.

'Only mad buggers venture out in this weather,' Gil said.

'Yes. Mad or lonely. And there aren't enough of either tonight. I think I will close up early.'

When he got back to the house, the snow still lay undisturbed on the steps to Feray's flat. He wondered whether to go down and leave a note but he had nothing to say and he decided against it.

19

On Monday morning, Vivian got a call. Her father's operation was scheduled for the following afternoon.

'He's on the list for four o'clock,' the nurse said.

'Do I have to be there?' Vivian asked.

'Not unless you want to be. He's signed the consent forms but he asked me to let you know.'

'He didn't make a fuss?'

'Let's just say we managed to persuade him that a new hip is his best chance of getting back to normal.'

She suggested Vivian ring tomorrow morning to check that nothing had changed and that the operation was going ahead.

Her father had been subdued when she and Nick were there yesterday. Sherlock Holmes was on his locker, a slip of paper marking his place, but he didn't mention Gil. When Nick attempted to show him how to use the telephone – part of the bedside paraphernalia – he'd waved him away with a can't-be-bothered gesture. It was less stressful for everyone when he wasn't playing up yet it unnerved her to see him passive and compliant. He would need to put up a fight if he were to regain his independence.

Vivian had established that a hip replacement was a run-of-the-mill procedure. Generally, patients were discharged within a week. She guessed that this statistic applied to elective surgery where the operation only went ahead if, and when, conditions were favourable. It was possible that, in falling, her father had done something to complicate matters and thus make a repair trickier. Add to that his age and circumstances and it seemed unlikely that he would be fit to leave hospital before Christmas, now only twelve days off.

'But surely you'll go and see him tomorrow,' Ottilie said when

153

Vivian told her about the operation and her proposal to visit the following weekend.

They were in the kitchen. Howard, although easy-going about most things, couldn't bear the office looking 'like a student bedroom' and he insisted his staff confine flurries of 'artiness' to the pin board that ran along one wall of the kitchen. Ottilie had appropriated more than her fair share of the board, covering it with photos of her family and her boyfriend, Spencer. Feeling she had to contribute something or risk being thought aloof, Vivian had dug out a reproduction of a Martin Parr photograph showing a group of Korean tourists standing in front of the Parthenon, and a sample of Pantone 3425 C – her favourite colour, despite its being the green used on the Starbucks' logo.

'I can't spare the time,' Vivian said. 'I'm way behind on everything. And he's being well looked after.'

It was apparent from Ottilie's face that she was appalled by this callousness. She came from a large family all of whom seemed fond of each other. They went on holiday *en masse* and any occasion, no matter how inconsequential, was an excuse for a get together. She couldn't be expected to understand that she – Vivian – felt more connected to Friel Dravid Associates than to her own father.

Vivian got home at eight o'clock, around the time the nurses would be shooing visitors out of the ward. She thought of her father, in pain, probably frightened of what lay ahead, the target of jibes from those uncouth men. Perhaps she should have gone to see him this evening. But a brief visit from her could do nothing to alter his situation. Were their roles reversed, she wouldn't expect him (or anyone) to visit every day. Some things had to be borne alone. At least her father and she had one thing in common – a preference for their own company.

She worked for a couple of hours, bathed then went to bed, hoping to fall asleep over her book. It didn't happen. At one o'clock, tense and resentful, she mailed her half-brothers to let them know that the operation was going ahead. She didn't know what she expected, or wanted, of them but it was unjust that, simply because she lived in the same city as their father, she had to shoulder this alone.

The snow had been cleared from the basement steps and a sliver of light was visible between closed curtains. Gil had been sure – pretty sure, anyway – that there was no sinister reason for Feray's absence, all the same he was relieved to see that she was back.

A couple of weeks ago he would have run down the steps without thinking twice but now he hesitated, tempted to sneak up to his flat and defer a post-mortem on the weekend. Whilst he weighed it up, his phone chirruped and Feray's text made the decision for him. *Chilli tonight if you fancy some x*

'Wow,' she said when, seconds later, he knocked the door, 'that was quick.'

'I'm hungry,' he said.

She laid her hands against his ears. 'You're freezing too.'

He shucked off his coat and followed her down the hall to the kitchen. 'Dermatology' had kept him at it all day, photographing a cohort of patients taking part in a clinical trial. He'd barely had time to grab a sandwich. He was brain-dead and ravenous and the basement seemed wonderfully benevolent.

The kids were in James's room, engrossed in something on the PS.

'New game?' he said.

'Early Christmas present from Arzu.'

So that's where she'd been – in Essex, Basildon or Chelmsford, he couldn't recall which, with her sister.

'We had a great time,' Feray said. 'The kids got to toboggan and we made a snowman. Look.'

She pulled her phone from her bag, showing him pictures of

unidentifiable figures tobogganing down a field, and others of a snowman in the front garden of a boxy new-build.

They ate and, as the children enthused over their weekend, it came back to him. Feray complaining about 'another bloody INSET day', then deciding to make a long weekend of it at her sister's. ('They're going to Will's Mum's for Christmas this year. It'll be a chance to take their presents.') It had probably been flagged on the calendar if he'd thought to look.

James and Melissa drifted off to finish homework and get ready for school next morning.

'How was *your* weekend?' she said. 'Do anything exciting?'

He drew the last grains of rice together in the centre of his plate and coaxed them onto his fork. 'Not really. I went to Kevin's. To see the baby. He's been pestering for weeks. We had a few beers and it started snowing. So I stayed over.' The fiction slipped out easily.

'Nice baby?' she asked.

'Kevin and Debbie think so.'

He waited for her to follow up with a dig about the power his unborn grandchild would have to skew his objectivity. He braced himself, prepared for the inevitable questions about his plans, but instead she asked him to pull out the fridge so that she could retrieve a fork that had slipped down behind it.

They cleared the table. Feray washed whilst he dried, the ritual tripping memories of washing up with Vivian after yesterday's breakfast. His failure to be straight with Feray about Vivian had, in the beginning, seemed harmless. In the four weeks since the explosion, things had moved on. Become a lot more complicated. He couldn't backtrack now. ('Oh, by the way, I've been seeing a young woman I met at the hospital. Coffee. Theatre. Sleepover. Nothing worth mentioning.') If he couldn't get a handle on the situation, how could he expect Feray to? Besides, there must be stuff going on in her life that she didn't tell him. People filtered information all the time. They had to or the world would be bogged down in irrelevant crud. This sop to conscience lasted for about ten seconds. Filtering was one thing, lying was something different. Feray deserved better.

Needing to give her a reason to shout at him, he said, 'I won't be coming to your mum's on Christmas Day.'

She shrugged. 'Fine.'

He pushed it further. 'I just don't fancy it.'

'It's okay. I don't want you there if you're going to be a party pooper. I'll tell her you've had another invitation.'

He was close enough to smell her musky end-of-the-day sweat. The top buttons of her shirt were undone, revealing the lace along the top of her bra and the swell of her breast. He kissed her, forcing his tongue between her lips, running his hand down her back and slipping it inside the waistband of her jeans, pushing his erection against her belly. Why was he making such a big deal of this Vivian Carey thing? His past was littered with meaningless encounters so why not accept that she was merely another?

'D'you mind if we leave it tonight?' Feray said. 'Arzu's youngest had us up before six. I'm shattered.'

Her gentle but unforeseen rebuff was more painful than any set-to about Christmas.

When Vivian got to work, she rang the ward. Whoever answered confirmed that her father was still on the list for the afternoon. 'He should be in Recovery by eight o'clock if you'd like to ring some time after that.'

'Could you let him know I phoned?' Vivian said.

'Of course. Any message, Miss Carey?'

'Message? Oh, wish him good luck I suppose.'

It was only after ending the call that she realised she'd been expected to send her love.

The afternoon limped towards four o'clock. The operation

would either go well or badly. The matter was out of her hands. The hospital would let her know if anything went wrong so she should put it out of her mind and get on with some work. But again and again, the image of a shiny scalpel cutting into pale flesh came between her and what she was trying to do.

Gil mailed, asking how her father was and attaching the snow photographs.

She examined the pictures, recalling the fun they had making their snowman, returning to the close-up she'd taken of Gil's face. He was okay looking but there was no denying that he was on the short side and wore terrible clothes.

She mailed back, thanking him and adding that, as he'd predicted, her father's operation was scheduled for today.

Almost immediately he phoned. 'Let me know how it goes, won't you? And how are you doing?'

'Me? I'm fine.'

'Sure? You sound a little wobbly.'

His perceptive observation demolished her defences. Not wanting to be overheard, she grabbed her coat and went out into the street.

'I can't do this, Gil. I loathe everything about it. It's so…so banal.' She leant her forehead against the wall, the bricks cold and rough to her skin. 'I can't stop thinking of him, stuck in that place, being treated like a child. It's so undignified. And if he gets through this, which he will, to spite me, what's going to happen then? He can't go back to Farleigh Road. And they needn't think I'm going to look after him. Why should I?'

'Try not to jump the gun, Vivian. For starters, Social Services won't allow him out until they're sure he can cope.'

'Ottilie thinks I'm a cow.'

'Who's—?'

'D'you know what? It would be best all round if he dies under the anaesthetic. And don't tell me I don't mean it because I do.'

He let her cry for a while and then he said 'I won't insult you by advising you to "take one day at a time" but—'

'Good. I despise clichés.' She blew her nose. 'What would *you* do?'

'Me? I'm the last person to ask. First whiff of trouble and I'm off.'

'Please help me, Gil. I need to put some shape on the next few days.'

'Well. You could hare off to St George's now, but as it'll take twenty-four hours for the anaesthetic to clear his system, I doubt he'll register your presence. Why not go tomorrow afternoon? Before it gets dark. Hospitals seem worse in the dark. Stay for an hour. That'll be plenty long enough. Explain that you'll be back on Saturday. That way you'll be home by seven and you can have a normal-ish evening. How does that sound?'

She knew Howard wouldn't mind her leaving early. She could be in the office tomorrow morning by seven and put in a couple of hours before the phone started ringing. And sleeping, or even staying awake, in her own bed would be preferable to a night in Tooting.

'It sounds good. Thanks.' She took a few deep breaths. 'We made a great snowman, didn't we?'

'One of the all-time greats.' He cleared his throat. 'I've got your picture up on my screen now, as a matter of fact.'

'Oh.'

'You don't mind?'

'Why would I?'

When she contacted the ward later that evening, they told her that the operation had gone to plan. Her father was still in the recovery room which they assured her was normal.

'Could you tell him I'll be in to see him tomorrow afternoon? Oh, and could you give him my love?'

Then she went to bed and slept until the alarm woke her next morning at six.

*

After work, to keep out of the cold and occupy the evening, Gil went to the Odeon in Camden Town. The cinema was located directly opposite the coffee place where he and Vivian had shared cakes. He glanced in, on the off-chance, but tonight 'their' table was taken by a young man with a laptop. Rather than go straight home, he stopped off for fish and chips, eating them perched on a high stool, peering out through the steamed-up window at the fuzzy glow of traffic lights and street decorations.

When he got in, his flat was so cold that bed was his only option. He'd slept naked until he'd moved in here. Faced with winter and a badly insulated roof, he'd invested in a couple of pairs of cheap pyjamas. Tonight they did nothing to alleviate the cold and he pulled on a sweater and a pair of socks before diving under the duvet.

Initially, enthusiasm for the current 'proper winter' had rendered the nation nostalgic. Now it had worn thin. Weeks of sub-zero temperatures had played mayhem with transport and communications. Schools all over the country had been forced to shut, enabling thousands of kids to take to toboggans and ice skates (and going a long way to explain why fractures were up one hundred and forty-five per cent on the equivalent week last year). The papers were full of it. Insurance premiums were set to rocket as pipes burst and drivers failed to heed warnings of appalling road conditions. There was a spate of grit thefts from council depots. One such robbery went ironically awry when a stolen vehicle, overloaded with its stolen cargo, overturned on an icy stretch of the A40. 'How were they going to get rid of thirty tons of grit?' Gil asked Tyler the next time he visited him. The lad had no hesitation in supplying the answer. 'eBay.'

If he intended visiting Polly before the baby was born, he needed to get himself organised. Travelling to the far side of the world for ten days was insane but he'd run it past Kevin and that was all the leave he would sanction. Two days to get there, two days to get back – he'd have less than a week in Coffs, and he'd be wiped out for another week when he returned. But if it convinced his daughter that he loved her, it would be worth it.

First thing next morning he booted up his laptop and trawled through the 'cheap flights' sites, getting a feel of what was available. There were endless come-ons. Apparently he could fly to Brisbane and back for seven hundred pounds, but when he entered dates it was a different matter. He'd be lucky to get change out of a grand. Even taking into account his recent lottery win, it would be hard to rustle up that kind of money.

20

He was sitting up, a mug of something on the table affair across his bed. He raised a hand and smiled when he caught sight of her.

'How are you?' she said.

'Pumped full of drugs, so I'm feeling pretty chipper.' He pointed to a stack of chairs in the corner. 'Come. Sit by me.'

She set a chair next to his bed. His face had been grey when she last saw him but now there was a blush of colour in his cheeks. His hair had been combed and he was freshly shaven. He looked better than he had since his fall.

On her way to the hospital, she'd stopped to buy a bar of chocolate, a packet of digestive biscuits and a bottle of lemonade, and she placed these on his locker.

'Actually the food's not at all bad,' he said. 'We get given a menu and we have to tick what we want to eat next day. Quite a choice. Tomorrow I'm having soup for lunch – tomato, I think – and chicken for supper. Reasonable portions, too.'

She had been prepared for a grisly account of his operation and criticism of the nursing staff, but he seemed more interested in the catering arrangements.

'Are they pleased with you?' she said.

It was the question a parent asked a child after they'd handed in a school project, and she expected him to accuse her of condescension.

'D'you know, I think they are,' he said. 'And they won't credit I'm eighty-seven.' There was pride in his declaration.

She glanced around the ward. The objectionable man in the opposite bed had been replaced by an older man who was asleep. The other two, isolated by headsets, were watching television, light from the miniature screens flickering on their blank faces.

'Shall I sort out *your* television?' she said.

He shook his head as if she'd suggested something distasteful. 'No thank you. I've got the radio for the news and so forth. I'd appreciate some reading matter though.'

'What sort of thing? Biography? Travel?'

'I used to enjoy Westerns. Zane Grey. Owen Wister. Max Brand. Great yarns.'

'Westerns?' She started to laugh then saw that he was serious. 'Right. I'll see what I can do.'

Striplights cast a flat, feeble glow across the ward. The creamy-yellow wall paint might have looked homely on the swatch but here it was anaemic, showing every scuff and mark. An odour of ill health enveloped the place – staleness verging on decay. It was hard to imagine that anyone could thrive in this dreary environment.

Vivian explained that she couldn't stay long. 'I'll be back on Saturday.'

'I shall be fine,' he said. 'Don't you worry about me.'

She had been expecting one of his diatribes and now, relieved by his apparent contentment, she leaned forward and kissed his cheek.

'What's that for?' he asked.

'Can't I kiss my father?'

He looked at her and frowned, and she thought he was going to say something. Instead he said 'Which one will you bring with you on Saturday? The young one or the old one?' He winked. 'I like the old one better.'

He reached across for the bar of chocolate, removed the wrapper and snapped off a couple of chunks. 'Fancy a bit?'

The journey home gave her time to reflect on her visit. They'd passed the hour without getting into any sort of argument. Could the anaesthetic have rendered him amenable? Laughing gas, wasn't that what they used to use? He was perkier than she'd anticipated.

They'd had a go at the crossword – something she couldn't recall their ever doing before – and he'd cracked a couple of the clues. His request for cowboy books was bizarre but, with all the comings and goings in the ward, it was probably impossible to concentrate on serious reading. He'd remembered that Gil and Nick had been to see him even though he'd forgotten – or chosen to forget – their names. She hadn't minded the 'young one or old one' wind up. Young*er* or old*er* would have been kinder but that was a quibble. He was pretty much on the ball. Maybe she'd been overly pessimistic about what lay in store for him. And her. Yes. She was pleased she'd gone to see him.

When she got in, she bundled his washing into the machine and set it on quick wash. Half-watching the news, she flicked through the day's post. A couple of mailshots. Something from her bank about changes in terms and conditions. The rest were obviously Christmas cards. One had a German stamp.

Her aunt's angled script, so like her mother's, pulled her up sharp as it always did and she opened this envelope first, thinking it might contain a letter. But it was only a card (snow-covered fir trees under a starry sky) printed with a Christmas greeting – *Gesegnete Weihnachten und ein glückliches neues Jahr!* – and signed simply 'Tante Steffi'. Gil had remarked that it was a shame she didn't keep in touch with her German family. Perhaps, when things returned to normal, she should take a few days out and go to Munich. Establish, once and for all, why a good-looking young woman had abandoned her family and married an old, English divorcé.

She heard a tap on the door. It was Mrs Sachs from the ground floor flat. 'I heard you come in, dear. I signed for this.' She held out a bulging Jiffybag. 'Save you the fuss of collecting it.'

Vivian thanked her neighbour but did not invite her in. They spoke when they passed in the hall and performed small favours for each other but, by tacit agreement, they maintained their privacy. She'd only been inside the old lady's flat once. Mrs Sachs had been returning from holiday and Vivian, who happened to be going out, had carried her suitcase in from the cab.

The handwriting on the package was familiar but it wasn't until she opened it that she realised it was from Irene Tovey. It contained a white envelope and three items wrapped in Christmas paper, each labelled 'To Vivian, my dearest friend.'

Vivian sighed. She and Gil had presumed that, if they held their nerve and didn't respond to Irene's drivelling messages, she must eventually give up. She was proving to be thicker skinned than they had feared.

She set the packages to one side and opened the envelope. The card – a delicate yet energetic drawing of three angels – was quite lovely and undoubtedly expensive. A surprisingly stylish choice for someone who sent out tacky tracts. She turned it over. *Walter Crane 1845 – 1915 Artist and Book Illustrator.* The card contained the ominous message. 'We MUST get together very soon. Until then, God bless and much love, Irene.'

The washing machine chugged away but the hospital smell that clung to her father's things persisted. She sniffed her sweater. There it was, faint but distinctive. Eager to be rid of the disagreeable smell, she showered, washed her hair and put on her pyjamas.

She returned to the kitchen and dropped a couple of rounds of bread in the toaster. While the timer ticked away, she checked the calendar for the coming week. Mulled wine here. Nibbles there. Same old, same old.

One event she was looking forward to was Howard and Cara's party. Every year the couple invited the whole of Friel Dravid to their home for an old-fashioned Christmas party. It was more family get-together than office 'do'. Work talk was banned for the evening and a kind of swear box – five pounds per transgression, money going to charity – was placed on the piano as a deterrent.

Naturally they were all expected to lapse at least once or risk being labelled miser. They ate simple yet delicious food, played parlour games and there was a quiz, complete with trophy, for the winning team. The climax of the evening was a concert when everyone was invited – but never bullied – to 'do a turn'. Last year Nick had surprised her by reciting a chunk from 'The Lady of Shalott'.

The Friel's party was next Thursday, the day Nick was leaving for his skiing holiday. When he'd told her he was going away for Christmas, he'd promised that they would 'do something special' at New Year but nothing more had been mentioned. Yesterday, when he'd phoned to ask about her father, he'd been dashing off to some drinks party and they'd made no arrangement to meet.

She made a mug of tea, spread her toast sparingly with Marmite and carried her supper into the living room. After she'd finished eating, she called him.

'Hi. Where are you?' she said.

'In Charing Cross Road. On my way to a thing at Foyles.' A siren forced him to raise his voice. 'Where are *you*?'

'At home.'

'Lucky you,' he said. 'How's your dad?'

'Remarkably okay. Look, I was wondering when we might—'

'Hang on a sec. I've just seen someone I need to speak to.'

'Fuck you,' she said as the call ended.

His failure to invite her to his Foyles 'thing' rankled. He must know she was having a miserable time, yet he was making no effort to cheer her up. When he rang a few minutes later she diverted his call then deleted his message without playing it back.

She went to the window and pulled back the curtain. The street below was deserted, frozen and motionless beneath a starry sky. She felt suddenly lonely and, without thinking too much about it, she called Gil.

'I'm not interrupting anything am I?' she said.

'As a matter of fact you are.'

'No worries. I'll let you—'

'I was scraping lentils off the bottom of my soup pan. But I suppose I can spare a couple of minutes. What's up?'

'I went to see my father as you suggested. It was a good visit.'

'Glad to hear it. How is he?'

'Smug. According to him, the medics think he's some kind of Peter Pan. He loves the food. And he wants to read Westerns. I blame you for that.'

'Me?'

'You and Sherlock Holmes,' she said. 'Actually I was phoning about Irene.' She told him about the card and the parcels. 'I dread to think what's in them.'

'Gold, frankincense and myrrh?'

'Probably. Has she sent you anything?'

'No, but there's a package waiting for me at the depot,' he said.

'You gave her your home address?'

'Afraid so. I stupidly put it on a sponsorship form.'

'You sponsored her?'

'Don't ask,' he said.

'I'll let you get back to your pan,' she said.

'I'm glad your dad's doing okay, Vivian. But it's likely to be a long job. I'm afraid you're in for a lousy Christmas.'

There. That's all she'd wanted from Nick – some acknowledgement that things were tough.

She cleared her throat. 'Gil, would you like to come over?'

There was silence on the line and she thought they'd been cut off but then he said, 'Sure about that?'

'Yes, I am.'

Gil showered and, as he put on clean underwear and socks, fresh shirt and jeans, he tried not to get ahead of himself. Maybe she was feeling down about her dad, or her job, or that Nick bloke, and wanted to have a good old moan. Or maybe she needed help with something in her flat. Someone to hold the end of a Christmas garland, or put up a shower curtain. But if that were the case, wouldn't she have mentioned it?

He paused, one foot on a chair as he tied his bootlace. He'd dropped everything and gone to her before. The first time was the day after her father's accident, when he'd taken her home and fed her pasta. Then again last weekend when she'd been steamed up about visiting the hospital. On both occasions there had been a specific reason for his going. She'd been in a pickle. He'd gone because she'd needed him.

He shoved socks, underpants and toilet bag in his canvas satchel, not thinking too hard about his motive for doing this. He tucked his laptop under the duvet hoping to insulate it against the cold, something he'd started doing after hearing that computers could be fatally damaged by low temperatures. Finally, before closing the door, he tapped his pockets. Keys. Wallet. Phone. And hospital ID.

He left the house, pausing to look down into the basement area. Feray had tied a Christmas wreath on the front door. A smell of garlic, intense and robust, hung in the air. The curtains were closed but, where they didn't quite meet, he saw an unidentifiable form pass the gap. He'd not seen her since Monday evening when she'd more or less given him the brush off. In fact they hadn't made love for a week. He hadn't thought about it until now. Had she gone off him? The possibility needled a little. But as he walked away, it went some way to counter his feeling of guilt.

He set off at a lick but the pavements were treacherous and he found himself tensing, slowing down for fear of slipping. By the time he reached the main road, his thigh muscles ached and his feet were numb. He'd planned to go by bus but when a taxi pulled up at the Assembly House and four girls burst out he climbed in, occupying the scent-y warmth, glad that he'd called at the ATM on his way home and had enough cash for the ride.

The driver inclined his head towards the glass hatch but kept his eyes on the road. 'I'll stick to the main roads, if that's okay with you, guv.'

'You're the boss.'

The taxi crept along. Now and again, Gil felt the vehicle drift as it rounded a corner. The cabbie kept the revs down as they travelled gingerly up Haverstock Hill and when they reached Belsize Park, he wasn't keen to turn into Vivian's narrow street.

'I'll drop you here if you don't mind,' he said stopping on the corner.

Gil rarely used cabs. A couple of cab rides a week soon gobbled up his meagre surplus, and, as he handed over a ten pound note, it crossed his mind that his previous taxi ride had had been with Vivian. And the one before. And the one before that.

21

Gil stood in the porch. It was the best part of thirty years since his gut had churned with this mix of doubt and elation, and he was tempted to hang on to this delicious moment when everything was possible. A car crept past the house, its headlights probing the gloomy recess, reflecting off the glazed tiles and sending shadows gliding across the snow. Two bulky figures, androgynous in Arctic gear, glanced at him as they walked past. Skulk here much longer and he'd be arrested.

He pressed the doorbell and leaned close to the speaker. He'd grown accustomed to doorstep interrogations and he listened, expecting to hear Vivian's voice. All he heard was a muted buzz then a click, signalling the release of the lock. He pushed the door open and climbed the stairs to the first floor. The door to her flat was ajar but he paused on the threshold and, not wishing to startle her, called 'It's only me.'

'In the kitchen,' she said.

She was wearing a dark green dressing gown and, beneath it, striped pyjamas. Her feet were bare. This vision of her, with her odd hairstyle and boyish nightwear, tugged at his memory. *Christopher Robin. Those Shepard illustrations.*

A machine was grumbling away, an empty washing basket ready on the floor in front of it.

'Do *your* clothes smell weird?' she said.

She must have seen bewilderment on his face because she laughed and explained how both her father's clothes and her own were tainted with the same stale smell of hospital.

'The wards can be niffy,' he said. 'Bodies in beds. Bodily functions. I'm used to it, I suppose. Better than working in a chip shop.'

'Hospitals ought to smell healthy,' she said. 'Antiseptic and…'

'Minty?' he suggested.

'Yes.'

She opened the tumble dryer, pulled out a towel and held it against her cheek. 'Another ten minutes.'

He watched while she fiddled with the laundry, waiting for her to tell him why she'd asked him to come, but she seemed to have forgotten he was there. He began to fear that, unless he moved things on, they were in danger of spending the evening in the kitchen, discussing smells and washing.

'Did you want to go out for a drink? Or something to eat?' he said.

'No.' She pointed to his coat. 'Here. Let me take that.'

She hung his coat and bag on the rack in the hall. He noted that her outdoor clothes were all on hangers. A cycling helmet and an assortment of bags and rucksacks were arranged on the shelf above, her footwear lined up on the ledge beneath. Ordered. Neat.

She nodded towards the sitting room. 'Sit down. I'll get us a drink.'

'That'd be good.'

'Whisky? Wine?'

'Whisky, please.'

Gil had been in this room once before. On that occasion he'd concentrated on making her comfortable and cooking a meal, paying little attention to his surroundings. Looking around now, the room seemed almost sterile. No discarded newspapers. No used mugs on the table. No bags or books dumped on the sofa. Knowing that he was on his way, she might have blitzed the place but he'd seen enough hastily tidied rooms to guess that this one was never anything but tidy. Another thing. No decorations. Not even a swag of holly or a fancy candle. The only sign of Christmas was a stack of cards on the coffee table, largest at the bottom, smallest on top and, next to them, three small, gift-wrapped parcels.

Vivian returned with a tray on which were two glasses, a jug of water and a bottle of whisky – 'Auchentoshan Classic Lowland Malt' according to the label. She chose the armchair facing him, her slender feet planted, side by side, on the rug. Her toenails were unpainted. A faint grey rectangle curled around the outside of her foot near the base of her little toe – evidence of a sticking plaster. He found the sight of her naked feet intimate and touching.

She broke the seal on the bottle and poured two generous measures into the straight-sided glasses.

'Everything okay?' he asked.

'I'm not sure.'

He waited for her to expand on this but all she said was 'Water?'

'I'm told it's a no-no with malts but I'll risk a splash.'

He added a small quantity of water to his drink and raised his glass towards her. 'Here's to your dad's speedy recovery. And to us, of course.'

He took a sip but she made no move to join him in the toast. 'Something wrong?' he said.

'This "us". What is it?' She was sitting very still, clutching her glass, her eyes fixed on his face. 'If you and I were simply friends, I would have heard about your girlfriend from *you* not from Irene. I'd know her name and where she lives. I'd know what you were giving her for Christmas. We might even have met.'

Thanks, Irene.

'What's this about, Vivian?'

'I don't know. That's my point.'

He took a gulp of whisky, gaining a moment to gather his thoughts. 'Okay. I have a girlfriend. Her name is Feray. She's Turkish, forty-something, divorced with two kids. She lives in the basement, I live on the top floor, and I don't have a clue what I'll give her for Christmas.'

'Does she know about me?'

'No.'

172

She shook her head. 'So how does it work? On Saturday night, for instance. Didn't she want to know where you were?' She sounded genuinely curious.

'We have an open relationship. We don't keep tabs on each other.' It sounded feeble and he could see she didn't believe him. 'While we're on the subject, does *Nick* know about me?'

'No, he doesn't.'

'So how does *that* work?' It was petty, playground stuff but he couldn't stop himself.

'That's what I mean. You and I have both kept this…this…' She leaned back in the chair setting the whisky sloshing in the glass. 'See? I don't know what to call it.'

'Does it need a label?'

'Yes, if we're to avoid misunderstandings.'

'What's wrong with things as they are?'

She shrugged. 'What? The two of us floating around in some kind of furtive bubble?'

'I thought it suited you that way.'

'I think it suits *you* that way,' she said.

He stood up and drained the remaining whisky, the liquor numbing his tongue and burning the back of his throat. 'Perhaps it's best if I go.'

'You're running away?' she said.

'No point in staying if we're going to fight.'

She replaced her glass, untouched, on the tray and went into the hall, returning with his bag.

'What did you bring?' she asked.

'What?'

She dangled the bag by its strap, jiggling it so that it danced like a fish on a line. 'What's in it?'

How long was it since he'd been standing in the porch, brimming with adolescent anticipation? Fifteen minutes tops? He tried to decode the expression on her face. Not anger, more exasperation.

'You didn't explain why you wanted me to come,' he said. 'I thought there might be bad news from—'

'I didn't say I *wanted* you to come. I asked you if you'd *like* to come. You came. And now I want to know what you brought with you.'

If he responded with anything less than the truth it would be the end of it. He took the bag from her, opened it and began placing its contents on the table. Tattered *A-Z*. Toilet bag. Electric razor. Underpants. Torch. Socks. Camera.

She studied the items in silence and he knew she was waiting for him to explain.

'I hoped you'd want me to stay,' he said. 'I won't pretend I didn't.'

She picked up the socks, freeing them from their loose ball, holding them close to the lamp. 'One's black, one's navy.'

He took them from her and dropped them in his bag. When he reached for the rest of his things she laid a hand on his arm. 'I want you to stay.'

She looked calm and solemn yet her proposal was so improbable that he wouldn't have been surprised if she'd clapped her hands and yelled *fooled you*.

'I'm confused,' he said.

'Labels prevent misunderstandings. Remember?'

They took a step towards each other, meeting in a clumsy hug. He felt her ribs and shoulder blades beneath the bulky dressing gown. It was like holding a cat.

She rested her chin on his shoulder. 'You don't smell at all weird.'

He lifted her hair away from her ear and kissed her temple. 'That's a relief.'

In Caffè Nero, when she'd halved those pastries, he'd known that this *unlabelled* thing would be on her terms. Each time they met, he braced himself against the disappointment of it being the last time. Being with her had never been difficult. There had been no question of his having to try extra hard, or to modify his behaviour to any extent – surprising considering that she wasn't a straightforward person. In fact she *was* straightforward, which was what wrong-footed him now and again. For the most part he found her unorthodoxy refreshing but tonight he wished that she would be a tad more conventional. Take things more slowly because this felt reckless, as if the whole thing were racing away too fast.

'There are half-a-dozen reasons why this is a lousy idea,' he said.

'Be specific.'

She was demanding that he list his own shortcomings and, God only knew why, he was going to do as she asked.

'You'll hate me for snoring. And for being too short. My music will drive you nuts and my nose hairs will disgust you.' He held her away from him so that he could see her face. 'I'm too old for you, Vivian. Remember how you despised your parents.'

'This is different.'

How different? Temporary? Casual?

'What about your boyfriend?' he said.

'That's over.' She fixed his eyes with her frank gaze. 'I think you and I have to sleep together.'

'What?' He laughed, breaking off only when he realised that she meant it. 'You're serious, aren't you?'

She nodded and gave a bleak smile. 'I think you should find out what having sex with me is like.'

'Vivian, Vivian. Couldn't we drift into this like other people do? Work it out as we go along?'

'That's not my style,' she said. 'Can we please stop talking?'

He held her face in his hands and kissed her, this time parting her lips gently with his tongue. Again he thought of a cat, tense and ready to bolt.

Vivian locked the door and sat on the edge of the bath. Poor Gil. Her proposition had shocked him, but if they were to continue seeing each other, they would have to face the issue of sex sooner or later. It was inevitable. When he'd come through the door, bag on his shoulder, she'd known that it should be tonight.

She thought it through once more – to be sure herself, and to give Gil a little time to get used to the idea.

She'd barely seen Nick in weeks, what with those unavoidable work dos and his 'new client'. He'd certainly failed to take on board the ramifications of her father's accident. She should be angry with Nick – disappointed by his lack of support, distressed by his probable infidelity. But she wasn't. If she felt anything it was sadness that their relationship had petered out almost without their noticing. Tomorrow she would tell him it was over and he could go off on his skiing holiday, fancy free.

But this didn't explain why she was drawn to Gil Thomas. She'd met all her boyfriends – five counting Nick – through work or mutual friends. She'd never been picked up by, or picked up, a stranger – because in effect that's what had happened. And such an insignificant stranger, too. Had she been sitting opposite him on the Tube, he wouldn't have warranted a second glance. She'd read somewhere that it was common for strangers who had shared the same trauma – a hijacking or a serious accident – to forge a bond, sometimes to the point of fixation. Could that be what was going on here? It certainly explained Irene's bizarre behaviour.

She brushed then flossed her teeth.

She sensed that he'd wanted her when they were making the snowman, and she'd rather enjoyed the feeling it had given her. But she wasn't prepared to – how did he put it? – 'drift into it, like other people.'

She took off her dressing gown and pyjamas, folding them and putting them on the shelf before turning to scrutinise herself in the long mirror. Pale. Skinny. Gawky. He must take her as she was.

Gil was sitting in her bed, the duvet drawn up to his waist.

'Hello, you,' he said.

'D'you need anything?'

'Do I?'

She took a small tin from the bedside drawer and handed it to him. 'Condoms,' she said.

She'd debated this when she was cleaning her teeth. She had to assume he was sexually active with this girlfriend of his and that was entirely his business. She wasn't going to discuss it with him – not now, anyway.

'Light off?' he said, his finger poised over the switch on the Anglepoise lamp.

'Please.'

She slipped into bed. Moonlight filtered through the curtains, enabling her to make out his shape against the white bed linen. Even with her eyes closed she would have known that this wasn't Nick lying beside her. Gil smelled different – less citrus, more spice. He took up less room in the bed although she guessed he was holding back, waiting for a cue from her.

She turned towards him. He echoed her movement and they faced each other, barely touching. He ran a hand across her back, doubling back again and again as if to make sure he hadn't missed anything important. Surely he must hear her heart, hammering away.

'You're tense,' he said.

'I know.'

He pulled her against him. He was slighter than Nick. Less hair on his head and more on his body. He kissed her. His lips weren't as soft as Nick's yet his kiss was gentler.

'You only have to say and I'll stop,' he said.

He went on stroking her back, her thigh, her breasts. He was slow and tender. Considerate. He was trying to calm her, to get her to let go. And it was working. Thoughts were dissolving before they could consolidate. By the time he entered her, gentle yet insistent – 'You're sure you want this?' 'Yes.' – she could think of nothing at all.

177

22

Gil stretched out his right arm. Vivian was no longer next to him. Somewhere close by water was coursing through pipes. She must be in the shower or doing something in the kitchen. What time was it? He switched on the lamp, angling his watch to catch the light. Seven o'clock. He'd give it five minutes.

He wasn't accustomed to down-filled duvets. Too hot, he'd woken several times in the night, in no hurry to get back to sleep, content to lie in the dark, his thigh touching hers. Once she'd murmured something but he hadn't caught what she'd said. Perhaps she dreamed in German. He must ask her sometime.

Vivian had been tense during their love-making and he'd been anxious not to get it wrong. He hoped it had been okay for her. Afterwards they'd barely spoken but for a whispered 'goodnight'. She'd fallen asleep straight away. Or found it easier to pretend. She couldn't be more different from Feray who was transformed from anxious mother to audacious lover once the bedroom door was shut.

He'd vowed to keep his London life simple. And he'd pretty much succeeded until now. He and Feray had grown fond of each other but theirs wasn't the Great Romance. What kept them together was good sex and convenience. Infidelity was toxic. If he went anywhere near Feray again he might as well say goodbye to Vivian and he couldn't bear that.

He got out of bed and pulled on his jeans and shirt. Vivian was in the kitchen, already dressed, her hair wet.

She glanced up from her bowl of muesli. 'Coffee?'

'Fantastic. Vivian, please don't feel you have to—'

'I don't feel I have to do anything.' She handed him a mug of black coffee. 'Thank you for making it so easy.'

Although he wasn't sure what 'easy' meant, he guessed that she intended it as a compliment and he felt insanely proud that he'd earned this. 'Do I have time for a shower?'

'I leave in ten minutes but you're welcome to hang on here.'

He wanted to go with her. To stand next to her whilst she locked her front door. To walk alongside her to the Tube.

'I'll only be a couple of minutes,' he said.

Belsize Park station – a two-storey building, faced with brown glazed bricks – was set back from the main road. A stream of commuters headed for the entrance and the foyer was already backed up. As they jostled towards the barrier, Gil began feeling anxious, wishing he'd owned up to his claustrophobia. Before he knew it, he was slapping his Oyster card on the reader, pushing through the gate, following her towards the lift that would take them down into the ground. He began to sweat. Too many people in too small a space. Unpleasantly, suffocatingly warm. Not enough oxygen. He took a few deep breaths. The air smelled of metal and perfume. The doors of the lift opened and the crowd began shuffling forward. His heart was racing.

He tapped her shoulder. 'I don't feel great. You go on. I'll get some air.'

She nodded and he stepped aside, watching her join the crush in the windowless box. The doors closed and she was gone.

He doubled back, pushing against the flow of bodies, mumbling something to the attendant at the barrier who let him through. As soon as he was outside, he felt better but now he was cross with himself. He should have been honest with her about his problem. It needed sorting or it was going to spoil things.

He hurried down the hill to the bus stop, visualising Vivian somewhere beneath his feet, her train careering through the warren of tunnels, racing towards Kings Cross. The bus came and, grabbing a *Metro* from a pile on the raised baggage area, he climbed the stairs to the upper deck. He found a seat and glanced

179

at the date on the paper. Thursday 16th December, 2010. He flicked through the pages. Assange out on bail. Retail sales down. The weather. The cricket. Tittle-tattle and bad pictures of celebrities misbehaving. This was a day like any other although it didn't feel that way to him.

He'd switched off his phone in the cab last night and now he jabbed the button, waiting for it to jangle into life. There was much to be said for those not-so-distant days when he could legitimately be off radar. Now his mother, his ex-wife, his kids, his boss all lost their rag if he failed to 'get back to them' within minutes of their call. He checked. One text – from Irene – her usual nonsense about getting together. No missed calls. Nothing from Feray.

He must talk to her tonight. It would be difficult. He liked her, and her children. He liked his flat, too, but if his being there caused her distress, he'd find another place.

The bus headed down Haverstock Hill towards Camden Town. To the east, dawn was streaking the sky with greenish gold and, beneath its mantle of snow, London looked spectacular.

Ottilie appeared with a notepad. 'You're coming to the party aren't you? Cara's asked me to do a head count.'

'Of course,' Vivian said.

'And Nick?'

'He'll be away.' She paused. 'I might bring someone else.'

Ottilie raised her eyebrows, plainly disappointed when Vivian failed to supply details.

The office was Vivian's natural habitat. She felt more comfortable here than anywhere in the world. Here she knew what to expect, and what was expected of her. Here problems had solutions. Generally, she found it easy to separate work and home but not so today. As she sifted through contractors' schedules, Gil and her father and Nick percolated her thoughts.

Finishing with Nick wouldn't be pleasant. For one thing, he'd demand to know whether she'd found someone else. Had she? She'd certainly found someone who made her feel different. Lighter. If she tried telling Nick that he'd think she was losing it. The best she could hope for was that he would take it gracefully – and gratefully – because, after the initial knock to his pride, he would be relieved.

She mailed him. *Are you free this evening? We should talk. V*

He came straight back to her and they arranged he would pick her up from the office at six-thirty.

'What news of your father?' Howard asked after winding up the weekly practice meeting.

'He's doing okay, I think.'

He touched her arm. 'Don't be too independent, Vivian.'

There was no word from Gil. This didn't surprise her. Both of them needed time to reflect and both of them had matters to resolve.

She'd liked having him next to her last night, even if he did snore. His love-making hadn't released a hitherto elusive passion in her – she hadn't expected it would – but it had been perfectly agreeable. After her rant about labels and bubbles she was surprised that he'd been able perform at all. He must have thought her deranged, but next time they could skip all that. Of course he might weigh it up and conclude that he preferred things as they were, and that the Feray woman offered a better deal. Apart from anything else, she lived right on his doorstep.

'Where shall we eat?' Nick said.

'Somewhere near.'

The first restaurant they tried was full, a couple of rowdy office parties already under way. They walked on until they found an Italian place with an empty table.

'Probably means the food's ghastly,' Nick said when they sat down.

'It's fine. I'm not hungry, anyway.'

'Hey.' He reached for her hand across the table. 'You look exhausted.'

She'd forgotten how good-looking he was. How women glanced approvingly at him when they passed him in the street. Good-looking and tall.

'I am,' she said.

The waiter brought the wine list and two menus. She watched Nick run his finger down the list, interrogating the waiter about this wine and that. What on earth had she been thinking? She couldn't sit here, drinking Barolo and eating fancy pasta, knowing that she was going to dump him.

'Decided what you're having?' he said.

The waiter was hovering, ready to take their order, and she signalled he should give them a few minutes.

'I have something to say,' she said.

Nick looked up from the menu and smiled. 'What's that?'

'It hasn't been right between us for a while, has it?' she said. 'I think we should call it a day.'

She hoped to see relief or, at the very least, comprehension on his face. Instead he looked bewildered. 'What?'

'Us. It's over.'

He shook his head. 'Vivian, sweetheart, you're tired. You're having a lousy time and I'm really sorry I haven't been around more. It's been crazy at work, but it'll calm down after Christmas.' He tried to grab her hand but she pulled away. 'Shall I drop out of this skiing trip? Is that what you want? You only have to say the word.'

She could say yes, then watch him squirm as he concocted half a dozen reasons why he couldn't pull out. But all she wanted was to finish this.

'It has nothing to do with your trip,' she said.

'What is it to do with then?' He leaned back in his chair, studying her face. 'Are you seeing someone else? Is that it?'

The frostiness of his tone strengthened her resolve. 'Are *you*?' she said.

He glanced down at the tablecloth, brushing away non-existent crumbs.

'It's okay,' she said. 'I don't mind. In fact I'd be pleased.'

'Why's that?' he said. 'You still haven't answered my question. Is. There. Someone. Else.'

He had raised his voice and the four women at the adjacent table had fallen silent, watching the unfolding drama.

'Not in the way you mean. I doubt you'd understand—'

'Try me. And don't forget I earn my living from fiction. So you'd better make it convincing.'

'You're behaving like a child,' she said.

'Don't be so bloody superior, Vivian. It's one of your less attractive traits.'

She took out her key ring, detached the keys to his flat and slid them across the table. 'Let me know when you want to collect your things.'

She was glad that it was ending in a spat. It was easier to walk away when he was being an arse. And those gawping women were on hand should he need consolation.

She arrived home to find a message from Richard on her landline. 'How's Dad? I spoke to the hospital this morning and they said he was "comfortable", whatever that means. Could you ring me when you've a moment to spare?'

She'd intended calling him last night but it had slipped her mind and, feeling a little guilty, she called him right away.

'Richard? It's Vivian.'

She told him that their father had been in good spirits when she'd visited yesterday. 'I don't think they're allowed to give out information over the phone. We might be anyone.'

He laughed. 'I can't imagine Philip Carey's health is of the slightest interest to anyone but his family.'

He was right but implied in his remark was criticism of her readiness to comply with a flawed system. 'I'm sure they'd be in touch if there was cause for concern,' she said.

'I'm sure they would. And how are you bearing up? It can't be much fun.'

'No, it's not.'

'You have no idea how long he'll have to stay in hospital?'

'None at all.'

'Well, if there's anything he needs…or you need…'

'He's asking for cowboy books.'

'Cowboy books? Good grief. Right. I'll get on to that. Anything else?'

She had him on the hook now. 'He'd appreciate a visit. It's difficult for me to get there in the week.'

'He'd probably assume he was dying if I turned up. But if you think it's a good idea I'll come down next week. Stay a couple of nights. I can probably schedule a meeting or two while I'm in London.'

She'd expected him to come up with a stream of excuses – distance, Christmas, bad weather – and she was thrown by his willingness to come, irritated by the way he made it sound so easy.

'Visiting's between three and eight,' she said.

'I'm sure they'll be flexible if I explain that I've come from the frozen north. Perhaps you and I could grab an hour. Talk things through. See how we can make things easier for you.'

They agreed to speak again at the weekend when she had a better picture of their father's progress.

Gil's day, which had begun so promisingly, went progressively downhill. Every clinic sent every patient to be photographed, or so it seemed. His lunch was a Mars bar. When he popped his head in to see Tyler, he learned that 'an anomaly' had shown up on the lad's latest scan. Gil had learned to see past medics' bullshit and

184

nurses' bluster and things weren't looking good. Tyler's goal was to get back on a bike. It was what kept him going, and over the weeks it had started to look like a possibility. Bloody cruel if this 'anomaly' buggered that up. And then there was Feray...

When he finally shut down his machine, he was in no hurry to get home. As he was leaving the building he bumped into the crowd from X-ray who invited him to join them for 'a few jars'. He needed little persuading. The pub was warm and welcoming. He'd forgotten how good it was to be out with mates, talking a lot of rot about things that didn't matter. He wasn't much of a drinker – not these days – and a couple of pints on an empty stomach had him pleasantly woozy. Kevin, who also seemed loath to go home, wouldn't let him leave until he'd bought him a double whisky, and by the time he floated out into the cold it was well past eight.

When he got off the bus he bought a tray of chips, ambling home, hoping the food and the cold would sober him up before he confronted Feray. Their liaison existed because it suited them both. But it no longer suited him. Of course she'd want to know why, and he couldn't hope to explain something that he, himself, didn't understand. He guessed she'd take it badly – no one likes being dumped, no matter how gently. Whatever happened they must try to keep any nastiness away from Melissa and James.

His children had been roughly their age when his marriage failed. He and Janey had tried to save their ferocious rows for when they were alone but the kids weren't stupid – or deaf – and they soon latched on. It had hit them for six. Polly, who was fourteen at the time, ran wild whilst the boys became morose and withdrawn. Their schoolwork – Polly's in particular – went down the pan, and all three of them played him and Janey off against each other. His sister, Louise, was the only person they'd treated with respect, which drove a second wedge between him and Janey. They'd turned on him, big time, when some kind person informed them that he'd been seen in a car with the mother of Adam's best friend.

He tossed the polystyrene tray into a skip. Maybe Feray wouldn't care. No point in anticipating trouble.

Feray opened the door a few inches. 'Quick. Come in before we lose heat.'

'Where are the kids?' he said.

'Doing their homework. Have you eaten? I could make you an omelette.'

'I'm fine thanks.'

'Coffee?'

'No thanks. I can't stay. I've got to…sort a few things out.' Now he was standing in front of her he felt wretched.

Appearing not to have heard, she took an envelope from her bag and offered it to him. 'I got this today.'

It was a letter from her employer, explaining that they were 'rationalising' the business and that the branch where she worked would be closing at the end of January.

'There have been rumours but still it's a shock,' she said. She moved towards him and there was nothing for it but to put arms around her. She'd clearly been holding herself together for the kids' sake and the relief of offloading released her pent-up stress. She began to cry.

'Will you stay?' she said.

'I really ought to…'

She kissed him. 'Please, Gil.'

23

The first thing Vivian did was tell Ottilie that she and Nick had split. By lunchtime, everyone in the Elephant House would be privy to the news and that would be another thing done.

Ottilie made a 'what a shame' face. 'Poor you. Poor Nick.'

'We're both fine. Honestly.'

Ottilie fiddled with the coffee machine, waiting a decent interval before asking 'So who's the new guy? The one you're bringing on Thursday.'

'He's not the *new guy*. He's a friend.'

'*Friend*. Right.'

'And I haven't invited him yet.'

Christmas was only a week away, a horror that she could no longer ignore. A couple of days with her father at Farleigh Road had presented a grim prospect but nowhere near as dismal as that which now faced her. Unless she was prepared to be branded an unfeeling monster, she would be spending a good part of Christmas Day at St. George's. If that weren't bad enough, a click on tfl.gov.uk confirmed that there would be no trains or buses on Christmas Day. She would have to spend a night – no, *two nights* – in Tooting.

In the middle of the afternoon, a courier delivered flowers to reception.

'For you, Vivian,' Ottilie shouted up the stairs.

She assumed the flowers were from Gil, although she wouldn't have thought him one for such an unimaginative gesture. Nevertheless, when she read the message on the card she was disappointed. *'Friends? I hope so. Nick x'*. From the look of the flashy bouquet he was over the initial knock to his pride and relieved – around fifty pounds' worth of relief, she estimated – to be a free man.

187

At the end of the afternoon, Ottilie pointed to the bouquet still sitting in the kitchen sink. 'They'll get mangled on the Tube. You'll have to take a cab.'

Vivian had already considered the problem of getting the flowers home. 'I'm at Dad's this weekend. I'll leave them here,' she said.

It was over twenty-four hours since she and Gil had parted at the Tube station. She was surprised that he hadn't made contact. By the time she got back to her flat, she'd convinced herself that he was waiting for reassurance that she didn't regret sleeping with him. Confirmation that she wanted to see him again. She texted him. *Party Thursday evening if you have nothing better to do. V x*

His reply came back immediately.

Will be in touch as soon as I've sorted things out. G x

He could blame it on the drink but that was pathetic and didn't alter the fact that he'd slept with Feray last night. Once they were in her bedroom, his body had taken over and the outcome was inevitable. He hadn't slept well, waking several times and cursing himself for being a weak-willed coward. He'd had the opportunity this morning to tell her the truth but he'd lost his nerve. What a shit. He deserved the sickening hangover that was making his day so bloody miserable.

'You look like death, mate,' Kevin said when they met in the gents. 'I thought you Aussies could hold your drink.'

Gil felt like punching him.

At lunchtime, he wandered down Tottenham Court Road. It was a harsh place at the best of times – an unremitting stream of traffic lined with hi-tech shops, sandwich bars and uninspired architecture. Today, beneath flat grey skies, it felt particularly soulless and the wall-to-wall Christmas tat made everything look tawdry.

He bought a coffee from a kiosk on the corner of Goodge Street and found a wall to sit on. All he had to do was answer one simple question – *What do I want?* If he was still set on the unfettered, uncomplicated existence he'd been chasing when he left Australia, his only hope was to start over again. But where? A monastery perhaps, because it was becoming clear that women – Polly, Vivian, Feray – were screwing things up. Correction. He was *allowing* them to screw things up. And Irene Tovey was still hanging around like a bad smell.

He walked on, away from the hospital, not caring that he was going to be late back. The world would turn without another set of morbid photographs. Crossing the road he headed south, towards Centrepoint, then, to escape the traffic, he took a left along Great Russell Street. Before long he was in front of the British Museum, not his favourite place. It was too impenetrable – physically and culturally – for Gil's taste and it was always awash with aimless tourists, oblivious, most of them, to what they were looking at, content to spend an hour out of the rain or the sun or the traffic.

Today, however, he was pleasantly surprised. Visitors were thin on the ground, Christmas shopping, he guessed, triumphing over culture. He mooched through a gallery or two until he reached the central courtyard. Now this he did like. The tessellated glass roof allowed daylight to pour in, a shot of adrenalin to the heart of the gloomy edifice. Visitors were drawn to the courtyard, attracted by its brightness, the aroma of coffee and the clamour of voices.

If he were going to be late back, he might as well be spectacularly late. He decided to waste time in the gift shop. This was incorporated into the monumental stone drum that sat in the centre of the courtyard and housed the Reading Room. He browsed the shelves. Guide books in a dozen languages. The Rosetta stone in a variety of sizes and materials. Egyptian cats, Lewes chessmen, Aphrodite's head, Hermes's foot. Chinese and Indian paintings – small, medium and large. Reproduction jewellery. The Fuji Wave on a collapsible umbrella or a set of coasters. The whole lot was bland and scarily overpriced. (A scarf for *four hundred pounds*?) Even postcards and pencils were twice what he might have expected.

He inspected the jewellery locked away in glass cabinets and suddenly he realised why he was loitering in the gift shop. When he and Janey had taken the kids to a museum or gallery, they'd often played the 'if-you-could-take-one-thing-home' game. They would stand in front of a display of artefacts or an array of paintings and, on the count of three, point to the thing that they liked best. Not only did it amuse them but it made them look closely at exhibits which they might otherwise hurry past. Long before that, he and his mates had done the same thing, scrutinising the girls at the local dance.

Now here he was, playing a variation on the old game, this time choosing not what he would take for himself, but for Vivian. It was childish but it gave him an excuse to think about her. To picture that Egyptian knot bracelet around her wrist. That turquoise and pearl necklace encircling her neck. Eventually he settled on art deco earrings – discs of intense green jade suspended from platinum and diamond studs, fake of course. These earrings – unfussy, bold, geometric – would perfectly suit her hair and her style. He checked the price on the tiny label. Seventy-five pounds. Yeah, well.

When Gil swanned in fifty minutes late, Kevin wasn't a happy man. He was prepared for a set-to but his boss simply adopted a martyred look saying that he'd had to miss an H&S meeting in order to clear the backlog of patients.

The afternoon dragged on and the most rudimentary tasks became an effort. He wasn't concentrating when Irene's call came through and, without thinking, he accepted it.

'Gil? I'm glad I caught you. I had to let you know we kept going for over three hours.'

'Sorry?'

'The sponsored singing? We sang for three hours, twenty minutes.'

'Well done,' he said.

'And we had a lovely meal at the Spaghetti House. I got a picture frame from Secret Santa and Tina loved her candle.'

'Look Irene—'

'I know you're busy but I had to thank you for sponsoring us.'

'My pleasure. Now I really—'

'Have you been in touch with Vivian? I sent her a card and some little gifts but I haven't heard from her. I do hope she's all right.' She cleared her throat. 'Did *your* parcel arrive? I'm only asking because things go missing in the post. And I was thinking that the three of us should get together for a little drink if you're free at all this weekend. What d'you say?'

He closed his eyes, picturing her thin lips greasy with crimson lipstick. And he lost it. 'No, Irene, I don't want to meet for a drink. I am not your guardian angel. Or your best friend. Our paths happened to cross but I promise you there was no celestial power involved. I wish you well, I really do, but I'm a busy man. I'm going to end this call now. Please don't contact me again.'

He switched off his phone, burying it deep in his pocket as if fearing that Irene's willpower might somehow triumph over Samsung technology. Probably, at some point, he'd feel bad about speaking to her like that but he had enough on his plate without adding a delusional old biddy to the mix. She'd be hurt but she'd get over it, and she could spend Christmas slagging him off to…whoever.

Vivian had daydreamed, briefly, about a second Tooting weekend with Gil. When they returned from the hospital, they would cook supper and sit by the fire with the papers or listening to the radio. They might even sleep by the fire. But after his two-day silence she had to face the fact that this wasn't going to happen.

On Saturday morning, anticipating a Spartan weekend, she got up late, soaked in the bath then went out for breakfast. Richard had promised to buy books for their father but, reluctant to go empty-handed to the hospital, she dropped in at Daunt Books where the assistant recommended *The Complete Western Stories* of Elmore Leonard.

She took a minicab from the Tube station to Farleigh Road, asking the driver to wait while she offloaded her bags and took a quick look around. The house felt warm and everything seemed to be in order. The temperature had barely risen above freezing all week and the snowman was still there. He'd shrunk a little and was leaning forward, as though trying to catch whatever she might have to tell him and she noticed that he was stippled with tiny specks of dirt.

The driver dropped her off outside the main hospital entrance and she joined the steady stream of visitors pushing through the revolving door. After the bracing chill, the air in here was stale and tepid. The instant she started down the corridor, lethargy enveloped her. God, it was dreary. She took the lift to the fifth floor and turned left, then left again through the swing doors. She massaged her hands with alcohol gel from the dispenser on the wall outside the ward then pressed the entry pad and waited for someone to release the security lock. For the first time she'd found her way here without consulting a single sign.

Her father was sitting in a winged chair next to the bed. A pale blue blanket was draped across his lap and he was reading the *Telegraph*. Like the snowman, he seemed to have shrunk since she last saw him. He looked both pathetic and defiant as he did his best to isolate himself from his surroundings, and she felt her resentment waver.

'Good to see you out of bed, Dad,' she said.

'What day is it? I've lost track.'

All he had to do was check the front of the paper but she let it go. 'It's Saturday. How are you?'

'I've been better.' He smiled and reached for her hand. 'You're cold.'

'It's freezing outside. You're lucky to be in the warm.'

He let her idiotic remark pass and signalled for her to bring up a chair. He looked tired but surprisingly cheerful as though, in escaping from the bed, he were already half way home.

'They've got me doing exercises.'

He pointed to his right foot, rotating it slowly at the ankle, repeating the movement with the left. As he did so, the blanket fell away from his legs and she saw that beneath his dressing gown he wore no pyjama bottoms. She caught a glimpse of the dressing, covering most of his thigh, and the catheter tube snaking down from the region of his groin. She felt revulsion, followed swiftly by embarrassment and guilt. He was an old man in pain and in trouble. He hadn't wanted this to happen any more than she had. Ottilie would have come out with a quip about 'showing off your bits' or 'don't frighten the horses', but the best she could do was pull the blanket back into position.

'This one's a bit trickier,' he said, edging his foot forward from the knee, wincing slightly as he did so. 'Good for circulation, apparently. Helps healing.'

The determination and concentration required to execute these minute actions brought home to her the scale of the mountain he faced.

She gave him the book – 'Just the ticket.' – and his mail, which included a few Christmas cards from neighbours who lived near the old house and who had known her mother.

'Can't think why they bother,' he said, tossing them on the bed.

'Well I think it's a kind gesture.'

He squinted at her. 'D'you send cards?'

'No.'

He laughed – a mirthful laugh – and she found herself joining in.

193

They chatted about the comings and goings in the ward. He seemed to have taken a shine to one of the nurses – Anthea or Alicia – the only one who made time to chat with him. He showed Vivian two 'get well' cards he'd received, one from Richard and the other from Mrs Francks. She told him that she'd spoken to Richard and would be reporting back to him this evening, but she didn't mention his planned visit in case it didn't happen.

At five-thirty, when it was time for his evening meal, she left him to it and went to find the coffee shop on the ground floor. It was incorporated in a small but well-stocked M&S Simply Food and she took the opportunity to pick up a few bits and pieces to get her through the weekend.

By the time she returned to the ward, her father was back in bed, his covers tidy.

'No Bill today, then?' he said.

'Gil, Dad. No. But he sent his best wishes.'

'Perhaps he'll come next time.'

After she'd eaten, she rang Richard, feeling like a naughty child to be doing so without having her father's permission to use the phone.

'He was out of bed. And they've got him doing exercises,' she said.

'That's good news. Did you manage to talk to anyone about his progress?'

Gil had mentioned that hospitals did little more than tick over at the weekend and there had been no sign of a doctor on the ward but it seemed a thin excuse.

'No, I didn't.'

'That's a shame,' he said and once again she felt her competence undermined.

'I'm staying at Farleigh Road tonight—'

'Is that necessary? It seems tough on you.'

She'd all but forgotten why she'd decided on these stopover weekends. 'I don't like leaving the house unoccupied for too long. Especially when it's so cold.'

'That's very thoughtful. Did you mention my visit?'

'No. Are you definitely coming?'

'Yes. It's all sorted. I'll fly down on Monday – back on Wednesday. I'm staying at the Hilton, Green Park. I was hoping we could meet for lunch before I go to the hospital.'

He made it sound as if all this were merely a logistical problem.

24

Feray had been drinking. Her cheeks and neck were flushed, and when she kissed him – a sloppy, brazen kiss – he tasted wine on her tongue. She led him through to the kitchen where two women were sitting at the table, glasses in hand. In front of them were two bottles – one empty and the other well on the way.

The older woman grinned. 'You must be Gil.'

'I must be.'

Feray made the introductions. 'This is Mags and that's Sinita. We work together.'

'Not for much longer,' Sinita said. 'We'll be getting our P45s after Christmas.'

Gil offered his commiserations and Feray took a glass from the shelf, emptied the bottle into it and handed it to him.

His stomach griped with the first sip of the plonk and, under the pretext of washing his hands, he tipped most of it down the sink.

'Where are the kids?' he said.

'Kennedy's got them. For the *whole* weekend.'

He was surprised that she hadn't mentioned this last night, especially as she'd always been sceptical of her ex-husband's childcare credentials.

The women were warming up, opening another bottle that Sinita produced from an outsize handbag. Having wrestled with the problem all afternoon, he'd decided the simplest way to break with Feray was to confess to having an affair. No point in trying to explain the unfathomable setup between him and Vivian. If she went ballistic, he'd take it on the chin. The essential thing was to end it. To do this he needed to get her alone and sober (and thinking back to last night, well away from a bed) but there was no chance of that at the moment so, after wishing them a great evening, he took his leave.

*

He waited until mid-morning before going down to the basement. When he rang the bell there was no reply and he let himself in. The kitchen light was on and the table was still laden with glasses and empty wine bottles.

'Feray?' he called. 'Anyone at home?'

Silly question. Her friends looked like party girls and he imagined they were, all three of them, sleeping it off somewhere.

As the day wore on and there was no sign of her, he grew impatient. He could understand why people were dumped by text message. He wasn't going to do that – not yet anyway – but he might change his mind if he didn't get hold of her soon.

He was rinsing out a couple of pairs of socks, when Louise phoned. Hearing his sister's tentative 'Hello? Is that Gil?' his first thought was that there was something amiss.

'What's happened?' he said.

'Can't I ring my big brother for no good reason?'

They chatted for a while. The weather in London. Their mother. Dan and children. Their tortuous Christmas arrangements.

'Rachel's gone totally OTT. I've been instructed to coordinate my gift wrap with her tree decorations.'

'Are you going to?'

'I suppose so. What are your Christmas plans?'

'I'm hedging my bets,' he said.

'Nothing new there then,' she said. 'How are things between you and Polly?'

'Not great. I can't get through to her. I've tried but we end up bickering. I'm going to come over in the New Year if I can. For a quick visit. See if we can work something out.'

'That's good.' She paused. 'D'you have enough for a ticket? Maybe I could—'

'Thanks, sis, but I'm loaded. Honest.'

'You'll give me fair warning, won't you? I'd like us to spend a bit of time together.'

'It's a date.'

In unveiling his shapeless plan to his sister, it became something that had to happen.

'Does Mum really not know Polly's pregnant?' he said. 'She used to spot nicotine stains at a hundred paces.'

'Smock tops are very "in" over here. It's easy to hide a small bump. Of course she's bound to latch on soon, but Polly's a grown-up. They'll have to sort it out. What about Chris and Adam?'

'I get a "how's it hanging" email once in a while.'

'No mention of the baby?'

'Nope. I reckon they're embarrassed. Something like that's a bit too real for seventeen-year-old blokes.'

'Real?'

'I'm sure they think about sex non-stop, but there's no way they'll connect their own urges to what's happened to their sister.'

'Maybe they're waiting for you to say something.'

'I'm going to pass on that one.'

They wound up the call. Gil promised he'd call on Christmas Day, when they were at Rachel's, and Louise promised that she would leave it to him to disclose his plans once he'd lined up the dates.

When he was hatching his getaway plans, he hadn't considered how Louise would take his leaving. So many people had been sticking their oars in that he'd overlooked her, making no fuss, standing quietly in the background. She simply hadn't come into his reckoning. He hadn't realised how much he'd counted on her rock-steady support – not entirely objective support, perhaps, but DNA should be allowed to tip the scales, shouldn't it? She'd been the one he turned to when his marriage was heading down the pan and his kids were drifting away. She'd told him he was being an arsehole but she'd done so with regret not malice. Yet he hadn't had the decency to ask whether she'd mind if he walked out of her life.

It would be good to sit in a pub with his sister, pint in hand, and tell her about Vivian. The whole story from the moment the bomb went off. Every little detail. Not that the women would get on. Louise would be intimidated by Vivian. She wouldn't 'get' her detachment, her circumspection, her European – yes, that's what it was – sensibilities. And he couldn't imagine what Vivian would make of his sister – a plump, forty-seven-year-old bottle-blonde with a harsh Aussie twang and hands coarsened by cleaning products.

He'd dumped the contents of his laundry basket on the floor and was working out what he needed to wash for the coming week, when the doorbell rang. It wouldn't be Feray – she had a key. Cold callers, peddling religion or politics, tended not to hang around. Once they'd tried all the bells without success, they moved on. This particular caller was persistent and, after the third ring, he went down to see who was visiting him on a Saturday morning.

He was nonplussed to find Irene Tovey on the step.

'Hello, Gil,' she said. 'Surprise, surprise.' She stamped her feet. 'Brrr. My feet are blocks of ice.' She was wearing ankle-high bootees with fur trim and, as she stamped, Gil couldn't help thinking of hooves.

Oskar chose that moment to appear and there was a mumbled exchange of greetings. Gil's neighbour, obviously assuming that Irene was on her way in, stood aside to let her pass before going out and pulling the door shut.

Now she was in, Gil could hardly bundle her out again. 'You'd better come up,' he said. Almost before the words were out, he regretted the invitation. 'Just for a few minutes. I've got an appointment.'

She followed him up the stairs, her bootees squeaking on the vinyl treads. By the time they reached his door she was breathing heavily and, clamping a hand to her chest, she said, 'I can see what keeps you so trim.'

Once they were inside, he said, 'Didn't I make my position clear?'

Ignoring his question, she pulled off her sheepskin mittens and placed them between the handles of her bag.

'I don't have much time,' he said. 'What exactly are you doing here?'

'Poor Gil. Always on the go.'

She began unbuttoning her coat. (That knee-length coat, the brooch on the lapel – *marcasite, was it?* those bootees, the wretched handbag – the whole lot belonged on a 'vintage' rail.)

'I've come to apologise,' she said. 'Naughty, naughty me.' She slapped herself on the back of her hand, a hard slap disturbingly evocative of flagellation. 'I shouldn't have phoned you at work. I caught you at a bad moment, didn't I? I could hear it in your voice. It's all too easy to have misunderstandings over the phone. I said to myself, the only way to put things right is to go and talk to Gil in person.'

'Ten minutes later and I'd have been out.'

'But you weren't, were you?' She gave a smug smile. 'I knew you'd be in because God told me to come this morning.'

She glanced around the room. 'What a homely place you have. I've often tried to picture it. A person's home says so much about them, don't you think?'

A mound of soiled shirts and underwear. Socks dripping into the sink. Bed unmade. Last night's dirty dishes on the draining board. He hoped this told her he didn't give a flying fuck about what she thought.

'Don't be ridiculous,' he said, 'it's a dump.'

Without being invited, she plonked herself down on the bed. He found her invasion of the place where he slept and occasionally made love quite shocking. He was even more shocked when she patted the rumpled duvet with her podgy hand, indicating he should sit next to her. He took a step back, putting a couple more feet between them.

'Look,' he said. 'I'll spell it out. Our paths happened to cross. That's all it was. In my job I meet dozens of strangers every day. Sometimes they've had bad news, or they're in pain, or they're scared. Or they might even have lost a handbag. I do my best to make things easier for them. And they're grateful. But we don't start exchanging presents, or meeting for drinks, or turning up on each other's doorsteps. We pass the time of day and move on. End of.'

She continued to smile her indulgent smile and he wondered if she'd taken in a word he'd said.

'Strangers are simply friends waiting to happen,' she said. 'That's what our minister tells us. Don't you think that's an uplifting thought?'

Gil shook his head. 'I think your minister is full of crap.'

She flinched. 'That's a wicked thing to say. I'm disappointed in you Gil. You've strayed from the path of righteousness. Your soul is in mortal danger.'

'You can't win 'em all,' he said, heady with success at ridding her face of that simpering smile.

She stood up. 'I don't know what Vivian's going to make of this, I'm sure.'

'What's Vivian got to do with it?' he said.

'Obviously, as her friend, I'll have to warn her you're not the nice man we thought you were.' She pulled on her mittens. 'I shall pray for your salvation, of course. It's never too late—'

'I think it is.' He held the door open. 'Would you leave now, please?'

He listened as she clomped down the stairs, waiting until he heard the front door shut. Then he went to the window and looked down into the street, watching her disappear around the corner.

Gil texted Feray several times without response, finally making contact with her on Sunday morning. After three days rehearsing his exit strategy, the whole thing had become huge in his mind. It might be best if they met on neutral ground, somewhere where there were people around to limit histrionics and minimise the possibility of physical contact. He'd made one mistake and he didn't trust himself if she started crying.

'Why are we meeting here?' she said when she joined him in the coffee shop.

The lighting was unflattering, accentuating the lines around her eyes and at the corners of her mouth. A few millimetres of grey were visible at the roots of her dark hair and her index and middle fingers showed traces of nicotine staining. She looked weary.

'You've started smoking again?' he said.

'Just one, now and then.' She pushed her hair back, looping it behind her ears. Usually she wore earrings but today only purplish pinpoints showed where her ears had been pierced. 'I'll pack it in when I get another job.' She looked him full in the face, daring him to criticise.

The girl came and Gil ordered a small black coffee – cheap and quick to drink. He was eager to get this done but Feray said she was famished. Her panini took forever to come, and forever to eat. At last she pushed her plate away and he could say his piece.

'There's no right way to say this...The timing's bloody awful...' He floundered, willing her to put two and two together and do his dirty work for him, but she wasn't going to make it easy. 'I've met someone,' he said.

'Someone?' she said. 'You've met "someone". Aren't I "someone"?'

'Of course you are. You're a wonderful woman. But we both knew that it wasn't a forever thing, didn't we?' It was dialogue from a second-rate movie. 'Didn't we?'

The seconds ticked away until he could bear her silence no longer. 'Say something, Feray.'

'It's been *three years*, Gil. It was starting to feel like a forever thing. To me anyway.' Her voice was getting louder. 'Who is this "someone"? Is she young? Yes? And rich? I expect so. Does she have kids? I don't think so.'

'I didn't go looking for this, Feray. I was happy with things as they were.'

'So why didn't you walk away from her? Does she have you by the balls? Where was Miss Someone on Friday night, when you and I were fucking?'

Before he could reply she kicked him hard beneath the table, catching his shin with the toe of her boot.'

'Jeez, Feray.'

'Fuck you, Gil,' she screamed. 'Don't come near me or I'll call the police.'

The proprietor of the café had left his coffee machine and was coming towards them, wiping his hands on his apron. 'Everything okay here, folks?'

Customers caught up in the drama, stared into their coffee cups.

'A misunderstanding,' Gil said. He took a ten pound note from his pocket, standing up and offering it to the man. 'This should cover it.'

He hurried out of the café. Picking his way over the banks of filthy snow, he crossed the road and jumped on the first bus heading south. His shin was throbbing and when he eased up the leg of his jeans he saw that Feray's kick had caught him squarely on the shinbone, half way between knee and ankle, breaking the skin. Although the wound wasn't deep, it was weeping watery blood and he dabbed it with his hanky hoping to prevent the denim from sticking to it. He should be grateful that she hadn't picked up the fork that was lying on the table.

The bus was going to Trafalgar Square and, needing to take his mind off the scene with Feray, he made for the National Portrait Gallery. He'd been there not so long ago but he never tired of studying faces. After revisiting his favourites – Jane Bown's Jagger, the pencil sketch of T. E. Lawrence, Hilliard's exquisite miniatures

– he checked out the photography exhibition that was causing such a stir in the Sundays. The photographers were at least twenty years younger than he and memories of his own abandoned aspirations weighing heavy, more than a little demoralised, he came away after half an hour.

By four-thirty it was dark, the temperature plummeting, and his stomach was grumbling. There were plenty of eating places in the vicinity but, even if he went for the most basic, by the time he'd finished he would end up shelling out another ten quid and he had to watch the pennies. He kept a supply of tins in the cupboard and he'd stocked up on vegetables only yesterday. He'd go straight home and make corned beef hash – enough for two days.

Thoughts of food made him hungrier and he made his way up Charing Cross Road towards his bus stop. It was hard going. The pavements were mobbed with Christmas shoppers dawdling, walking three abreast, half of them talking into mobiles. Seeing all those bulging bags it was difficult to believe that money was tight.

When his bus reached Warren Street, the lights were red. Within hours of the explosion, this had become a place of pilgrimage. Dozens of bunches of flowers were lashed to lamp-posts and heaped around traffic bollards. He'd watched the offerings mount. They'd taken a hammering from weather and passing traffic, and, after six weeks, nothing much remained but cellophane and synthetic ribbon. This flower obsession had taken off big time when Diana died and the whole world had been shown what to do. Flowers – always left in the wrapper. Mawkish messages. Teddy bears and balloons. Reverence for the dead? Sympathy for the survivors? No. It was a superstitious urge to offer up thanks that Death had, on this occasion, passed the donors by.

There had been little information released on the investigation. The whisper was that the bomber was 'white Caucasian'. It was likely that the explosives strapped to his torso had been detonated by a malfunction of a mobile phone. Gil wondered why this hadn't been leaked to the media but maybe it suited the powers-that-be to let the public assume the bomber to be of Middle Eastern origin.

25

Vivian wondered whether she would recognise Richard. It was five years since they'd met at her mother's funeral. It had been all she could do to get through that awful day and she had scant memory of it.

She needn't have been concerned because as soon as she entered the restaurant a man stood up, hand raised in greeting.

'Vivian. Hello,' he said. 'I hope this place is all right. I haven't eaten here before.'

An odd statement coming from a man who lived in Edinburgh.

'Are you in London often?' she said.

He looked sheepish. 'Every couple of months. Usually here and back in a day. I don't get to see Dad as often as I should.'

She wondered if her father knew that his son regularly came within a few miles of his house. 'As often as I should' implied that Richard did, now and again, get to Farleigh Road although her father had never mentioned these visits.

She studied the man sitting opposite her. His hair was white now but she recalled the sandy-haired young men who had occasionally come to the house when she was a child. In her mind's eye they were remarkably tall – but then everyone's tall when you're five years old. In middle age, Richard bore a strong resemblance to their father. They shared the same prominent nose and rudiments of a cleft chin, the same tapering fingers and flat fingernails.

'Was he pleased to see you?' she said.

'Hard to say. He kept telling me I shouldn't have bothered "fagging all the way down".'

'He loves playing the martyr. How was he?'

'Tired. Old. A wee bit confused.'

'Confused?'

'A few non-sequiturs. Repetitions. I collared a doctor. She assured me he's going on well. When I mentioned the confusion thing, she said old people often become disorientated when they're removed from familiar surroundings.' He shrugged. 'It sounded reasonable, but it all came out a bit pat.'

They ordered food and he asked how she was coping. She explained that she would only be able to get to St. George's at weekends. 'I'm afraid he won't get many visits in the week.'

'Don't beat yourself up,' he said. 'By the way, I called in at the house. Everything looked to be in order. Your snowman – I'm assuming it's yours – gave me quite a start.'

He laughed, as if he were indulging a juvenile prank.

'You have Dad's keys?' she said.

'Yes. He gave me a set when he moved in.'

Her father hadn't told her this – but there was no reason why he should. In the normal run of events, Richard would have no more use for keys than she did. And when things went awry, as they had done now, it was as well that they could both access the house.

'Wine?' he said, raising the carafe.

She held her hand over her glass. 'Not at lunchtime.'

'Very wise.' He smiled and poured himself a liberal measure. 'From what I read, the building industry's taking a battering. Your firm's okay?'

'We've been lucky so far.'

She told him about the competition win and how she was scheduled to run the Cologne office after Christmas. 'Someone else will have to do it.'

'You mustn't jeopardise your career for Dad,' he said. 'I don't intend doing that so why should you?'

He wiped a piece of bread around his plate. 'We should start thinking about a care home. He won't be able to look after himself much longer and, let's be honest, we don't want him living with us, do we? John feels the same.'

The thought had been at the back of her mind. Nevertheless it was a shock to hear it expressed in such bald terms, and to know that her half-brothers had been hatching plans even before they'd been told the prognosis.

'Dad wouldn't like it,' she said.

'Maybe not. But he just might have to lump it.'

'Doesn't he get a say?'

'Of course. But let's not forget he's eighty-seven. And we have no idea how this is going to pan out. He may be thankful to have an excuse not to struggle on alone. He can't be getting a lot out of things as they are.'

Richard was clearly unaccustomed to having his pronouncements questioned. He seemed altogether too ready to make judgements on a life with which he'd chosen not to engage. Her own involvement had been reluctant but she had made the effort to visit every few weeks. It seemed wrong – underhand – for the two of them to be sitting here consigning their father to a geriatric home.

He folded his napkin into a neat square and set it alongside his plate. 'I don't know if you're aware of this, Vivian, but after your mother died Dad assigned me enduring power of attorney.'

'What?'

'Ahhh. He didn't tell you.'

'Obviously not.'

He gave a nervous smile. 'Look, Vivian. This doesn't change anything.'

She had only a sketchy idea of what 'enduring power of attorney' entailed – but enough to know that, if their father became incapacitated, Richard would have the authority to handle his finances.

'I think it does,' she said, 'especially if you're suggesting he's becoming incapable.'

'I'm not suggesting anything. And I certainly wouldn't take action without consulting you first.'

His disclosure had wrong-footed her. She'd been too eager to see him as an ally but how could she trust him now?

She glanced at her watch. 'I must get back.'

Opening her purse, she took out thirty pounds and placed it on the table. 'I hope that covers it.'

'Don't be silly,' he said, pushing it towards her.

'You think I'm silly?'

'Of course not. Vivian—'

'Tell Dad I'll be in to see him on Christmas Day,' she said.

She'd begun to hope Richard might share this with her. Now it seemed that his motive for coming to London was to check on their father's state of mind.

When she phoned Gil, he didn't ask about Nick and she didn't asked about Feray, but he seemed his old self again and she assumed that he had, as promised, 'sorted things out'. They talked about her father's progress and Richard's visit. Gil told her how he'd finally lost it with Irene, warning her to expect a phone call. And he said that he would love to accompany her to the party tomorrow.

Now she was having doubts about the wisdom of her invitation. Her 'he's just a friend' approach hadn't convinced Ottilie. The presumption would be that Gil was Nick's replacement. The assembled company (the women anyway) would measure him against Nick and almost certainly find him wanting.

They arranged to meet after work. Although they'd spoken, she hadn't seen him since their night together and she was feeling apprehensive. Even a little shy.

Vivian was wearing the green coat, the one that would set off those jade earrings. She looked tired. And edgy. No matter what she'd said about their failing relationship, finishing with the Nick bloke couldn't have been fun. On top of that, she was bearing the brunt of this business with her father – a double bind if she felt nothing for him. He thought Philip Carey was a game old codger, but it was easy to like other people's parents.

'So, your brother turned up,' he said.

'*Half*-brother. Yes.'

'That should make things easier for you.'

She shrugged. 'Let's not talk about it.'

They drank coffee and again shared cakes, and he didn't care that his shin was throbbing or that he was spending way, way over his daily allowance. Every time they met he had that delicious sense of starting something from scratch. Of not knowing where it was going – or whether he would ever see her again. Maybe this should bother him but he was happy simply to go with it.

'Tell me what happened with Irene,' Vivian said.

He gave her a full rundown on Irene's phone call and visit.

'I can't believe she turned up after what you'd said to her,' she said.

'Irene Tovey and God – not to mention the pastor, or whatever she calls him – make a relentless team. They don't give up easily.'

'Surely she'll leave you alone now,' she said.

'You'd think so, wouldn't you?' He scooped up the last crumbs of cake. 'D'you know I actually wanted to hit her? Sitting on my bed. Simpering away like…like Mrs Doubtfire.'

Vivian laughed. 'Don't.'

'Apparently I'm a son of Satan. I'm surprised she hasn't been on to you already.'

'She will, I'm sure.' She popped a sugar lump into her mouth. 'About tomorrow. The party. You don't have to come.'

He was prepared for this. He didn't blame her for having second thoughts. An office party was about as public an arena as you could get – the mother lode of gossip for the year to come.

'I'm flattered that you invited me but I can see it might be tricky for you,' he said. 'It's not easy when two parts of your world collide.'

'I really do want you to come,' she said, 'but…'

'But?'

'When I told Ottilie – she's our office manager – that I was bringing a friend, she did that eye rolling thing.'

'Eye rolling, eh? Not good.'

She laughed and seemed to relax a little.

'Why not tell them how we met?' he said. 'It would explain why you've invited me. Besides, one look at me and Ottilie will know there can't be anything between us.'

'You'll come then?' she said.

'I'd love to. Where? When?'

'Queens Park. Seven-thirty.'

'Dress code?'

'Oh. Informal.'

'I guess we're not talking sweat pants.'

She frowned. 'Architects love grey. No logos. No patterns. Nothing shiny.'

'Sure you're not confusing them with fog?'

They exchanged the café's fragrant fug for the chill of the street. Looping her scarf around her neck, she shivered. 'I'm going back to work now.'

He didn't like the idea of her alone in what wasn't the most salubrious area and he thought about offering to walk her back to her office. But he didn't want her thinking he was angling to spend the night with her.

'You'll be all right?' he said.

'Of course.'

She took a step towards him and kissed him on the lips – a lingering, unambiguous kiss and he watched her stride away, waiting long enough to know that she wasn't going to look back.

What had they talked about for the past hour? Nothing much. As ever, their conversation had been sparse – more like verbal impressionism. Take that weekend at her father's house. They'd spent a lot of the time in silence. In his experience silence was not the default female state. Polly would accuse him of gender stereotyping but he felt qualified to defend himself. A recent study in a well-respected journal reported that, in any one day, the average man says seven thousand words – the average woman, twenty-one thousand. Vivian bucked that trend. But she'd grown up without siblings and with a father who apparently had nothing to say to her. This might explain a lot.

Gil stepped down from the bus and cautiously picked his way home. The country was, it appeared, still in the grip of a rock salt shortage. Camden was being frugal with its supplies, gritting only the main routes, leaving side streets crusty with ice. In the past couple of weeks, he'd seen enough plastered limbs to know that it wasn't only OAPs who were coming a cropper.

Hands deep in pockets, shoulders tensed against the cold, he stood on the pavement looking up at the house. The tired old building looked almost grand under the inky sky, its flaking paint and stained brickwork restored by soft street lighting. Oskar's curtains were open, his room illuminated by the glow of a TV set. In the room below, Christmas lights, poor imitations of icicles, dangled across the head of the window frames. And at the very top of the house, his dormers were dark and lifeless.

The lights were on in the basement. Feray and the kids would have eaten by now and were probably watching television. He hadn't seen her since Sunday. He'd been expecting her to have another go at him, to launch a second attack, but nothing so far.

He wondered how she would explain his absence to the kids. They were used to his casual involvement in their lives and they seemed to like him. Kids of their age were savvy and they'd have worked out that he and their mother were having sex – although he and Feray had done their best to be discreet. So what would she tell them? That he was a two-timing creep? He'd be sad if she did, but they were her children and she must decide what line to take.

He unlocked the front door and climbed to the top of the house. Having his own place had been at the heart of the dream that he'd hauled half way around the world. On that first day, when he'd unlocked the door to this flat – his very own place – he'd been elated. But recently, instead of feeling liberated by solitude he was beginning to feel limited by it. As he switched on the light, he saw his dream world for what it was – neglected and makeshift. The furniture, the pans and crockery that he'd so diligently accumulated, were second-hand junk. His clothes were other people's rejects.

Still wearing his hat and jacket he sprawled on the bed. What the fuck was going on? Taking against his home? It was as bad as taking against himself. Perhaps Feray was in the basement sticking pins in his effigy. Or Irene, riffling through her tracts and calling hellfire down upon his heathen head.

Feray used to come up here once in a while to share a bottle of wine and make love. She never held back with her condemnation of the place. The mouldering mastic around the shower tray. The ill-fitting blinds. The damp patch behind the bed-head. She hated the carpet, which caused a shower of sparks to fly when they pulled off their clothes in the dark. He christened the phenomenon 'the North London Lights' and let her criticism wash over him, much as a teenager tunes out parental disapproval.

One day Vivian might ask to see where he lived. He pictured her, standing just inside the door, saying nothing but taking it all in, her silence a hundred times more potent than Feray's tirade.

He washed the crockery that had accumulated on the draining board, dried it and put it away. He returned books and CDs to the shelf. Then he emptied the contents of his bedside chest – the one he'd scavenged from a skip – on to the floor. Mismatched socks. Off-white underpants with ruptured waistbands. Misshapen T-

213

shirts. Scabby sweaters. Discarding two odd socks and a sweat-stained T-shirt he folded everything and put it back. Now at least it was tidy crap.

He turned his attention to the party. Grey. Plain. Matt. He checked his hanging rail almost wishing he hadn't asked for a steer. Unless one of Irene's miracles had taken place while he wasn't looking, he wouldn't find anything like that here.

26

Gil showered and changed in the staff cloakroom. He'd gone for his blue shirt – the one he'd worn to the Roundhouse – and black jeans. He was in two minds about a tie. Wear one, then whip it off, or go without and have a standby in his pocket? He plumped for the former – a slim, woven silk job in shades of orange which Feray had bought him for his birthday and which he'd worn only once. He scrutinised the man in the mirror. Not bad.

He returned to the office to collect his anorak when he spotted an overcoat draped over a chair. It was tweed – *grey* tweed – with a crimson lining, and when he tried it for size it fitted perfectly. The pockets contained half a packet of Polos, a flyer for a computer repair business and a betting shop pen, but nothing to identify its owner. The H&S crew were long gone, heading for yet another Christmas party. He'd have the coat back by eight-thirty tomorrow morning – no harm done.

By a stroke of luck, overground trains from Euston to Watford stopped at Queens Park and by seven-twenty he was standing in the Tube station entrance, watching passengers coming through the barrier. They emerged in batches, slapping Oyster cards on the readers, pulling up coat collars against the sudden blast of cold air before filtering out into the night.

Most mornings, on the way to work, Gil studied his fellow travellers. The folks sitting on the top deck of his bus weren't hedge fund managers or barristers or chief executives, they were the drones who kept the capital functioning. They couldn't afford to buy London property but there was work for them in this city and they shelled out rent for tiny flats or tinier bedsits, sharing rooms and making do. Day after day, they turned out – clean and decent – heading for sandwich bars, hotels, stations and hospitals in order to make little more than the minimum wage. He had to hand it to them.

He checked his watch. Seven-twenty-eight. Another batch came pushing through, and there she was, in her rust-red coat – the one she was wearing when they first met.

'Hi,' he said.

He was tempted to touch her – her hair, her ear lobe – but there were people around and he didn't know how she felt about public demonstrations of affection.

'Hi,' she said. 'You're sure you okay with this?'

She was giving him a final chance to change his mind. Naturally he'd prefer to have her to himself this evening but that wasn't on offer.

'Let's do it,' he said.

She smiled and caught his arm, steering him out into the street. They passed a parade of seedy shops then turned into a wide road flanked by municipal-style blocks of flats, three or four storeys high. A stream of cars and buses trundled past, pumping out fumes and spewing up filthy water, and he positioned himself between her and the traffic, recalling how his father had done the same thing whenever he walked alongside a woman.

'Who'll be at this party?' he said.

Aside from Ottilie, and Howard Friel, Vivian hadn't mentioned her colleagues.

'Just Friel people. Ottilie has thirty-eight on her list.'

'Did you tell her how we met?'

'No. You didn't come up.'

'I sound like a boil,' he said.

The story would soon be out, of course. 'How do you two know each other?' was a classic icebreaker. He would tell them how they'd both ended up in A&E after the explosion and thus explain away Vivian's unlikely 'new friend'.

'Down here,' she said, pointing to a turning on the right. 'Kingswood Avenue.'

They exchanged mucky pavements and grinding traffic for a

broad, tranquil street. Two-storey terraced houses ran down one side and some kind of dense hedge – perhaps four feet high – lined the other. On the far side of the hedge, skeletal trees loomed, caught in the glow of the streetlights.

'What's over there?' he said pointing to the trees and the darkness beyond.

'The park. Queens Park.'

'Makes sense.'

Roads joined Kingswood Avenue at regular intervals, dividing the houses into groups of eight or ten, avoiding the sense of monotony in what was turning out to be a long, straight street.

Every house in Coffs Harbour, give or take, stood in its own plot. For most part they were sprawling, single-storey affairs, built of timber with roofs of corrugated sheeting. Even those in the West End, the least prosperous part of town, had their own gardens complete with palm tree and miniature pool for the kids.

It had taken Gil a while to get used to London's tight streetscape – to read the clues to the status of an area and its residents. The houses in Kingswood Avenue weren't large but they were gracious and well maintained compared with the pinched terraces of his own neighbourhood. He saw shrubs and hedges in front of these houses, not discarded mattresses and bin-bags of decaying litter. Properties here hadn't been desecrated by jerry-built extensions and gimcrack modifications. He'd never studied house prices – what was the point? – but he'd suffered enough mind-numbing conversations with Kevin to know that a house in Kingswood Avenue would command an astronomical sum.

He pointed to an estate agent's board in one of the gardens. 'How much would this one set me back?'

'A couple of million,' she said, 'perhaps more.'

He laughed. 'That'd buy you a whole street in Coffs. Not that you'd want one.'

217

The Friel's house was a couple of hundred yards down. Lights glowed in the ground floor windows and over the front door.

'Stylish,' he said pointing to a tapering column of snow, perhaps five feet tall, to one side of the garden path.

'Howard's been on about it for days. It's a scale model of Cleopatra's Needle. He barrowed snow over from the park.' She frowned and her mood changed, as if a bogeyman had stepped out of the shadows. 'Richard saw our snowman. He thought it was funny.'

Gil smashed his fist into his palm in mock fury, eager to lift her spirits. 'Bastard. We'll hide the next one under a tarp. What d'you think?'

'I think we should get inside before we freeze.'

She rang the bell and a man – forty-ish? gay? – opened the door.

'Hello, darling,' he said, brushing her cheeks with his lips. 'Cara's made me bellhop for the evening.'

Vivian made the introductions. 'Ralph, this is Gil. Gil, Ralph.'

The men shook hands and Ralph held his arm out for their coats. Gil watched him glance at the label in the borrowed coat but couldn't tell whether he was impressed or not.

Glasses of wine stood on a tray in the hall and they helped themselves. The house was filled with a delicious winey, garlicy smell. Murmuring voices and the strains of something easy – Jamie Cullum? Brad Mehldau? – leaked through an open doorway. Vivian guided him into a dimly lit room.

He'd assumed the Friels would go for modern stuff. Steel and leather. Monochrome. Stark and uncomfortable. What he saw surprised him. Rich red walls, overstuffed armchairs, patterned rugs on polished boards, paintings and knick-knacks – bourgeois more than Bauhaus.

Nine or ten people were sitting on sofas ranged around an open fire.

'Vivian. Hi,' one of the women called out, beckoning them. 'Budge up everyone.'

Vivian squeezed onto the sofa and he perched on the arm next to her.

'This is Gil,' Vivian said.

One by one, like well-schooled children, they gave their names. 'Alex.' 'Celine.' 'Thalia.' 'Fareed.' The roll-call continued but, after 'Chris', Gil stopped trying to remember.

They resumed their conversation, discussing travel plans for the coming holiday. The best route to Dorset. The disparity in train ticket prices. Whether it was better to travel overnight. They moved on to reminiscences of nightmare journeys and Christmases trapped with feuding families in remote locations. Gil half-listened, more interested in watching Vivian. She was absorbing it all, occasionally laughing or nodding but she made no contribution to the exchanges. These were her workmates, people with whom she spent every day, yet a distinct *something* separated her from them. He couldn't, for instance, imagine them teasing her or including her in office tomfoolery. Maybe they found her intimidating. Maybe they felt sorry for her. It was difficult to put a finger on.

The sofa contingent dispersed to refill glasses and inspect the giant Christmas tree that occupied the bay window. He and Vivian lingered by the fire, stoking it with coal from an iron bucket. Vivian nodded towards a black woman on the far side of the room who appeared to be arguing with a beefy young man.

'That's Ottilie,' she said.

'The bloke?'

'Spencer. Her partner. I'll introduce you.'

He laid a hand on her arm. 'Not yet. I need to hone my small talking skills before I tackle Ottilie.'

She stood up. 'I'm going to the loo. You'll be okay?'

'I'll do my best.'

He was on his way to find another glass of wine, when a tall man came towards him, hand outstretched. 'Howard. Howard Friel.'

'Gil Thomas.' They shook hands. 'Thanks for inviting me.'

'Thank me at the end of the evening, after Cara has browbeaten you into doing things grown men don't normally do.'

'Sounds alarming.'

'It is. You've seen this evening's timetable?' Friel pointed to a hand-lettered poster that was fixed to the wall above the piano. 'It's all there. As you see, we eat at eight. Games start at nine.'

'Games?'

'"Charades." "Who am I?" "Mafia Murder." "Bang." A word of warning. Not knowing how to play isn't an acceptable excuse. We wind up with a concert. This, you'll be pleased to know, *is* optional. Cara isn't quite that cruel. Kicking out time – midnight on the dot.'

'Interesting.'

'It seems cold-blooded but it ensures that everyone knows what's what and, more importantly, when to go home.'

Gil congratulated Friel on his snow sculpture and they discussed the pitfalls of working in a medium that was prone to melting. They moved on to the drawbacks of smokeless coal – 'efficient but aesthetically unpleasing' – and the characteristics of the perfect Christmas tree. It was party drivel – verbal gymnastics, one-upmanship in wit. Friel didn't ask what he did for a living or refer to his Australian twang – the usual topics when meeting someone for the first time. Yet he had the feeling that Friel was trying to trip him up. Vivian clearly rated him but Gil's first impression was that there was something slippery about the man.

At eight o'clock, everyone filtered through to the kitchen where Friel and an arty-looking woman were stationed behind a table, ladling food into deep bowls.

Ralph was in the queue behind Gil. 'Cara doesn't hold with finger food, thank God. She favours *food* over *cooking*.'

This evening's choice was between vegetable curry and goulash. Gil chose the latter then went in search of Vivian whom he found sitting on the stairs, bowl balanced on her knee.

She had a knack of making the simplest outfit look out of the ordinary. Tonight she was wearing what was, in effect, a grey sack with sleeves, her only adornment a long silver chain, the links the diameter of ten pence pieces. As far as he could make out she was without makeup. She made the other women look overdressed.

'You look very lovely,' he said.

'Thanks.'

She moved up a few steps, making room for him to sit below her on the stairs.

'Who've you been talking to?' she said.

'Ralph. And your boss. And someone called Andrea who lives in Oxford.'

He hoped she wouldn't ask what he thought of Friel. He could hardly confess that, on the strength of one fatuous conversation, he hadn't taken to the man. On the other hand, he didn't want to lie to her. He'd been less than straight about his relationship with Feray and it hadn't felt good.

'Should I start sweating about these games?' he said.

His diversionary tactics worked and, while they ate, she gave him a rundown on the party games.

In the kitchen Cara Friel was blackmailing people into taking second helpings. 'My freezer's bursting. This will all go in the bin if you don't eat it.'

She smiled when she saw Vivian.

'Sorry, darling, I haven't had a moment. Once we've got pudding out of the way, I can join the fun.' She plopped a spoonful of trifle into a bowl. 'Is Nick around? I haven't seen him.'

Although Gil was standing alongside Vivian, Cara hadn't registered that they were together, and he saw the colour rise in Vivian's cheeks.

'Actually, Nick and I have split up. I thought you might have heard.'

Cara looked anguished. 'No. Howard is hopeless when it comes

221

to telling me the important things.' She put her arms around Vivian and patted her on the back. 'You poor thing. Are you all right?'

'I'm fine. We're both fine. Neither of us has time at the moment. My father's in hospital and—'

'Now Howard *did* remember to tell me that. You must be frantic with worry. How is he? I must send a card.'

'He's making progress.'

Gil moved closer to Vivian, leaving her no choice but to introduce them.

'Cara, this is Gil,' she said.

He gave what he hoped was a winning smile. 'Delighted to meet you, Mrs Friel.'

'*Gil*. What an interesting name. And it's Cara.' She raised her eyebrows. 'Are you an architect, Gil?'

'Afraid not. I'm a medical photographer.'

'Thank heavens,' she said. 'Medical photography. It sounds fascinating. When we have a minute, you must tell me all about it. So Gil, how d'you know our lovely Vivian?'

'Gil was one of the people at the crossing when the bomb went off,' Vivian said. 'We happened to be in A&E at the same time.'

Cara's face crumpled. 'Awful, awful business. When we heard how close Vivian came to...' She shook her head. 'I don't even want to think about what might have happened. It must be a tremendous help, having someone to talk to, someone who's been through the same trauma. One's own little support group.'

Vivian's concise account of their meeting was accurate, and Cara clearly found it a reasonable foundation for a friendship. Fine. After all, he'd suggested that it would be enough to appease the curious. And yet...

All evening Vivian felt she was holding her breath. Only when Ralph handed them their coats did she find it possible to relax.

There had been no need for disquiet. Gil had chatted, stacked the dishwasher, not tried too hard when they were playing games, and had the decency *not* to volunteer for the concert.

'Where do you live, Gil?' Cara said when they were leaving.

'I'm in Kentish Town.'

'Not too far from Vivian then?'

Vivian knew where Cara was going with this, and why. A young landscape architect had gone missing in Bristol. It was four or five days since she was last seen buying a pizza on her way home from work. The circumstances of her disappearance pointed to abduction, or worse, and every front page showed her picture – an innocent face glowing with optimism.

'Gil's promised to see me home,' Vivian said.

'Good. Perhaps you two could share a cab with—'

'It's all sorted,' Vivian said. 'Goodnight everyone. Have a lovely Christmas, Cara.'

'Yes. And thanks for a great party,' Gil said.

She grabbed his arm and they started back the way they came.

'Was that okay?' she said.

'It was fun. They're a nice crowd.'

They walked on, their breath condensing in the sub-zero air.

'There's something I have to tell you,' he said.

Her stomach flipped. 'Oh.'

'I may be – in fact I'm sure I *am* – claustrophobic.'

She stopped and, laughing, kissed him on his lips. 'Is that all?'

'You don't understand,' he said. 'It means I don't go by Tube and—'

'The last Tube's gone anyway. We'll get the bus to Finchley Road.'

She took out her phone, opened the London Transport site and checked the timetable. 'There's one due in six minutes.'

On the bus they discussed the party. Gil had chatted to most of her colleagues but, from the way he glossed over his conversation with 'Friel', she guessed that the two men hadn't hit it off. Maybe Gil was envious of their longstanding friendship and daily association. She wondered, too, whether Howard had sensed that there was more to her friendship with Gil than she'd suggested. He could sometimes be over-protective.

They got off the bus at Swiss Cottage and walked up the hill towards her flat. Lights still blazed in the big houses in Buckland Crescent and Belsize Park, party music seeping from open windows.

'You'll stay?' she said when they reached the front door.

'If that's okay with you.'

'I wouldn't have asked if it weren't,' she said.

She watched him hang his coat in the hall. He'd been to her flat several times now but she wasn't yet accustomed to seeing him there. He looked out of place – like a pencil in a cutlery drawer. They fitted together best on neutral ground. Walking down the street or sitting on a bus. Even in her father's house because she, too, was pretty much a stranger there.

'That's a nice coat,' she said.

'It is. Pity it's not mine.'

He explained how he'd requisitioned it for the evening, making her laugh at his dithering over what to wear. He was good at telling stories, of spinning the ordinary into something amusing and she was sorry that she'd worried him with all that nonsense about grey.

Howard had told them all to have a lie-in and that he wouldn't expect them until mid-morning but tomorrow would be a normal working day for Gil.

'What time d'you have to be in?' she said.

'Eight-thirty.'

'We should go to bed.'

The last time he was here she'd seduced him (that's what it boiled down to) and she wondered whether he was waiting for her to take the lead again.

'I'm staying because I've had to share you all evening and I want you to myself for a little while,' he said. 'We don't have to make love. In fact I'm not sure I'd be up to it.' He grinned. 'No pun intended.'

She nodded. 'D'you need anything?'

He produced a toothbrush from his pocket. 'A squeeze of toothpaste, if you can spare it.'

Whilst he was in the bathroom, she undressed, put on a nightshirt and slid into bed. Nick hadn't collected his things yet and she wondered whether to offer Gil his pyjamas but when he came into the bedroom he had stripped off to a white T-shirt and boxer shorts. He climbed in beside her and switched off the lamp. They weren't touching but they were close enough for her to feel the warmth of his body.

'Irene rang this morning.' She had been on the point of getting into the shower. Calls at seven in the morning tended to be important and without checking she'd accepted it.

'Vivian? It's Irene. I'm so glad I caught you.'

She knew – or thought she knew – what was coming.

'Actually, Irene, I'm behind schedule. Could you possibly—'

'It won't take long. And it's vital you hear this before it's too late.'

'Look Irene, I really don't have time—'

'I don't want to alarm you, dear,' Irene said, 'but you must steer well clear of Gil Thomas.'

'Gil?'

'Yes,' Irene said. 'We thought he was a good Samaritan, didn't we? Prince Charming. Well he fooled us. He's evil. Worse still, he's devious.' Irene raised her voice. 'First he suggested we meet after work for a little pre-Christmas celebration, as he put it. He pretended he was interested in the missionary work our church does. He even made a donation. Nice as pie. Grooming. Isn't that what they call it?' Now

225

she was gabbling. 'Then, the other day, he invited me to his flat. I had no qualms about going. It wasn't as if he were a stranger. I was too trusting. I should have left the minute I saw the bed.'

'What?'

'Well, dear, I don't want to distress you but he tried to touch my…private places.' She paused, obviously waiting for the full horror of it to sink in. 'But don't worry. I was able to get away.' She paused again. 'Our Lord taught us to turn the other cheek but I'm sure He doesn't mean where perverts are concerned.'

Vivian wanted to laugh and tell her not to be ridiculous but something stopped her.

'Sorry, Irene, my cab's here,' she said. 'I've got to go.

Vivian related the conversation.

'Wow,' he said. 'She's certainly got it in for me.'

'The scary thing is, I'm sure she believed what she was saying.' Vivian found his hand and squeezed it. 'I should have told her she was lying.'

'No,' he said. 'You did the right thing. I don't want her starting in on you. The woman's toxic.'

'She can't be allowed to go around making that sort of accusation. What if she—'

'Shhh. Let's worry about that when it happens,' he said. He folded her in his arms. 'I've been thinking. I know you'll be at your dad's place for Christmas. How about I keep you company? You'll want to spend time at the hospital but you have to eat and I'm happy to act as catering manager. I'd like to pop in and see him too, if that suits.'

'You can't, Gil. It'll be miserable.'

'Cheerier than a bedsit in Kentish Town.'

'I wouldn't bet on it. I haven't even thought about food or—'

'Easy. We shut up shop around midday on Christmas Eve. Just give me a list.'

226

The explosion had been, as Cara said, a terrible thing. Had she arrived at the crossing a few seconds earlier, she might have been one of those bodies on the traffic island. A few minutes later and she would have run in the opposite direction. But she'd arrived at exactly the right time to meet Gil Thomas.

She kissed him. 'I shouldn't accept, but I will. And thank you, thank you, *thank you*. You're a lovely man.'

'Not a sex-crazed pervert, as Irene would have you believe?'

'In my experience, sex-crazed perverts don't wear boxers to bed.'

It wasn't long before a slight snoring indicated that he was asleep. She lay in the darkness, taking pleasure in his being at her side, realising how isolated she'd come to feel since her father's accident.

Her father. She should have checked with the hospital but, after the conversation with Richard, she was furious with him for his evasiveness. Let his beloved son take responsibility for a couple of days since they were such great buddies.

27

Gil, who knew about such things, had explained how, whenever possible, patients were 'allowed out' over Christmas. 'Good for morale. And it takes pressure off the staff.' 'They wouldn't send Dad home, would they?' she'd asked. 'Unlikely. His wound's not healed. And he's not mobile. They wouldn't risk it.' She was relieved, happy to trade off time in the ward against responsibility for her father's safety, and the physical intimacy that went with tending to the sick.

At two o'clock, after champagne and mince pies, Howard wished his staff a happy holiday and closed the office until the New Year. Vivian had taken her holdall to work and she went straight from the Elephant House to Farleigh Road. Gil was coming via Sainsbury's and while he was busy with food shopping, she would get the house ready.

There were a few pieces of mail on the mat, and a note from Teresa – Vivian had forgotten the cleaner – saying that she'd turned up *twice* and been unable to get in. (Naturally her father wouldn't trust a cleaner – albeit *his* cleaner – with his house keys.) She phoned to apologise and let her know what had happened. Although sympathetic, Teresa was understandably unhappy at losing two weeks' pay and they agreed that Vivian would pay her half her usual wage until she was needed again.

The only evidence that Richard had been to the house was a pile of junk mail left in the centre of the kitchen table. She'd not heard from him since their lunch, which didn't surprise her as they'd not parted on the best of terms. Until her name had appeared in that 'next of kin' box, wherever possible she'd avoided involvement in her father's affairs. And that had suited her fine. But the situation was different now. No one could be sure how quickly, or how well, he would recover. He'd had plenty of

228

opportunity to tell her about this power of attorney business. To explain why he'd chosen Richard. Oversight was one thing but secrecy was another. As soon as Christmas was out of the way, she would tackle him on the subject.

Despite the continuing cold, the snow was melting. Outcrops of clumpy shrubs and islands of flattened grass had appeared spoiling the unblemished whiteness of the back garden. The snowman was shrinking and leaning precariously. Another old man on the brink of falling. She hadn't caught the weather forecast but the sky was gunmetal grey. If it snowed again, they would be able to restore him and maybe fix him up with a companion.

Gil texted. *At S'burys. Long q s. May be some time x*

Her decision to take Gil to the party had been the right one. They could have allowed things to continue as they were, but a covert friendship could never be quite healthy. Her colleagues had said nice things about him the following day, and they'd accepted the explanation of their friendship – no bawdy remarks, no eye rolling.

Humming to herself, she went upstairs to her father's bedroom. Net curtains obscured the windows, cutting out what little daylight remained. A fringed lampshade dangled from the central light fitting. Mismatched furniture – a wardrobe, a couple of upright chairs, a tallboy with flimsy metal handles – was placed randomly around the room. Cough sweets, indigestion tablets, a magnifying glass, a torch and a copy of Whittaker's Almanac were piled on the bedside table.

Her father spent night after night alone here. His days were spent alone too but she knew how darkness crystallised hazy apprehensions into full-blown fears. What did he think about, lying in this bed in the dark? The future? Not a great prospect – and that was before his accident. The past? She couldn't imagine whether that brought comfort or distress. She'd been determined not to feel sorry for him but now he'd ambushed her with a packet of indigestion tablets.

She stripped the double bed of its winceyette sheets, substituting white percale from her holdall. Long before they became the default in Britain, the Carey family had slept beneath duvets – proper ones, filled with feathers, not synthetic substitutes. After her mother died, her father had abandoned his duvet for sheets and grey blankets – suspiciously ex-army-looking. She'd never bothered to ask why.

She gathered up his bits and pieces, clearing the surfaces that he used as a dumping ground, finding a place for everything in the bottom drawer of the tallboy. Then she used a pillowslip from the laundry basket to dust the room. *There.*

She'd spent yesterday lunchtime looking for a gift for her father. What would a bed-bound octogenarian – and a bolshie one at that – appreciate? She'd seen a dozen things that Gil might like – a down-filled jacket, a chromatic harmonica, a grey tweed cap with a button on top, a natty little rucksack – but she'd resisted because they'd made a pact. Each would give the other one of their possessions. The suggestion had been his and she'd agreed, assuming that he was short of funds. On reflection, she saw that it had little to do with money. This hand-me-down *thing* should embody the essence of themselves, or at the very least be meaningful. It was a test, almost Arthurian in ambition, and it had taken her some time to decide on the appropriate item.

But what to buy her father?

In the end, she'd dashed into Boots and grabbed an Imperial Leather gift set, three flannels and a tube of hand-cream. Surely he couldn't find fault with such a practical present. As an afterthought, to offset this utilitarian selection, she'd spent over the odds on a red cashmere scarf in a trendy shop on Haverstock Hill. 'What's this? I already have a scarf.' She could hear him now.

She lit the fire, sitting cross-legged on the hearth rug, listening to the crackle and spit as the kindling caught light. After a few minutes, yellow-grey smoke was twirling up from the coal, giving off the sulphurous smell particular to a freshly lit fire. At last a single flame licked up, and then another, and another, until a flickering halo capped the mound of coal.

She went around the house gathering table lamps which she set on the floor, their mellow glow camouflaging the drab surroundings. Something was missing. *Green.* There should be foliage. Bracing herself against the cold, she cut swags of shiny-leaved laurel from the back hedge and laid them along the mantelpiece. After she'd added clusters of tea lights, it looked as festive as any Christmas tree.

Gil crossed the items off his list. <u>*Small*</u> *chicken* (that had been a tricky one). *Fish* (for this evening). *Vegetables, salad things and fruit. Butter. Milk. Bread. Wine – one red, one white. Christmas pudding. Mince pies.* Cheese? Did she forget cheese? Or maybe she didn't like cheese. How little he knew about her. And what about cooking oil? The old man must keep a few essentials in his cupboards. He decided to stick to the list. They wouldn't starve and there was always a Spar open somewhere.

Sainsbury's was crammed with frazzled shoppers. The checkouts were backed up causing gridlocked frustration in the aisles. It was too hot in here. And his rucksack wasn't helping. He was tempted to abandon his trolley and head for the exit. But he'd promised her he would do this. He closed his eyes, breathed deeply and shuffled forward. His turn came and he loaded his shopping onto the belt. The checkout girl – 'Kasha' – processed his goods faster than he could pack them, her torso twisting as she passed each item from right hand to left. Without looking, she presented each barcode towards the scanner. Did checkout staff acquire a sixth sense? Butter. *Bleep.* Tangerines. *Bleep.* Milk. *Bleep.*

'Fifty-eight pounds sixty-three,' she said, indicating the card-reader. 'Nectar?'

He shook his head, entered his PIN and confirmed the total – more than twice his weekly food allowance.

Having fulfilled his mission, he wanted to be with her right away. The carrier bags were heavy, the handles stretching and cutting into his hands – a good enough reason to lash out on a mini-cab. When he reached the house he dumped the bags on the doorstep, allowing himself a few moments to anticipate the starting-over moment before knocking the door.

'Hello,' he said. 'I bring gold, frankincense and milk.'

He thought she was going to kiss him but instead she picked up a couple of bags. 'Was it horrible?'

'Grim.'

They unpacked the shopping, checking the cupboards to see what was there and what they might be short of, the commonplace task giving them time to adjust to being together. And, as he watched her emptying oranges into a bowl, it came to him that he was in love with her. He loved her. The realisation thrilled and terrified him. He didn't want or need this. This wasn't in his plan. But it had happened and it was somehow wonderful, and anyway there was nothing he could do to change it.

They made tea and toast and took it into the living room to eat in front of the fire. Dusk was fading into darkness and they drew the curtains. Four-thirty on Christmas Eve.

He pictured his children, on the far side of the world, sleeping their way into the heat of Christmas Day, immediately editing the image as he remembered the child in Polly's womb. North of Coffs, in Grafton, his sister Rachel was almost certainly awake, worrying about the catering, fretting about table napkins and timings. Louise – sweet, conciliatory Louise – would soon have to rouse her family and convince them that Christmas at Rachel's was going to be *much more fun* than a lazy day at home. Once she'd got them sorted, she'd collect their mother then drive the fifty-odd miles to Rachel's place. What a palaver.

'It's already Christmas in Australia,' he said, 'and it'll be hot.'

'Do you – *did* you – spend it on the beach?'

'Not until I left home. When I was a kid we had a proper English Christmas. Turkey, mince pies, Christmas pud, the works. All sweltering around the dining table. Mum and Dad were replicating their own Christmases, I suppose. It's hard to break the chain.'

'We always opened our presents on Christmas Eve,' she said. 'I've never spent Christmas with anyone but my parents. It's too… personal to share with strangers. Being with another family, seeing all their rites and rituals, would seem like voyeurism.'

Thirty-six Christmases with her parents – that was hard to comprehend. 'You never went to your mother's family? Christmas in Germany would have been quite something I should think.'

'No.' She frowned. 'We never had much to do with them. I'm not sure why.'

She stood up and fiddled with the candles on the mantelpiece. 'Have you seen the matches?'

He washed their plates and mugs then went upstairs to the bathroom. The house was by no means large but, compared with his bedsit, it was palatial. It struck him how rarely he went into a house that was a home. Kevin's a few times – the Friel's place – and here.

Above the sink, a shaving mirror – a magnifier on a swinging bracket – was fixed to the wall. He adjusted its angle so that his features filled the reflecting disc. There was no escaping its brutal honesty. Thickets of nose hair, wrinkles like trenches, blood vessels snaking across his eyeballs, that warty eruption on the slack skin beneath his left eye – everything rendered several times life-size but no doubt visible to the naked eye of a young woman with twenty-twenty vision.

'How d'you see it going?' he said when he returned to the kitchen. 'Do we need a Friel-style schedule?'

He meant it in a jokey way but somehow he got the tone wrong and it sounded mocking.

'You don't like Howard, do you?' she said. There was no antagonism in her question, merely curiosity.

'I hardly know the man.'

'But it's obvious you don't like him.'

He regretted referring, even obliquely, to Friel. Disharmony between two people was, more often than not, sparked off by a third party. He'd learned this even before he and Janey got together. He wasn't foolish or love-struck enough to imagine he and Vivian could sidestep these snares. *You don't like Howard, do you?* It seemed they had already been blighted by the phenomenon.

He held his hands up in surrender. 'I'm jealous of the guy.'

Something else he'd learned – along with men who cried and men who were comfortable with small babies, women couldn't resist men who owned up to their frailties.

Vivian was searching for a heavy pan for the fish when the senior ward nurse phoned.

'No cause for alarm, Miss Carey. Your dad's running a bit of a temperature. We've moved him to a single room. Just a precaution until we indentify the problem.'

'He's not in danger?'

'No. But he asked me to let you know. He didn't want you coming in and finding an empty bed.'

'Thank you. I hope he didn't nag. He can be very…'

The nurse laughed. 'Yes, he can.' She paused. 'Any idea when you'll be in?'

Hospitals were busy places. They didn't have time to satisfy an old man's whim. And now this offhand question. Something wasn't right.

'I could come this evening if…' She left it hanging, waiting for assurance that tomorrow would be soon enough.

'He'll be pleased to have a visitor. And someone can have a little word with you.'

She recounted the conversation to Gil, doing her best to conceal her irritation with her father for managing to spoil their evening, not wanting Gil to think her selfish.

'Why don't you go now?' he said. 'We can eat later.'

It was six-thirty by the time she got there. It was busier than she'd previously seen it, the corridors jammed with people carrying holdalls and parcels. There was lots of laughter and silly hats and piped music, as though illness (and bad news) could be warded off by Christmas ritual.

When she reached the ward she was directed to the room adjacent to the nursing station. The door was shut, the sign on it restating hand-washing instructions and telling visitors to report to a member of staff before entering.

He seemed to be linked to a great deal of equipment – tubes, wires, screens flashing unfathomable yet ominous numbers. The raised cot sides made him look helpless. His hand, resting on the blanket, twitched spasmodically but otherwise he was perfectly still. She glanced around. The room contained nothing even vaguely homely – no get well cards, no patterned curtains, no crumpled newspapers or packets of sweets. This was a place dedicated to illness.

She pictured his bedroom at Farleigh Road, regretful that she had, a few hours ago, done her best to eliminate him from it. She took his hand. It was cool and dry which surprised her as he had, according to the nurse, a raised temperature.

'Dad?' she said, squeezing his hand. 'Dad.'

He opened his eyes and stared at her but there was no recognition in his gaze. 'Where's my wife?'

'It's me. Vivian.'

He shook his head violently, waving her away as though she were an impostor, then he closed his eyes and was still again. Were it not for her pounding heart she might have imagined his disquieting reaction.

She sat next to the bed. He was breathing steadily and deeply, sunk back into sleep. Sometimes, coming out of a dream, she needed time to orientate herself. Had she roused him from a dream about her mother? Was that it?

A nurse slipped into the room. 'You found him, then,' she said, as if that were the solution to the problem.

'What's wrong with him?' Vivian said. 'He asked for my mother. She's been dead for five years.'

'It's not unusual for older people to get a bit…muddled.'

'Muddled? What are you saying?'

The nurse's face was set in a vapid smile. 'It's easy for those closest to miss the signs. Little slips, here and there. A bit forgetful.'

'He wasn't muddled until he came in here.'

'Well…Would you like a cup of—'

'You're doing tests. Tests for what exactly?'

The nurse's smile had faded. 'I'll fetch someone.'

This suggestion that confusion was acceptable – inevitable even – made Vivian cross. And uneasy. *Had* she failed to spot something? Richard had mentioned that their father was confused but she now knew he had a financial motive for planting that seed and didn't trust him.

A young woman came in and introduced herself as Doctor Halliwell. Her hair was tied back in a ponytail, drawing attention to the crop of spots on her forehead. She looked tired and scruffy and barely old enough to have left school. She was holding a ring binder and as she flicked through the loose leaves Vivian noticed her bitten nails.

'Right. Okay,' she said, 'you're…' She flipped back to the cover of the binder.

God. She doesn't even know his name.

'You're Philip's daughter?'

236

Vivian might not know her father well but she did know that he deplored familiarity, particularly the compulsion to call old people by a first name, 'as if we no longer warrant respect'.

'I'm *Mr Carey's* daughter,' she said, a correction almost certainly wasted on Doctor Halliwell who was still flicking back and forth through sheets of paper.

It seemed that all had been going well, if a little slowly – 'everything takes longer at your father's age' – but last night his temperature had risen sharply, suggesting an infection somewhere.

'We've put him on antibiotics,' she said. 'That should sort it out. And we'll run a few tests. To be on the safe side.'

'The safe side of what?' Vivian said.

The young woman looked uncomfortable, stuck for words, as though they had deviated from the established script. Vivian felt almost sorry for her – working on Christmas Eve, bolshie visitor, zits. But she must save her sympathy for the old man in the bed. 'Another thing. Why have you moved him out of the ward?'

The girl came up with a couple of woolly reasons – 'quieter for him', 'easier for the nurses to keep an eye' – which didn't seem quite good enough to explain his occupying a premium spot in a busy hospital. She glanced at her watch. 'I'm afraid I need to get on with my ward round,' she said. 'I'm sure you want to spend some time with your father. Will we see you tomorrow? You can come in whenever you like. It's open visiting'

After she'd gone Vivian sat with her father for another ten minutes. Should she wake him and see whether he recognised her this time? No. It would be cruel to drag him back from wherever he was. Tearing a page from her notebook, in large, clear script she wrote *Popped in but you were sleeping. See you tomorrow. Vivian xx*. Then she tucked the note into his hand and headed back to Farleigh Road.

28

Enough light penetrated the curtains for Gil to find his way to the bathroom without switching on the light. He checked the time. Two-forty in London – gone noon in Australia. When he'd promised Louise that he would call today, he hadn't anticipated being away from his flat. Using his mobile would cost a fortune – money he didn't want to spend. But if he failed to meet his promise, they would simply nod their heads and add another black mark to his tally.

Vivian was awake when he returned.

'Did I wake you?' he said.

'I wasn't asleep.'

She'd returned home in some distress. Over a belated meal, she'd told him what she'd found when she got to the hospital. What seemed to disturb her most was her father's demand to see his wife and his failure to recognise her – his daughter. A matter of weeks ago, she'd insisted that she and he were, in effect, strangers. Listening to her detailed account of her visit, he'd sensed a change in her position, as if she were nudging closer to the old man. Vivian always seemed sure of her opinions, which made this apparent shift puzzling. Then again did it matter *why* a young woman went from loathing to tolerating her father? Wasn't it enough that she did?

He got back into bed, keeping to his side of the mattress, making sure not to crowd her.

'Want to talk?' he said.

'Not really.'

'Okay.' He turned on his side, facing away from her. 'Give me a dig if I snore.'

When he was a young man, relationships had started with sex and usually not progressed much further. Then Janey came along and it had been a case of good sex followed by bad luck – if you could call 'forgetting' to swallow a pill *bad luck*. After Polly was born, when bed had become a place to sleep and not much more, he'd drifted in and out of a number of rather public affairs. Janey hadn't seemed overly bothered but, for some reason which he couldn't recall, they'd given it a second go resulting in the twins, and confirmation that it was never going to work.

Things had been different when he came to London. He was older, of course, but he'd partly attributed his dwindling libido to the climate – less bare flesh and more intellectual distractions. His ad-hoc arrangement with Feray had been ideal.

Sex seemed inconsequential to Vivian. (Was that what she'd tried to warn him of?) They'd made love just that once – 'to see if it works' – and at the time, he'd got the impression that it did. Now he didn't know what to think. Tonight they'd undressed in silence, separated by the width of the double bed. It was as if she'd forgotten he was there.

She fidgeted for a while, then edged towards him until they were lying back to back. 'I'm cold,' she said, touching his calf with an icy foot.

'Here.' He rolled over and gathered her against his shoulder. 'How's that?'

'Nice.'

'You mustn't upset yourself,' he said. 'He's being well looked after.'

'Is he? People are supposed to get better in hospital, not worse,' she said. 'If he's to die I wish he'd died in the garden. They say that hypothermia is just like falling asleep.'

'He's not going to die,' Gil said, 'not yet anyway.'

He had no idea if this were true. Mention of an infection coupled with his transfer to a single room rang warning bells. There were plenty of 'nasties' lurking in hospitals and he was a frail old man.

'I hate that place,' she said. 'It's where they took my mother. She was dead before the ambulance arrived but I suppose they had to take her somewhere.'

He pulled her against him in a hug. They stayed like this, their bodies growing warmer. But she remained tense.

'It's no good,' she said at last. 'I'm going to make some tea.' She sat up and as she leaned across him to switch on the lamp, her breast brushed his arm. He felt himself stir and turned away, hoping she hadn't noticed.

They bumped up the central heating and lit the rings on the gas cooker, sitting in the kitchen, waiting for the house to warm up. She looked forlorn and he set about cheering her up.

'Tell you what. Let's have breakfast,' he said.

'It's *three-thirty*.'

'Haven't you heard of the "all day breakfast"? C'mon. Live a little.'

They ate porridge followed by bacon sandwiches smothered in ketchup and, by the time they'd finished she looked less troubled.

'I have something to ask,' he said. 'Strictly speaking, I should ask your dad—'

'For my hand in marriage?'

Her response, frivolous and flirty, threw him. His face must have revealed this confusion because she said 'I'm only *half* German. I am allowed to make jokes.'

Of course she was teasing. Yet her words had flipped his guts and set his heart thudding

He recounted his promise to Louise. 'Would it be okay to use the landline? It'd be a couple of calls. Coffs and Grafton. I'll pay.'

'Don't be silly,' she said. 'When would be a good time?'

'Now, if that's okay. They'll still be recovering from lunch.'

She yawned. 'I feel sleepy now. I'll leave you to make your calls.'

'I'll be up soon,' he called as she went up the stairs, taking pleasure in the intimacy of the simple words.

He dialled Rachel's number, checking each digit against the entry in his diary, thinking how few times he'd phoned her since coming to England. They'd never been close, their lack of fondness made more apparent by his warm relationship with Louise. Even as a child Rachel had been inflexible, unable to accommodate opinions and attitudes that conflicted with her own. They'd found it easier to keep out of each other's way. These days they exchanged perfunctory emails but they both knew that it wouldn't take much for them to lose touch.

'Rache? It's Gil. Merry Christmas.'

They exchanged greetings, skirting around the fact that he was, for no good reason in her eyes, on the far side of the world. They soon ran out of small talk and Rachel handed over to Louise.

'Merry Christmas, Gil,' she said.

'Hi, Sis. Bearing up?'

'We're having a terrific time. Rachel's put on a fantastic spread.'

The brightness in her voice told him that she was getting through the day as best she could. They talked about the weather and the laptop that Dan had bought her. He would have asked her about Polly but he assumed the others were listening to the conversation and he didn't want his daughter's pregnancy to become the focus of the family gathering.

'I'll ring you at home,' he said, 'and we'll have a proper chat.'

'That'd be nice. Mum? Come and talk to Gil.'

His mother sounded frail and although the line was clear, a time lag – no more than a fraction of a second but nevertheless disruptive – meant that they were constantly talking over each other or failing to catch the tail end of a remark. As usual she was fussing about the cost of the call, telling him goodbye before they'd had time to say anything. She'd never challenged his decision to leave, and he loved her for it, but he knew that she must wonder if she'd done anything to drive him away.

'You have a great day, Ma,' he said. 'Actually I'm coming over soon.' He hadn't meant to blurt it out but it suddenly seemed important to give her something on Christmas Day. 'Before the end of January, probably.'

He allowed time for his words to reach her and time for hers to come back.

'Thank you, Gil,' she said. 'It'll give me something to look forward to.'

'Take care, won't you Mum? We'll speak again soon.'

'Thank you,' she said. 'You're a good boy.'

He pictured her pulling a hanky from the sleeve of the cardigan she wore even on the hottest day of the year, and he felt empty.

In her most recent email Janey had mentioned that the kids – *his* kids – would be spending Christmas with her and Alan. Where else would they be? Before he had time to chicken out he dialled her number. With luck they'd all be outside and not hear the phone. He'd leave a message and have fulfilled his obligations.

'Hi.' It was a man's voice.

'Hi. Is Polly there by any chance?'

The time lag and then a tentative 'Dad? It's Chris. Dad? Are you still there?'

The *man* was his son and it shook him a little.

'Chris. Hey. Merry Christmas. How's it going?'

'It's good.'

He waited, forgetting that teenage boys (his, anyway) never volunteered information and needed to be interrogated. 'So who's there with you?'

'Mum, Adam, Polly, Alan. Chloe and Mark from next door.'

'Quite a party then. I expect you had a slap-up dinner.'

'Yeah.'

'It's the middle of the night here,' Gil said.

'Cool. D'you want to speak to Adam?' Chris said. It was obvious his aim was to get off the phone as quickly as possible.

'That'd be great,' Gil said. 'And Polly too, if she's around.'

Mention of Polly ignited a glimmer of interest. 'Can you imagine her with a kid, Dad? It's weird. She keeps nodding off and snoring. Like an old woman. She looks gross too.'

Chris and Adam had spent their childhood tormenting their sister. It was their fallback position when they had nothing better to do. They weren't cruel boys but younger brothers were programmed to torment. Polly was no pushover and the ensuing battles – physical, verbal and psychological – had been hard fought and often distressing to witness. When he'd left (or been thrown out, depending who was telling the story), the three kids had joined forces and turned their anger on him. Understandable but nonetheless hurtful.

'Don't be too hard on her, Chris. I don't suppose she's thrilled about the way things are.'

A sigh of exasperation reached him from the far side of the planet and he was on the point of reminding his son that he was seventeen, not seven, and that he should be looking out for his sister because the baby's father wasn't around. But he let it go, anticipating Chris's *and where's its grandfather?*

He heard – faint but clear – the sound of laughter. Janey lived on Firman Drive, overlooking Diggers Beach. Late December it was probably up around eighty degrees. Wooded slopes running down to the shore. Pink sand. Azure sea. White-tops flipping onto the beach. Some people might call it Paradise.

'Hey, I'll be over soon,' he said.

Either Chris hadn't heard or wasn't interested because all he said was, 'Here's Adam.'

Gil went through a similar exchange with his other son, this one involving an element of bike talk. The boys were non-identical twins and bore little physical resemblance to each other, but they had – or had cultivated – the same nihilistic take on life.

'Is Polly there?'

243

'Yeah. Uhhhh. No. She and Mum had a row. She went off in her car.'

'A row?'

'Yeah. Mum wouldn't let her have a drink. Because of the baby. This baby thing is freaking me—'

'But she didn't have a drink?'

'Daaad. She's thick but she's not *that* thick.' He laughed as though he'd said something clever.

'Is Mum there?' Gil said.

'No. She's gone after her.'

'Right.' *Right.* 'Could you let them know I called?'

'Sure. Look, I've gotta go, Dad. There's another call coming in. Oh, Merry Christmas and all that stuff.'

Vivian had pushed the pillows away from her, wedging them against the headboard. She was deep in sleep, spreadeagled on her front in the centre of the bed and, reluctant to wake her, he went looking for somewhere else to sleep. The neighbouring room contained, amongst other things, dining chairs, a stack of cardboard boxes, a filing cabinet and a rolled rug. The junk room. He tried the next one and found a single bed.

The bed was comfortable and he was bushed but, when he closed his eyes, no matter how hard he tried, he couldn't stop Polly's car spinning off the road.

29

Gil woke to find Vivian standing next to the bed holding two mugs.

'Did I drive you out with my snoring?' she said.

He heaved himself up. 'You were sleeping when I came up. I didn't want to wake you. What's the time?'

'Eight o'clock,' she said. 'Coffee?'

She sat on the end of the bed. He must be looking pretty crumpled and he was glad that she hadn't switched on the light.

'Merry Christmas,' she said.

'Merry Christmas, Vivian.'

'You spoke to your family? Were they pleased to hear from you?'

He'd given her the expurgated version of his family circumstances. Now might be the time to fill her in on how it really was. But on Christmas Day? Maybe not such a great idea.

'Yes. Thanks,' he said. 'I must give you something for the calls.'

Over breakfast they made a plan, deciding to cook their meal in the evening. Vivian was doing her best to be upbeat, but he could see that she was dreading visiting her father.

'We could call in this morning. Check how he's doing,' he said. 'If we don't want to traipse back here, there's sure to be somewhere we can get a bite of lunch.' (For Gil one of the wonders of living in a multi-cultural city was the availability of anything at any time.) 'Then we could go back and spend a bit more time with him.'

'Or we could stay here.' She sighed and shook her head, as if to dislodge temptation. 'Let's leave at eleven.'

'Sounds good.'

She held out her hand. 'Shall we go back to bed?'

Her invitation took him by surprise and he felt himself harden as he followed her upstairs.

She was tense and tentative. Apologetic. Her timidity seemed to rub off on him and what should have been a Christmas gift turned into an unsatisfactory fumble.

'I'm sorry,' he said. 'I rushed it.'

'No. It's me. I can't seem to…'

He wondered why she'd suggested they come back to bed. He hated to think that she felt she owed it to him. That he expected it. Most of her difficulty stemmed, he was sure, from too much thinking. But trying to convince her with words would only add to the tangle of thoughts that constrained her. And assuring her it would be better next time – well, that would be patronising. He held her close, regretting that he couldn't simply flick a switch that would allow her to let go.

It was quiet there in the bedroom. Quiet and still. No ticking clock or drone of a plane, only the sound of her breathing. She felt suddenly heavier in his arms. He couldn't see her face but he guessed she'd fallen asleep. Her head must be pressing on a nerve in his shoulder because his hand was starting to tingle. But he didn't move.

Her father was sitting up in bed, connected to an array of monitors, staring towards the window, which was obscured by vertical blinds. He paid no attention to them as they washed their hands, only acknowledging them when the stood at the bottom of his bed.

'Good,' he said to Vivian. 'You're here.'

'Merry Christmas, Dad. You're looking better.'

He nodded towards Gil. 'You've brought him.'

Gil held out his hand. 'Hello again, Mr Carey. How are you doing?'

The old man frowned. 'Do I know you?'

'It's Gil, Dad,' Vivian said. 'He brought you the copy of Sherlock Holmes. Remember?'

Ignoring her question, he said 'Has he got the van? Can he bring it round under the window?'

Vivian was staring at her father, silenced by his rambling.

Often in his job, Gil had to deal with confused people – old and young – and he'd learned that the best strategy was to take the lead from them and go cautiously with the flow.

'The van's off the road, Mr Carey,' he said. 'Carburettor trouble.'

The old man frowned and raised the bed covers, peering at whatever was – or whatever he imagined was – beneath them. 'I've got to get this stuff out.' He turned back to Vivian. 'Did you bring my clothes? I need to go home.'

She glanced at Gil and he winked, encouraging her to go along with the Alice in Wonderland conversation.

'They'd like you to stay a bit longer, Dad,' she said. 'Besides, you haven't had lunch yet. They do a very nice lunch here.'

He pointed towards the carrier bag in her hand. 'Are those my clothes?'

'No. They're presents. For you. It's Christmas Day.'

She took several gift-wrapped parcels out of the bag and handed them to the old man who tore them open, tossing the contents on the bed without seeming to register what they were.

'Toiletries,' she said. 'Not very exciting, but always useful. And the scarf's a cheery colour, don't you think?'

The old man inspected the scarf. 'Red. Roses are red. Blood is red. Tomatoes are red.' He raised his finger. 'And books are read, too.'

'That's a good one,' Vivian said. She seemed to be getting the hang of it now.

Gil pulled his ID tag from his pocket and looped it around his neck. 'I'll nab someone. See if I can find out what's going on. Won't be long.'

'I'd understand if he were delirious,' Vivian said. 'But he's so calm.'

'Infections cause all sorts of symptoms,' Gil said.

'So everyone keeps telling me.'

They were sitting on the wall that surrounded the visitor car park, drinking foul coffee from the vending machine in the foyer.

Despite his ID tag and charm offensive, he hadn't established much. Bloods, urine and swabs had gone off for testing. He guessed that, having isolated the old man, the urgency had gone out of their investigations. It was Christmas, after all, and the staff had enough on their hands. The labs would be closed for days to anything but emergencies. Old man. Bit befuddled. Hardly priority.

'If the wound's infected, wouldn't it be obvious?' she said.

'It may not be the wound. It could be a urinary infection. They're very common.'

Gil's stint at UCH had been akin to a medical apprenticeship, albeit a haphazard one. He'd photographed an assortment of bizarre and banal conditions and, listening to the top guys explaining things to patients and students, he'd picked up a fair knowledge. Were he a gambling man, he'd bet a fiver that the medics were looking for a super-bug. If this turned out to be the problem, the prospects weren't great for Philip Carey.

'What d'you want to do now?' he said.

She grimaced. 'Fast forward six months.'

He thumbed an imaginary remote control and shook his head. 'Batteries are flat. How about we look for something to eat?'

They headed towards Tooting Broadway. It was as if a curfew had been imposed and only a few defiant souls had dared venture out. Without the usual bustle, dilapidation and graffiti were what caught the eye, and the area looked depressing and a little menacing. As they passed one shuttered shop window after another, Gil wondered if he'd been optimistic in thinking that they would find somewhere to eat. They'd all but given up, when they came to a pub that was open for business. The Star was on the rough and ready side and it appeared that all the misfits in the

Borough of Wandsworth had been lured by its beery fug. He recalled last year and his two-day pub crawl around Kentish Town with Andy. They'd been like the blokes he saw around him in this bar, doing their level best to eradicate Christmas and all its attendant baggage. But it was a relief to be out of the cold and comforting to be somewhere dingy and insanitary after the bland hospital environment.

The only warm food on offer was, according to the chalk board, 'Christmas in a bun' which the barman explained was turkey, stuffing and cranberry sauce in a bap.

Vivian wrinkled her nose but Gil persuaded her to chance it and they ordered one each, and half pints of beer to wash them down.

'About this morning…' Vivian dipped her head.

'No worries,' he said.

He waited, giving her time to say more. When it was clear that she wasn't going to, he reached out, wiping a non-existent trace of cranberry sauce from the corner of her mouth, suddenly wanting to connect with her in an intimacy that had nothing to do with sex.

'Shall we go back?' he said.

'I don't want to but I suppose we should.'

When they arrived, two nurses were fussing around the old man, checking the equipment and tidying his bedclothes. He was awake, staring at the ceiling.

'Did you have a good lunch, Dad?' Vivian said.

He smiled but said nothing.

The younger nurse tutted then, speaking loudly and slowly, she said: 'Come along, Philip. Tell your visitors. Did you eat all your dinner?'

Gil reached for Vivian's hand. She was going to find this whole hospital scenario harder to handle than most.

They made their way back to the house. More people were around, more traffic on the move. Dog walkers. Kids wobbling along on oversized bikes. Teenagers escaping. Grandparents (or parents – not always easy to tell) pushing strollers. The citizens of SW17 had been allowed out after the Christmas morning lockdown.

They passed a woman whose wild, dark hair made him think of Feray. She and the children would be with her parents, somewhere out near the North Circular. He hoped they were having a good time and that, if she weren't able to forgive him, at least she could forget him for the day. After Christmas, he must try and patch things up with her. He hadn't planned to go through life hurting people and letting them down. His mother. His wife. His children. A string of lovers – although they probably had expected no better from him. Now Feray had joined the list.

Vivian had stopped to read a 'Lost Cat' notice stapled to a plane tree.

'Some crazy woman's offering two hundred pounds for information,' she said.

He waited for her to catch him up.

'It's not even a pretty cat,' she said.

'But it's *her* cat,' he said. 'It could be her only reason to get up in the morning. The thing that keeps her going.'

'A cat? Oh, come on.'

'Think about it', he said. 'She has a run of bad luck. Her family moves to…I dunno…Timbuktu. Her friends let her down…'

'So she gets a *cat*?' she said.

'We deal with things the best way we can,' he said. 'And getting a cat beats getting religion, don't you agree?'

They turned into Farleigh Road and spotted another notice fixed to a fence. Gil studied the image of the timid-looking animal

– predominantly white with a smatter of tabby smudges. 'You're right,' he said. 'It's pretty ugly.'

'If I'm ever reduced to getting a cat,' Vivian said, 'it'll be a chocolate-brown tom. With turquoise eyes. And whiskers this long.' She held the palms of her hands six inches apart.

Vivian had never imagined that this house could become a safe haven. Yet, as she and Gil prepared their meal, the tension gripping her shoulders eased.

Her aversion to the hospital had developed into loathing. The smell, the heat, the faulty lifts; the makeshift signs and pathetic Christmas decorations; the confrontations and unanswered questions; the lack of privacy, the bewildered visitors, the elusive staff. All those sick people. It was too much.

She'd never had to confront the kind of degeneration that was gaining hold of her father. Death, when it swooped in and took her mother, had been instant and immutable. Vivian had been called on to do nothing but survive. It had been cataclysmic yet somehow honest by comparison with her father's degrading – and probably futile – ordeal. Were his hip to mend and he regain his senses, the best he could look forward to was a limited and dependent life. *Dependent* – that menacing word again.

Gil touched her arm. 'Penny for 'em.'

She shook her head. 'Let's eat in the dining room.'

They set the table with a white linen cloth, which she found in the sideboard drawer along with her mother's favourite bone-handled cutlery. After they'd added candles and a sprig or two of holly, the austere little room felt surprisingly festive.

They opened the wine and a jar of olives and pottered in the kitchen, the aroma of roasting chicken intensifying as they discussed the best way of achieving crisp roast potatoes and whether the carrots should be cut into discs or batons. By the time they'd finished, every surface was strewn with the aftermath of food preparation.

'I can't believe we've made such a mess,' she said.

'Cooking's like making love,' he said. 'If you're not making a mess, you're doing something wrong.'

Her cheeks were warm from alcohol and cooking, but she felt them flush further.

Last night she'd left him downstairs, making his calls, and she'd lain in the dark, waiting for him. The last thing she recalled was his voice murmuring up from the hall and, when she'd woken this morning, she'd found herself alone in her father's bed, wondering why he wasn't beside her. He explained that he hadn't wanted to wake her. This was perfectly reasonable but not the way she'd anticipated their Christmas Day starting. After breakfast, she'd attempted to reclaim him but the spectre of her father (they were in his room and in his bed) had paralysed her into failure.

She hadn't realised how hungry she was and she'd forgotten how delicious home-cooked food could be. More often than not, she and Nick had eaten out or picked up something for the microwave. They'd rarely cooked together. In fact, it was hard to remember what they *had* done together.

When they'd finished eating they decamped to the sitting room and pulled the sofa close to the fire.

'Let's do presents,' she said.

They placed their parcels side by side on the hearthrug. They'd both chosen green wrapping paper – his to her, metallic and tied with silver string; hers to him, dark green, dotted with cotton wool snowflakes.

'Have you ever opened a present that lived up to expectations?' he said.

'Yes,' she said. 'A fountain pen. From my mother. I still use it.'

For her thirteenth birthday, she'd asked for a fountain pen, one with a refillable reservoir. She already owned several 'cartridge' pens whose scratchy nibs dug into the paper and whose narrow bodies were difficult to hold. She'd explained this to her mother but when she saw the small parcel sitting next to her breakfast plate she'd been frightened to open it in case it was the wrong one. She needn't have worried. Inside the sleek snapping-jawed presentation box lay a Pelikan Classic 200. Marbled grey with a gold nib that flexed with the pressure of writing. Fat enough to sit comfortably between her fingers. When she'd gone into W H Smiths to buy a pot of black ink she'd checked the price, guessing that her mother had concealed the cost of it from her father.

Gil handed her his parcel. 'Quick. Open it before I chicken out.' He kissed her on the cheek. 'A small thing but mine own. Merry Christmas, Vivian.'

From its size and heft, she guessed it was a book. She was right. The corners of its cream linen cover were battered – one appeared to have been chewed – and the front was stained with a coffee-coloured circle. The title running down the spine read A DREAM TOO FAR by Elspeth McKendrick.

She must have looked puzzled because he reached across and flicked back the cover. Inscribed in the top corner of the flyleaf in precise, rounded handwriting was 'Helen Thomas. Christmas 1958.' Then, below it, in the same handwriting but this time larger and more confident-looking, 'To Gillon – may God keep you safe. Ever your loving Mother. June 2005.'

'I was going to be "Peter" after my granddad until she read that,' he said. 'She had a tough labour by all accounts so when she came up with Gillon, Dad didn't have the heart to argue with her.'

Vivian riffled through the yellowed pages, pausing now and again to scan the text. 'Gillon. There it is. Gillon. And here. Gillon.'

'Mum gave it to me when I left,' he said.

She ran her hand across the cover of this book, which had been in the world longer than he had. 'I love it. But I can't accept it. It should go to your daughter.'

He laughed. 'She'd lob it straight in the garbage can.'

She lifted it to her nose and caught the unmistakable scent of old book. 'Have you read it?'

'I gave up after ten pages. It's drivel.'

'I'm not sure I'd feel the same about you if you were a Peter.'

'That settles it. It's yours.'

She'd imagined that choosing what to give him would be fun. But, the more she'd thought about it, the more impossible it became. She'd mulled over things they'd talked about, places they'd gone together, hoping that the perfect object lurked amongst these memories. During the process she'd realised that, astonishing though it was, their shared history spanned less than two months.

She'd looked around her flat. Books. Music. Pictures. She'd contemplated giving him the musical box that had belonged to her mother. It was in the form of a traditional Bavarian house complete with balcony and tiny dancing bear. It was special to her but, unlike the book which virtually contained him, it would mean nothing to him. A piece of jewellery? A photograph of her as a child? What about her favourite pyjamas?

'Merry Christmas,' she said, watching as he eased the wrapping off the small package, fearful that she'd got it wrong.

'This is perfect,' he said.

She'd cut the hair from behind her ear where she hoped the irregularity would go unnoticed. 'A lock of hair' conjured up a blonde curl trapped in a locket or the back of a gold pocket watch but her hair was black and straight, and when she'd placed it in the plain silver frame it had looked more like the business end of a watercolour brush.

'It doesn't seem arrogant?'

'Not at all. Your hair, your amazing, beautiful hair, was the first thing I noticed about you. And the fact you were making *notes*.'

'If you'd prefer my notebook…'

'Shhhh,' he said.

This time it was easy. Gil's patience, his soothing and encouraging voice and, yes, his expertise, played their part. But the simple truth was that she wanted him.

Afterwards, they went upstairs and she steered him into the spare room, away from everything to do with her father. They spent the night pressed close to each other, murmuring apologies as they attempted to accommodate knees and elbows.

30

It had snowed overnight, only a couple of centimetres but enough to conceal the blemished remnants of earlier falls. As they walked to the hospital, it seemed to Vivian that the world was new again – sprinkled with possibilities.

Her father seemed pleased to see them, although she wasn't sure he knew who she was. He was still muddled, today convinced that he was a guest in a hotel and that Gil was one of the staff, but as long as they took their cue from him, they were able to carry on a bizarre, shifting conversation. There was no reference to a van but he spent a considerable time discussing the pattern on his pyjamas. 'I'm not sure I like stripes. Paisley. That's the one. I used to like stripes. Not any more.'

Vivian promised that she would track down some paisley pyjamas and bring them with her next time, which seemed to satisfy him.

'I'm going to sleep now,' he said after they'd been with him for barely an hour. 'Can you put me straight before you go?'

Taking this as a signal that they were dismissed, they tidied his bed, scrubbed their hands and escaped from the ward. The coffee machine had an 'out of order' sign on it today but Tartine on the High Street was open and doing brisk business. They ordered coffee and croissants, and found a table near the window.

'How does he seem to you?' she said.

'Happy enough.' He smiled at her. 'And you're doing fine.'

'Am I? I feel I'm playing a game without knowing the rules.'

'Isn't that the human condition? A lifelong game where you're never given the rules?' He shook his head. 'Jeez. I sound like Irene.'

'No,' she said. 'Irene knows all the rules, thanks to Moses. When d'you go back to work?'

'Tomorrow. There won't be any clinics for a couple of days but they need a photographer to cover emergencies. I volunteered so Kevin could spend time with his family.'

She'd assumed that he would have a few more days off and last night, nestled against his back, she'd planned how they might occupy the week. They could walk on the snowy Heath. Watch old movies. Cook delicious meals. If Gil was up for it, they might even go to Cologne. She would buy his ticket. She could show him the gallery site. And the cathedral. And the thousands of padlocks – 'love-locks' – fastened on the Hohenzollern Bridge. None of that was going to happen.

'That was sweet of you,' she said.

'Not entirely. I need to chalk up a few brownie points before I push off to Australia. What about you?'

'Howard shuts the office between Christmas and New Year. He's a generous employer.'

He raised his coffee mug. 'Good old Howie.'

She remembered his dig at Howard after the party. 'You *are* jealous,' she said.

'How could I not be? The man leans over your drawing board. Takes you to building sites. You have intimate conversations about…' he waved his hands in the air.

'Sections. Elevations. Fenestration. Building regulations.'

'Stop,' he groaned.

He was teasing, of course, nevertheless his readiness to admit to jealousy made her feel something close to adolescent excitement.

Over a second coffee they discussed how to spend the remainder of the day.

'I'm happy to go back to the hospital,' Gil said.

They'd left her father calm and on the verge of sleep. It had been an okay visit – certainly better than yesterday's.

'I think I'll quit while I'm ahead,' she said.

'Any idea when you'll next be here?' Gil said, as they were packing up.

'Not tomorrow. Tuesday, maybe? Am I being callous?'

'Not at all. You're wise to pace yourself.'

She told him of her intention to get Richard more involved. 'I'm sure he'll call in here. That's why I want to leave the house tidy.'

As she was returning the cutlery to the sideboard drawer, her mother's voice came, soft but clear, telling her to put away her toys before her father came home. *Schnell, schnell. Wir müssen alles tipptopp machen bevor dein Vater kommt.* She shivered.

They were nearing the Tube station when she remembered Gil's confession.

'We can take the bus,' she said.

'It would take forever. Anyway, it's time I faced up to this.'

'Sure?' she said.

They entered the station and were caught in the wind tunnel of stale air funnelling up from the platforms. Gil grimaced and she grabbed his hand, and they stood side by side on the descending escalator. A Sunday timetable was in operation and they had to wait eight long minutes for a northbound train. By the time it emerged from the tunnel – a giant piston, shunting lukewarm air ahead of itself – a crowd had assembled on the platform.

The train slowed to a stop and the doors slid open, the surging crowd sweeping them into the carriage. All but a few seats were taken and they stood near the door, Gil's eyes fixed on her face, his hands clamped around the pole as if at any moment he might be swept away. His forehead was slick with perspiration and she got ready to bale out at the next station if he couldn't handle it.

'Okay?' she said, resting her forefinger on the back of his hand.

'Piece of piss,' he said.

Once through the West End, the crowd in the carriage thinned. Gil had willed himself into something akin to a fugue state, where it was all going on around him but he was somewhere else. By the time they were nearing Camden Town, the point at which the Northern line forked into two branches, he felt wrung out. This train continued via Kentish Town – his stop – but Vivian needed to change here for Belsize Park. When the doors opened he expected her to make a move but she stayed where she was.

'I'll be fine from here,' he said.

She shook her head. He knew arguing would be a waste of time and, to be truthful, he wasn't sure he was quite ready to go solo.

They reached their stop and left the train. The dead air grew sharper and fresher as the escalator trundled them up and up, and, when they reached the ticket hall, it was all he could do not to raise his fist. For forty minutes he had held it together, focusing on the next blob on the Tube map but now, almost out of the blue, he was in Kentish Town with Vivian and no idea what might happen next.

'How far to your flat?' she said.

'Not far,' he said, scanning the street for somewhere to get a coffee. But apart from a couple of convenience stores, everything was shuttered and he had no alternative but to add 'Would you like to come back?'

'I would,' she said.

He'd known that, sooner or later, she would come to his flat. They were friends – lovers – whatever – and it would be weird if she didn't. But he'd imagined he would get fair warning. Time to square the place up. Stock the fridge. His mother would have clucked disapproval. In her book, being caught with a grubby bathroom was second only to dropping dead in dirty underwear.

They called in at Saeed's for bread, milk and eggs and he watched her studying the stock as though the tins and cartons on the dusty shelves were archaeological specimens that might reveal something of civilisation in these parts. When he paid for his goods, Saeed's eyelid dipped in a wink and Gil knew it wouldn't be long until news that he'd been buying groceries with a young woman filtered back to Feray.

Until now they'd inhabited Vivian's world – her flat, her father's house, her boss's party. During their spell south of the river he'd had the feeling they were laying down the foundation for something that might last but he was no longer sure of that because, by a twist of fate, she had strayed onto his territory.

'This is it,' he said pointing to the steps up from the pavement. 'I'm at the top.'

The gloomy hallway reeked of Oskar's garlic-heavy concoctions. The floor tiles were cracked and curling, the paintwork grubby. As they climbed the stairs, he couldn't help but see it through her eyes. Contrast it with her spotless home.

When they reached the top landing, he was dismayed to see his portrait of Feray leaning against his door and, alongside it, an Argos carrier bag on top of which was his striped robe. She must have dumped his stuff here before leaving for Christmas. Pushing the bag and the picture to one side, he opened the door and shepherded Vivian in.

The place was a tip. Unwashed crockery. Unmade bed. Drawer emptied on the floor in his search for matching socks. Clearing the armchair of accumulated clothing, he gestured for her to sit down.

'I don't get too many visitors,' he said.

She pulled up her coat collar. 'I'm not surprised. It's freezing in here.'

He plugged in the oil heater and lit all four gas rings, then took the duvet from the bed and tucked it around her knees. While the kettle boiled he scooped up his socks and stuffed them back in the drawer.

'Back in a sec,' he said.

Once in the bathroom, he replaced the used hand towel with the most respectable one from the shelf, rooted out a new bar of soap and flushed a double dose of bleach down the lavatory. But there was nothing he could do about the stained lavatory pan and the blackened mastic around the shower tray.

When he returned Vivian was holding the portrait of Feray.

'I brought your things in,' she said indicating the bag which now lay on the bed. 'She's beautiful.'

'I guess she is.' He attempted to keep his tone light and neutral, waiting for the next comment.

'She must be very angry to have left your stuff out there like that.'

'She's entitled to be angry,' he said, feeling the need to defend this woman whom he had so recently failed. 'She's rearing two kids on her own. Her job's on the line. Her ex doesn't pay his whack. Actually, her life's pretty shitty at the moment.'

'But why take it out on you?'

He shrugged. 'Who else is there?'

She shook her head, dismissing his lame explanation, clearly expecting him to come back with something more plausible. But he felt wiped out – the sleepless night and the ordeal of the Tube – and he didn't have the energy, or the necessary ammo, to put up a fight.

He raised his hands. 'Okay. I wasn't entirely straight with you. We had a bit more than a casual thing going. It was easy and it suited us both. But we'd made no promises to each other.'

'She has a sensuous mouth,' she said, studying the photograph. She looked up, fixing him with her gaze. 'Was she good in bed?'

He could say that it was none of her business, or parry her question with something similar about Nick Mellor.

'Yes,' he said and when she nodded, in what he felt was acknowledgement of his honesty, he was glad that he hadn't tried to sidestep her question.

'So why give her up?' She sounded genuinely puzzled.

'Simple. A bomb went off, and I met you and… Look. Are we

having a row? Because if we are, I think I'm entitled to know what it's about.'

'I don't know what you expect from me,' she said.

'Don't you get it? I don't *expect* anything from you. Nothing at all.'

She looked again at the photograph, as if determined to fix every detail in her memory, then she leaned it, face inwards, against the wall.

'That's easy then,' she said.

'It can be if you'll let it.'

She took hold of his hand and kissed it. 'I'm ravenous.'

He wasn't sure what had happened there – whether he'd set her mind permanently at rest – but he didn't much care because they'd come through the skirmish and she hadn't walked out on him.

They ate scrambled eggs on toast and followed it with tinned mandarin oranges. Afterwards she inspected his bookshelf and his album collection, wrinkling her nose at his choice of music. He insisted she listen to Jimmy Guiffre, jubilant when she admitted to 'quite liking' 'The Train and The River'.

For two days, cocooned inside their private Christmas, they hadn't listened to the news. When he switched on the TV, they learned that yesterday at around the time they were eating breakfast, the body of the missing girl had been found by the roadside in Bristol. The police were appealing for information, displaying family photographs of an open-faced girl, laughing at the camera. And there was CCTV footage – jerky and grainy – of her buying groceries on the way home to her flat and her fate.

'It's too sad,' Vivian said.

'It is,' he said, thinking how often Vivian was alone, a soft target for anyone on the lookout for young women.

31

Richard's phone was going straight to voice mail. Vivian left increasingly vehement messages and when he finally got back to her, she told him that their father had lost his mind.

'He's disorientated, I'll give you that,' he said. 'But let's not forget he's an old man, in unfamiliar—'

'I don't forget things,' she said. 'For instance I haven't forgotten that you were the one who first said he was confused.'

'Confused, yes, but I wouldn't say—'

'I spent Christmas listening to his ramblings. Believe me, Richard, he's lost his mind.'

She ended the call before he could tell her to calm down.

Her outburst was effective and, presumably not relishing a slanging match, he mailed her, promising to come to London before the end of the week.

Vivian's abhorrence of the hospital was mutating into stoicism and the next time she visited she made it as far as the ward before the heebie-jeebies set in. In the forty-eight hours since she was last there, her father had changed. He looked thinner. Smaller. His eyes were dull and sunken, crusty at the corners. The skin on his arms was flaky and dry to her touch. He barely acknowledged her. There was no babble about vans or pyjamas. In fact he hardly spoke, responding to her questions with 'yes' or 'no' or nothing at all, smiling occasionally and wistfully at some invisible thing (or being) beyond the foot of his bed.

A nurse arrived to check the various bags and monitors. Despite the woman's steady wittering, he continued to stare ahead. Vivian wished he were playing one of his games but she knew he wasn't.

'Could you make sure he takes these, dear?' the nurse said, handing her a plastic cup containing several pills.

'Okay. Are his results back?'

The nurse took a ring binder from the window sill and flipped through it. 'Mmmm. Doesn't look like it.' She smiled brightly. 'But it's Christmas, don't forget.'

'Really?'

Vivian's sarcasm was rewarded with a nervous glance.

After she'd gone, Vivian inspected the tablets – two white, one blue and a red-and-yellow capsule. Hard to believe these harmless-looking objects were capable of halting an old man's slide towards disaster.

She tipped them onto her hand and offered them to him. 'Tablets, Dad.'

He watched her warily, making no move and saying nothing.

'Come on,' she said.

She wished she could walk away. Leave this to someone who knew what they were doing, someone who wasn't repulsed by flaccid lips and toothless gums. Steeling herself, she pushed the blue tablet into his mouth, her stomach heaving at its warm, damp pliability. When he showed no signs of swallowing, she tried flushing it down with a drink of water, her attempt resulting in a regurgitated tablet and wet pyjamas. She retrieved the tablet, draped a towel around his neck and tried again, her revulsion to some small extent counteracted by satisfaction in success.

'There. That wasn't so bad, was it? Three more and we're done,' she said, surprised to hear herself murmuring trite reassurances.

She checked the locker. She must tell Richard to bring more pyjamas and moisturiser for his skin. She was bundling washing into a bag when she became aware that he had turned his head and was watching her.

'You're Vivian,' he said and smiled, as though she had emerged, without warning, from dense fog.

'Yes, I am.'

She kissed him, not minding his sour breath, ashamed that minutes before she'd made such a big deal about touching him.

264

'We should have...' he said. 'We should have...'

She waited for the rest, and when it didn't come she prompted 'What, Dad? What should we have done?'

Perching on the edge of the bed, she held his hand and talked, telling him that the house was fine and that Richard would soon be in to see him, hoping that her voice and mention of familiar things would strengthen his grip on the world. But as the bland expression settled back on his face she knew he had slipped away again.

She spent a day at work, delighting in the peace of the deserted office. She liked working alone and had, once or twice, considered setting up her own practice. But a one-woman band, were it to survive, would attract only minor commissions and she would miss the challenge and buzz of major projects.

Gil was always somewhere in her consciousness – a version of Wolfi, the constant (and invisible) friend who had kept her company when she was a child. Her father had finally banished Wolfi with 'Carry on like that, Vivian, and it'll be the loony bin for you.'

She regretted pushing for the invitation to Gil's flat. He'd been humiliated by the squalid state of the place. It *was* dire. She'd made matters worse by quizzing him about Feray, but the sight of that sensuous face staring boldly at the camera had rattled her. Although she believed him when he said the affair was over, she wished the woman would move to the other side of London.

As she was leaving the Elephant House, Gil phoned and she suggested she meet him from work. When she got there he was waiting in the foyer.

'Can I see your office?' she said.

'Sure. It's not very exciting but it's tidier than my flat. And warmer.'

They took the lift to the second floor and he led her to the

265

corner of a soulless room, more warehouse than office. She noted where he hung his jacket; where he sat when he emailed her; the postcards Blu-Tacked to the wall alongside his desk. No photograph of her or Feray. Now she would be able to picture him both at home and at work and she liked that.

They discussed what to do and decided to go to the Everyman on Haverstock Hill. The film was about a lone hiker trapped when a boulder fell onto his arm – a true story. When it came to the scene where he severed the arm with a penknife, she buried her face in Gil's sweater, waiting until he signalled the all-clear. Afterwards they went back to her flat to cook supper and he revealed the secret of his carbonara sauce (a pinch of celery salt, a small jar of which he swore he always carried in his bag). He stayed the night and, when he left for work next morning, she missed him.

Since their split, she'd scarcely given Nick a thought. It was over and that was that. Consequently she was surprised when, later that morning, he turned up with a flashy box of chocolates and the bits and pieces she'd left at his flat.

'I happened to be coming over this way,' he said, making no effort to verify the improbable excuse.

'Really? How was your holiday?'

'Good. Perfect snow.'

'And the company?'

He glanced away. 'Okay, I suppose. Any chance of a coffee?'

She put the coffee on and, without being asked, he cleared the table and refilled the milk jug. It felt as if he were reclaiming lost territory and she didn't much care for that.

'Any plans for New Year?' he said.

So. Things weren't working out with his 'new client'.

'Yes,' she said.

Ignoring her reply, he ploughed on. 'Thea and Ivan are having a party. I thought you might like to come along. It'll be the usual crowd.'

'As I said, I have plans.' She took the empty mugs to the sink. 'I'll find a bag for your things.'

'Great.' He cleared his throat. 'Look, Vivian…'

'Oh, and I think you still have my keys.'

She waited while he fumbled her keys off his overloaded key ring.

'Happy New Year,' she said.

'And you.'

When he leaned towards her she turned her face and his kiss landed near her ear.

It was only as he was leaving that he asked after her father and she took pleasure in telling him that he was probably dying.

As Gil anticipated, it was a quiet week. The mood across the hospital was low-key, the post-Christmas flywheel barely getting going before it slowed again for New Year. He had time to catch up on paperwork and tackle long overdue 'housekeeping'. Kevin put in a couple of days at the end of the week. With time on their hands, Gil was unable to avoid a blow-by-blow account of baby Jack's first Christmas – all caught on camera.

He also had time to think about Vivian.

The other morning, they'd parted without making arrangements to meet. Maybe this was how it was going to be. He could hardly complain. There had been plenty of times when this kind of freewheeling approach had suited him. But this was different and he found the vagueness unnerving.

He was glad that she'd been to his flat. It had been hairy while it was happening but he could see now that a week's warning would have made things worse. He might have shoved a few things out of sight, and possibly contrived better heating but, short of total refurbishment, the place would never be more than a dump. The Feray business had been unfortunate. He wasn't sure if he'd put Vivian's mind at rest with his explanation but at least she knew a bit more of the background, and the matter was out in the open where it was less likely to cause damage.

He'd not made contact with Feray since their bust-up but he'd bumped into the kids in the shop so he knew she was around. The youngsters treated him as they'd always done and he hoped this meant she hadn't lumbered them with another anxiety. He couldn't fathom why she'd returned the photograph. It wasn't as if he figured in it. He felt sorry and sad that she had because, despite all her bluster, she lacked self-esteem and confirmation of her beauty might help her feel good about herself.

New Year's Eve loomed, inflated with unrealistic expectations. While Tunisia boiled with civil unrest, the office resounded with resolutions to get 'rat-arsed', 'slaughtered', 'wasted'. Gil was invited to umpteen parties and accepted all the invitations, hoping that he would be with Vivian and not have to go to any of them.

According to Louise, their mother was stocking her freezer with cakes and crumbles in anticipation of his visit. Janey mailed saying that the boys were looking forward to seeing him but not, it seemed, sufficiently to mail him themselves. Nothing from Polly – no surprise there – but at least she'd not freaked out.

The best deal for a ticket turned out to be a couple of hundred quid more than he could afford. But he couldn't wriggle out of it now and once Kevin had okayed his leave, he went ahead with the booking. Vivian knew that he was planning the trip. Originally he'd told her that it would be the end of January but he'd saved a bit on the fare by bringing his trip forward a few weeks. He would be away from her – or the possibility of being with her – for eleven days. What could happen in eleven days? To get the measure of it, he rewound eleven days. The weekend before Christmas. His split with Feray. Friel's party. Christmas. His experiment in time travel did nothing to reassure him.

Richard phoned to let Vivian know that he was already in London.

'It's New Year's Eve,' she said. 'Isn't that sacrosanct to Scots?'

'Yes,' he said. 'But Christmas must have been a non-event for you. You deserve some fun. I thought you might like the weekend off.'

That was precisely what she would like. And yet. There was a competitive edge to his offer. A sense of stakes being raised. *Whatever you sacrifice, I'll sacrifice more.*

'I'm not sure,' she said.

She had never watched death creep up on someone like it was creeping up on her father. Deaths that had impacted on her – there had been remarkably few – had been sudden, or distant. Her mother. A work colleague. The bomb victims. Observing the process of dying was disturbing, humbling and, yes, fascinating. Before long her father would know the answer to the ultimate riddle. What could be more fascinating than that? She'd never expected to be involved in his dying. If she'd thought about it at all, she'd imagined that she would get a call from someone (a doctor? a neighbour?) telling her that he was dead. The end of a process in which she'd played no part. No part in his living – no part in his dying. A reasonable symmetry. Now here she was, wanting to ease his departure from the world. Not in a murderous way – although there had been times… What could be more absurd than to start caring about the man when he no longer recognised her or, for that matter, any element of the real world. It was ridiculous.

'Up to you,' he said. 'I shall be here until Monday. Look, if you *are* going to be around we should get together. What if I go in now and report back when I see how things are? I'll ring you tomorrow and we can take it from there.'

It was a logical suggestion yet she resented his turning up like some superhero ready to save the day. *Hah.* Once he'd seen their father, he wouldn't be so bloody sanguine.

'Will you stay at the house?' she said.

'I may.'

A second wave of resentment caught her as she pictured his trespassing on what she'd come to think of as her domain.

'He needs more pyjamas,' she said.

'No worries. I picked up a couple of pairs before I left. Towels, too.'

'Oh. Right. I should warn you he won't wear stripes.' *That'll catch you out.*

'Just as well I chose plain ones,' he said.

She drank a cup of green tea and listened to the news. In Finland birds were, for no apparent reason, dropping out of the sky. A footballer had been arrested for drink-driving. Snowstorms had left part of Wales without electricity. A euro was worth eighty-six pence. Why had she imagined that the last day of two thousand and ten would be different from any other?

She checked her watch. Gil was probably getting ready for a boozy night out with the legendary Kevin. When they'd spoken yesterday he hadn't mentioned anything. But that was fine. He probably assumed she would be at the hospital. Or doing something with the Friel Dravid crowd.

She'd never cared for New Year – surprising considering her European pedigree. Every year, on this night, hopes were ramped up beyond reason. No event could ever match expectations. Normal etiquette didn't apply and nothing seemed off limits. People – men generally, but not always – felt at liberty to kiss her on the lips and pass inappropriate remarks or ask impertinent questions. And underlying the alcohol-fuelled joviality lurked a feeling that everything could, at any second, hurtle out of control. No, it really wasn't her thing.

Her phone chirped. When she checked it was only a HNY text from Cara and Howard who were on a Paris-bound Eurostar.

Footsteps sounded on the stair. She held her breath but they continued up the next flight. Malcolm. She'd already heard Mrs Sachs's muted radio and the clatter of a pan. She suddenly pictured the front wall of the house swinging open like a dolls' house to reveal three flats stacked one on top of another, each inhabited by its solitary occupant, all three preparing to navigate the evening alone.

How would she get through it? Supper, her favourite music, a lazy bath, bed with a book. She'd be asleep by eleven and when she woke all this nonsense would be over. She studied her stock of individual meals. Fish pie with green beans or frozen peas on the side. That would do. She would eat around eight. She poured a glass of white wine and scrolled through her iPod. Gillian Welch. Melancholy yet unsentimental.

She was opening a bottle of wine when her phone rang. It was Gil.

'Hello,' he said. 'Where are you?'

'At home.'

'Good because I'm outside, freezing to death.'

She went to the window and pulled back the curtain. There he was, on the opposite side of the street, clutching something.

'You didn't phone,' she said.

'Isn't that what I'm doing now?'

'I meant earlier. Why didn't you—'

'Any chance we could discuss this inside? The curry's getting cold.' He held up a carrier bag.

'You've brought a takeaway?'

'Well there won't be a table to be had tonight. Now could you please let me in?'

32

'I might have been out,' she said. 'You should have called.'

Before buying the curry he'd walked past and, seeing the lights in her living room, had taken a chance.

'Wouldn't be the first curry I've eaten in a bus shelter,' he said.

They agreed to argue about who should have contacted whom after they'd eaten but, by the time they were bagging up the empty cartons, it no longer seemed relevant.

'Any change with your dad?' he said.

'Not really. At one point I think he was trying to tell me something but…'

She explained that Richard was in London and had volunteered to take over hospital duty for a few days.

'He says I should take the opportunity to have fun,' she said.

'Good on him.'

She laughed.

'What?' he said.

'You sound so *Australian*.'

'I doubt my family will think so.'

'You're going, then,' she said.

'I have to, Vivian. I need to talk to Polly before this baby's born.'

'When?'

'Next Saturday.'

She frowned. 'So soon?'

'Sooner I go, sooner I'll be back,' he said. 'You won't have time to miss me. C'mon. What shall we do?'

'Can we play Scrabble?'

He slapped a palm to his forehead. '*Scrabble*. You must be psychic. It's my all-time favourite way of celebrating New Year.'

'Fool,' she said and went to find the box.

He loved that she took the game so seriously, playing to win, challenging hard when he stretched the rules, admonishing him when he cheated on the arithmetic. She insisted on timed play, using her phone as a stopwatch, stopping the clock when texts came through – 'It's from Ottilie. "Have fun, hun." I suppose she means h o n. Or maybe she doesn't.'

Gil had switched off his phone to avoid having to explain why he hadn't turned up at any of the parties. New Year had the knack of distilling emotions until they were caustic and he was also concerned lest Feray choose this evening to let off steam. They still hadn't spoken but he'd spotted her in the supermarket yesterday. Her trolley was loaded with cans of beer and it looked as if she were stocking up for a party. She'd been standing with her back to him, talking to someone. A man.

Long before the game was finished it was obvious that Vivian was the winner but she insisted on playing it out, triumphant when he picked up a last-minute 'J' and had to deduct eight points from his score.

'Loser decides what we do next,' she said, gathering up the tiles.

Her artlessness (another of her traits he loved) ruled out laddish suggestions. 'Okay. Let's watch Jools Holland,' he said. 'We'll show Richard and Ottilie we know how to have fun.'

They sat together of the sofa, not touching but close enough for him to catch the smell of her shampoo. He questioned her liking for Vampire Weekend – 'Kids' stuff. Vacuous pop.' – and she mocked his enthusiasm for Rico Rodriguez – 'Ska? Ughhh. Makes my flesh creep.' They agreed that Kylie could belt out a song – even if what she sang was naff.

At midnight and they kissed and clinked glasses. (They'd chosen whisky to toast the New Year – poured from the same bottle she'd opened that first night. *A good omen?*)

'Here's to the coming year,' he said.

'Let's not think about what's coming,' she said. 'Not tonight, anyway.'

'Okay. Let's drink to this moment.'

'Two thousand and eleven's a prime number,' she said.

He laughed and shook his head. 'How d'you know that? *Why* d'you know that?'

'I just do.'

They put the lights out and went to the window, pulling back the curtains, watching as bursts of fireworks illuminated the sky. When there was no more to see, they went to bed. And, for the first time, he was absolutely sure she took pleasure in their love-making.

'How about we kick off this *prime* year with something exciting,' Gil said next morning.

They were sitting in bed, drinking tea. The curtains were open and, above the rooftops, ragged clouds were scudding across a pink-tinged sky.

'Like what?' Vivian said.

He pretended to mull it over but he'd cooked up a plan yesterday in the hope it might be needed. 'How about a trip to…Brighton?'

'Brighton?'

'Yep. Pier. Beach. Big pavilion. You know the one? And before you dream up any excuses, yes, trains *are* running today.'

She took a sip of tea. 'But what if—'

'We can be back in London in an hour if needs be.'

When they were on the train, she presented him with a navy hat with a fleecy lining. According to the wrapping, it came from Cologne. It looked and felt expensive, and it crossed his mind that she'd bought it for Nick. No matter because now she was giving it to him and he accepted it gratefully.

By eleven-thirty they were battling along the promenade, fighting the gusting wind. The sea was yellowish-grey. Bubbly spume whipped off the waves looking to Gil horribly like washing-up water. They ventured to the water's edge. The sea thundered onto the shore, sucking up pebbles as it drew back before dumping them on the beach again. The incessant noise – wind, waves and clattering stones – made conversation futile. Vivian, spray-drenched hair whipping across her cheeks, stood gazing out to sea. She turned to him and smiled, mouthing 'thank you' and blowing him a kiss.

Taking his old hat from his pocket, he tried to hurl it into the English Channel – an offering to whoever was responsible for unforeseen moments of euphoria. As it left his hand, the wind tossed it over his head and it landed behind him. Absurdly convinced that failure to complete his mission might blight the future, he loaded the hat with pebbles and tried again, twirling around like a shot-putter before releasing it to soar into the air, watching as it plummeted into the boiling sea.

'That was perfect,' Vivian said.

They were on the train back to Victoria. Vivian was sipping hot chocolate from a cardboard cup. The salt wind had tangled her hair and raised the colour in her cheeks and she looked younger, less composed, than usual. For the umpteenth time, he marvelled that he was the man she had chosen to be with.

A crumpled copy of yesterday's *Metro* protruded from the pouch on the back of the seat in front and he fished it out. It featured a list of New Year resolutions made by 'celebrities'.

'Good to know that Rihanna intends to see more of her mom and grandparents this year,' he said. 'And, hallelujah, Heidi Klum – *Heidi Klum?* – is going to be good to the people around her.'

'Have you made a resolution?' Vivian said.

'No. But maybe I ought to.'

'What would it be?' she said.

'I should probably try not to piss so many people off this year.'

Dribbles of condensation running down the windows. A child

singing 'Bob the Builder'. Vivian's lip pressed to the non-spill cover of the cup.

'I hoped Irene had gone away,' he said, 'but I may have been overly optimistic.'

Vivian half-turned to face him. 'What's happened?'

He wished he didn't have to tell her, but it would surely come out before long. Best she hear it now, from him, in case Irene decided to drag her into it.

'She's written to the hospital,' he said. 'She claims I made "inappropriate remarks". That I wasn't to be trusted with female patients.'

Kevin had relayed this information yesterday. 'Don't worry mate. We'll sort it out,' he'd said, 'I told them straight out she's a nutcase.'

From day one, Gil had kept his boss abreast of Irene's attentions. Kevin was fully aware that she'd been pestering him and Vivian since the night of the explosion. Gil was sure he was in the clear. For starters, he wasn't permitted to photograph patients without there being a 'chaperone' present – a nurse or a medical student. Nevertheless, it wasn't nice knowing that she was out to get him.

'What?' Vivian said. 'How can she say that? She isn't even a patient at UCH. You've never photographed her. They must know she's lying.'

'She *was* treated there on the night of the bombing. If they check, her name will come up on the database.'

'But all she needed was a couple of sticking plasters,' Vivian said.

'That's true. And, once they've established the facts, they'll dismiss her accusation. But you know how it is. There are procedures to be gone through. It may take a while.'

'It's my fault,' she said.

'How d'you work that out?'

'If I hadn't waited with her—'

'You would have gone straight home,' he said, 'and I would have gone straight home, and we wouldn't be sitting on this train together.'

Richard was waiting in the hospital foyer.

'Good of you to come,' he said as though this were her first visit. 'They're looking after him very well.'

'Oh? What makes you say that?' she said.

Clearly he hadn't expected to be asked to validate his statement and he smiled nervously. 'Well. They make sure he's comfortable. Check him frequently. The sheets get changed every day.'

'Really? Gosh, I hadn't spotted that.'

Richard Carey wasn't a bad man but he'd somehow become her adversary in some kind of battle over their father. He probably didn't want to win the contest any more than she did but, once engaged, it seemed that neither could back down.

Their father's room was quiet after the bustle of the ward. The lamp attached to the back of his bed was dimmed as though bright light might damage him. He was sleeping, the trace on the monitor the only proof that he was alive.

'I don't suppose his results are back,' she said.

'As a matter of fact they are,' he said. 'It's MRSA.'

'Oh,' she said, annoyed that he hadn't told her right away.

He must have read her thoughts because he said 'I didn't want to ruin your day with bad news. Apparently the infection's deep in the wound.'

'Right. So what happens next?'

'They're talking about operating again. Apparently the MRSA bacteria gather around "foreign bodies" – in this case, the replacement hip. They want to take it out, flush the area with antibiotics, then put in a new joint. It's called "washing out", I believe.'

'That's revolting,' she said.

He shrugged. 'No choice, I'm afraid.'

277

'There's always a choice.'

He shot her a glance and she realised he thought she was suggesting they leave the man to die.

'I mean, can't they inject something into the joint?' she said. 'Does he have to go through it all again?'

'That was my first question.' He nodded towards the drip. 'Intravenous antibiotics – which amounts to the same thing – would have worked by now if they were going to.

'But can he take another anaesthetic?' she said.

'It's a risk.' He paused. 'Actually, there is another option.'

'What?'

'They could take out the joint and…not replace it. It would offer a better chance of eliminating the infection.'

She absorbed the information, trying to block an image of her mother, boning a leg of lamb ready for stuffing, the ball-joint coming away from the raw, fatty meat.

'But how would he—'

'He wouldn't. He'd be confined to bed.'

They stood, silently watching the prone figure. This old man's fate lies with us, she thought.

Their father chose that moment to rouse himself and start pushing at the sheets as if preparing to get out of bed. The cot-sides were raised to prevent his tumbling out but they also gave him something to grab onto and he summoned enough strength to pull himself up to sitting. Still with his eyes closed, he shouted 'Heaven. Heaven. Heaven.'

Vivian was astounded yet filled with delight. She wanted to cheer. They'd written him off but here he was, refusing to surrender, sounding like a hellfire-and-damnation evangelist.

'Christ,' Richard said.

Vivian barely managed to stop herself laughing at his reaction.

'Can you help me?' he said, prising the old man's hand off the rail. 'He needs to be lying down.'

'Why?' she said. 'Look. He's awake. That's good, isn't it?' She turned to her father who had opened his eyes and was peering crossly at them. 'Hello, Dad. Happy New Year.'

He looked startled and started scrabbling at the covers again.

'I'll get someone,' Richard said and disappeared from the room.

Alone with her father, she willed him to spit out a scathing remark about Richard, or wink to let her in on whatever game he was playing.

'Dad,' she said. 'It's Vivian.'

'Vivian.' He pronounced it slowly and without inflection, as if it were a made-up word.

'Yes.' She paused. 'Last time I was here, you started telling me something important.'

He shook his head.

'Yes, you did' she said. 'You kept saying "we should have..." Come on. Please try.'

He'd stopped his restless movement and was leaning back against the pillows. She laid her hand on his arm. His skin was translucent and a livid bruise spilled across his wrist from beneath the binding that secured the business end of a syringe to the back of his hand. She opened the locker and saw that Richard had, as instructed, brought in a tube of moisturising cream. Squeezing a blob onto her palm, she massaged it gently into the paper-thin skin. He let out a sigh and she felt him relax.

'It's okay, Dad,' she said. 'It doesn't matter.'

33

New Year had fallen on a weekend and therefore Monday was designated a holiday. Richard was travelling back to Scotland by train and he and Vivian met in Starbucks at Kings Cross.

'Sorry to abandon you,' he said. 'I'll be down again as soon as I can. Did I mention that John's coming over? Probably next week.'

Vivian had almost forgotten John. A second patronising half-brother on the scene was a disquieting prospect.

'D'you think Dad'll make it?' she said.

'We just have to hope for the best,' he said.

'Best for whom?'

Vivian had decided she neither liked nor trusted this man and she enjoyed watching the shadow of discomfort cross his face.

'Did you get any sense out of him?' she said.

'Not really. He was away with the fairies most of the time.'

They discussed a few practicalities. Quarterly bills would soon start turning up and they agreed that, for the time being at least, she should settle these and he and John would reimburse her.

'I can't imagine why he hasn't set up direct debits,' he said.

She'd had this out with her father and been exasperated by his unwillingness to trust British Gas, npower, the TV licence people, Thames Water, and pretty much the rest of the world, all of whom he was convinced were out to fleece him. All the same, she stood up for him.

'Checking bills, going to the bank, things like that make him feel he's in control. And it gives him something to do. It's worked fine until now.'

'Well that will have to change,' he said, slamming his palm down on the table.

They talked about work and, when they'd exhausted that, moved on to Richard's daughter and family who lived in Glasgow. Their lives sounded successful and well ordered, but they were of no interest to Vivian and she was thankful when an echoey announcement interrupted the conversation.

'That's my train,' he said. They hugged awkwardly. 'Oh, I've had the hospital add my name to yours as next of kin,' he said. 'I hope that's okay with you.'

'Why wouldn't it be?' she said.

He squeezed her hand, insinuating that they were in something together. But they weren't. He was scurrying back to Scotland whilst she was left here, on permanent duty.

Kings Cross was no distance from the Elephant House and Vivian contemplated putting in a couple of hours on the Cologne job, but her conversation with Richard had stirred unsettling thoughts and she doubted whether she would be able to concentrate. It was still bitterly cold but the wind had dropped. The sun – the first London had seen for weeks – was casting a watery glow across the sky and, needing to think things through, she set off to walk the three miles home.

Why on earth had Richard chosen to stay at Farleigh Road? He had every right, of course, but he wasn't short of money so why choose the gloomy, draughty house over the comforts of a hotel? She didn't like the idea that he'd had hours to snoop around. Had she left anything there that she'd rather he didn't see? Which bed had he used? She and Gil had made love in both and it was excruciating to imagine him smirking as he spotted a stain on the sheet or a grey hair on a pillow.

In Camden Town the shops were open and doing brisk trade. She didn't stop but bought a coffee from a kiosk and strode on towards Chalk Farm.

A little way ahead of her a couple were picking their way along the uneven pavement. The woman was towing a wheeled shopping bag, her free hand tucked beneath the man's arm. It was obvious from their caution and their gait that, beneath padded coats and

281

woolly hats, they were old. Old and frail, and probably frightened of what the New Year might bring.

Her mother hadn't chosen to die. She hadn't chosen to leave her – Vivian – as Philip Frederick Carey's 'next of kin'. But, when all was said and done, he was her father. And he was going to die. He was going to die very soon. Microscopic organisms were consuming him. Already there was nothing much left of him. Certainly nothing left to hate.

By the time she reached the bookshop, she'd made up her mind to decamp to Tooting.

Each evening, after work, she went directly to the hospital, sitting with her father until eight o'clock. (Visiting times, relaxed over Christmas, were being enforced again.) By the time she got back to the house and ate supper, she was ready for bed. Three days in to her new routine she was exhausted, no longer sure why she was doing this.

Sometimes, when she perched on the bedside chair, studying her father's emaciated figure, his eyes would be open (although there was no telling if he was seeing anything). Sometimes, when she took his hand in hers, his grip tightened. Sometimes he murmured, or pushed at the covers. He seemed not to be in pain and she liked to think that wherever he was – because it certainly wasn't here – was a pleasant place.

Whilst she sat, she sometimes thought about Gil. For her eighteenth birthday, her parents had given her driving lessons. She'd been a nervous pupil and her instructor had reassured her that, were she or another motorist to make a terrible mistake, he could take over the 'dual controls' and avert disaster. This had never happened but it calmed her enough to get her through the test. Knowing that Gil was there – or at least in the same city – calmed her, too. If she were in a pickle, he would come – no questions asked. It frightened her to think that he would soon be thousands of miles away.

UCH was in full swing again after the break, consultants fired up to meet unachievable targets – or so it seemed to minions like Gil forced to run around after them. To keep up with the flood of patients needing to be photographed, he worked through his lunch hours and, as if he didn't have enough to do, Kevin volunteered him for a couple of early morning theatre sessions. It was full on.

Kevin was confident that nothing would come of the Irene business.

'You told them about the angel claptrap?' Gil said.

'And the parcels. Everything. I made sure they knew she'd been trying to make something of this from day one.' Kevin paused. 'Best not let on that you're going to Oz next week though. They might think you're doing a runner.'

Gil laughed. 'Save them the hassle of transporting me.'

He felt thoroughly miserable at the prospect of leaving Vivian and spent the front end of the week making deals with the Devil. Icelandic ash clouds, please. Wrongful arrest. A dose of something contagious (but not serious) if that's what it took to keep him in London. He felt bad (and spooked) when reports began coming through of flooding in Queensland following freak summer rains. He might not want to go but neither did he want people losing their lives and their homes. So accepting that, like it or not, he would be flying to Australia on Saturday, he made 'to do' and 'to pack' lists.

He'd not seen Vivian since their outing to Brighton. Apparently, after Richard had vacated Farleigh Road, she'd moved in to make visiting her father easier. By all accounts, the old guy was semi-comatose. If that were the case, he wouldn't have a clue whether he had visitors or not but she was doing what she felt was right and one day she might take consolation from that.

He would be away for just eleven days. That said, they would be eleven decisive days. The odds on his straightening things out with Polly were slim but he had to give it his best shot. However it played out, his relationship with his daughter would be different by the time he returned. The next couple of weeks would be critical for Vivian, too. It wasn't looking good. A 'wash out' was bad news for an old man in Carey's condition, although he didn't tell her that.

The prospect of leaving without seeing her made him feel despondent. Yet he'd made a point of playing down his trip and he didn't want to make a song and dance of the temporary separation. In the end he called and asked about her father and, as if it were an afterthought, added 'How are you fixed this week? Perhaps we could get together.'

'We could meet for lunch,' she said.

He wanted to sit with her. Talk to her. *Be* with her. A scant hour in a coffee shop wasn't what he had in mind.

'What about after work?' he said.

He pressed his phone tight to his ear, hoping to detect a hint of eagerness in her voice but the traffic grinding along Euston Road drowned out any nuances in her response.

'I go straight to the hospital,' she said.

'How about I meet you there?'

'It's a real schlep for—'

'When would suit you?' he said. 'Today? Tomorrow?'

'Won't you be packing tomorrow?'

'Today it is then.'

'Okay,' she said.

One of Gil's commissions took him to the trauma ward where he'd passed occasional lunch hours with Tyler. When he last inquired, the lad was having problems and Gil was mindful that he'd failed to check on his progress. After he'd finished on the ward, he went to the nursing station.

'D'you know what happened to the biker?' he said.

All they could tell him was that Tyler had been transferred to

284

the Spinal Injury Unit and Gil returned to the basement feeling rotten that he'd not seen the kid to wish him well.

Messages from Coffs filtered through. They were all looking forward to his visit. He'd grown accustomed to being the black sheep, the fall guy, and their enthusiasm was unexpected and slightly puzzling.

With a few days to go, Polly suspended her silent protest, finally mailing him after a sustained period of non-communication.

dad. no questions. no lectures. no bullying. no bribery. ok? p x

He could go with that. At least she'd spared him a kiss.

34

Vivian was starting to understand how the hospital worked. The hierarchy. The routine. The shifts. The layout. She recognised a number of the staff, and they her, when they passed in the corridor. She noted how wiped-out they looked when they snatched five minutes in the cafeteria or shivered in the 'smoking shelter'. It was hard to believe she'd made such a fuss about visiting her father during those first days when he was lucid and bolshie. It would be a pleasure – yes, a pleasure – now to sit at his bedside, having a set-to about this or that. *We should have.* He was right. Whatever it was, they should have.

Gil joined her in her father's room. He looked tired and, to be honest, old.

'How's he doing?' he said.

'He needs a transfusion before they operate.'

'Any idea when that'll be?'

'All they'll say is "when he's strong enough."'

They were standing, side by side, at the foot of the bed and Gil draped an arm across her shoulder. 'And how are *you* doing?'

Out of the blue, she was deluged with sadness. 'Better than he is,' she said.

Gil pulled her to him and she buried her face in his shoulder. His jacket was still cool from the outdoor air and smelled faintly metallic.

'I hate all this,' she said.

'Yeah. It's a bummer.'

She pulled away from him. 'You don't know what I'm talking about,' she said, annoyed by his automatic assent.

'So d'you want to tell me?' he said.

You are leaving. My father is dying. And, after I'm dead, no one will remember my mother.

286

She blew out her cheeks. 'Sorry. I'm shattered, that's all. We'll go in a minute.'

Gil was helping her on with her coat when her father coughed and stretched out a wasted arm. She took his hand. It felt clammy and insubstantial, as she imagined a featherless, freshly-hatched chick might feel.

'Anna? Annaliese?' His voice was plaintive.

'No, Dad. It's Vivian.'

Everything but his ears and nose seemed to have shrunk and his skin was taut on his skull. She moved closer, hoping he would recognise her, or at least realise that she was not his wife.

'It's going to be fine, Dad. They'll soon have you sorted out.' Given the circumstances, the lie seemed forgivable.

'I'm sorry,' he said, lisping through flaccid lips.

'It's not your fault. It was an accident.'

He pointed towards Gil. 'Who's that?'

'It's Gil. He brought you the Sherlock Holmes book. Remember?'

'Elementary', he said, a rasping noise which might have been laughter coming from his chest.

Fearing that he would at any second slip back into his dream world, she turned to Gil. 'Will it do any harm to keep talking to him?'

'It might tire him but I can't see it'll do any damage. Look, shall I leave you two for a while?'

Dear Gil. Considerate as ever. But thinking she might need help in understanding her father's mutterings, she asked him to stay.

She perched on the edge of the high bed. 'Is there something you want to tell me Dad?' She waited, eventually prompting 'Something you should have done, perhaps?'

With that he became agitated, clutching her hands, trying to pull himself up.

'Father,' he said. 'Baby.'

'What's the matter with him, Gil?'

'He's frightened,' Gil said. 'You could try holding him.'

She eased an arm beneath his head. This wasn't easy. He seemed so breakable and she was nervous in case she detached the tube from the back of his hand.

'That's it,' Gil murmured.

She held her father in the crook of her arm and he grew gradually calmer, his breathing less laboured. Before long he was asleep and she was able to extricate herself.

'I'm useless at this,' she said.

'You did just fine.'

The bell rang, signalling the end of visiting time and they joined the troupe of visitors heading for the lifts. The doctor who had told her about the blood transfusion was standing at the nurses' station, writing in a file.

He glanced up and smiled. 'Hello, Miss Carey. How is he?'

A couple of weeks ago she would have snapped *you tell me* but now she knew that his smile masked exhaustion. 'He said a few words.'

The doctor glanced at Gil, as if in two minds whether to proceed.

'Gil's a good friend,' she said. 'My father liked – *likes* him.' How easy it was to consign a life to the past.

'He's very weak,' the doctor said. 'He's been through the mill. And now this infection…'

She nodded. 'It doesn't seem fair.'

'We see a lot of "not fair" in here I'm afraid. We'll do our best for him.'

'I know you will,' she said.

Compared with being born, dying seemed a hit and miss affair. If he weren't to die alone, how would she know when to stay? Tonight? Tomorrow night? It would be typical of him to wait until she'd gone for a coffee *then* die so that, for the rest of her life, she would feel guilty.

A crowd was gathering in the lift area. Amongst them was a young woman wrestling with a baby, his (the blue snowsuit suggested a boy) plump cheeks flushed from the heat. The child quickly became more fretful, throwing back his head and arching his back. He began to wail. The woman's embarrassment increased when he suddenly kicked out and, in an effort to hang on to him, she dropped her bag and its contents – keys, phone, lip salve, coins, hairbrush, more than it seemed possible the bag could contain – spilled across the floor.

'Shit,' she said.

'Here,' Gil said, holding his arms out to take the child. The woman looked doubtful then, recognising that there were enough people around to ensure this stranger did her baby no harm, she handed him over. 'Thanks.'

While she scooped up her things, Gil laid the child against his shoulder where he could see his mother. Vivian watched him swaying to and fro, whispering in the child's ear. This either calmed or shocked the baby into silence and, by the time the woman had retrieved everything, he was well on the way to falling asleep.

'You've got the touch,' the woman said, smiling at Gil. 'I guess you've been there.'

'A few times,' Gil said. 'Look, why don't I carry him down for you?'

The lift stopped and they shuffled in. By the time they'd reached the ground floor, the child was heavily asleep, barely stirring when Gil handed him back to his mother.

'That was sweet of you,' Vivian said as they watched the pair disappearing towards the exit.

'Guilt. That'll be Polly in a few months time. C'mon. Let's find somewhere to eat.'

Gil steered Vivian towards an Italian restaurant tucked round the corner from the Tube station. It was an unpretentious place –

scarcely more than a café – and the menu was limited, but she was shivering and it was clear that she needed to eat. The food came quickly. It was delicious, and the Sicilian plonk wasn't bad.

'I was hungry,' Vivian said, tucking into a wedge of lasagne.

He guessed that she'd not been eating properly, or sleeping well either by the look of the shadows beneath her eyes.

'I'm not nagging,' he said, 'but you must promise to look after yourself. Maybe you should eat a proper meal at lunchtime.'

'Define nagging,' she said.

Half-a-dozen customers arrived whom the proprietor seemed to know well. The conversation in Italian grew louder and livelier, and the atmosphere became rather jolly.

'Don't you want to know why I'm staying at the house?' she said.

He took her hand. 'I did wonder.'

'It's what my mother would expect me to do. She was very particular about doing the right thing.'

'I'm sorry I never met her,' he said.

'Well at least you met my father when he was still…himself.'

Her cheeks had a little colour in them and she seemed more at ease. It was a shame to leave this cosy place and they lingered over tiramisu and coffee.

After the snug restaurant, the house was chilly and inhospitable.

'Shall I light the fire?' he said.

'Quite honestly I'm ready for bed.'

'We could sleep down here. By the fire. You have a bath and I'll sort out a mattress.'

'That *would* be lovely,' she said. 'But it's a lot of—'

'I'm on it. Off you go.'

His mission started well but when the mattress – thank God he'd only attempted the single – wedged on the bend in the staircase, his confidence faltered. Somehow he managed to slide past it, then yank it down to the hall and drag it into the living room. The fire was reluctant to get going and he used a candle as a firelighter.

Ten o'clock now and Vivian had said they should leave at seven. That meant they had nine hours together. Jeez. He was being pathetic. Convicts on death row, soldiers heading off to Afghanistan – they had good reason to count the hours. He was simply going to visit his family. Unless some random catastrophe struck, he'd be home in eleven days.

By the time she came down, a bed, complete with pillows and duvet, was positioned in front of a fire that now burned as brightly as anything on a Christmas card.

She shrugged off the robe, which he guessed was her father's. Beneath it she was wearing the sort of old-fashioned nightdress his mother wore. He stripped down to boxers and T-shirt and they lay together beneath the duvet, watching the fire.

'Thanks for this,' she said. 'You always know what I need.'

He felt a surge of pride. 'If it's too cramped I can put a few cushions at the side. Like an extension.'

'We managed fine last time,' she said in a matter-of-fact voice.

'You always tell it like it is, don't you?'

'Isn't that good?' she said.

'On the whole, yes.'

'D'you tell it like it is?'

'Not always,' he said.

'D'you lie to me?'

He turned so that he was facing her. 'I have done. But I give you my word, I never will again.'

'Good,' she said.

They were so close together that there was nothing else for it but to kiss. As their kissing became more passionate, he felt her hand easing down his boxers, caressing his backside and his thigh.

Afterwards, when he was sure she was asleep, he stoked the fire. The flames leapt, sending sparks eddying up the chimney, casting enough light for him to see her face, her hair and her knee protruding from the covers.

Kevin packed him off an hour early. The night with Vivian had left him way behind on his travel preparations and he was glad to have the extra time. He'd tidied the flat and was crossing the hall on his way to the bin with a black bag, when he bumped into Feray.

'Hi,' she said, 'I was checking the mail.' She held up an envelope as if to prove her right to be there.

'How's things?'

'Good,' she said. 'You?'

'I'm okay, thanks.' He cleared his throat. 'Actually I'm glad I've seen you. I'm going away for a couple of weeks. Wouldn't want you thinking I'd done a moonlight.'

'Anywhere nice?' she said, a tight, bright smile on her face.

'Oz. To see Mum and the kids.'

'Everything going on okay with your daughter?'

'Far as I know. Matter of fact, that's why I'm going. See if we can patch things up before the baby arrives.'

Her expression softened. 'That's good, Gil. Families are the most important thing.'

They talked about Melissa and James, and Feray's job – which it seemed was secure for the next six months pending union negotiations. She'd had a good Christmas. And New Year.

'I'd best get on,' he said. 'I haven't started packing yet.'

'D'you want me to keep an eye on the flat while you're away?' she said.

He remembered her fury that day in the coffee shop. Boy she'd been livid. And those bags outside his door weren't a peace offering. But she seemed perfectly calm now. And hell, what was the worst she could do?

'That'd be great. Thanks.'

35

Louise had offered to pick him up from Brisbane airport but it meant her taking time off. Besides, it was a lot of driving – five hours each way. The train took half that time and he was glad to have a chance to get his head around being here.

He'd come with only a small backpack. (Shorts, a few T-shirts, flip-flops and his cozzie.) This had raised eyebrows at the Heathrow check-in desk. He was tempted to point out that it was none of their business, but it didn't do to get smart at airports these days and instead he'd shown them his return ticket and explained that his mother kept a heap of clothes for when he visited, a plausible lie.

He left the train station and walked up Camperdown Street towards Harbour Drive. It was the middle of the afternoon yet the broad streets were deserted. School was on summer break until the end of January and the majority of families would be taking their annual holiday. Stopping to catch his breath, he looked up at the sky. Seen through the cat's cradle of power cables and phone wires, it was the unsubtle, uniform blue of a nursery toy. To his right lay a patchwork of shallow-pitched roofs punctuated by scrappy palm trees and telegraph poles. Beyond lay the sea, a slash of turquoise blending to dark green at the horizon.

When he'd left his flat yesterday morning – no, it was the day *before* yesterday – he'd shivered beneath a sweater and anorak. The Heathrow train was hot, the airport hotter and the planes stuffy. *En route*, he'd stripped off what he decently could and stuffed it into his backpack. Twenty-eight hours flying hours and ten time zones later, he was sweltering in T-shirt and jeans, his feet sweaty inside his sensible shoes. He toiled on up the incline. The parched air dried the lining of his throat. His eyes ached and his head throbbed. He dug around in his pack for hat and sunglasses.

By the time he reached the top of the rise, he felt groggy. Recognising the symptoms of dehydration, he made for the bar he used to frequent when he was in this neighbourhood. In the two years since he last visited, 'Pete's Pad', which he'd liked for its hippy-ish ambience, had become 'Pirate Pete's', complete with fake parrots and treasure chests. He craved cold beer but knowing that alcohol would finish him off, he ordered lemonade and a cheese burger, and sat in a gloomy corner, enjoying the air con.

He texted Louise to say that his flight had been delayed and that he would be getting in later than anticipated. He needed a couple more hours to acclimatise. Surface too quickly and he'd get the bends.

He had a few dollars in his pocket, enough to pay for his snack, but he needed more cash. The bloke behind the bar directed him to the nearest ATM.

'You can leave your pack here, if you like,' he said. 'Save you hauling it.'

It took Gil a beat to remember that he was in Coffs not in Camden. 'Thanks, mate. Is there somewhere I can get out of these togs?'

The barman indicated the restroom.

Before leaving, he changed, sluiced his face and cleaned his teeth. Now wearing shorts, flip-flops and a fresh T-shirt, only his pallid limbs labelled him a tourist.

Keeping to the shady side of the street, he walked east down Harbour Drive, past a longboard shack, a seafood cafe, a pet store and a 'healing centre'. He paused at the bus stop outside 'Ray White – Real Estate' and confirmed that the bus would drop him within walking distance of his mother's house. He located the machine and tapped in his PIN. He'd checked his balance before leaving London, even so he was relieved when a hundred dollars appeared from the slot.

Free of his pack, he felt a lot better and he set off at a brisk pace, heading down to Jetty Beach. The beach, protected from ocean swells by a breakwater, provided safe swimming and easy windsurfing and was popular with young families. This afternoon, the car parks were chocker and the beach, backed by low dunes, was as crowded as Gil had ever seen it. Along the shallow curve of the bay, children were splashing, screaming, digging and generally tearing about. Apart from pop-up tents and anti-UV suits, it was a timeless scene.

When they were still playing at happy families, he and Janey used to bring the kids down here at weekends. Polly had been a real water baby – fearless, even when the wind whipped up a swell. The boys, on the other hand, hadn't been so keen. They'd always been happier on wheels – bikes, scooters, go-carts, skates. Let them loose on an expanse of tarmac and they were in their element. Still were, or so he'd heard.

Beyond Mutton Bird Island the sea, a dozen shades of azure, was stippled with white-tops. In the past hour, something had happened to the sky and it had softened to forget-me-not blue grading through pale turquoise to near green at the horizon.

He was debating whether to walk out along the old jetty when his phone rang.

It was Louise. 'Where are you?'

'Just got in. I'm…walking up Camperdown.'

'Walking? Are you nuts? Stay right there. I'll pick you up.'

'Why don't I meet you at that bar on Harbour Drive? Next to the post office?'

'I think I know the one. I'll be there in twenty minutes. Gil?'

'Yeah?'

'Welcome home.'

He was sitting at a table overlooking the road by the time his sister was parking her decrepit Commodore. He watched as she got out and locked the car. She'd lost weight by the look of it and her face looked drawn. She'd dyed her hair and it was an unlikely shade of reddish-brown. She looked older than her forty-seven years.

When she spotted him, she shrieked with delight. They hugged, cried, laughed and talked a lot of nonsense, and he wished he hadn't kicked off his visit with a falsehood.

After a beer they discussed his plans. 'I'll see the boys, of course, but my priority has to be Polly. I may have been a tad...negative about the baby. She needs to know I'm totally on side now.'

Louise nodded. 'That's great. So when are you seeing her?'

He wasn't prepared to confess that his hopes were riding on one frosty email. 'We haven't firmed anything up. I'll call her from Mum's.'

'You and I can grab a few hours, can't we?' she said.

'Definitely.'

Had it been up to him, he would have stayed at Louise's place. His mother would fuss and prattle and take too much trouble but he couldn't disappoint her. He'd come to Coffs to smooth things over so he must grit his teeth, eat whatever his mother put in front of him, and do his best not to piss anyone off.

'You look pale,' Louise said as she started the car.

'I'm okay. A bit tired. A decent kip and I'll be rarin' to go.'

In fact he wasn't feeling wonderful. What with the beer, the lack of air-con in the car and the whiff of Louise's spaniel coming off the blanket on the back seat, it was all he could do not to throw up.

His mother's house was on the other side of the highway that ploughed through the middle of Coffs and continued up the coast to Brisbane. He'd been astounded when she'd upped and moved here. It transpired that, not long before his father's fatal stroke, his parents had discussed what was to be done when one of them was 'left', agreeing that the survivor should sell the family home and buy something more manageable. And his mother had done just that. The house and garden were considerably smaller. And there was no pool to worry about. It was handy for the library, the botanic gardens and the cemetery where his father lay. The move had been a wrench but it made sense and, four years down the line, she seemed reconciled to her new situation.

'Be patient with her, won't you?' Louise said. 'She comes out with some real corkers. I used to argue but...' she shrugged 'it wouldn't do for us to fall out so I let it wash over me now.'

'Corkers?'

She laughed. 'You'll find out soon enough.'

'Polly implied she's losing it.'

'She gets a bit muddled at times but I wouldn't say she's losing it.'

'Muddled?'

'She mislays things. Forgets names. Misses birthdays.'

'Sure you're not talking about me?' he said. 'So you think she's coping?'

'Seems to be. She eats well. Does the crossword most days. Reads a lot. She's joined an art class.' She paused. 'One slightly weird development. She's taken to going to church on Sundays.'

'Mum goes to *church*?'

'Like I said, you're going to have to let stuff wash over you.'

They turned into Prince James Avenue. The single-storey houses looked flimsy, as though they were constructed of foam board. They varied in design but the impression was one of uninspired uniformity. Corrugated tin roofs added an air of impermanence, as though these nondescript dwellings were temporary and could be easily swept away whenever someone came up with something better.

Louise stopped outside number twenty-three. 'I'll wait here,' she said. 'Let you have a few minutes together.'

Yanking his rucksack off the back seat, he started down the concrete path. His mother must have been watching from the window because suddenly the front door opened and she was coming towards him, arms outstretched. He'd been so preoccupied with leaving Vivian and worrying about how things would go with Polly that he hadn't prepared himself for this.

His mother looked unfamiliar in what he guessed was her best frock. For one thing, she wasn't wearing her pinny, the declaration of her intent to cook, or clean, or get on with something useful. For most of his life, Gil had found it convenient to think of his mother as a flinty pioneer. Indestructible. Enduring. But he could no longer escape the truth. His mother was an old lady.

'Hey, Ma. You're looking gorgeous,' he said, adopting the twang he'd spent the past five years losing.

'Gil,' she said. 'My Gil.'

Dropping his pack, he took her in his arms, breathing in the cheap lavender scent she saved for special occasions. They stayed like this for some time, her head pressed against his chest, her fingers clutching his arm.

She set about fattening him up, producing meals that she was adamant had been his favourites. Insisting that he do something to earn his keep, he persuaded her to list things that needed doing around the place. This wasn't entirely altruistic. A trip to the DIY store (Louise had arranged insurance on his mother's car) for a tap washer or pig netting for the fence was a legitimate reason to escape when her witter and reminiscing got too much.

His sons were like sniffer dogs, frequently turning up to visit their grandmother when a meal was in the offing. They seemed unfazed by his presence as though he lived down the road and dropped in every day. There was a lot he wanted ask them. How was school? What were their plans? How did they feel about their sister's pregnancy? But if he went at them too hard, they might stop coming, and he was getting to enjoy their being around. As agreed, he spent time with Louise, Dan and the kids who also made no big deal of his being there. As ever, Rachel was 'busy,

busy', promising that, if she could 'rearrange a few things', she would drive down from Grafton at the weekend. He shared several beers with an old friend who'd heard he was in town, doing his best to look interested in gossip about people and places he couldn't remember. Janey called but he managed to duck out of speaking to her, not wanting his meeting with Polly (assuming it happened) to be coloured by his ex-wife's opinions.

Resolved not to put pressure on his daughter, he waited to see whether she would get in touch. When, after a couple of days he'd heard nothing, he began to worry she might hold out and he capitulated and phoned.

'I wondered when you'd get round to calling,' she said. 'It sounds pretty cosy over there.'

The boys might appear to be oblivious but evidently they were reporting back to their sister.

'I'm sure you'd be welcome,' he said. 'Look, I don't know how you want to do this. Maybe we could go somewhere quiet for a chat.'

'Neutral ground, you mean.'

'If you like.'

'So why don't you pick me up from work this afternoon? I finish at four.'

'You're still working?' he said.

'See? Why d'you always have to do this?'

He wasn't sure *what* he always did but he apologised anyway and said he would be there.

He'd assumed that Polly had stopped work. She still had a couple of months to go but he didn't like to think of her being at everyone's beck and call. He didn't like to think of her working at the wretched supermarket, full stop. What had started out as a stopgap – 'while I work out what I want to do with my life' – appeared, somewhere along the line, to have become permanent.

As four o'clock approached, he grew more nervous. Should he

swing by a store and buy her a gift? Flowers? Something for the baby? He'd better get this right. She wouldn't fall for any bullshit.

He parked near the front entrance, scanning the women leaving the store. What if he didn't recognise her? What if she'd changed her mind and wouldn't talk to him? He switched off the engine and got out of the car. Sun, reflecting off every shiny surface, dazzled him. The expanse of tarmac acted as a vast storage heater, pumping out heat upon heat.

He closed his eyes, evoking the watercolour palette of London in January. Brick-built terraces. Steeply-pitched roofs. Congested streets. Buzz. Hassle. Grimy snow on Tooting Bec Common. And there, in her green coat, Vivian striding to the Tube.

As soon as he'd arrived at his mother's, he'd checked that the picture frame containing her hair was undamaged, then tucked it back in the pocket of his rucksack. When they'd parted at Kings Cross, in the chaos of Friday morning's rush hour, they'd agreed that phoning would be tricky. 'Email?' she'd said. 'Mum's not online.' 'No worries, Gil. It's not long.' 'So I keep saying. But you'll get in touch if…?' 'Of course.' Seven miles above the Arabian Sea, he'd made a deal with himself. While he was in Coffs, his head must be one hundred per cent *in Coffs* – or what was the point of this? He placed his hand on the roof of the car, the discomfort of the hot metal yanking him back to the southern hemisphere.

She appeared from the side of the building. The red supermarket tabard was tight across the bulge of her belly. Her hair was dragged back in a ponytail. Her face was plumper and she wore no make-up.

He'd thought about this for too long – rehearsing what he might say, what she might say. Now that it came to it, he couldn't speak.

'I hope you're not crying, Dad,' she said.

He saw tears well in her eyes.

'I hope so too,' he said.

300

He tried not to crush her belly as they came together in a hug. 'You're hot,' he said.

'Hot. Bloated. Covered in stretch marks. Peeing every five minutes. It's a barrel of laughs.'

He held her tighter. There was nothing he could say to make it better.

She pulled the band from her ponytail, shaking her head to loosen her hair. 'Can you help me off with this?' she said, indicating the fastenings on the tacky nylon tabard.

Beneath it she was wearing shorts and a white T-shirt, her bump and protruding navel visible through the stretched fabric. She stared at him, defying him to comment, and he wanted to thump the shit who had done this to her.

'Okay. Where shall we go?' he said.

She pretended to think but he was sure that she already had it planned.

'Could we go out to Mutton Bird?' she said.

He'd expected he to suggest somewhere cool, a restaurant maybe or a shaded spot, certainly not a nature reserve where there was nothing but scrub and rocks.

'It'll be scorching out there.'

She shrugged. 'So why bother asking me?'

They drove to the Marina, parking the car and walking along the boardwalk that gave access to dozens of moored boats and linked Mutton Bird Island to the mainland. A slight breeze, blowing off the sea, went a little way to alleviate the heat but the sun was unremitting.

'You're going to burn,' she said.

He pulled a bottle of Factor 50 from his pocket – his mother had insisted he bring it – and slathered it over his arms, legs and face. The wholesome aroma transported him back twenty years.

'I was down here the other day,' he said, pointing towards Jetty Beach. 'Remember how you hated wearing a cozzie?'

'Remember how *you* hated coming to the beach? You'd stick it for ten minutes then bugger off with your camera.'

Was that how it had been? Maybe, maybe not, but it was enough that Polly remembered it that way.

'Let's not fall out about the past,' he said. 'It's what happens from here on that's important.' His words might have come straight from a self-help manual.

'The baby's okay?' he said. 'You get regular checks? Blood pressure. Urine.'

'Dad. I'm not a complete moron.'

'No. You're not.'

Were he to tell her that one day she would fuss this way over her own daughter she wouldn't believe him.

He ploughed on, steeled for the next rebuke. 'Everything's good at home?'

She shrugged. 'It's hard after having my own place. Don't get me wrong, Alan's been great. And I know I'm lucky to be living rent free, blah, blah, blah. Mum can be pretty controlling, though. *You* must know that.'

'Yeah. Well. Someone had to take control.'

They found a patch of shade under the wooden walkway leading up from the shore to the path running down the spine of the island. A previous visitor had faked up a seat from a pile of rocks and a plank of sea-smoothed timber, and Gil took his daughter's arm, steadying her as she lowered herself onto the makeshift bench.

'So. How would you like things to go from here?' he said, hoping to guide her gently toward telling him what she wanted from him. Instead she took off in another direction altogether.

'D'you have a magic wand handy?' she said. She picked up a stone and threw it at a gull that was tormenting a small brown bird. 'I don't think I can do this, Dad. What if I can't stand this baby? Like that woman in the book? What if I'm a bad mother? I'm not going to breastfeed, that's for sure.'

His daughter's hands were cradling her belly as if to shield her unborn child from what was being said.

'You can do anything you want to do, Polly.'

'That's crap, and you know it.' She closed her eyes and massaged the back of her neck. 'I can't put my life on hold for the next eighteen years. I can't.'

'It won't be on hold.'

'Yours obviously wasn't,' she said, 'but then you're a bloke, aren't you?'

Children's voices carried across the water. A tourist boat – big and ugly – manoeuvred into the harbour.

'Isn't this when you're supposed to tell me how *wonderful* parenthood is? Everyone does. But I sit at my checkout, day after day, seeing all those miserable women with their screaming babies and that's not the message I get.'

He took her hand. 'I don't have the right to advise anyone on parenthood. I was rubbish at it. I don't know why. I had a terrific role model.'

'Gramps was a good dad?'

'The best.'

They sat in silence and he knew she was remembering the kind grandfather whom he resembled slightly, or so everyone said, who'd always had time to play or to read or to talk to her.

'I so miss him, Dad.' She wiped a tear from her cheek. 'Shit. That's another thing. I keep crying.'

'Hormones,' Gil said, putting his arm around her.

They walked slowly on up the path to the highest point of the island, pausing now and then to let Polly catch her breath. She pointed back towards the town. 'Coffs looks pretty good from here, doesn't it?'

He couldn't deny that from a distance the town, rising up the hill from the white sands of the bay, backed by the misty ridge of the Great Dividing Range, looked idyllic.

She closed her eyes and flexed her neck.

'You okay?' he said.

'No. My back's killing me,' she said. 'Can we go now?'

The path was peppered with protruding stones lying in wait for the unwary. But when he offered his hand she didn't take it. As they made their way back, he attempted to pick up their conversation, hoping to discover whether he even figured in her future.

Eventually she said, 'Can we not talk, Dad? I've been up since six. I'm shattered.'

He dropped her back at the supermarket car park, holding the door open as she manoeuvred herself behind the wheel of an old Mazda.

'See you soon?' he said.

She gunned the engine and, without replying, drove off.

He'd expected a shouting match. Tears. Polly raking up every teenage grudge. Maybe, if she got really steamed up, physical violence. Instead he'd been faced with a frightened girl who was convinced that she'd blown her chances of a happy life.

Overwhelmed with sadness, he watched her car filter into the traffic and disappear down the highway.

Next morning, on the way to Bunnings Warehouse for a hacksaw blade, he stopped at the internet café. He'd resisted until now but seeing Polly, realising how scared and miserable she was, had unleashed a pack of black thoughts. Needing to know that Vivian wasn't trying to contact him, he logged on and scanned his unopened mail. His inbox was jam-packed with dross but there was nothing from her. They'd agreed – more or less – that she would get in touch only if her father died. Her silence, although disappointing, had to be good news. Sitting in front of the machine, he wanted, more than anything, to mail her. To let her know that he was counting the days. But superstition triumphed.

Renege on his deal with the gods – *one hundred per cent in Coffs* – and even the slightest chance of making things right with Polly would be scuppered.

Louise asked him whether he could bear a family get together. 'Rachel's coming down at the weekend. It'd be at our place. Lunch. Nothing fancy.' She paused. 'It'd mean the world to Mum.'

'Great idea,' he said.

'Really?'

'No. But you're right. We should do this.'

'Thanks, Gil. It might be the last—'

'I know.'

Time was racing away. Good as it was to see the rest of his family, that wasn't why he'd come here. He had to see Polly again but whenever he called she was either at work or 'going out'. During one particularly frustrating phone call, he was a whisker away from telling her that he'd flown half way round the world, and spent a grand that he didn't have, in order to see her. Maybe she was testing him. Maybe that was exactly what she wanted him to do. But after Mutton Bird he no longer had confidence in his own judgement.

Not knowing what else to do, he contacted Janey. 'Could we meet?' he said. 'I'd really appreciate an update on the kids. Your take on how they're doing. The boys seem fine but it's blood out of a stone when it comes to hard information. And Polly. I'm not sure what's going on there. She seems very down.'

Janey was a nicer person than she used to be. He attributed this to his successor – solid, dependable Alan. Alan's first marriage had been childless and, when he and Janey got together, he'd taken to the kids, and they to him. Gil might have resented this but in fact he was grateful to the man who had created a stable home for them.

They met in Janey's lunch break, on the trade park where she worked as office-manager for a building supplies firm.

'Good to see you, Janey,' he said.

She laughed. 'Liar. You've been avoiding me all week.'

'You know what a coward I am.'

'I do.' She placed a hand on his knee. (Her hand was so familiar but what happened to *their* ring?) 'It's fine, Gil. It's been fine for years. What about you? Is your new life living up to expectations?'

'It has its moments.'

They sat on a wall in the shade of a eucalyptus tree, sharing her sandwiches while she gave him a rundown on their sons. Chris found schoolwork easier than his brother but was slapdash. Adam had a flare for design. They should both achieve grades that would take them to university if that were the way they wanted to go.

'You're doing a great job, Janey,' he said.

'That's not what you said when you heard about Polly. You practically accused me of child neglect.'

'Yes. Well. I was totally out of order. Do we know anything about the father?'

'No. And I advise you not to go there. She's very tetchy.'

'Was it a one night stand?' he said.

'I don't know. Horrible to think that, but it might be easier in the long run.'

'She seemed so excited when she wrote telling me. I had to be happy for her. She made out you were over the moon.'

'That was wishful thinking,' she said.

'I'm not hearing that now. She's full of doubt. What's changed?'

'Reality's kicked in.'

'Shame it didn't kick in sooner,' he said.

'No point going there either. We have to take it from where we're at.'

'She's going to need a lot of support.'

'We'll manage. Alan's a sucker for babies.'

Her reply – rather smug, he thought – came back in a flash. He recalled Polly's assertion that her mother could be controlling and it struck him that Janey might, in fact, relish the prospect of becoming indispensable.

'And what about money?' he said. 'She won't be earning for a while.'

'You're going to write her a big fat cheque?'

She stood up, shaking the crumbs from her yellow dress. 'I've got to go, Gil.'

'Thanks for coming. Oh, by the way, has she said anything about me?'

'Aaah. Now I get why you wanted us to meet up,' she said. 'You may not want to believe this, but no, she hasn't mentioned you.'

He and his mother had rubbed along better than he'd anticipated. As Louise warned, she did get muddled at times – usually when she was tired or had woken from a nap. And she did come out with inappropriate remarks – 'corkers' – about immigrants and gays. But Gil didn't reprimand her. In her eyes, the world had changed for the worse, and she needed to find a reason for that.

He noticed how often she touched him. An errant clump of hair was clamped down. A smudge of oil wiped from his cheek. A leaf brushed off his T-shirt. Any excuse to make contact. On Friday, after they'd cleared breakfast away, she led him to the box room and pulled out the bottom drawer of the chest. The empty drawer was lined with floral paper, which he thought he recognised as the wallpaper from the old house.

'Why don't you leave your things here?' she said. 'Ready for next time. Lavender bags will keep the moths away.' She smiled a hopeful smile.

A few T-shirts, a couple of pairs of shorts – all fit for the rag-bag...

'That's a great idea, Mum,' he said.

Preparations for the 'nothing fancy' party occupied most of Saturday. Although Gil wasn't looking forward to it, it took the heat off him and for that he was grateful. And there was an unexpected bonus. Amidst the fetching and carrying, he was able to grab the odd half-hour and slink off in the car. When he got on that plane, he had to be sure that he was carrying the *real* Coffs back to London, not some picture-postcard version. With that in mind, he steered clear of the beaches and spectacular views, instead tooling around residential streets, retail zones, malls, sun-scorched parks, confirming what he already knew to be true. There was too much space, too much sky here and not enough – for want of a better word – *soul*.

By Sunday morning, his mother could no longer hide her misery. Several times he found her weeping.

'D'you want to go to church, Mum?' he said, hoping to divert her attention from his leaving. 'I'll pick you up after the service and we could go to the party from there.'

'Good heavens, no,' she said. He might have suggested she visit a strip club.

Louise's garden was festooned with bunting and balloons, as if they were gathering to celebrate an arrival not a departure. He glanced around. Here they all were. His family. Chris – squatting on the decking under the awning, showing Louise's kids his mobile phone. Adam – messing about with a football. Rachel – organising their mother. His brother-in-law fussing with the barbecue. But no Polly.

He scanned the garden again, hoping he'd missed a figure in the shadows. He could understand why she wouldn't come. Being gawped at, being the subject of speculation (because that's how it would feel to her) would be an ordeal. Why would she put herself through that?

Rachel waylaid him. 'The man of the moment,' she said. 'Polly not here? I'm not surprised. I expect she's embarrassed.'

He mimicked her scrutiny of the garden. 'And no Denis?'

'Not everyone can drop things at a moment's notice, even for the prodigal's *temporary* return.'

Gil held up his hands. 'Let's call a truce, Rache.'

'I don't know what you're talking about,' she said and hurried off to do something vital.

His mother had settled in an upholstered chair, a little distance from the action. She was clutching her handbag and smiling as she watched her family partying around her. In a couple of months, she would be a great grandmother and he a grandfather. How could that be?

'Photo time?' Louise said once the leftovers were cling-filmed and safely stashed in the fridge.

Gil had already taken some photographs, zooming in close when no one was paying attention. But he guessed his sister was after photographs to place on the sideboard alongside the weddings, christenings and graduations. He wasn't keen on these pieces – all forced smiles and unnatural poses – but he wanted to please her and together they staked out the garden, looking for a suitable backdrop. Again he noticed how worn out she looked. Although they'd seen quite a lot of each other during the week, there had always been people around and he hadn't had the opportunity to ask her about herself.

'Here? In front of the hibiscus?' Louise pointed to a rangy, dark-green shrub, spattered with scarlet blooms.

'Perfect,' he said.

He switched his camera to 'remote' and located the gizmo to activate it. Dan rustled up a tripod. Lazy contentment had settled over the afternoon and when Louise announced that it was 'photo time', there more than a little resistance. But Rachel soon wrangled them into place.

They grouped, and regrouped. Everyone together. His mother and her three children. He and his mother. He and his sisters. He and his sons. Between shots, he returned to the camera to make sure everything was as it should be, scurrying back to join in the ten-second countdown.

When they'd finished, he scrolled quickly through the images. Not bad. But he was sad that Polly wouldn't be on the sideboard with the rest of them, regretful that he hadn't taken a camera to Mutton Bird Island. The most up to date picture he had of her – a squinting, laughing close-up taken, he guessed, with a mobile phone – had arrived with an email six months ago or more. Low resolution made for a lousy print but, wherever she was and whoever she was with, she'd been happy and he loved it because of that.

The party began to wind down. Gil noticed his sons exchanging how-do-we-get-out-of-here looks. His mother kept dipping into sleep, startled each time her head fell forward, jolting her into wakefulness. Louise's kids mooched off to watch television.

'I'm heading home now, Gil,' Rachel said.

'How long will it take you?' Not that he cared but they might as well part on a civil note.

'Not much over the hour, if the traffic's moving. Have a good trip, Gil. A shame you couldn't stay longer.' Her lips barely touched his cheek.

'Well. You know how it is.'

She didn't of course. Nor did any of them.

Then there was Louise, shoving a container of chocolate brownies into his hands, smiling and crying. 'London sounds heartless,' she said. 'I don't like thinking of you all alone. You do have…someone?'

'Don't worry about me,' he said. It was too late to get into that now. 'Everything's okay with you, isn't it?'

'Yes. Of course. It's just…'

'What?' But he couldn't get any more out of her.

Parting with his sons was more of a tug than he'd anticipated. He'd grown close to them during the week, getting to know these boys who, while he wasn't around, had become young men. Chris – so like Janey in looks and temperament. Adam – the daydreamer with a dry sense of humour. It must all have been there, dormant in the bud of those babies he'd grudgingly pushed in their double stroller. He wished he could explain to them how not to make the mistakes he'd made: the two of them were, in a way, a mistake, conceived as they'd been to bring Janey and him back together. The three of them ended up shaking hands and making mannish promises – 'take care', 'see you later' – as if he were popping down to the garage for a carton of milk.

By the time he was parking in Prince James Avenue, his mother was out for the count. (Why was it that in sleep, children looked younger and old people, older?) Had she been seven not seventy-odd, he would have carried her into the house and popped her straight into bed. He was sitting in the car wondering what to do, when a car pulled up tight on his rear bumper. Feeling slightly threatened, he kept his eyes on his mirror. After what seemed too long, the door opened and the driver got out. It was Polly.

'Hey,' he said, getting out of the car. She was only a few yards away but he had the feeling that if he rushed her she might take off. 'You've got a new car.'

'It's Mum's,' she said. 'Mine wouldn't start. How was the party?'

'Okay, I suppose.' He didn't refer to her absence, fearful of putting her back up.

She nodded towards his car. 'Is Gran okay in there? Not too hot?'

'She's fine. For a while, anyway.'

'You're off early tomorrow?'

'Yup. My train leaves at six-fifteen.'

His stomach was knotting. Unless he could hold her attention, she would say goodbye, get back in the car and drive away.

'Can I tell you something that happened to me?' he said.

'Okay. But can we sit down? My back's killing me.'

They perched on the wall and he told her about the bomb. He tried to make his account amusing – the stuff about Irene's handbag, and Vivian making notes in A&E, and how the three of them had ended up having breakfast in an all-night café.

'Why didn't you tell us?' she said.

'No point. Besides, you had plenty going on here.'

'The women sound like a couple of weirdos,' she said.

'Irene's definitely a weirdo. She started stalking me.'

'Really?' She sounded almost interested. 'How?'

'She kept turning up. Sending presents. Generally pestering. In the end I told her to bugger off.' He stopped short of mentioning the accusation of assault.

'And the other one? Vivian, wasn't it? Have you kept in touch?'

It was the first time 'Vivian' had been said in this place and he envisaged the syllables of her name rippling out, planting the notion of her here.

'We meet now and again for coffee, and to slag off Irene. Her office isn't far from where I work.'

'Has she got kids?'

'She's not married.'

'What's that got to do with it?' she said and he regretted his thoughtless remark.

'When I was a kid I thought I was special,' she said, 'that I would do something amazing with my life.'

'You *are*. You *will*.'

She prodded her belly. 'I don't think so.'

36

Vivian was at work when the call came advising her to come to the hospital.

'Take a cab,' Howard said. 'I'll pay.'

'Tube's quicker.'

'Should I come with you?' he said.

'No,' she said. 'It's not as if it's a shock.'

It wasn't a shock but now that it was happening she felt shaky. She'd grown complacent – even comfortable – inhabiting the limbo-land of her father's illness. He in that little room, being cared for by people who didn't mind doing the rotten job. She sitting with him for an hour or so every evening. Then back to Farleigh Road for a bite to eat, bath and bed. It wasn't so bad.

Never having watched anyone die, she dreaded what awaited her at the hospital. In fact when she saw him, he looked no different from yesterday. What *was* different was the ambience within the room. Today there was none of the customary bustle and banter. Nurses came and went quietly, carrying out their duties with calm purpose, keeping up a stream of reassurances that Vivian doubted he could hear but which *she* found comforting. The staff showed concern for her, too, frequently asking whether she needed anything. Tea? A sandwich? They produced a pillow and blanket so she could nap in the chair. It was peaceful and not the least bit frightening. And there was a sense of inevitability as they moved towards the end.

Daylight was draining from the flat, grey sky and they were alone when her father stirred and said, 'Have you cancelled the milk?'

His words, loud and perfectly articulated, made her jump. She wanted to laugh. *There.* They must be mistaken. Dying people didn't fret about milk deliveries.

'Yes, Dad. And the papers,' she said. 'You mustn't worry. Everything's taken care of.'

She leaned towards him and stroked his hand, expecting more questions. Was the house okay? How long had he been here? Why wasn't she at work? She waited, the minutes seeping away in silence, until her back ached and she began to think she'd been dreaming.

Someone brought her more tea. She glanced at the free paper she'd picked up on the Tube. Another 'flu death. Celebrities she didn't recognise. A foolproof new diet. More flooding around Brisbane.

Gil would have been in touch if he'd failed to make it to Coffs Harbour. She missed his mails and calls but this was turning out to be such a weird week she wouldn't have had time for him even if he were in London. Anyway, he'd be back soon.

Tired of reading, she went to the window. It was dark and beyond the rooftops she could make out Sainsbury's illuminated sign. Now and again, she caught a glimpse of a bus moving along Tooting High Street. Out there, people were walking dogs, picking up takeaways, going to the pub.

She curled up in the chair, watching the blip fluttering across the monitor, simultaneously bored and on edge. Murmuring voices filtered in from the corridor as the late shift was briefed on the patients entrusted to their care for the next eight hours.

A nurse popped her head around the door. 'Everything okay, dear? Can I get you anything?'

Vivian's mouth still tasted of the tuna fish sandwich she'd eaten an hour ago. What she wanted most was a toothbrush, but that wasn't the sort of thing the nurse was offering.

'I wouldn't mind getting a breath of air,' she said.

The nurse took her father's hand, pressing the inside of his wrist with her dark, elegant fingers, her lips moving silently as she checked his heartbeat against her inverted watch.

314

'You should be okay,' she said.

Vivian stood outside the main entrance. It felt good to return to the world. She pulled her coat around her, filled her lungs with fresh, cold air and thought about running away. A mini-cab to Belsize Park might cost forty pounds, but it would be worth it to escape from this and sleep in her own bed. Her father didn't know she was here. It would make no difference to him – although there was something sad about anyone dying alone. And what would Richard say? *Richard*. She should have contacted him this morning.

His mobile was off and she tried his landline, letting it ring until the machine cut in. She left it a few seconds then dialled again. This time he answered.

'He won't last much longer,' she said.

'Vivian? Right. I see. Where are you now?'

'At the hospital.'

'Okay. Let me think.' His voice was gruff with sleep and she imagined him, wiry hair sticking up, struggling into a tartan dressing gown. 'What if I catch the six-twenty-five? I'd be there by midday.' He sounded unsure, as if he wanted her to tell him what he should do.

'Up to you,' she said.

The moon was a silvery smudge behind a veil of cloud. Frost sparkled on the handful of cars in the car park. As she looked up at the ugly slab of the building with its rows of dimly lit windows, a man emerged from the front door. A phone cast its glow on his cheek and he was speaking urgently in a language she couldn't identify. *Arabic? Farsi?* He finished the call then sprinted across the car park, got into a car and drove away.

She'd expected the final breath to rattle out of him but he left silently and without a fuss. It was hard to explain but, despite his showing no signs of life for hours, his absence was palpable. He was there. And then he wasn't. It was the strangest thing.

315

He lay on his right side, legs drawn up so that he reached only halfway down the bed. She knelt on the floor, the better to study his face. His eyes weren't quite closed, his lips drawn open in a pinched 'Oh'. She touched his forehead. *Warm.*

Minutes ago, this had been a human being. Now the essence of this *being* had evaporated. Gone. Where? *That film. The weight of a human soul.* God. What was the matter with her? She'd just watched her father die and she was trying to recall a film title.

She fetched the nurse who, having checked the monitor and his pulse, put a motherly arm around her shoulder and led her to the day room, telling her to wait there whilst a doctor… She didn't catch what the doctor had to do. She looked around. Fake wooden tables. Vinyl flooring. It was a dreary place, made even drearier by fierce strip lights. And there was that all-pervasive hospital smell.

She phoned Richard. This time he picked up immediately.

'He's dead,' she said.

'Poor old Dad.' He paused. 'Still, not a bad innings. How was it?'

For her or their father?

'Easier than I'd feared,' she said covering it either way. 'You'll still come, won't you?' He was, after all, also 'next of kin'. Why shouldn't he put in a bit of effort?

'Of course, of course. Let's meet at the house. As there's no great rush, I'll sort out a few things here and catch a later train.'

The far corner of the room was set up as a play area with a miniature table and chairs moulded from yellow plastic. At first glance, it looked inviting but on closer inspection she saw that the books on the shelf were tatty, the toys in the dumpbins cheap and unappealing. There were several jigsaws in boxes on the table and she chose an underwater scene with mermaids, fish and shells. But the pieces showing the mermaids' faces were all missing which made it look as though they'd been decapitated.

After some time, the nurse returned to tell her that her father was 'ready' now. She must have looked confused because she said, 'We've tidied him up for you.'

They'd turned him onto his back, and raised his head on a pillow. He was wearing fresh pyjamas. His arms were outside the covers, lying at his side. His mouth was still open as if he'd been caught in the middle of saying something. He looked cross and a little bewildered.

The scenery had changed too. The medical equipment had been removed. The tissues, moisturiser and bottle of water were gone from the top of his locker, replaced by a vase of imitation flowers and a table lamp.

'He looks peaceful, doesn't he?' the nurse said. 'You'll want to say your goodbyes. Take as long as you like.'

'Thanks.' Vivian nodded towards the plastic flowers. 'And thank you for…'

'Our pleasure, dear. Last moments are so precious.'

Alone again with her father, she wondered what she was supposed to do. She guessed people talked to the body, or wept, or even laughed. She stood at the foot of the bed, expecting to feel something. Dislike? Not anymore – not for several weeks in fact, although she couldn't say why. Grief? Compassion? Pity? Sadness? Relief that he was dead and that she was free? Nothing really, except exhaustion and maybe curiosity. She looked slowly around the room. Odd to think that she wouldn't come here again. She touched his face. He was cold now. Not a person at all.

After what seemed like a decent interval, she took a last look at the husk of her father and went to find out what happened next.

She left the hospital at five-forty armed with a form stating that Philip Frederick Carey had died of sepsis, a leaflet entitled 'What to do after someone dies', and a sports bag containing soiled pyjamas, spectacles and dentures. It was Thursday 13th

317

January, 2011, and she was an orphan. It was an exhilarating thought.

As she passed the Tube station, she shoved the holdall into a litter bin and then walked back to Farleigh Road.

She heard a key in the latch. It was dark and, for a few seconds, she couldn't think where she was.

'Vivian?' Richard's voice rose up the stairs. 'It's only me.'

She checked her watch. Four-thirty. She'd slept for six hours.

'Down in a minute,' she called, shivering as she pushed back the duvet.

Richard was in the kitchen, rooting around in a cupboard. 'Sorry if I woke you.'

She couldn't avoid his hug and as he held her, she caught the astringent whiff of coal tar soap.

'You must be exhausted,' he said. 'I'm making toast. D'you fancy some?'

Within minutes of being here, he'd taken command. She shouldn't mind. In fact she should be grateful because now she could hand all this over to him.

They sat in the kitchen and she told him how it had been, leaving out the bit about the milk delivery, determined – she wasn't sure why – to keep this memory for herself.

'John's hoping to fly over on Saturday,' he said. 'And we should make a list of people to notify.'

'People?'

'Friends. Neighbours.'

'I suppose we should tell Mrs Francks, next door. She called the ambulance. And the woman who cleans – *cleaned* – for him. Apart from them…'

He frowned. 'Doesn't he have a cousin in Wales?'

Does he? Despite being dead, her father had the power to humiliate her.

'His address book's next to the phone,' she said. 'It'll be in there I expect.' She pushed the death certificate and 'What to do' booklet across the table. 'The hospital gave me these.'

He studied the certificate. 'Ahhh, *sepsis*,' he said, as though the cause of death made some kind of difference.

Setting it aside, he began reading aloud from the booklet, underlining sections with a red pen. This required no input from her and, as he droned on, she drifted.

I should go in to work. The contractor needs that list of door furniture – although I'm still not entirely sure about those handles. If Howard's around, we can go through it again.

'Okay with you?' Richard's voice brought her back to the kitchen.

'Whatever you think's best,' she said.

He was so like their father. Dogmatic. Overbearing. She couldn't imagine his ever admitting to being wrong. (Of course when her father was Richard's age, she had been only eight years old. What had her parents been thinking?)

'Right.' He slapped the table with the palms of his hands in a *that's-settled-then* gesture, although she had no idea what had been settled. 'Before we talk to anyone, we need to decide whether it's burial or cremation. Did Dad discuss it with you?'

She remembered how she and her father used to sit in this kitchen, discussing the rats in the shed or what he owed her for a jar of jam.

'No,' she said.

'Mmmm. Maybe he wrote something down. The filing cabinet's the obvious place.'

'It's locked,' she said. She was sure of this because, curious to know what the ugly grey thing contained, she'd tried it only a few days ago.

Pulling a bunch of keys from his pocket, he isolated a flat, silver key, holding it up as though he'd done something heroic. Of course he had a key. He would have been given it when he became attorney.

Her father had been a systematic and unimaginative man, and, when Richard unlocked the cabinet, she wasn't surprised to find his tax documents filed under 'T', water bills under 'W', and so on.

'D for death?' she suggested. 'F for funeral? H for heaven?'

Richard put a hand on her arm. 'You must be out on your feet. Why not leave this to me?'

She could no longer remain in the house with this bumptious bore. 'I'm going home now,' she said. 'I'm sure you and John will do a perfect job. Let me know if you need me.'

She lay in bed. She was hungry but couldn't be bothered to do anything about it. When she swallowed, her throat had that raspy tickle that preceded a cold. It was Thursday, wasn't it? Somewhere amongst it all, death had stolen Wednesday.

At St George's, the night staff would be coming on. Some other sick person would be in that little room, hitched up to monitors and drips. So where, exactly, was her father's body? In one of those refrigerated drawers, perhaps, with a tag on his toe – or was that just in movies? It seemed impossible that he could make the journey from wherever he was into a hole in the ground (or an urn on Richard's mantelpiece) without a hitch. But undertakers did all that, didn't they? Amazing, considering how hard it was to find a reliable plumber.

She had no recollection of undertakers or registrars or anything much in the period following her mother's death. She'd floated near the ceiling for days on end, watching a zombie masquerading as Vivian Carey, going through the motions. Those drugs were strong. This was nothing at all like that. A sick old man had died. It was the natural order of things.

She turned over, yanking the duvet up over her head, breathing the warm scent of her own body. Tomorrow she would go to work and soon everything would return to normal.

37

Howard pressed her to take more time before coming back to work, but she was adamant that she wanted to get back to normal. However it appeared that 'normal' was out of the question. Throughout the day, her colleagues sidled up mumbling condolences, Ralph near to tears as he recounted what he'd gone through when *his* father died. She felt embarrassed and fraudulent.

True to form, Ottilie's concern manifested itself in a relentless supply of coffee and snacks, and an offer to listen if she 'needed to talk'.

'Thanks,' Vivian said, 'but I'm fine. Really I am.'

'You *think* you are,' Ottilie said. 'When Duval passed, Ma kept right on going, as if nothing had happened. Three months later…' She pursed her lips and shook her head.

To Vivian's satisfaction, Richard seemed disturbed by her abrupt departure. He phoned several times to check that she was 'coping' and to update her on the 'arrangements'. Death commanded an abundance of euphemisms. He and John had decided on cremation, he didn't explain why. The funeral would take place in ten days time, somewhere out beyond Morden. There would be refreshments – 'sandwiches and cakes, nothing elaborate' – at the house for anyone who cared to go back. He didn't say who would do the catering and she didn't ask.

Before leaving Farleigh Road, she had picked up her father's address book, saying she would contact those that needed to be informed. Richard seemed reluctant to let the book out of the house but she'd held her ground, insisting that he already had enough to do. Also, unbeknown to him, she had taken her father's keys. She'd happened across them in his overcoat pocket and guessed he'd forgotten to replace them on the hook after his final expedition. Amongst them was a small silver key, which she now knew belonged to the filing cabinet.

On Saturday she spent the morning food shopping, cleaning and catching up with the washing, finding these humdrum chores improbably agreeable after the disruption of the past weeks.

After lunch, she sat down with the address book. According to the flyleaf, her father had started this book a matter of months after her mother's death. She could picture the old one now, well-thumbed and disintegrating. What had become of it? As she flicked through its pages, the sight of her father's writing pulled her up short. Striding across the paper, bold and old-fashioned and so very particular to him, it was like hearing his voice. He'd maintained that 'ballpens' had been the death of good handwriting and had always used a Waterman fountain pen – a retirement gift from his work colleagues. The entries in this address book had been made with that pen and, judging by their uniformity, might have been written at one sitting.

It didn't take long to go through it. In fact there were so few names, so few crossings out to indicate a move or a death, she wondered whether he'd kept it up to date. Apart from her half-brothers and their families, and her aunt in Munich, the addresses were all in the south east of England, the majority in London. Her father's cousin – if he existed – must surely be in here somewhere. But there was no one in Wales or, come to that, anyone west of Reading.

She'd planned to phone around but the only phone numbers recorded were those of the family. It was a striking omission, as if he didn't want or need to speak to any of his 'friends'. Undeterred, she composed an obituary notice, including details of the funeral and adding her name and phone number. She printed a copy for everyone in the book and used her own fountain pen to address the envelopes.

Next morning – Sunday – she couldn't summon the willpower to get out of bed. A dull ache had spread across her lower back and a sore throat was affecting her voice, making her sound like a stranger. She suspected that there was some truth in Ottilie's warning although she'd hate to give her the satisfaction of knowing it. She slept the morning away and, after a bath and a couple of Nurofen, her backache eased and she relocated to the sofa. Searching for something to occupy her, she picked up Gil's Christmas gift.

A Dream Too Far was, as he'd warned, sentimental tosh. Yet it was easy to see why its protagonist had appealed to the pregnant Helen Thomas – not much more than a girl – daydreaming of her unborn child and hoping that, were it to be a boy, he would grow up to be a dashing young doctor like Gillon Fraser. Fifty-odd years ago, 'Gillon' must have caused a stir but Helen had stuck to her guns and Vivian admired her for that.

London was shockingly cold and by the time Gil reached home, he had donned every item of clothing he had with him.

He'd anticipated returning to a chaos of ransacked drawers and unwashed crockery but his flat was disturbingly tidy. A loaf of bread sat on the worktop, the fruit bowl was fully stocked and there was a Tupperware container of what looked like chilli in the fridge. *Feray.*

To stand any chance of getting to work on time tomorrow, he needed to sleep. Pulling down the blinds he fell, fully clothed, into bed. As soon as he closed his eyes, he was bobbing on a gentle swell which, had he been on a boat, might have been soporific but here, three storeys up, it was disconcerting. After a restless hour he got up and made a bowl of porridge. As he aimlessly trickled a syrupy *Gil* across its surface, he recalled his breakfasts with Vivian. The bland, warm food steadied his gut but now she was in his head and he wouldn't sleep until he'd spoken to her.

Returning to the warmth of his bed, he called her.

'Where are you?' she said.

'At home. My body is anyway. It'll be a while before my brain catches up.'

'My father died,' she said. 'I know I said I'd mail but there was no point.'

Voices murmured in the background. She must be at work.

'I'm so sorry,' he said. 'When was it?'

'Thursday. I was with him.'

'That's good,' he said.

'Yes.' She paused. 'I found it weirdly fascinating.'

'Most people do, although they won't admit it. It's the ultimate mystery, after all.'

'Yes. It really is.'

'So when's the funeral?'

'Tuesday.'

'You've been busy then,' he said

'No. I've handed over to John and Richard. All I have to worry about is what to wear.'

'Well, I'm glad you're okay.'

'Did you sort things out with your daughter?' she said.

'I'm not sure.'

Then someone called her name and she had to go.

He was late getting to the hospital next morning. He'd fidgeted around the bed for what seemed like hours. 'Too tired to sleep', his mother used to say. Eventually he'd given up and watched a no-star movie on Channel 5. The last time he'd checked it was near midnight but soon after that he'd fallen into a dreamless sleep, not waking until nine. Kevin huffed and puffed but a few strategic enquiries about baby Jack, along with an offer to cover evening work for the remainder of the week, put things right.

In a quiet moment, he mailed Polly. They had – or so he liked to think – reached an uneasy peace, but he'd seen how touchy she was, how ready to take offence, and he kept his message short, avoiding saying anything that might rub her up the wrong way.

My dearest Polly. It was wonderful seeing you last week. Thanks for taking the time. I often think about our walk to Mutton Bird and the things we talked about. You are never far from my thoughts. Love to my very special daughter – and her very special daughter. Dad xx

He wasn't exaggerating. Thoughts of his daughter were ever present, like the hum of a fridge. Occasionally the hum stepped up to a roar and he was overwhelmed with anxiety. It sickened him to think that she was resigned to a mundane future. And she was obviously scared of the birth itself. Janey had been the same when she was nearing her due date, terrified that she wouldn't be able to expel the 'thing' inside her that was getting bigger and bigger by the day. The second time, enormous with the twins, she'd been quite serene. Once Polly was safe in her crib, at least Janey had had someone with whom to explore the unmapped territory of parenthood. For a while, anyway.

But it wasn't as if Polly would be going it alone. Janey would be there. And *good old* Alan too. Alan had been ready to support Polly through her pregnancy – no small commitment – and doubtless he'd be delighted to play grandfather when the babe was born. The kid wouldn't be short of grandpas – even if the *bona fide* one lived on the other side of the world.

The trip to Coffs had been a mental and physical drain. (He must have been crazy to think he could take it in his stride. Ten years ago, maybe.) But it had been unexpectedly good to see his family and he was glad that he'd gone. By the end of the week, he was over the worst of his jet lag. He still woke at odd times in the night and felt bushed in the afternoons, but the dazed feeling had faded and his metabolism was returning to normal.

Before he could settle back into his London life, a couple of issues needed to be resolved. First there was Irene. There had been no developments while he was away and Kevin advised him to do nothing. Why stir things up needlessly? Reasonable enough although he would prefer the matter to be cleared up, not left to lie in wait like a malevolent redback.

Feray, too, was causing him slight concern. She'd offered to keep an eye on his flat and, loath to hurt her feelings, he'd accepted. He hoped she realised there was no more to it than that but, on his return, he'd been thrown to find that she'd been in and tidied the place up and he'd dropped a rather formal note through her door, thanking her and enclosing a fiver to cover the groceries.

He'd not spoken to Vivian again but it was clear from her emails that she was glad to be back home and able to concentrate on her work. Their dates – if they could be called that – had, in a weird kind of way, been contingent on her father. With him gone, things would be on a very different footing – one which had yet to be established.

When Friday evening came and they still hadn't arranged to meet, he called her.

'Hey. I was thinking. It'd be good to catch up. Could we get together over the weekend?' He felt like a kid, arranging a first date. 'That's if you're not tied up.'

'I have things I need to do on Saturday,' she said. 'Sunday? We could go for a walk.'

'Terrific. I'll come over around eleven.'

It was snowing again and Feray was scattering salt on the steps.

'No let up,' he said, pointing to the low, grey sky. 'Thanks again for…'

'It took only a few minutes,' she said.

She asked about his trip. He asked about the kids. Then they stood awkwardly, neither of them sure how to wind up the encounter.

'Need anything from the Co-Op?' he said.

'I'm good,' she said. 'But thanks anyway.'

She smiled and he remembered how beautiful she was and how good things had been with her.

'Look, Feray. This sounds creepy but I'm going to say it anyway. I'm really, really sorry. You and the kids deserve a steady bloke. Someone who'll commit.'

'We do,' she said. 'You're a shit, Gil. A nice one, but all the same a shit. I was very, very angry—'

'And then some. I haven't dared show my face in that coffee shop.'

'Yes, well. You know I've got a temper on me. Now I've had time to get used to it, I think it's good we finished. And I don't have the energy to stay angry.' She glanced away and he had a hunch what was coming next. 'Actually, I've met someone. He works with my brother-in-law.'

Gil remembered the man he'd seen her talking to in the supermarket. 'That's wonderful,' he said.

'Maybe not wonderful but he's kind and reliable. He's got a couple of kids too, so he knows what that's like.'

Another loser must have been written across his face because she added 'His wife died. Breast cancer. We're taking it slowly but so far...' she held up a gloved hand to show crossed fingers. 'You?'

'It's good. I'm good. It's all good,' he said.

Their falling out had troubled him and he was grateful to her for letting him off the hook. So much so that he bought a bunch of anemones from the stall near the Tube and left them on her doorstep.

That evening, Janey phoned.

'Polly's okay?' he said.

'She's fine,' she said. 'And the boys are fine. They're all still in bed.'

'So what's up?' he said.

As usual, the time lag punctuated their conversation with silences, no longer than a beat yet enough to dislocate the flow.

'I need to ask you something,' she said.

'Ask away.'

This time the pause was a little longer.

'Did Polly say anything about not keeping the baby?'

'Not *keeping* it?'

'She says she's going to give it up for adoption. She didn't mention it to you?'

'No. *No*. Hell. I would have told you. She was apprehensive. Scared that she'd be a bad mother. But you and I talked about that, didn't we? When did she tell you this?'

'A few days ago,' she said. 'You know what a drama queen she is, I assumed she was trying to get attention. But now she says she's been talking to a social worker.'

'I take it you think she should keep the baby?'

'Of course I do. It's our granddaughter we're talking about here.' The old antagonism had crept back into her voice but it was tinged with panic. 'What are we going to do, Gil?'

'Look,' he said, 'I need time to get my head around this. I'll phone you back.'

Why the hell would Polly do this? She couldn't think that the child would stand a better chance with a couple of strangers. Janey and Alan were more than willing to give her a safe, loving home, and all the support she needed. When he'd gone to meet Janey for lunch that day she'd seemed quite excited about being involved. Could that be it? Was Polly punishing her mother for – how had she put it? – being 'so bloody controlling'. Threatening to give the baby away did give her immense power. She had two months to weigh it up – or maybe to *wind them* up. One thing was for sure, it was her decision.

When he called back, Janey picked up straight away.

'Okay,' he said. 'Here's what I think. We have to back off. If we don't crowd her, I'm sure she'll come round.

'Are you?' she said. 'Well, here's what I think. She was okay until you turned up. By the way, why *did* you come?'

'C'mon Janey. I wanted to see—'

'*You* wanted. *You*. Did you really think a flying visit from you was going to make everything right? I don't know what you said, or didn't say, but she sees you and starts talking about adoption. Coincidence? I don't think so.'

'I refuse to get into a fight, Janey. You can't lay this on me.'

'I can and I do. You're selfish, Gil. I suggest you spend a little time thinking about other people for a change. Daughters are supposed to worship their fathers but Polly despises you. Perhaps you aren't aware of that.'

38

Richard phoned to let Vivian know that he and John were flying to Edinburgh for the weekend. 'John wants to catch up with friends, and I need to collect a few things. There's nothing else to be done before the funeral. We'll be back on Monday morning. Let's touch base then.'

She made a plan. While they were away, she would go to Farleigh Road. It might be her only chance to look around before everything was bundled up and dispersed to charity shops or the tip. She might even locate that old address book. She couldn't say why but its disappearance seemed significant. She considered inviting Gil to go with her. But this visit was about drawing a line and it wouldn't be right to turn it into an outing.

'I have things I need to do on Saturday,' she told him when he called. 'Sunday? We could go for a walk.'

Richard had been busy in the house. The coats were gone from the hallstand, leaving it naked and anonymous. Tea towels were now in the drawer beneath the draining board. The shoe-cleaning kit was relocated under the stairs. Extra lavatory paper was no longer in the landing cupboard but on the shelf in the bathroom. He had reset the heating, too, and the place was cold.

The letterbox rattled and she jumped, fearful that her half-brothers had cancelled their plans. When she went into the hall, she found a handful of flyers on the mat but her heart was pounding and, to put her mind at rest, she phoned Richard with a spurious question about funeral flowers.

'How's Scotland?' she said.

'Colder than London, if you can imagine that. We're in Glasgow just now. At my daughter's.' On cue, a child began singing in the background.

'Well, enjoy your visit,' she said, pleased with her newfound surveillance skills.

She set the heating back on 'constant' and wandered through the house, repossessing it. It was impossible to believe that, only six weeks ago, she hadn't known where her father kept his pyjamas, or which denture cleaner he used, or that he read Westerns.

The dining table was covered with labelled pocket-files containing correspondence and bills. 'Gas', 'Electricity', 'Pension', 'Tax'. A dozen or so in all. She was surprised that they'd been left out like this, but when she looked inside, she saw that the documents were all photocopies.

She turned her attention to the missing address book, scanning shelves and rummaging through drawers. There was no reason to think he'd hidden it so, if it were in the house, it shouldn't be hard to find. Drawing a blank in the dining room, she tried the sitting room and then the kitchen. *Nothing*. In all probability, he'd got rid of it (although that did seem a strange thing to do).

The filing cabinet in the junk room was locked but the silver key opened it as she'd known it would. A riffle through the suspended pockets released a not unpleasant whiff of pencil-sharpenings and damp paper, but none of them held anything as bulky as a book.

She moved on to the bedrooms. Richard's objectionable Fair Isle sweater was on the back of the chair in her father's room but, apart from that and a towelling dressing gown, he appeared to have taken everything with him. John had changed the bedding in 'her' room and her linen lay neatly folded on a chair. She'd neither seen nor spoken to John during their father's hospitalisation (or, in fact since their mother's funeral). She remembered him as being taller and more reserved than his older brother but it had become easier to lump them together and picture him as a clone of Richard.

A search of both rooms produced nothing unexpected except,

in the bottom of the wardrobe, an album containing holiday snaps of a couple with two young boys. The man – clearly recognisable as her father – looked to be in his thirties. The surprising thing was that the whole family was laughing. She eased a few photographs out of the old-fashioned mounts, but there was nothing to indicate where or when they'd been taken. Replacing them, she returned the album to the wardrobe, vaguely affronted that her father had kept no equivalent record of his second family.

Before abandoning her search, she gave the filing cabinet one more try, this time starting at the end of the alphabet and taking a closer look at the documents – the originals of the ones downstairs – contained in each buff-coloured pocket. 'Water', 'Tax', 'Pension', 'Mortgage' (paid off thirty years ago yet the paperwork still all there), 'Marriage'. *Marriage?*

'Marriage' contained two certificates. The first recorded the marriage of Philip Frederick Carey to Elspeth Mary Jamieson at St Brides Church, Dumfries, on 16th April, 1949. (Elspeth hadn't taken it with her as a memento, then.) The second showed that Philip Frederick Carey had married Anneliese Birgit Krüger at Wandsworth Register Office on 21st March, 1974.

Vivian frowned. No, no, no. Her parents were married in 1973 and she was born fifteen months later. Her birth certificate proving this was locked in her desk drawer.

She sat on the top stair, checking and rechecking the date. She'd imagined her parents' courtship to have been a conventional business – engagement, marriage, sex. In that order. It seemed she was mistaken. Premarital sex implied passion. Lust. Now *that* had never figured in her imaginings. What she'd always thought had been her parents' selfish decision to have a child had, within the space of minutes, become something entirely different. She had not been an old man's indulgence but an accident. A slip up.

Had they married for love or because her mother was pregnant? She couldn't imagine her mother blackmailing her father into it.

He belonged to a generation for whom 'failing to do the decent thing', was unthinkable. Perhaps he couldn't face the shame.

She made a quick calculation. Richard had been twenty-three, John twenty when she was born. They must have known their father was remarrying but had they known his new, young wife was pregnant?

When she was seven or eight, confined to bed with something or another, to occupy her, her mother had produced her wedding photographs. They were little more than snaps, and she remembered being disappointed that there had been no flounced white dress and no veil. She closed her eyes, trying to see them again. Her parents were standing in front of a big, grey building. Her mother wore a kaftan – blue, patterned with yellow flowers – and a white hat with a floppy brim. She was holding a bouquet of sunflowers. A kaftan. Perfect camouflage.

She folded the certificate and put it in her pocket then locked the filing cabinet.

Before leaving she checked that everything was as she'd found it – the central heating controls ('timed'); the lavatory seat (up); the back door (locked). Glancing out of the kitchen window, she saw that all that remained of the snowman was a mound of ice. The next time she stood here, her father would be a mound of ashes.

Gil wasted ten minutes in the bookshop, timing his arrival for eleven on the dot.

When Vivian opened the door, she was wearing her coat and gloves. 'We'll get coffee on the way,' she said.

No kiss. No 'I'm glad you're back'. Only the suggestion of a smile, then straight in as though he'd returned after collecting something from another room. He wondered whether it was her way of concealing emotion.

'Sounds good,' he said.

Snow still hung about in odd corners and crevices but the pavements were clear. They walked along in silence, she almost outpacing him with her long-legged stride, he working hard to keep up. He'd grown accustomed to her silences but this one seemed excessive.

'Are you okay?' he said.

'No,' she said, 'but it's not what you think.'

He caught her hand and they stopped walking. 'And what *do* I think?'

'You think I'm upset because my father died.'

'Aren't you?'

'No.'

'C'mon,' he said, pointing to the coffee shop on the far side of the road.

It was one of those fancy places where coffee was overpriced and the staff were patronising, but it was warm and he needed to get to the bottom of this.

'Tell me,' he said bracing himself for news that she was ill or had lost her job. When she told him that her parents had been married for only three months when she was born, he almost laughed. But she was obviously shaken.

'That was an awfully long time ago,' he said. 'Does it really matter?'

'How can you even ask that? They let me think I was planned. *Wanted.* But I wasn't.'

'You're being a bit harsh. They got married and stayed married. They wouldn't have done that if they hadn't wanted you, or cared for each other.'

'Why didn't she tell me?' she said.

The penny dropped. It was her mother's role in this that she was finding so hard to handle.

'Maybe she didn't think it was important.'

She glared at him.

334

'I know how much you admired your mother,' he said, 'but she was human, Vivian. You have to allow her that.'

They sat, looking everywhere but at each other. He didn't have the energy for this. He'd barely slept after the conversations with Janey. Thirty-something years ago, her parents had jumped the gun. So what? If she were determined to get steamed up about something, kids in Africa were dying of malaria. The planet was heating up. Polly was going to give his granddaughter away.

He stood up. 'Look. I'll head off home now. You've got things on your mind. We can do this some other time.'

He'd gone a couple of hundred yards by the time she caught up with him.

'Can we pretend that never happened?' she said.

'*What* never happened?' he said, slightly disappointed in himself for capitulating so readily.

She pushed her arm through his and they continued up the hill, commenting on window displays and hideous dogs and ridiculous hats, in an attempt to salvage their morning. But something had shifted – only slightly, yet enough to make him feel apprehensive.

At the junction of Gayton Road and Well Walk, the road widened. Yellow-brick terraces gave way to imposing, red-brick houses with pillared entrances and elaborate pediments. Magnificent London planes lined wide, raised pavements. They crossed the road and followed a well-worn path on to the Heath. This was a popular weekend destination – understandable considering that the majority of Londoners had no access to a garden. Clearly Vivian was familiar with the paths and tracks criss-crossing the Heath and she took the lead. The ground was still frozen and pockets of snow remained here and there. Scruffy, leafless trees and thickets of brambles lined their route. The track became narrower until they were forced to walk in single file and soon all that proved they weren't the only people left in the world was the distant shriek of a child and the occasional barking of a dog.

335

They'd been walking for ten minutes or so when the track opened into a clearing in the centre of which stood a massive tree.

'I thought you'd like this,' she said, pointing to its trunk.

At first he thought it was lichen but, as he got closer, he saw that the grey, circular patch, about two feet in diameter, consisted of gobs of chewing gum. He looked up into the branches of the craggy tree. 'It's an oak isn't it?'

'Yes. The locals call it "the gum tree."'

'What's the story?'

'Stick your gum on the tree and make a wish.'

'Sounds reasonable,' he said.

She pulled a pack of chewing gum from her pocket and held it out.

He had no idea why she'd brought him here, but seeing as she had, he might as well put on a show. Taking a stick of gum from the pack, he chewed methodically then placed the resulting gobbet of at the top of the circle and pushed it into the bark. With his thumb still on it, he closed his eyes, as a child would. *Don't make me choose between them.*

'Your turn,' he said.

She shook her head. 'Wishes are for dreamers.'

'You must have made wishes when you were a kid.'

'Yes. But they never came true.'

Leaving the unkempt woodland, they rejoined the Sunday strollers and continued north towards Kenwood House.

'What's happening about Irene?' she said.

'Nothing,' he said. 'It's gone quiet. But Kevin's heard a rumour that she's pulled this kind of stunt before. Some poor sod at Barts. I don't know the exact circumstances.'

'That's appalling.' She paused. 'I tried to get in touch with her when you were away. I thought maybe I could persuade her to withdraw her accusation.'

'That's sweet of you,' he said. 'What did she say?'

'Her phone kept going to voicemail. And she hasn't replied to my messages or texts.'

'That's not like our Irene,' he said.

'That's what I thought. In the end I phoned her office.'

'And?'

'She hasn't been to work since before Christmas,' she said.

'Is she ill?'

'They said they couldn't give me any details.' She paused. 'So I wrote to her. I used the excuse of telling her about my father. Don't worry. I didn't mention you.'

'Did she reply?' he said.

'Not so far, which I find unnerving. Death's an open goal for her. I expected to be inundated with scratch-and-sniff tracts and pithy epigrams. But nothing. Irene gone to ground is more disturbing than Irene on the rampage.' She wrinkled her nose. 'I wonder whether we should have been more—'

'We've both had a lot of stuff going on, Vivian,' he said.

'I know. And she really is a dreadful woman. All the same—'

'Hold it,' he said. 'She has a sister. She has work colleagues. She has her beloved minister and his posse of holy rollers. Irene Tovey has a whole gang of people looking out for her. She'll be okay.'

'Mmmm. I suppose you're right,' she said.

Vivian's uncertainty was out of character. But she'd been through an ordeal during the past weeks. Hospital visiting. Watching her father's deterioration and his death. And she still had to face the funeral. The odd wobble was understandable. (It would also account for her overreaction to the birth certificate.)

He clapped his gloved hands together. 'Come on. I'm getting chilly. Let's up the pace.'

They completed their circuit of the Heath, ending up at the Garden Gate at South End Green. The pub was hot and noisy, there was nowhere to sit and the food had sold out.

'Polly's talking about giving her baby for adoption,' he said.

This was neither the time or place for this – but that's what happened when he drank on an empty stomach.

'How d'you feel about that?' she said.

'Feel? Scared. Angry. Responsible. But mainly scared. Apparently my daughter hates my guts.'

Something trickled down his cheek and he realised that he was crying. 'Can we get out of here?' he said.

When they got back to her flat, she persuaded him to sit on the sofa and watch the tail end of a movie while she cooked cheese omelettes. After they'd finished eating, she showed him the two certificates, pointing out the offending dates. 'See?'

He regretted his earlier impatience. 'Your mother would have told you one day,' he said. 'On the face of it, she had another thirty years.'

'I suppose so. And I've been thinking. Maybe this was what Dad was trying to tell me.'

'Could well be,' he said. 'I'd like to come to the funeral, if it's okay with you.'

'Of course,' she said. 'Gil, would Polly and I be friends?'

He thought for a second. 'No. I don't think you would. She's flighty. Irrational. Wilful. In fact she's pretty obnoxious.'

She gave a sad little smile. 'And you love her, don't you?'

'I suppose I do.'

39

Gil's journey involved a bus to Waterloo, a train to a place he'd never heard of, a ten minute walk down a suburban street and a short cut across a recreation ground. He'd expected the North East Surrey Crematorium would be a new-ish building – '60s, maybe, painted magnolia, with a chimney masquerading as a bell tower. But what he found was a substantial Victorian edifice with buttresses, twin spires and stained glass windows. No chimney to be seen.

He arrived in good time and sat on a bench, skimming the newspaper he'd picked up on the train. Hearing voices, he looked up. Four people were coming from the opposite direction. As they drew nearer he recognised the Friels, Ottilie and one of the men from the party. Friel was holding forth, pointing at something on the roof of the building, and none of them spotted him. They stopped to check the noticeboard at the entrance, then went inside and, after a minute or two, Gil followed. He chose a seat several rows behind them and, unbuttoning his jacket, studied the service sheet. *Philip Frederick Carey. 7th August 1923 – 13th January 2010. RIP.*

It was all depressingly humdrum. Anodyne music. Muted décor. Sickly scented flowers (or air-freshener). A couple of attendants – looking alarmingly like bouncers – hovering near the entrance.

He had been fourteen when he'd attended his first funeral. The dead man was a workmate of his father's – a man whom he'd never met. 'Best see how it's done when you're not grieving for the poor sod in the box,' his father had said. Wise advice. He wished he'd done the same for his own children before they'd had to face their grandfather's funeral.

Inevitably, thoughts of death crept in. If he died tomorrow – it could happen – who would sort things out? There had to be a procedure for dealing with unclaimed bodies. He'd be disposed of by some means or another that was for sure. He might even end up here, in this vast cemetery. Now that would be weird. Of course he wouldn't be 'unclaimed' unless he'd totally pissed off every one he knew – more than likely, the way things were going. Maybe he should put something in writing.

Vivian watched the undertaker's men slide the coffin out of the hearse. It was pale not unlike laminate flooring and with gold-coloured handles, and three white wreaths balanced on top of it. The four men manoeuvred it deftly onto a trolley – waist height with spindly chrome legs – and propelled it towards the entrance. The whole thing looked insipid and comic, and to be honest, feminine. Decidedly inappropriate for the old man who lay inside. But having opted out of those decisions, she had no right to criticise. Besides, the whole lot would be gone within hours.

She'd had no response to her obituary letters and she'd fretted all week that no one would come. Howard had reminded her that funerals weren't RSVP affairs, and that it was simply a matter of crossing one's fingers that someone turned up on the day. As they followed the coffin down the aisle, she was relieved, therefore, to see a handful of people – Gil, Howard and Cara, Ottilie and Ralph, Mrs Francks (how had she found her way here?) and a group of elderly strangers – already in their places.

The service was formulaic, the singing pathetically thin. A man who had never met her father said complimentary things about someone she didn't recognise. When he instructed them to 'take a few minutes to remember the man you knew and cared for', she wondered whether anyone here *had* known or cared for Philip Carey. Finally, accompanied by mundane music and the hum of an electric motor, curtains surrounded the coffin.

The small congregation was steered out through a side entrance, into a courtyard where piles of wreaths indicated that this was one of many funerals today. A young man in a dark suit was in the process of placing the family wreaths alongside one other, the card on which read 'Deepest sympathy from all at Friel Dravid', Ottilie's influence unmistakable in its deep reds and purples.

It turned out that the strangers – two couples and an old man – were ex-neighbours of her parents. They'd spotted the obituary in the local paper. When Richard thanked them for coming and invited them back for refreshments, they declined, explaining that Ken, who had driven them down, wanted to get home before the rush hour. After a few minutes, Ottilie and Ralph made their excuses and headed off, leaving Howard, Cara, Mrs Francks and Gil as the only customers for the sandwiches sitting on the table at Farleigh Road.

'You'll come back to the house?' Vivian said, half-hoping they wouldn't.

'Of course we will, darling,' Cara said. 'Who needs a lift?'

John stepped in. 'We'll be going in the limousine. If you could bring Mrs Francks and…' He raised his eyebrows and nodded towards Gil.

'Gil. Gil Thomas,' he said.

Vivian guessed from Gil's face that he was expecting her to elaborate but she couldn't put the right words together and the moment passed.

As Howard led the little party towards the car park, Gil turned and raised his hand.

The return drive through Morden and Colliers Wood seemed never ending. Vivian stared out of the window, detaching herself from the Scottish foursome and their prattle. 'That went off well, don't you think?' 'Not a bad turnout, considering.' 'I wouldn't want to live here, on this busy road, would you?' Now and again, when they stopped at traffic lights, she caught the eye of a pedestrian whose pitying, grateful expression showed relief that that they weren't in the funeral car.

341

When they reached Farleigh Road, Howard's car was already outside the house. Richard ushered everyone in whilst John dealt with coats. Joan and Penny ('the wee wifies' – John's phrase) took orders for tea and coffee.

Vivian watched the facets of her life collide. The Friels, like a Hollywood couple on a mercy mission. Richard, challenged by their urbanity, getting more pompous by the minute. Gil doing his best to fade into the background. The 'wifies' shocked yet fascinated by Cara's bad language. Mrs Francks gamely chomping her way through salmon sandwiches. Occasionally Gil glanced in her direction, but she ignored his unspoken invitation to come and stand next to him. She didn't know why but she just couldn't.

Cara cornered her. 'I didn't realise you and Gil had become such good friends.'

'It's been tough,' Vivian said, 'and he's been incredibly supportive.'

'Well all that's behind you now, darling,' Cara said, disposing of Gil with a wave of her hand. 'I hear you're off to Cologne soon.'

'Yes. In a couple of weeks.'

'How exciting. I can't wait to visit.'

Vivian and Howard had finalised the arrangements yesterday. She hadn't told Gil yet. But it shouldn't come as a surprise. He'd always known she was going to do this.

A headache was starting and she went upstairs to find something for it. The bathroom cabinet still contained her father's first-aid supplies. Cough syrup had oozed from a bottle and the box of paracetamol tablets was glued to the shelf.

She began dropping things into the waste bin. A discoloured crepe bandage. A tin of Germolene. Athlete's Foot powder. A squeezed-out tube of Anthisan. She tipped liquids – Optrex, calamine lotion, TCP – down the lavatory and flushed several times to get rid of the stench of antiseptic. At the very back of the shelf was a tube of Savlon. She was about to toss it in the bin when she noticed the use-by date. 04/2005. Three months before her mother died. *God.* Her mother had bought this. Her mother had held this in her hand.

Vivian remembered many details of that July day. Ants swarming on the front path. Her father polishing his shoes. Her own hands holding a lace-edged handkerchief. Strangers laughing in the kitchen. There must have been a coffin, and cars, and weeping, and wreaths, but when that had been going on, she'd vacated her body and gone somewhere else – she couldn't say where.

The stairs creaked and she shoved the tube into her pocket.

'Vivian? Are you up here?' It was Gil.

'I'm clearing the medicine cabinet,' she said.

He must think her mad. This was her father's wake and she was in the bathroom chucking things out. But all he said was 'Can't you slip away? We could catch a movie. Or get something to eat. Whatever you fancy.'

That's what he said, but she knew he meant *can't we get back to how we were* and she wasn't ready to deal with that.

'I can't,' she said. 'There's family stuff to discuss.'

After he'd gone, she realised she hadn't asked about his daughter.

The others were shaping up to leave and Friel offered to drop Gil somewhere.

'Thanks, but I could do with a walk,' Gil said. He couldn't face any more of the man's condescension. Of course Friel was in love with Vivian. It was obvious from the way he kept putting his arm around her and looking at her whenever he said something funny.

He wondered when she would get around to telling him the Cologne date had been fixed. On the return drive, he and Mrs Francks had ridden in the back of the car. (He'd expected her to twig that he was the man who had offered to clear the snow from her path – but of course *that* man had been Polish.) Cara Friel had treated the journey as a travelling cocktail party, playing hostess and making small talk. *Do you have family in London, Mrs Francks? How was your Christmas, Gil? Shame there weren't more people at the service. Oh, and wasn't it good news that Vivian felt up to starting in Cologne.*

He'd known she was lined up to run the German office. She'd explained about the flat and how she would return home regularly to check her place and visit her father. But now he was dead, it seemed, there was nothing – *no one* – to stop her from going. To be realistic, their relationship might stagger on for a few months. He'd end up arranging his life around her schedule, on the off-chance that when she was in London she might spare him a moment. The disappointment – the resentment – when she didn't would be destructive. Let's face it, he'd come to London to escape that sort of crap.

He got in to find two emails from Janey, the first was rambling and melodramatic, filled with spite. Apparently this adoption crisis was entirely his fault. Everything had been going smoothly until he turned up. And while they were at it, why *had* he run out on his children? His selfishness was to blame for Polly's going off the rails. In ten years time, when – demented with self-loathing – she flung herself off Sydney Harbour Bridge, he would be responsible for that, too.

He assumed Janey had been drunk when she'd written it. If not, she was out of her mind.

The second mail, sent six hours later, was short and to the point. Polly had been keeping a list of girl names, adding to it whenever she came across one that appealed to her. Janey had just found the list in the waste paper basket, ripped into tiny pieces. He had to agree that this was proof she was going to give the baby away.

Destroying baby names was the kind of chilling act that figured in psycho-dramas. But leaving the debris where it could be spotted? *Nah.* This was part of Polly's wind-up campaign, along with telling him his mother was 'losing it'. Either way, what the fuck did Janey expect him to do?

He switched on the television, flicking from channel to channel, but nothing held his attention. He checked the time. Polly should be at home now. He could ring her. But what would he say? *Please don't give your baby away?* Yeah, brilliant. That should do the trick.

He'd promised her that motherhood wouldn't mean putting her life on hold. Of course that was twaddle. A baby was a burden. Physically. Mentally. Economically. (Look at Kevin and his wife – two of them to one scrap of baby, yet they were struggling to stay sane.) No matter how much help she had from Janey and the sainted bloody Alan, no matter if some day a nice fatherly guy came along, this kid would always be her responsibility. What he couldn't explain – and wouldn't even try – was that this burden would be far outweighed by unconditional love. What parent wouldn't take a bullet for their child?

Is that why you walked out on us, Dad?

40

They met at the solicitors' office in Balham.

After introductions and condolences, Sonja Olsen, whom Vivian placed in her mid-forties, ran through a checklist of what needed to be done before they could apply for probate.

'It's very straightforward,' she said. 'You'll be able to do most of it yourselves.'

She held up a large cream envelope. 'I have your father's will here.' She turned to Richard. 'You're his executor, Mr Carey. Did he give you a copy?'

'As a matter of fact he didn't,' Richard said. 'He informed me you were holding it, but we were surprised not to find any reference to it amongst his papers. Is that going to be a problem?'

They'd talked about this last night, along with what should happen to the contents of the house and what Vivian was owed for utility bills. Despite a trawl through the filing cabinet – Vivian holding her breath for fear they noticed that the marriage certificate was missing – they'd found neither the will nor any reference to it.

'It's customary,' the solicitor said 'but in some cases clients prefer their wishes to remain private until after their death. It's a personal choice.'

She handed Richard the envelope. 'Maybe you'd care to look at it while you're here. If there's anything you don't understand, I'll do my best to clear it up.'

She installed them in a quiet room, and the receptionist brought a tray of coffee. Richard made a performance of opening the envelope, running his pocketknife under the flap, pulling out a sheaf of paper with a theatrical flourish. Along with the original will, there were three copies, each of their names written in the top corner in their father's slanting script.

'I suggest I read it aloud whilst you follow your copies,' Richard said.

He cleared his throat and began reading, projecting his voice as if he were addressing a board meeting. Vivian hadn't given much thought to the will. She'd vaguely assumed that it was a formality and that everything would be divided between the three of them. But after a paragraph or two of standard preamble, it became apparent that it wasn't going to be at all like that.

'"I bequeath to Vivian Johanna Carey, daughter of my late wife Anneliese Birgit Carey (née Krüger), free of all taxes and death duty, the sum of five thousand pounds."'

Vivian stared at the page. *Daughter of my late wife*. What an odd way to put it.

Richard must have thought so too because he stopped reading, the absence of his voice making way for the *purr, click; purr, click* of a photocopier somewhere nearby.

And then she understood. There was nothing odd about it. It was the truth. The wonderful, obvious truth. She was not Philip Carey's daughter. He was not her father. To be absolutely sure, she re-read the whole sentence, checking each syllable of each word. And, as she did so, the cords binding her to him stretched and stretched until they snapped.

Richard and John must have worked it out too. Silent and motionless, they watched her, waiting to see how she would react, no doubt expecting her to fall to pieces. When she didn't, John began fidgeting, flipping through the photocopied pages.

He cleared his throat. 'Maybe we should take a few minutes to…'

'No,' she said, switching her gaze between these men who it seemed were, miraculously, no longer her half-brothers. 'Carry on please, Richard.'

Richard rattled through the rest of it, stumbling over the antiquated terminology, plainly desperate to get it done. It didn't take long. The estate was to be shared, equally, between 'my sons, Richard James Carey and John Philip Carey'.

'Did you know?' she said when he'd finished.

Richard looked as though he were going to vomit. 'Of course we didn't. And besides we shouldn't jump to conclusions.'

'Oh, come on,' she said.

John took it up. 'Dad…I mean…maybe he left some kind of explanation. We should check.'

'Check what?' she said.

'Well, we ought at least to—'

'Check that I have no valid claim on his estate?'

'That's below the belt, Vivian,' he said.

Richard signalled his brother to be quiet. 'Assuming this is true, he must have had good reason to keep it to himself.'

'How about this?' she said. 'When my mother died, he lost his support system. It suited him to have me stick around. He knew if I learned the truth, I'd never go there again.'

'Dad could be selfish but you're making him out to be a scheming tyrant,' Richard said.

'It's feasible,' she said.

'Maybe,' John said. 'But when it boils down to it, it was your mother's place to tell you.'

Vivian couldn't have that. 'She failed to tell me and then she had the nerve to die. Another black mark for Mum.'

'I didn't mean it like that,' John said.

'He made this will after my mother died, knowing I wouldn't learn the truth until today. You think that's acceptable? Because I don't. It's cowardly. Spiteful.' She couldn't breathe properly and she was near to tears. 'He must really have hated me.'

As her composure slipped further she sensed the men closing ranks. Determined not to allow them the satisfaction of seeing her lose control, she excused herself and went to find Sonja Olsen.

'All done?' the solicitor said, looking up from her papers.

'Not quite.'

'Something I can help with?'

'Did he leave anything else?' Vivian said. 'A letter? Or another document?'

The solicitor picked up a file from a stack on the floor. Taking out a fat manila envelope, she checked the label. 'These are the deeds to the house in Farleigh Road.' She peered into the file. 'No. Nothing else here. Is something missing?'

'The thing is,' Vivian said, 'the thing is, it appears that Philip Carey isn't – wasn't – my father.'

Sonja Olsen looked expectant, as though waiting for the punchline of a joke.

Vivian offered her the will. 'I'd be interested in your opinion.'

From the first-floor window, she watched Balham going about its Wednesday business. A white van was parked on the pavement, two policemen talking to the driver. A mother was pushing an empty buggy and carrying a screaming toddler. A young man in shirtsleeves hurried out of Starbucks, balancing four cups in a cardboard tray. Sketchy clouds were thinning, revealing patches of blue sky. Anyone who didn't know might think it an ordinary day.

'Well, it would certainly seem…' Miss Olsen broke off mid-sentence as if Vivian might find the rest of it too hurtful.

'John thinks I'm jumping to conclusions,' Vivian said, 'but what with "daughter of my late wife", and the bequest, I can't see any other explanation.'

'I take it you are in possession of your birth certificate?'

'Yes. I was looking at it only a matter of days ago. Philip Carey's definitely registered as my father.'

Sonja Olsen took refuge in the legal technicalities. 'That proves nothing except his willingness to accept paternal responsibility. Of course there's always the option of DNA testing if you wish to challenge—'

'You don't understand,' Vivian said. 'I spent my childhood – my whole life, in fact – wondering what I'd done to make my father dislike me. Can you imagine how that feels? How it's affected me? Discovering he's *not* my father…I don't know…this sounds melodramatic but it's like being reborn. Does that make sense?'

The solicitor nodded but looked uneasy.

Vivian smiled. 'Don't worry. I shall be fine. Honestly.'

Sonja Olsen paused for a second before resuming her mantle of professionalism. 'Well if you do have any further questions or want to discuss anything – anything at all – please don't hesitate to get in touch.'

When Vivian returned to the room, the men had donned their overcoats. They were doing their best to look benevolent but they resembled a couple of conspirators.

'Any joy?' Richard said.

'He left no other documents, if that's what you mean by joy,' she said.

'We thought we'd go back to Farleigh Road,' John said. 'Work out where we take it from here.'

'Take what?' she said. 'I don't want to take anything anywhere.'

Richard put a hand on her shoulder. 'We understand how you must be feeling, Vivian.'

She took a step backwards, out of his reach. 'In that case, you'll understand why I shall open a bottle of champagne this evening.'

Vivian had planned to go straight to work once the business with the will was done. But that was out of the question now. Howard. Ottilie. Ralph. Wanting to know about her 'inheritance'. Guessing how much the house might sell for. Before facing them, she must work out a strategy and, on her way to the Tube, she contacted Ottilie.

'I have things to sort out,' she said, which was true. 'Tell Howard I'll be in first thing tomorrow.' She ended the call before Ottilie could ask any questions.

She left the crisp, bright day and descended to the platform, the elation that had kept her going for the past hour or so leaching away, leaving her drained of feeling. The overhead matrix flicked away the minutes until the next train was due and she fixed her eyes on it, waiting for some sort of emotion to engulf her as it surely must.

When the train arrived there were plenty of empty seats and she chose one mid-carriage. She seldom had the opportunity to study her fellow travellers, crammed together as they generally were in the rush hour crush, everyone resolutely minding their own business. She glanced around. On the adjacent seat, a young man flipped through a printout of a Powerpoint presentation. *A job interview?* Opposite, two middle-aged women, wearing too much make-up and cheap jewellery. *Probably heading for Oxford Street.* Standing near the door, a man in a padded coat, tracksuit bottoms and dusty, toe-capped boots with a hefty-looking toolbox on the floor between his feet. *Plumber? Electrician?*

Her gaze wandered from one person to another, and occasionally to her own image reflected dimly in the carriage window opposite where she sat. What did these people make of her? An unfair question when she no longer knew what to make of herself.

The train stopped at Clapham South and several passengers got on. Amongst them was a man with a child in a buggy. He sat on one of the flap-down seats near the door, manoeuvring the buggy so that it was close to him. It was stuffy in the train and the child – Vivian had no idea how old it was – one? older? – muffled in winter clothing, struggled to escape, arching its back and tugging at a red knitted hat. The hat came off came, revealing spindly plaits and hooped earrings. *(A girl.)* Nothingy-blue eyes. Pasty face with patches of dry skin on cheeks and chin. Crusty nostrils. A plain child.

The man unclipped the harness and scooped his daughter – it

had to be his daughter – onto his knee. Steadying her with one hand, he deftly removed her coat and cardigan with the other and stowed them in the buggy, all the while murmuring reassurance. 'There you go. How's that? Better?'

The child stared solemnly up into his face. He bent and kissed her on her forehead, and she raised her hand and brushed his lips. He opened his mouth and she inserted her fingers and he pretended to nibble them, drawing his lips over his teeth to protect the tiny digits. Vivian expected the child to giggle or complain but instead she nestled into her father's shoulder, her eyes fixed on his chin. He nibbled gently and soon her eyelids dipped. When it was obvious she was asleep, he removed her hand from his mouth but kept hold of it.

He must have sensed Vivian watching him from the other side of the carriage because he glanced across at her and smiled, as if they shared a secret. She smiled back, wishing that she could tell him that he was giving his plain-faced daughter a wonderful gift.

As soon as she got in, she took out the wooden box in which she kept her mother's things. There wasn't much. A wristwatch with a tiny face and delicate gold strap. A purse. A couple of passport photographs. An appointment diary with pathetically few entries. A pair of sunglasses. An unremarkable selection of jewellery. She'd studied these items dozens of times and knew that she wouldn't find the answer here.

Nor did she think it – whatever form it might take – could be at Farleigh Road. She'd rifled through pretty much everything when she was there. Of course there was the possibility that he (what should she call him now?) had hidden something in the attic or beneath the floorboards. If that were the case, she would never find it because she would never go there again.

Taking the tube of Savlon, which she'd salvaged yesterday, she dropped it in with the other things, and she was returning the box to the cupboard when it came to her. *This* was what he'd been trying to tell her as he lay dying in that claustrophobic room.

As a small child, she'd known that he *couldn't* be her father. For one thing, she looked nothing like him. (Nor like her mother, but that relationship wasn't in dispute.) He'd tolerated her, but hadn't loved or even been interested in her. To be fair, he'd never abused her, unless imposing his hands-off Victorian standards and depriving her of the unconditional love to which any child was entitled could be termed abuse. She'd never confided this knowledge to a single soul. They would have thought her wicked or mad. Worse than that, it might have got back to her mother thus hurting the only person who loved her.

At some point, her child's eye view of her situation had become less black-and-white and this conviction had been replaced by resignation and resolution to keep out of his way. On the whole this had worked but she saw now that she had simply been marking time until she could leave home and escape his grinding censure.

Although today's disclosure didn't excuse Philip Carey's treatment of her, it went some way to account for it. What she didn't understand was why, even when she was old enough to deal with it, her mother had failed to tell her the truth. John had been right, of course. She should have told her. She must have been conscious of the damaging effect his conduct was having on her daughter. The truth, no matter what it was, would have been preferable. But whatever else happened, she must keep faith with her mother. Trust that she had, for whatever reason, made a good decision in marrying – and sticking with – Philip Carey. Doubt her mother and her life would have no datum line.

She closed her eyes and cast her mind back. Maybe she'd missed something – a hint or a clue.

There had been something odd. She couldn't recall why this had come up but, not long before her mother's death, they'd discussed

353

the choices available to women these days. (Career. Motherhood. Marriage. That sort of thing.) During the conversation, she'd asked her mother why she hadn't gone back to work once she – Vivian – had started school. 'Your father provided for us, and I looked after us. That's how we'd agreed it would be.'

How we'd agreed it would be.

The obvious reason for an agreement between a pregnant woman and an old man was that the woman needed respectability and security, and the old man needed a housekeeper. *Surely* that couldn't be it. Things like that happened in Hardy novels not in Tooting. Not in 1974. After all if her mother had felt herself incapable of raising a child alone, she had family in Germany. Single mothers wouldn't have been *that* frowned upon – even in Bavaria. On top of that, to remain with this old man for thirty-odd years…

Her thoughts raced, scattering in all directions. Had her birth father been the love of her mother's life? Or a one night stand? Darker possibilities lurked were she brave enough to go there. Rape. Incest. Human life came about as readily from acts of violence as acts of love.

She took a notebook from her bag and began jotting down thoughts and questions as they occurred to her – anything which might cast light on this revelation. It was the same notebook she'd been using in A&E, when Gil had insisted she eat his crisps.

Gil. If he were here, he'd laugh and accuse her of treating this like a forensic investigation which, of course, it was. 'You'll be setting up an incident room next.' That's what he'd say.

She put the notebook down, found her phone and scrolled through her contacts. But when Gil's number showed on the screen, she hesitated. Tell him now and he'd offer suggestions. Solutions. He'd assume he could put himself in her place. But how could he do that when she wasn't anywhere? She would tell him. But not yet. Not until she'd worked out where she was now and where she wanted to be.

41

According to Kevin's big book of rules, Gil wasn't eligible for time off to attend Carey's funeral and he'd been forced to call in sick.

'Don't push your luck,' Kevin said next morning. 'They've got their eye on you. What with *one thing and another.*'

That was as near as Kevin ever got to a reprimand. He couldn't handle confrontation and to avoid it he'd perfected a nod-and-wink technique. Despite having assured Gil there was no need to worry, it looked like he planned to hold the Irene Tovey business over him until it was formally settled.

Gil had several other things on his mind, one of which was the letter in his pocket. His mother had written it the day he left – around the time his plane was taking off.

Dearest Gillon,

I hope you are over your jet lag and that the weather in London has improved.

It was lovely to have you here this week. Thank you for doing all those jobs. It is such a relief not to have that tap dripping all the time.

It's hard for teenagers to express their feelings but I know Chris and Adam liked having you around. I hope they won't stop coming over to see me.

I think you should know Louise and Dan are going through a bumpy patch. She didn't want to worry you with it so please don't say anything if you speak to her. I am sure it will blow over. I was surprised when she offered to throw the party but she was determined to have a family get together. She is very fond of you, you know.

Now we have the new baby to look forward to. Me a great gran. Imagine that.

That's all for now. Take care of yourself, won't you? All I ever
wanted was for my children to be healthy and happy.
Ever your loving Mum. xxx

What a killer.

In the course of hunting for a screwdriver, Gil arrived at the
conclusion that he had too much stuff. Before he knew it, he'd
filled three black bags with junk – impressive for a man who, in
theory, had few possessions. The lack of clutter inspired him to
give the flat a good going over. He even unearthed the spray polish
he'd splashed out on when he was renovating his chair.

Cleaning occupied his time but not his thoughts. Vivian had all
but ignored him after the funeral. He didn't think she'd set out to
hurt him, all the same it hadn't been great. He could kid himself
it was because she was distressed, or cross with him for dismissing
her parents' shotgun marriage as no big deal. He doubted it was
either. It had been okay to take him to Friel's party – the stand-in
for the boyfriend who'd gone skiing. The bomb had still been news
at the time making him something of a novelty. Now that the
bomb and Mellor were history, her friends would start asking why
this Aussie bloke kept showing up.

He'd seen her only twice since returning from Coffs Harbour –
their walk on the Heath, and at the funeral – but that was enough
to prove that they were slipping away from each other. She'd
complained that he and she were floating around in a bubble. She'd
wanted to 'label' their relationship and he'd talked her out of it. He
regretted that now. It was hard to ignore something which had a
name, or lose something which had a label attached to it.

Then, as he was thinking about going to bed, she rang. She had
something to tell him, something she couldn't discuss on the
phone. Was he free tomorrow? Her tone was oddly upbeat for a
woman whom he feared was about to dump him.

'Why don't you come here?' he said. 'I promise it'll be tidier than last time. And warmer. If you're good, I'll let you choose the music.'

'Midday?'

'Perfect,' he said.

He stood at the window, looking down at the street, expecting her to come round the corner. At twelve-ten, he texted her his address in case she'd forgotten. By twelve-twenty, he had her crushed beneath a bus. Then suddenly there she was, striding towards the house, carrying a bunch of flowers.

He waited until she rang the bell before going down, not wanting her to know that he'd been watching out for her.

'Yellow for wisdom,' she said holding out the bunch of daffodils.

She had painted her nails. Nothing outrageous, in fact not far off their natural colour. (Polly's nails had been dark blue. It looked as if her fingers had been crushed in a car door.) But Vivian – *his* Vivian – didn't paint her nails.

He took her coat and draped it on a coat hanger, then found a jug for the flowers. Slanting sunlight fell across the freshly laundered bedspread. The room smelled of coffee and furniture polish. What with the tidy flat and the flowers, it seemed very grown up and weirdly unreal.

'Sorry I haven't been in touch,' she said.

'I expect you've been busy. There must be a lot to sort out.'

'Not at all. In fact I don't have to sort *anything* out.'

'No?' he said.

'No. Because…' She clapped her hands and smiled triumphantly, like a schoolgirl who'd proved the teacher wrong. 'Philip Carey wasn't my father.'

Before he had time to question this astonishing statement, she was telling him the story, her words spilling out in a breathless torrent. When she'd finished, she went through it again, as if a

357

second telling made it doubly credible, this time showing him the will, running her finger along the critical words.

'You know what this means?' she said. 'I never have to think about Philip Carey again. I never have to see Richard or John Carey again. Or set foot in that horrid house ever again. You can't imagine how good that feels.'

Her cheeks were flushed and she was talking too quickly. His instinct was to try to calm her down. To hold her and stroke her as one might stroke an agitated animal. But she was so fired up she would probably freak out if he touched her.

'When did you find out?' he said.

'Wednesday morning.'

'That's three days ago,' he said.

'I was going to phone you, but then I realised I have to work this thing out for myself.'

'It's quite something to work out,' he said.

'I thought so at first. But then I realised that I don't have to work *anything* out. I don't have to *do* anything. I don't have to *tell* anyone. As far as the world's concerned, I shall be no different.'

'Right,' he said, 'I hear what you say but…'

'But?'

'It's too theoretical. Clinical. Okay. The world needn't know. But *you* know, and you can't fool yourself into believing nothing's changed.'

'There,' she said, 'that's exactly my point.'

'Excuse me?'

'I tell you and right away you're telling me what I should do and how I should feel.'

'That's not fair, Vivian,' he said. 'I only want what's best for you.' It sounded trite. Patronising.

'Good.' She closed her eyes as if she were in rapture. 'I feel fantastic. Clean. Light. Free.'

'Well that's wonderful,' he said. 'I'm delighted for you. Really I am.'

'I hoped you would be.' She stretched, reaching up, her fingertips almost touching the ceiling, smiling as though she'd woken from a satisfying sleep. 'I need the loo.'

'Carry on. I'll start lunch. Steak and salad okay?'

Now that he had a few minutes to organise his thoughts, his primary feeling was one of concern. She was being totally irrational which, considering her usual cool-headedness, was disturbing. This revelation vindicated those weird feelings she'd had about Carey but, by anyone's reckoning, she'd received earth-shattering news. The ramifications were mind-blowing. Surely she couldn't imagine something so fundamental could be dismissed so lightly. She didn't really believe she could carry on as before.

But the last thing she needed at the moment was someone to drag her off her cloud nine. He'd simply have to go along with her for the time being.

She returned and, while the steak was cooking, they compared recipes for vinaigrettes. He opened a bottle of wine and she helped set the table. It was like any run-of-the-mill Saturday lunchtime.

They had started eating when her phone rang. 'It's Richard,' she said, rejecting the call and tossing her phone back into her bag. 'He can't accept that I'm delighted that Philip Carey, Farleigh Road and the two of them are nothing to do with me. I've decided not to talk to him or John ever again. I've wasted too much time being Philip Carey's daughter. Now that I'm *not*, I refuse to waste any more.'

She drained her wineglass and refilled it. 'Can we talk about something else, please?'

'Sure.' He sliced through his steak, watching the pink juices puddle on the plate. 'I gather you're off to Cologne soon.'

'Yes,' she said. 'A week on Monday.'

So cool. So matter-of-fact. She didn't even ask how he knew.

'Looking forward to it?' he said.

'Yes, I am. The timing couldn't be better.'

They talked about protests in Egypt. The arrest of a neighbour for the Bristol girl's murder. Floods around Brisbane. Three short weeks ago they'd slept, side by side, in front of the fire. Now they were strangers.

Whilst he struggled through his steak, she cleared her plate.

'You're not hungry?' she said.

'I had a late breakfast,' he lied.

He carried the dishes into the kitchen and opened a fresh pack of coffee. The kettle was boiling, making its usual racket, and she said something he didn't catch.

'Sorry?' he said, stepping back into the living room.

She was facing away from him, lowering the stylus on to an LP. Billie Holliday. 'God Bless the Child'. She couldn't know what that voice, this track, did to his gut.

She turned and held his gaze just as she had when they were making the snowman and he took her photograph. 'You have to go back to Coffs Harbour.'

'Do I?' he said. He could feel a gob of steak wedged in his gullet.

'Of course you do.'

'Why's that?'

'Because I had the father I hated,' she said, 'and Polly doesn't have the father she loves.'

He wanted to laugh but he could see that she was serious. 'Oh come on, Vivian. What kind of cockeyed logic is that? You know it doesn't work that way.'

'How *does* it work?'

'Well there's certainly no divine being sitting up in the sky, weighing out fathers on some celestial scales of justice. As it happens you're wrong. Polly doesn't love me. She despises me. And she's bloody stubborn. Once she's made up her mind, nothing will shift her. My going back wouldn't change a thing. It'd probably make it worse.'

'You can't know that,' she said.

'I know she didn't ask me to go back.'

'Were you listening? *Really* listening?'

He took a step towards her, hoping to put an end to the exchange, but she held up her hand to stop him.

'So you're telling me you don't intend doing anything,' she said. 'You'll carry on as if nothing has happened.'

He couldn't let that pass. 'Hold on. Something pretty fundamental's happened to you too but you're allowed to do nothing and I'm not?'

'Our situations are entirely different. You have it in your power to change the future. I can't change the past. Your decision affects half a dozen people. Mine affects no one but myself.'

How carelessly she trampled on his heart.

She pulled her coat off the hanger. 'If I stay any longer, we'll fall out. And I couldn't bear that.'

'Really?' he said. 'You seem more than happy to get rid of me.'

'I didn't say your leaving would make me happy. I said you have to go.'

That evening, Gil visited most of the pubs in Kentish Town. When he finally made it home, he played his way through his Miles collection until Oskar knocked the door, pointing out it was past midnight. Gil apologised, invited him in, and they listened to Coltrane and finished off the dregs of a bottle of brandy.

Next morning he bumped into Feray in the shop.

'You look terrible,' she said. 'And what's that all about?' She pointed to the packet of cigarettes in his hand.

Before he knew it, they were in her flat, drinking sweet gritty coffee, and he was telling her about Polly's threat to give away his granddaughter.

'Does she really mean it?' she said.

'Poll's always been a drama queen,' he said. 'But she's not a kid any more. This is a real life changer. The problem is, she's boxed

361

herself into a corner. Time's running out and I'm scared she'll go through with it.'

'You and she talked?' she said.

'Yes. A couple of times. To be honest it wasn't great. She was frosty to say the least.'

'What did she say about the baby?'

'She's worried she won't make a good mother. But this adoption business only flared up after I left. Janey's blaming me, of course. She insists everything was trotting along nicely until I turned up.'

Melissa appeared, still wearing her pyjamas. When she saw him she smiled, apparently unfazed by his reappearance in their kitchen after so many weeks.

'Hi, Gil,' she said then turned to her mother. 'I can't find my black leggings, Mum.'

Feray sighed and went to address the crisis leaving Gil thinking how easy it was to talk to her and, bearing in mind their history, how generous she was to listen.

'All sorted?' he said when she returned.

'In her drawer, of course.'

'I've been banging on about myself,' he said. 'How are you? Still seeing that guy?'

'Yes, I am. And we're still taking it slowly.'

'That's terrific.'

'And your girlfriend?' There was no resentment in her voice.

'Vivian was never my girlfriend,' he said. 'I fooled myself into thinking she might be. She needed me for a while but now she doesn't.'

'I'm not sure I like this Vivian. She sounds selfish to me. But if she's the one you wanted, I'm sorry it didn't work out. More coffee?'

She refilled the long-handled copper jug and set it on the gas ring. 'You once told me you came to London to live your dream. Maybe it's time for a new dream.'

'Maybe.'

When Feray said that she'd love to have the portrait back, he knew she harboured no hard feelings towards him.

Kevin took his resignation pretty well. Gil had implied that his flit was down to 'women trouble' which ensured Kevin was on side, and which was true – although not in Kevin's terms.

'Might as well square the books mate,' Kevin said, rigging the dates so that three weeks' notice looked like the statutory four. 'Once the heat's off, you might want to come back.'

42

'I wasn't sure you'd want to come,' she said.

'Don't be daft.'

He took off his coat and she saw that he was wearing the blue shirt and bow tie he'd worn when they went to the Roundhouse.

'You look nice,' she said.

'Thanks.' He tugged the folds of the tie. 'Mmmm. Something smells good.'

'Goulash,' she said.

She'd wondered whether he'd want to risk another meeting and, rather than phoning, she'd emailed to give him time to consider. Her first attempt had included an apology and something about not parting on bad terms. But in the end she'd kept it short. *Come to supper on Saturday? V x*

'How was your week?' he said.

'I was fine. Richard's stopped calling, thank God. Work was manic – but that's how I like it. It's good to get back on track. Mrs Sachs came in for a coffee. She's going to keep an eye on the flat and put my mail to one side. And I've made a list of what to take. Just clothes really. Everything else is there.'

'So you're all set,' he said.

'I think so.'

She poured two measures of whisky. 'Have you heard from your family?'

'I had a letter from my mum. She says all she wants is for me to be happy. I don't even think she's being ironic.' He cleared his throat. 'Like you said, I've got to give it a go. Babies don't stick to a schedule so I need to get on with it. I'm leaving in two weeks.'

'You're doing the right thing,' she said, feeling a tug of regret. 'Sorry I've been so horrid.'

'No. Don't apologise. I appreciate your honesty. I needed the wake-up call.'

The flat was filled with the scent of paprika and caraway and, if she closed her eyes, she was a child, helping her mother set the table for Sunday lunch.

'I've started writing a story,' she said.

He looked puzzled. 'I didn't know you write.'

'I don't. But sometimes we need stories to help us understand things. See what you think.

'There was once a tall man with black hair, grey eyes and narrow feet. He was kind and clever. He loved drawing and numbers and finding out how things worked. One day he met a young German woman. I'm not sure where. Paris or Berlin or London. Anyway, they fell in love. Deeply, deeply in love. Then something terrible happened – I don't know what – and he disappeared. Vanished. Forever. Not long after that the woman discovered she was pregnant. Then…I think she must have gone a bit crazy.'

His eyes were fixed on her face and she knew he was waiting to see how she would tackle the next part – the unfeasible part – of her story.

'That's as far as I've got,' she said. 'It'll do for now.'

He reached out and touched her hair. And somehow, without discussion, they accepted their separate futures.

After supper, she showed him the letter that had arrived two days earlier.

Dear Miss Carey,
I hope you don't mind but I opened your letter to my sister. I'm dealing with Irene's mail as she's not up to it at the minute. She's not been at all well and the doctors don't want her being on her own, so she's staying with us here in Maidenhead. I don't know how much she told you, but she's not had an easy life. I think the terrible

business of the bomb affected her more than we all realised. We're
crossing our fingers that she will soon be better. She often spoke to
me about your kindness. Thank you.
Best wishes
Lillian Dobson

'It's sad,' Vivian said.

'It is,' Gil said, 'but I can't say it comes as a shock.' He handed back the letter. 'Her sister sounds like a nice woman. It's some responsibility she's taken on.'

'Yes. I hope it pans out for them both.'

'Me, too,' he said. 'The truth is we're all a whisker away – or should I say, a lost cat away – from becoming an Irene.'

They'd opened a second bottle of wine and were both a little intoxicated. She must be careful what she said now. It would be too easy for alcohol to get the better of her. There had been moments when she'd come *near* to loving him. But she didn't love him and it would be unforgiveable to mislead or confuse him with an ill-considered remark.

'I read the book,' she said. 'It was appalling. But I see why your mother called you Gillon.'

'She's a romantic at heart, bless her,' he said.

She took the book from the shelf and offered it to him. 'One of your children – or grandchildren – should have this.'

He shook his head. 'I'd rather you binned it than they did.'

'I won't bin it,' she said.

She couldn't say where the time went. They didn't talk much – in fact barely at all. But it was exactly how she'd hoped it would be.

'Will you stay?' she said.

This had been on her mind all evening and was part of the reason she'd drunk more than she might have done.

'I'd like that,' he said. 'On one condition. No, two.'

366

'What?' She couldn't imagine what he was going to say.

'You wear those stripy pyjamas. And we sleep – as in *sleep* – together.'

'You'll make me cry,' she said.

At some point in the night she surfaced. She was curled on her side, Gil pressed close behind her, his deep, regular breaths warm on the back of her neck.

The next time she woke it was light and she was alone in the bed.

'Gil?' she said then tried again, a little louder, 'Gil?'

When she went to find him, his coat had gone from the hook.

He'd held it together pretty well, he thought. His exit had been on the cheesy side but he wouldn't have got through breakfast without making an idiot of himself. Now all he had to do was get his head round the fact that he'd never see her again. She *wasn't* going to come with him to Coffs. Polly *wasn't* going to phone to say she was keeping the baby. Or that she wanted him to stay in London and be happy.

He wondered how to tell the family he was coming back. It was a tricky one. It mustn't look as if he were expecting a medal, or a guarantee that his return would put everything – or indeed anything – right. Rachel's 'prodigal' dig was still raw in his memory. Maybe it was best to turn up unannounced. It was a tad melodramatic – *here comes the cavalry* – but once they knew he'd given up his job and his flat they'd realise he intended sticking around.

Then there was the problem of cash. He was broke. His mother would put him up for as long as he wanted to stay, he was certain of that. But he couldn't sponge off her for long. He'd have to find work straight away. In a bar or supermarket – anything would do. And – this was the big one – he didn't have enough to cover a plane ticket.

He'd recently audited his worldly goods but he did it again on the off-chance he'd overlooked something. The only items of value were his camera and his laptop. The laptop was nothing special. It would fetch a couple of hundred pounds at most. On the other hand, the camera and lenses should raise enough for a one-way fare. He was reluctant to part with it. It was a nice camera and might be the means of earning a few quid but he had no alternative, and within twenty-four hours of pinning a 'for sale' card on the staff notice board, he'd had several enquiries.

He was reasonably on track with his leaving schedule, when Louise Skyped. She assured him that it was a social call, but he suspected there was more to it. They limbered up with small talk about the floods and their mother's upcoming trip with her quilting group. When he could no longer avoid asking after her family, she said they were fine but in the next breath blurted out that she and her husband were having problems.

'Big problems?' he said.

'I don't know. He won't talk to me. He's preoccupied. Not sleeping. Snappy. The kids have started to notice.'

She dipped her head, her image on the screen freezing and tearing but he knew she was crying.

'I'm sorry, Gil. I didn't mean to dump this on you.'

'Dump away,' he said. And despite his earlier resolution, he told her that he was coming home in a couple of weeks. Home for good.

His news brought on more tears. 'That's wonderful,' she said. 'It'll mean so much to Mum. To all of us, in fact.' She looked up and smiled. 'I feel better already.'

Once he got in the swing of it, distributing his possessions turned out to be fun.

He gave his jazz albums to Freddy Kimura. Gil had picked them up in charity shops and he'd more than had his money's worth of enjoyment from them. Freddy – a vinyl nut – insisted on paying him a hundred pounds. It was reward enough seeing them go to a good home but, given that Freddy was a surgeon and that he – Gil – was strapped, he accepted.

The television went to Feray (for her bedroom). Also the best of the crockery and kitchen stuff. The kids were thrilled to have his posters. As recompense for putting up with years of his music, he gave Oskar his guitar. He left a box of books on the front step with a sign inviting passers-by to help themselves. (And they did.) The furniture would have to stay. Everything else – bedding and clothes he wasn't taking – could go into black bags at the last minute.

He and Vivian hadn't discussed whether they would stay in touch. It would have come up over breakfast – another reason why he'd left the way he had. A clean break was brutal, but he knew himself well enough to know that it had to be that way if he were to commit to life in Coffs. He mustn't cling to one single atom of hope. Vivian would understand.

So when, a few days later, he received a letter from Germany, he was more than a little shaken. The envelope contained a cheque for five thousand pounds – Carey's legacy he assumed – and a note.

Use what you need for your plane ticket. The balance is to go to your daughter. It might tip the scales. V x

If you don't accept, it'll go to the cats' home.

During his final days at the hospital, dozens of people stopped him in the corridor or dropped into the studio to wish him well. Kevin saw to it that there was a card – slightly obscene, of course – signed by all those who'd contributed to the whip-round of four hundred pounds. With everything else going on, he hadn't thought much about leaving this place and these people. When he went out through the revolving door for the last time, he felt unexpectedly sad.

369

The four hundred pounds had come out of the blue and it wasn't too difficult to persuade himself it would be okay to spend some of it. He took Feray and the kids out for a farewell lunch at the local pasta place. Feray happened to have a two-for-one voucher so the bill was less than it might have been. The kids said they'd like to go to Australia one day and prattled on about crocodiles and poisonous spiders and surfing. As the meal progressed, they grew more talkative whilst Feray ate next to nothing and barely said a word. She and the children were *en route* to her parents and, when they could sit in front of empty coffee cups no longer, he walked them to the Tube where they said their goodbyes. Another tough one.

From there, he carried on down to Camden Town. The route took him past half a dozen of his favourite charity shops but he resisted setting foot inside any of them – excellent training in self-denial. Camden Town was throbbing with crowds heading for the Lock and he was glad to be going in the opposite direction.

By contrast, the British Museum was blessedly calm. He strolled around for half an hour, stopping when something caught his fancy. His meanderings led him, as he knew they would, to the shop. The earrings were still in the display case – green and stylish – and still seventy-five pounds. He made a quick calculation. Thirty-odd cups of coffee. Hell, if he drank water he'd recoup that sum in less than six weeks, and his abstinence might absolve him of this brief but premeditated lapse in his vow not to think of Vivian.

On his way back to Tottenham Court Road, he passed a gift shop. Normally he wouldn't give a place like that a second glance but something made him stop. In a couple of days he would jet out of this city, just like the gaggle of tourists poring over the tacky goods on display. One window was devoted to teddy bears in various sizes and predictable guises. Pearly kings and queens. Policemen. Beefeaters. Bowler-hatted businessmen. Even the

Queen. In amongst them, he spotted one small bear wearing a bow tie and a knowing smile. He was maybe six or eight inches high – perfect for a tiny hand.

The bus took him past Warren Street station and the traffic island. The damaged railings had been replaced and there was nothing except the pads of fresh concrete at the foot of the pillars to indicate that anything unusual had happened there.

43

Vivian bought a newspaper, picked up a coffee and made her way back to the office. The International Sweets and Biscuits Fair was in full swing at the Koelnmesse. In the Alter Markt, as part of the razzamatazz, confectioners were handing out goody bags, and the air smelled of caramel.

She had been concerned that, in dividing her time between the two cities, she might feel she belonged in neither. Quite the opposite. Cologne was beginning to feel like home and spending time away from London had increased her appetite for what it had to offer. (When she was there last week, she and Ralph had gone to the Cottesloe.) An unexpected spin-off of the new routine was that she, Bella Sachs and Malcolm had struck up quite a friendship.

Things were progressing well on site. The weather had improved and, after a bad start, the contractor was back on schedule. Friel Dravid's little outpost on Lintgrasse was already making its mark. A couple of jobs had come in and the firm had been invited to submit a scheme for a library at Bremen University. Howard was coming over later in the week for a progress meeting. Ottilie had booked him a room at the Mercure but Cara had decided to come too and persuaded her to switch it to the Excelsior.

Gil had once tried to convince her that, had her mother survived Philip Carey, she would have revealed everything. Maybe. Maybe not. If she wanted answers, the place to start would be Munich, with Tante Steffi. But it would be dangerous to invite the past to consume her when the future was so interesting.

Vivian was sorry that she wouldn't see Gil again. He was a wise, kind man. She wouldn't have got through that hard winter without him and she would never forget him – although she could no longer quite picture his face. There was no question of their keeping in touch. There would be too much sadness in it. If she had learned anything in the past few months it was the importance of knowing when to let something go.

The earrings were beautiful. She wore them most days. Her new hairstyle – boyish and asymmetrical – showed them off to advantage and she'd had a number of flattering comments. It had taken her a while to get used to her new look but today, glimpsing her reflection in a shop window, she liked what she saw.